I0678845

Simple Affair
C.R. Misty

Also, by C.R. Misty

Deeply Bound
Something Desired

Simple Affair
C.R. Misty

Simple Affair

C.R. Misty

Cover Design by Lady Maverick Publishing

Published by Lady Maverick Publishing

The International Boundaries Series | Book 1

Chapter 1
Opening

I sit here alone at my desk and let a gentle sigh escape my lips. I wonder how I should start this because all of it has been so hard. I could just make up a bullshit tale of love and romance and being swept off their feet from the hands of their lover, but that tale is told a thousand times over. I will let you take what you will with this one, this could be a real story or just another made up mess. In the end, I will never confirm and instead let you put it together. I take a shallow breath, here it goes.

This was a year of change for me. I was making my dreams happen. I had two goals for the New Year, one to become a published author and two to become a mother. The first goal happened. I felt a flood of accomplishment when I published my first book. It is an ultimate high even if it was a solo celebration. My family and friends didn't really get my passion for writing. I got the feeling in countless conversations that they didn't see the hours upon hours of work in solitude and then publishing the book only to make minimal sales as something that was rewarding and would lure me to go back for more. I could never explain it to them other than it was something that made me happy and that is why I kept at it. To me, it was freeing and empowering in knowing that I could actually do it and it was even more amazing to receive some sales.

I am an author, maybe not the best one, my imposter syndrome, that shitty little voice in the back of my mind often creeps in and inserts doubt. I have to keep reminding myself why I bother, and unfortunately the second of my goals is still a work in progress. It was a hard truth to swallow. I don't think anyone can say that they enjoy failing and especially at something that should be easy and natural. It was harder than I could have ever imagined. I would go through a series of emotions, experiencing the feelings of hope, possibility, and anticipation that it could work and then the utter disappointment, sadness, and regret of getting my hopes up in the first place the moment it was known that it didn't work.

I know that not everything in life comes easy or even at all, though I was not going to let this be the end of the story.

I couldn't prepare for what was about to happen. Everything that I thought I knew and that I loved would soon come into question. I am not a bad person, but I believe after you read this some of you will hate me for what I did.

My name is Jordan Connor. I've spent my entire thirty-one years of life living within the nation's capital. I married someone that I had fallen deeply for fast, and we are going on seven years of marriage.

Josh and I started off in a lust filled relationship meeting up at the call center job that we used to both work at until we got higher paying jobs elsewhere. We soon spent our lunch breaks making his car shake and with time, love and friendship came.

Fast forward to now, we own a nice house and two cars. To everyone we lead a normal happy life. We laugh together, play together, make love twice a week and have no major worries. We fight, every couple does, and it would be weird if we didn't. It's not physical, it's always a fight of words. As I write this all down at my desk, it brings my life into perspective. I have done well for myself so far. It seems like a list of accomplishments as I re-read the words and I should be happy, fulfilled, and thankful.

We married within our first year of meeting one another, I knew that starting a family would be difficult. Josh has had a bad hand dealt to him in terms of health and to make a long story short he will never father a child. When I learned this, I was a twenty-four-year-old that was completely in love with her husband to be, I had no problem with it. I wanted to enjoy my twenties, focus on myself, my friends, this marriage, and concentrate on getting myself established into a great career before even contemplating bringing a child into the mix. The plan was at thirty, we agreed, I would seek medical help in order to get pregnant.

Thirty came and went and I never so much as tried. Josh had lost his job and we ran out of money. It was crushing to put the plan on hold indefinitely, but we had no choice but to wait. Therefore, in the time being I did the things that helped cheer my spirits, I spent time with my mom and dad, spent the weekends at camp with the extended family and did a lot of reading at the beach.

Back then, I had been thinking about it, writing a story, why not, I thought. I had nothing to lose. I loved reading and I could probably write a better story than the piece of garbage that is on my bedside table. My first attempt at writing began and this newfound hobby started a chain of events.

Chapter 2
Making Oneself

I spent hours downstairs in my home office writing. When away from home, if an idea, scene, or anything that I thought would be great for my book I would start a note on my smart phone and save it so that I could transfer it to my document later. I finished my first draft within months, a full length one hundred-thousand-word novel. I had the luxury of being able to hand my work off to friends and family to proofread and help edit. While I waited for their feedback, I started learning how to publish and market this book.

Marketing is a mystery to me but in knowing nothing about it and a combination of being part naïve and part fearless, I decided to get onto social media as a way to market myself while my novel was being reviewed. I started building my author profile by joining Twitter and creating a Facebook page.

You must be wondering why I am telling you this. What is the point of me giving the details into writing a book and wanting a family, and how does the social media side come into it? I may have lost you. My full lips press together as I sit here alone at my desk. I am certain that I have lost you or you are now totally bored with this story and are about to put it down. I ask you to read a little further because I promise that this will link together.

To summarize, I wrote a book, published it, and did all the marketing myself, so what right, so do a thousand others if not more. I am going to bring this story forward from November to July of the following year. In that time, I marketed myself as an author and gained thousands of followers on social media. I would not classify myself as a social media star, but I believe that my online presence was starting to snowball, and that summer was when I published my book. It generated a little extra pocket money which was an assurance that I was on track as a new author and that my book was a good start.

Did I get you back? I am crossing my fingers here at my desk hoping so. We are only a few pages in. Please read on a little further.

Chapter 3
Sharing

July was the most nerve-racking month of my life. It wasn't the publishing that had my nerves it was, finally, my fertility treatment, I was about to do a round of IUI, it stands for Intrauterine Insemination, the procedure was happening soon. Josh and I had to use donor sperm. We paid for the procedure ahead of time, picked the donor and we shared the news with our family and close friends. My feelings and nerves were all over the place. It was a combination of being over the top excited, happy, nervous, and ready to start the next chapter. We drove an hour to the doctor's office in the city on a warm July morning to undergo the procedure. It is a simple procedure; you lie on a table and the nurse comes in with the vial full of donor sperm. She puts it into some sort of elongated syringe, it is a long thin tube that goes into the uterus so that the sperm is placed as close to the egg as possible, sounds fun right? The procedure takes no more than fifteen minutes and most of the time is spent just lying on the table.

To be completely honest with you, it is an awkward procedure, you take something as intimate as lovemaking and it is turned into an uncomfortable encounter at the doctor's office. I lay still on the table for moments after the nurse removed the instruments from me. My stomach cramped a little and I was cold with only being clothed from the waste up and only having a thin sheet wrapped around my lower half. The nurse left the room for a few moments as Josh, and I waited for the time to pass before it was safe for me to get up. Josh held my hand the entire time. All at once I was happy, shy, and scared, as I stared at the second hand of the clock making the faint ticking sound on the wall across from the table.

We waited two weeks for the result, and I was to go back into the doctor's office to find out if I was pregnant. The thing is I started my period just days before the appointment and completely broke down, and with it, I lost care for the things that had made me happy.

The morning that I knew that it didn't work, I crept out of bed, clueless to what I was about to discover. In that moment, I felt good, happy and I had to pee, so I headed to the washroom. As I wiped, that is when I knew. No, this can't be happening, I sat on the toilet in shock at my unsuspecting discovery, minutes go by, and it sinks in. How could you be so stupid Jordan, I was excited for nothing. A tear runs down my cheek. I wasn't prepared to be disappointed. Minutes go by and I urge myself, okay I can't just sit here, I need to get up. I wash up and walk to my room, I can't face Josh; I can't. I crawl into our king size bed and start to sob uncontrollably, God I wanted this so bad. What do I tell him, what do I tell our family?

Josh is an early riser and had been up and doing stuff around the house. He must have heard that I was up and came into the bedroom moments later. His blue eyes meet mine. "Hey, I was waiting for you downstairs what's..." He sees my puffy face. "What's wrong?"

"It didn't work." I lift my head from the pillow. My brown hair falls behind my slender shoulder. It is hard to breathe let alone get the words out.

His scruffy light brown brows furrow, "What do you mean; are you sure?" He takes a seat on the bed next to me.

I whimpered, "Josh it's too heavy to mistake it for something else, it didn't work." Saying it over again doesn't help my state and I break down again and curl up into a ball.

Josh does what any man with a heart does; he stays and wraps his toned arms around me, which is always comforting. "Jordan it will happen. At least you know now and at least it never was it would be harder I think if you had actually lost a child." His blue eyes show concern and regret as they look into mine and he gently rubs my back.

"I know" is all I can say but his speech doesn't stop the tears rolling down my face. He stays with me for a while.

After some time, Josh with caution in his voice eventually says. "Jordan, I need to head into work, you can either stay here, and be upset over something that never happened or you can get dressed and make something of your day. It will happen." He stops rubbing my shoulder and gets off the bed to get ready.

In between sobs I say, "I know, I just need to get this out of my system, and I'll be fine."

It was hard in the beginning, telling my family and close friends that it had not worked. I got the encouraging speeches; then, it will work next time speeches etc. Hours turned to days, which turned into a couple of weeks, and I focused on my writing. I started promoting myself as an author and got myself prepared mentally to try again in a month or two.

At some point, before the weekend Mom and Dad invite me up to camp and I accept their invitation. I could use a break, besides Josh will be working at his new job, and I would rather not stay home alone. I look forward to seeing my mom and dad and spending the weekend up at the river.

Chapter 4
Follow, Copy, Paste

Saturday morning, I woke up in my mom and dad's camper. They have one of those goose neck trailers that has all the comforts of home. I am snuggled beneath the sheets on the pull-out couch in the living room area. Dad is up and is already outside. I can see him just outside my window, and the coffee machine is on and gurgling as it is brewing, the smell of a medium blend fills the air. I lay there in bed for a few minutes and grabbed my phone.

I open Twitter and see notifications of new followers. I send them each a message thanking them for following and providing a link to my book.

I follow, copy, and paste messages on that site, not knowing what would come out of a conversation with a complete stranger. I received a message back saying, "Hi there, thanks for following me back. You sure are popular. I write too. Here are my links, here are my websites, and I am also on Wattpad." He sends a flurry of messages, sharing his links and websites.

I politely respond, "No problem, happy to connect with someone who shares the same interests."

He replies, "I am so proud of my work, and I hope you enjoy what I posted on Wattpad."

I contemplate checking out his links, but I wonder if I have the time to commit to another book right now. I sit up and reply, "Your book sounds interesting, but I don't have Wattpad. I'll have to download it once I'm home."

He responds, "Oh, how are you enjoying the weekend?"

I pause and consider how much I should reveal. After taking a moment to look at his sites and verify his identity as an author with a decent biography, I decided to share a bit more. "I am spending the weekend up at camp with my parents."

He replies, "Oh, that must be nice. I used to live up north, not far from you, Rochester."

It seems he noticed my location from my biography. I answer, "Oh yes, I would be a few hours north of Rochester. So, I see that you live in Texas? P.S. Cowboys are yummy, just saying." I'm not sure why I wrote that, but out there now.

He responds, "Yep, been here for five years, but really I'm a Yankee. I miss it, the seasons."

I reply, "I love warm temperatures. You're lucky to not have to deal with snow."

He writes, "I admit the warm weather is nice, but I miss living up north."

I continue the conversation, "Have you seen the picture on my feed from last winter? All that snow. I can't stand cleaning the driveway."

He answers, "Yes, I guess that would be the not so fun part."

I want to wrap up the conversation, but I don't want to sound too curt. Feeling hungry, I write, "It is right around breakfast time. I'm going to step away to eat. I'll have to get Wattpad to read your work, and I'll get to it soon. Have a great day, and thanks for the chat."

I send the message and shortly after, he responds, "I'll take a look at your book too. Thank you and enjoy your weekend up at camp. Bye."

I put my phone down not thinking anything more. Mom is in the kitchen putting breakfast together.

She asks, "So were you looking at your book sales again?"

I stretch and say, "No just sending out messages to my new followers, that's all." I get out of the pull-out bed to join her in the kitchen, putting some bread in the toaster and I make a glass of chocolate milk. We eat, I go for a walk with mom down the dirt road. We return and relax, eat lunch then go to the beach to read, sunbathe, swim and then dinnertime arrives and soon we are into the later hours of the night. The day was a good one and by the next day I hate to say it, but the person that I had been talking to on Twitter I had already forgotten his name. I forgot about the promise I made to look at his work and download Wattpad. I forgot. I didn't mean to, it's just with family here social media takes a back seat to reality.

Chapter 5
Rinse and Repeat

A week goes by, and this weekend proves to be the same as the last. Josh is working the entire weekend again. I miss him. I miss us. He works so hard, and he is doing it to help us but at the same time even though it is for us, we hardly see each other. I can't stand to be alone, especially on the weekend and I already work forty hours a week, I don't have it in me to work a second job like Josh does. I never asked him to work a second job. We could get by without him taking on a second job, but he insisted. He wanted to do this, and I couldn't persuade him to relax on his days off so this weekend, I find myself back up at camp to spend time with my mom and dad.

I woke up all snuggled up in bed, with my parent's Chihuahua keeping me company this morning. I reached over for my phone that was charging on the shelf. I don't know why I feel the urge to check my phone. My friends are all busy with their own young families. It is unlikely that they would reach out, and besides the only people that would send me a message in the night or early in the morning would be my parents, who I am with or Josh and there is nothing. I decided to work on my author image, and I make the effort to be social on social media. I read the message in my inbox, and it's from him, Devon Chambers, the person I chatted with last week. I recognized his photo and his name. I realize that I forgot to look at his work, and now he might ask about it. I reply, "Hey, how are you?"

Devon responds, "I am good. It's a bright sunny day where I am. Are you up at camp this weekend?"

I'm surprised by his attention to detail. "Yes, just spending time up at camp with Mom and Dad."

He asks, "Oh, that must be nice. What are your plans for today?"

I think quickly and come up with a lie, not wanting to admit that I haven't read his work yet. "I've been having problems with getting Wattpad to download. I haven't read your sample yet, but I plan to." I feel guilty for making these promises I may not keep.

I wait for his response, and he replies, "That's okay. I want to tell you something, and I hope it doesn't bother you."

Curiosity piques within me, and I reply, "Okay." Is he going to comment on my own book?

He continues, "I hope you don't think any differently of me. There's a scene I'm writing, an intimate scene, and I hope that when you read it, it doesn't change your opinion of me."

What could he possibly be referring to? I hope he hasn't written something disturbing, a tinge of worry creeping in. I responded cautiously, "As long as it's not something bizarre like, you know, strange fetishes or... eating each other's poop, I'll be fine. Please don't tell me it's anything messed up." I held my breath, awaiting his reply, feeling the weight of anticipation, and nibbling at my nails.

He chuckled and reassured me, "Oh no, nothing like that. It's just a good old-fashioned passionate encounter. It's intimate and it's been my fantasy." I let out a sigh of relief; he still sounded like a regular guy. "Alright, that sounds acceptable. I'm actually looking forward to reading it," I replied, a hint of curiosity piqued. Suddenly, I wondered if I could access Wattpad with the spotty reception we had at camp. My phone was both a blessing and a curse – convenient yet frustrating at times. Despite the odds, I managed to search for the app, and it loaded onto my screen. What a relief!

"Devon?" I asked, eager to share my progress.

"Yeah, what's up?"

"I got Wattpad! I'm trying to find you. Did you use a pen name?"

"Yes, try searching for D. Chambers."

I located his sample and exclaimed, "Great, I found it!"

"Awesome. I'll make sure to find yours too. I'm on it."

"Thanks, Devon. I'll write a review once I'm finished."

"Sounds good. I promise to do the same."

"Alright then, I'll let you get back to your day. Talk to you later."

"Okay, bye."

I put down my phone after looking at his profile picture; he is pretty cute with his short brown hair, brown eyes, and clear complexion. He has that confidant masculine look to him, which is hot in my books. I wonder what he is like in person. Anyway, it's not like anything would come of it. I am married. I think he likes me; I can't put my finger on it, but I sense something and it's a nice feeling to know that I still have it.

The day passes by just as last weekend, which is a welcomed and loved routine with my parents. After dinner, I share a couple of drinks with Mom in the camper. We laugh together, talk, and eventually settle down for a bit. I pull out my phone to check Twitter as my mom fills her glass from a box of wine.

"I can't believe the number of people following you," Devon's message popped up. I couldn't help but smirk, sharing his surprise. It was inexplicable—I had amassed thousands of followers, gaining between thirty and fifty each day.

Deciding to respond, I typed, "Yeah, it's funny how it works. Once you hit a thousand, something changes. More people seem interested and willing to follow along."

A few moments passed without a reply from Devon. It didn't surprise me; his previous comment seemed to have been sent earlier in the day. Lost in my thoughts, my mom interrupted my daydreaming. "Hey, who are you talking to, Jordan?"

"Just my Twitter peeps, Mom," I replied with a chuckle.

She laughed and inquired, "How many do you have now?"

"Over six thousand," I beamed, amazed by the number. I didn't even know six thousand people personally: maybe four hundred at most. I realized that in the grand scheme of things, six thousand was just a fraction, but for someone like me who was just starting out, it was a great start.

Amused, she asked, "Why do you think they're following you? You're not famous or anything."

I shrugged and replied, "I don't know, Mom. I tweet messages every day. Maybe they like what I have to say?"

Curiosity piqued, she suggested, "Have you ever asked them why they follow you? It's not like you're a celebrity or anything." She said it playfully, fueled by a few glasses of wine. I chuckled at her lighthearted remark.

"No, I haven't. Would you like me to ask them?" I huffed jokingly.

"Sure, Jordan."

Devon still hadn't responded to my previous comment, but I decided to ask him anyway. I trusted that he understood my personality and wouldn't take offense. Sometimes, conversations with unfamiliar people could lead to misunderstandings. Intentions behind light-hearted remarks might be misconstrued. I believed Devon was the right person to provide an insightful answer.

"Hey, I have a question for you. I'm not drunk or anything—well, I did have a couple of glasses of wine with my mom—but I need to ask you something." I clicked send.

Looking up at my mom, she inquired, "So, what did they say?"

"I just asked the question. They might be away from their computers. Oh, wait, I have a message."

A surge of joy filled me as I saw Devon's reply. "Hey Jordan, ask away," he responded, accompanied by a smiley face.

With a mix of excitement and caution, I typed my question, hoping he wouldn't misinterpret my intentions. "My mom and I are curious to know why you're following me. We just can't wrap our heads around how I have so many followers." Fingers crossed, I hit send, praying my instincts were right and I wouldn't come across as conceited.

Amidst my nervous anticipation, Devon's lighthearted response brought a smile to my face. "Drinking, are we? I'm laughing. Well, I followed you because we're both writers; it seems we share the same interests."

Relieved by his friendly explanation, I looked up at my mom and exclaimed, "I have an answer!"

She leaned forward, her green eyes meeting my blue ones, and asked eagerly, "Do tell."

Reading Devon's response aloud, I realized our conversation wasn't over yet. He had his own question, "Why are you following me?"

"I followed you back for the same reasons," I replied. "I try to follow back people who follow me."

Devon expressed his flattery, smoothly adding, "I'm honestly flattered that someone as beautiful as you is following me. You're quite popular here on Twitter."

His words made me smile, and I responded, "Thank you, Devon. From your photo, you seem like quite a catch. And about the popularity, I actually don't receive a lot of interaction even though I reach out to people. Many of them are fellow artists, and their tweets are mostly promotional."

"Why thank you! I'm smiling," Devon replied. "Yes, Twitter can be that way. I seem to be stuck at the four-hundred follower mark, and none of them really engage. You're the only one I talk to here."

"Likewise," I chimed in. "I have some light-hearted conversations, but you're the person I talk to the most."

Devon's response warmed my heart. "I'm so flattered. I hope I'm not taking up too much of your time."

"Not at all," I reassured him. "I enjoy talking to you, and I always make time for things that bring me happiness."

"You seem like a genuinely wonderful person, inside and out. I'm grateful that we stumbled upon each other," Devon confessed.

I couldn't help but agree, feeling a sense of connection with this stranger. "Yes, me too. Well, as much as I hate to cut this short, I'm with family right now, so I need to go be social. I'll talk to you later."

"Okay, have a great night," Devon replied.

As I put my phone down, I couldn't help but feel a rush of emotions, like a teenager crushing on someone they barely know. It made no sense, yet here I was, developing feelings over a few light-hearted texts. I had to shake off these thoughts.

Mom broke the silence, suggesting, "I think Dad and your uncle have built a campfire. I see some light over there. Do you want to walk over and see what everyone else is doing?"

Smiling, I replied, "Yes, let's go be social."

The weekend went by, and I read Devon's work. His main character is a woman. This guy has to be off the market. My guess is his main character is based on a girlfriend. It must be, she has too much spunk and the feel of a real person with having likes, quirks, and a personality. His character does not fall flat. I find a lot of authors struggle with characters of the opposite sex, but this guy seems to have this girl down. I will need to ask him whenever we talk next. I am glad that I gave his book a chance and think I learned something about him by reading the sample.

After this weekend I do not forget my Twitter friend's name, Devon, sounds strong and he has a fire in his eye, I wonder how old he is? He must be taken and that is okay because what I am feeling with this little crush is nothing because it is only texts. Anyway, back to reality and I return home from camp to Josh.

Chapter 6
Summer

This summer has been challenging. I have not seen Josh much. He is always working, and when he is around, he is cranky, miserable and to be honest I begin to cherish the time that I have away from him. When we are together, it is as if he is always looking for something, anything to argue about, it could be as small as a dish being left out that sets him up for nagging. I hate it, dread it, and sometimes wish I could just leave, step out of my life, and never return, though that thought quickly leaves my head because I wouldn't know how to just leave. I created a life with Josh and half of what we have created together is mine. Sometimes I wonder if he even loves me anymore. How can someone be so mean to a person that he hardly sees? The extra job he is working he says it is for us but honestly the change in him with being so tired and so moody, working all the time for a little extra money isn't worth it.

Our relationship wasn't always like this. The man I had fallen in love with was once happy and outgoing. He was the one that would grab everyone's attention in a room and make others smile with his silly sense of humor. He was a kid at heart and most people when they first meet him end up liking him once they understand his playful manner.

I met Josh after graduating college with a diploma in computer science. My first job in the technical field was where I met Josh. I was training for an entry-level job in technical support, and he was a senior support staff and was a mentor for all of the new hires. At first, I took no notice of him, well I did notice him because I wasn't afraid to ask for help when I needed it but what I meant to say was at the time he was just another tech guy in the office, a handsome one, always well groomed, dressed nice and I didn't think anything more because he was a colleague.

Over the weeks as I progressed with the job, my questions slowed as I got more comfortable with my work, but Josh's presence was still as if I was on my first days. It wasn't long before we shared our breaks together. At first, it was just spending time together in the office cafeteria then it turned into trips to the local coffee shop and eventually turned into hanging out after work. First, it was at the local bar and grill but eventually it turned into sleeping over at his home.

Long story short, we were engaged after three months of dating and married within a year of meeting. We were hopeless romantics and crazy about each other back then. I wish that our relationship could take a step back in time so that I can feel that passion that we had once more.

Now the weeks are tiresome, we get up early, get ready for work and Josh begins the morning ritual with a, "Would you please do this first or why did you put that there?" It always sounds negative instead of a simple, "Good morning."

I can't take it. I just grind my teeth and do what he is nagging about so that I don't have to waste another moment with him. Almost seven years and I wonder how much longer I can deal with this, with him. Should I deal with it? I could leave him; I wonder sometimes what would my life be like if I left? I catch myself asking these questions often. Do I even love him anymore?

This morning we took separate cars to work, which is to my relief. I can enjoy the radio and the solitude. My mind starts to wander away from Josh as I make the commute to work along the highway. I should write a review for Devon, yes, I'm going to on my lunch break, why not, it was a good start to his story. It turns out it was just a sample of a few chapters, what a great tease. I should use Wattpad to sample my own work.

Lunchtime comes and I remain in the office. I write and publish a positive review. I wonder if Devon is notified of the review right away. I should send a message to make sure he sees it and if he hates it, I can remove it right away.

Excited to share my thoughts with Devon, I instantly sent him a text, "Hey Devon, I finally finished reading your sample and wrote a review. Take a look and let me know what you think. If you're not happy with it, I can remove it." I wondered how often he checked his messages, but I had work to address, so I focused on my overflowing work email.

After an hour or so, I decided to take a short break and checked my phone. To my delight, I saw a response from Devon. "Oh, hey Jordan, thank you so much. I just saw it. Can I ask you something?"

Curious, I replied, "Sure, what's up?"

"Would you mind if I posted your review on my website?" he asked.

"It's your review, so I don't mind at all," I replied.

"Thank you!" He expressed his gratitude.

Thinking about the captivating female lead character in his story, I couldn't help but ask, "So, I have to ask, is the main person in your story based on your girlfriend?"

Devon chuckled and clarified, "Ha ha, no, she's just a fantasy girl that I made up—my fantasy girl. It would be nice if my partner read my book, but she just isn't interested. It's a shame. What about you? Does your husband read your book?"

His question caught me off guard, reminding me of our ongoing conversations and flirtations over the past couple of weeks. With a tinge of disappointment, I reluctantly began discussing Josh. "No, well, he started to read my book, but he couldn't get into it and eventually put it down. It just wasn't his cup of tea. It's too bad because I did base a couple of my characters on him."

Devon empathized, saying, "Yes, that is a shame. You can't force someone to do something they don't want to do. I'm just really happy that you enjoyed my sample. I genuinely believe it's going to be my breakout novel. In the New Year, I'm planning a trip to Victoria. That's where I based my story. I'm going with my brother."

"I've been there," I replied. "You should visit the harbor, ride the ferries, and even though I'm from Canada, the west coast feels like another country."

Curious, Devon asked, "How is that?"

"In my city, we have a bilingual culture, English and French. But on the west coast, there's a vibrant Asian community," I explained.

"Sounds like a visit overseas?" he pondered.

"Precisely. It's funny how you can feel like a foreigner in your own country. I experienced the same feeling when I visited the United States. Even though I'm exposed to American television, being there is an entirely different world," I elaborated.

Curious to understand more, Devon inquired, "How so?"

Smiling, I responded, "Well, for starters, I noticed people riding motorcycles without helmets. How is that even allowed? And then there's the fondness for guns and the abundance of chicken joints."

Devon burst into laughter, typing back, "Oh my god, girl, you're cracking me up here at my desk!"

Devon's laughter subsides as he responds to my question. "The chicken, you're funny, girl. Smart and funny. And I'm going to say it, even if it's out of line, you're beautiful."

My heart skips a beat at his compliment. "Thank you, you're a handsome guy."

Blushing, Devon thanks me and continues, "How old are you?"

I smile and decide to be honest, hoping my age won't scare him away. "Thirty-one. And you?"

"Forty-two," he reveals.

I feel a moment of disbelief, carefully examining his photo again. He doesn't look forty-two. "You must use some really great anti-aging cream."

"Ah, thanks. You're too kind," he replies.

Laughing, I say, "I would have guessed you were in your twenties or early thirties."

Devon appreciates the compliment, responding, "You look younger too. I would have thought you were twenty-four."

I chuckle, "Ha ha ha, no, I wish. So, tell me about yourself. Do you have kids?"

"Yes, I have a boy. Well, he's twenty," he shares.

"Wow," I react, surprised by the revelation. "Yes, I know. I had him young. What about you?"

"No kids," I reply.

Devon elaborates on his situation, "I love my boy, but he lives with his mother."

Curious about his son's future plans, I ask, "Is he going to be going away to school soon?"

"Yes, I've supported him all his life, and I'll continue supporting him until he's of age. So, one more year. I love him, but his mother sprung this on me. Honestly, I had sex with her once, and that did it. Sorry, that's too much information."

Devon has no idea about the struggles I've faced over the summer, which are the opposite of what he's gone through. I sympathize and respond, "No, it's okay. I don't mind the chat.' You must have some really good swimmers."

He laughs at my comment, replying, "Yes, they know how to find the egg. No problems there."

Curious about his past, I venture to ask, "So, how long have you been divorced? You don't have to answer if it's too personal."

He reassures me, "No, it's okay. It's been years. To be honest, she just used me. She had a baby to get out of her parents' house. I hate to say it, but she admitted that to me years later. I love my boy, it's just that I hate that I felt manipulated by his mother. Anyway, how long have you been together with your husband?"

That is low, to feel used by the woman who brings his son into this world, my poor guy. I respond to him, "It is going on seven years."

"He's a truly fortunate man to have someone as extraordinary as you. I hope you don't mind me saying, but you're not just beautiful, you're intelligent and funny too."

Devon's compliments never fail to make me smile. A true Southern gentleman, I wonder if all men from that region possess such charm. A part of me fantasizes about a future with him.

I sense a genuine interest in his words, and my intuition tells me that something is shifting. In my nearly seven years of marriage, I've never entertained the thought of another man. But now, everything is changing. It both excites and unnerves me. I find myself drawn to Devon, even though our connection is solely through chat and a few photos from his websites. The attraction is undeniably mutual; I catch myself often gazing at his pictures.

Shaking off my daydreams, I remind myself to keep the conversation going. "Tell me more about yourself. I read some of your other books. Have you had experience in combat?"

"I was a combat helicopter pilot during the Gulf War."

His words hit me like a wave, and I can't help but feel a surge of excitement even while I'm at work. I'm conversing with an extraordinary person.

"I've never met anyone quite like you. It's incredible to think that you've been out there. Sometimes, those positions, like combat pilots serving their country, feel like they only exist in movies."

"They're very real. I started off fueling them up, then underwent training and ended up flying them for four years. I spent twenty-nine days in air combat."

I can't contain my enthusiasm. "I've always joked that if I ever won millions, I'd buy a helicopter and a tropical island. Now that I know about your experience, maybe you could be my personal helicopter pilot."

He replies eagerly, "I would absolutely love that and would be thrilled to visit your tropical island. You have no idea."

He knows exactly how to capture my heart. Alright, I should wrap up this conversation. A smile spreads across my face, despite being at work. "Devon, I have to get back to work now. Thanks for the delightful conversation. You've truly made my day."

"Likewise. Talk to you later."

I am just smitten. I hardly know him and there is something. I am all smiles for the rest of the day thinking about him. I know that I shouldn't be but who cares. As long as it's my secret it won't hurt anyone.

I am curious about him and now I am crushing hard. He keeps me company even though it's just through a virtual world and not real life. Maybe I could trade in my husband for this southern man. I have to stop thinking about it. This is so unrealistic. The rest of the day floats by and I am in my daydreams wondering. The evening proves to be another lonely one of doing some housework and a bit of writing. Josh is working late again tonight.

Chapter 7
What it became

I'm not sure when things took a change but over the course of the summer this person, Devon, and I, went from communicating and having chats on a weekly basis to talking pretty well every day. The things that I learn about him are that he was in the military and at one point, he was a bodyguard for a high-profile public figure. This man is captivating to me.

Devon was born and raised in the United States. He lived in Rochester until his parents divorced and then he moved around and eventually settled in Texas. He has one biological brother whom he is close to and several step siblings from his parents remarrying. His mother raised them from a young age after his parents' divorce. His father was a cop and was hardly around. When Devon was of age, he enlisted in the army. He explained that he hadn't seen death but was sure that the munitions from the helicopter killed enemy and explained that out there you don't hesitate, it's kill or be killed. I don't see a mean streak in him even though he has this background. Without reading his books, I would have never gotten the feeling that he had been involved in life-changing events. He is a father, a spouse, he found another love after the divorce from his son's mother, and he is a writer and works in the high-tech field, a polar opposite life to that of army and bodyguard work.

He is an accomplished writer and a modest man. I remember those early conversations about his books. Devon first made it out to sound like he was an aspiring author but after doing a little digging and him opening up with our conversations I discovered that he has been writing for years. He has received awards for his work, local newspaper articles were written about him. He has done book signings. He even has merchandise for his fan base.

He has yet to strike it huge like the success that mainstream authors reach, but I can see that he is on his way. I would have never known and that saying, "never judge a book by its cover", that is Devon. He has never boasted. To me he is a kind, supportive friend. He isn't fake or trying to gain something from our writing connection. He is just Devon, my friend, champion, and secret.

The thing that hurts is our reality, he has a spouse and so do I...

That is the barrier, besides the distance. I used to judge others for their marriages falling apart. When you find out that someone's partner was cheating. I would wonder how could they when they have someone who loves them. How do these married people find second lovers when others remain single their entire lives? I now see how. Devon and I were perfect strangers who stumbled upon each other based on like interests. This was completely by accident, please don't judge me and let me explain. It started with general talking and interaction, which evolved into chemistry and attraction and then it snowballs. I know at this point that he isn't an online predator or anything weird like that. Devon has opened up more in becoming a Facebook friend. I can see into his life and view his friends and family and he can do the same with me. He is just a normal man, with a network of friends and family and I am a normal woman with her own family and friends, we weren't seeking this.

Now we know each other's schedules, home addresses, where the other works and what we like and dislike. We are starting to know each other on a more intimate level. This is how it happens, and I have a husband but right now, my heart wants another, desires another. I can't get Devon out of my head. This is how cheaters become who they are and for me this was not intentional, it just happened.

Chapter 8
Long Hours

Josh is still working a lot of hours in his second job. During the week he is away maybe two or three evenings, and I can bet that every weekend he is working. Tonight, I find myself at home after a full day at the office and I just finished a simple meal, a bacon egg and cheese sandwich, having breakfast for dinner is so yummy. It is going to be a long evening alone; I am just lazing in my black leather recliner watching television in the living room when my phone lights up with a message.

"Hey Jordan, are you there?" I can't help but smile; he's my secret man. Maybe tonight won't be so dull after all.

I reply, "Hey Devon, yes, I was just about to message you. What's up?"

"I just want to ask you something, and I hope it doesn't come off as creepy."

"Go ahead, ask away."

"I was wondering if I could have one of your pictures for my friend's photo collection. I'll understand if you say no."

I already know what he wants with my photo. Men, always the same. I pretend to be oblivious and say, "Sure, I think most of them are already public anyway. Take whichever one you like. Just please don't use it as an avatar."

"No, I just want a photo of you for my personal collection. I know it's crossing a line, but you're stunning."

His compliment melts my heart. Who doesn't love hearing something like that? "Thank you, my hot cowboy."

He responds, "Blushing here. I have to ask, though, because I still don't get it. Do you find me attractive? Was it my profile picture that caught your attention?"

"Yes, you're quite a catch. Your profile picture definitely intrigued me."

"So, you've seen all my pictures. You know that I have a bit of extra weight. I'm working on losing it, though. Does that change anything for you?"

"Devon, I like what I see. A little bit of padding doesn't make a difference. I actually lost thirty pounds myself over the course of a year, so I understand the struggle. All I did was count calories, and now I'm at a normal BMI."

Devon replies, "My spouse uses my weight as an excuse to avoid intimacy. It's been three years since we've been intimate. I know it's too much information, but there you have it. I said it."

Normally, I would think that statement is an exaggeration, maybe implying a once-a-month kind of situation. But with Devon, he's always been honest, and I've never caught him in a lie. I have a sinking feeling that it's true. "Oh, my poor guy. Seriously? I can't even begin to imagine. I get frustrated after just a week. Wow."

Devon responds, "I know, it's my issue, not yours. She loves me, but she's much older than me, and well, it's just not something she wants anymore. We're more like roommates who get along rather than anything else."

That's a tough situation. Should I cross that line? It's harmless, we're friends. "If I were there, I'd give you some. Isn't that what friends are for?" I add a playful tongue-sticking-out emoticon to make it clear that I'm not entirely serious, unsure of whether he wants to take this further. He stays silent for a moment, and I guess it's just his flirtatious nature and nothing more. I definitely crossed the line.

Finally, I received a message from him, "You have no idea what you do to me. Looking at your pictures makes me aroused. I want you so badly. Care to guess what I'm doing right now."

My instincts were right. Who asks for pictures? Oh man, what should I say? Deep down, I'm turned on by it, wishing I could be there to fulfill his desires. My older man, and here I thought I was being inappropriate just moments ago.

I respond playfully, "I know exactly what you're doing right now. Should I cheer you on or something?" I include a smiley face. It's fun to know someone is pleasuring themselves to your photos. I leaned back in my recliner, waiting for his response.

Devon once again takes his time to answer, likely caught up in his own pleasure. I'm getting so aroused that I'll have to use a couple of fingers myself soon. Just the thought of it has me soaking wet.

Finally, Devon replies, "You have no idea what you do to me, girl. Well, now you do. And I bet you can guess what I use your photos for."

I'm flattered. If I were there, it could have been passionate lovemaking. I wish I could touch him and experience his passion. We're separated by borders and thousands of miles. Maybe it's for the best, keeping us both honest.

I joke, "Are you finished already? That was quick." I chuckle at my own comment. My man just unloaded to me.

"Ha-ha, you're too funny. I'd go again and again if I had you. Anyway, I have to go for now. Talk to you later."

"Bye Devon" I put the phone down, God I am soaked and need my own release, so my hands proceed into my pants to touch my small wet lips, my clit is hot and swollen. I imagine Devon on top of me with that handsome face and those passionate brown eyes staring into my blue eyes. I imagine him holding his length and being gentle at first and easing it in. I press my palm against my button, and with an index finger in my opening and middle finger on the other spot, I massage myself and close my eyes. Devon talking to me while he was at it, pressing his swell inside and closing his eyes with each slow but controlled thrust, he is careful not to lose his own release before I get my own. I imagine that he is asking me to come for him and I get my release.

Chapter 9
The Fine Line

Devon and I have started to walk a fine line. He is running through my head, I can't get him out, it's like high school all over again with this guilty obsession of ours. Our conversations are not just sexual; it's about everything that is going on in our lives. He has become my closest friend and knows pretty well all of my thoughts; my hopes and dreams and I have learned of his own personal goals. God, I keep thinking to myself, if we had met in real life, before we got tangled in our current relationships, things would be different if I had been with someone that I could be as opened to as I am with him.

This morning, I'm at my office desk, diligently working when I receive a message from him. "Hey, good morning. I hope your day is going well. Just wanted to let you know that I had to take care of myself before work."

I read the message on my phone, and it brought a smile to my face. I reply, "Hey, good morning. I bet you're feeling pretty pleased with yourself today. I wish I were there to share in the pleasure."

"I can imagine you enjoying it. I'm well-endowed and skilled at pleasing. I particularly enjoy going down on a woman."

His message makes me squirm in my office chair. I glance around to make sure my co-workers aren't around, and all I see are the dull grey walls of cubicles. I let out a sigh as desire starts to build, and I say, "I know I would enjoy it. God, I want it right now. Sometimes I'm glad I wasn't born a man because I get mine too easily, and I can be quite greedy. I would pin you down, climb on top, and satisfy myself before you could get yours."

He responds with a growl," Jordan, I'm practically pre-ejaculating at my desk here. I can't get up right now."

"Sorry, I suppose it's easier for us girls to hide it." I know I'm wearing a foolish smile on my face. I can't help it, and I think it's because he's a little older. He's more open with his emotions and more in tune with mine.

"I once had a relationship with a coworker. I know, a bad idea, right? Well, one day, she went under my desk and gave me a blowjob. Just as she was doing that, the boss walked in."

There's his dirty side coming out. I respond, "Oh my god, did you guys get caught?"

"No, the keyboard tray was enough to hide her."

Wow, I'm picturing it right now. If I were in that situation, I think I'd be terrified and would probably shit my pants (not literally, just hypothetically). "Oh man! That's intense. I could never do that. I'd be too chicken."

He quickly replies, "Ah, that's too bad. You could have come over and helped me out right now."

"I would, but not at your work." I think very few ever see this side of him, but I am flattered to be able to see it and that excites me. I get the impression that his family and friends see him as a squeaky clean up front, honest man. I can be a shy person but with him he is starting to push my own boundaries. It's not in a bad way, I don't feel pressured, I enjoy it because in some weird way I am now starting to feel more daring and confident in myself.

"Jordan, one day I would love to meet you. Maybe at one of my book signings or we could go out for a coffee?"

"I would really like that. Perhaps you could visit me here."

Devon had mentioned during the summer that his novel is set on the Northwest coast of the United States and the West Coast of Canada. He had plans to travel there for some book research and experience the actual locations. Although he hadn't given a definite date, the idea starts to take shape as he suggests, "Maybe I could change my trip from Victoria to Ottawa. Would you be interested in that?"

"I would be interested. We need to carefully consider and plan everything."

Devon replies, "I don't have any vacation time this year, so it would most likely happen in the New Year."

"Okay, that gives us time. We can see where this goes. You know how I feel about you. It wouldn't be too difficult to arrange. You could fly in, meet me at work, and we could spend time together during the day. I'm right in the heart of the city. We could even explore the sights if you'd like." My heart races at the thought of being with him.

"You have no idea how much I would love that." His comment brings a smile to my face, but at the same time, it scares me because I know deep down that I would cross that line with him and betray my marriage. Do I really want this? My heart desperately longs for it...

Chapter 10
Being Alone

The week rolls by with plenty of conversation from my passionate southern man, and before I know it the weekend is here, and Josh is gone to work for a nine-hour shift. The current state of affairs that Josh and I are in just sucks. I need him here with me, but I can't just ask for it because it irritates him. Josh is trying so hard to help us get ahead. It has been an expensive year with the IUI attempt and the repairs to our home. These long hours are pulling us apart and secretly I wonder if Josh is angry with me for spending my extra time writing novels instead of taking a second, steadily paying part-time job like him.

I am alone at home today, but it won't be for long. Suddenly, my phone lights up with a message from Devon. "Good morning, I hope you have an awesome day!" My sweet and thoughtful man. I can feel how much he cares about me, just as I am always thinking about him.

"Hey, good morning right back at you!" The conversations we've had this week have been intense and passionate. We both feel the pull, even though we haven't acted on it. We're slowly distancing ourselves from our loved ones. I should try to scare him off, to create some distance from this situation that's becoming harder and harder to resist.

Devon sends another message, "Hey, I've been thinking a lot about meeting you and there are some things I want to discuss."

"Sure, go ahead," I reply, feeling a mix of excitement and nervousness.

"If we meet, I don't want to use condoms. I don't like them, and I want you to be able to feel me."

I take a deep breath, unsure if he realizes the impact of his words on me. It's clear that he's carefully considering this. "I haven't used condoms in years, so it would be strange to start using them now," I respond.

"Good, I really want to feel you. I've never felt this way about anyone before. It's not just about the sex; I'm drawn to you in a way I've never experienced in my entire life." There's a pause, and I struggle to find the right words to respond. But before I can, he sends another message. "You know I enjoy going down on a woman. Would you like that?"

Finally, I gather my thoughts and reply, "I would." As I say those words, my heart skips a beat, realizing that this encounter might actually happen. But I need him to know something, something that might change his perception of me. Maybe it will even scare him off. So, I take a deep breath and say it.

"Devon, there's something you need to know, and it may change the way you think of me."

"Try me," he replies, as if he's daring me. He has no idea what's coming.

I take a moment to gather my thoughts, realizing that I need to be honest with Devon. I can't keep hiding behind my fears and uncertainties. So, I muster up the courage and reply, "Devon, um, well, I need to let you know that I can be a bit sensitive and sometimes it can be uncomfortable if you go too deep." There, I finally said it. It's not exactly what I wanted to say, but it's a step in the right direction.

As I hit send, a wave of relief washes over me, but also a pang of guilt. I wish I had the courage to tell him about the attempts to conceive, about the commitment I have in my marriage, but I chicken out. Maybe this piece of information will make the decision for me and scare him off. It sounds foolish, but it's my subconscious hope.

To my surprise, Devon responds immediately, alleviating some of my guilt. "That doesn't bother me in the least, Jordan. I want you, and I understand. I would start off slow for you, so you can get used to me." I read his words, and it's clear that he's not turned off or deterred in the slightest. It's as if he has blinders on, fully focused on the possibility of being together. It's both exciting and terrifying at the same time.

There is that maturity of him. To be honest, I'm not used to it. I fell for him that much more and am now wet at the thought. After our conversation, I have to calm myself down, and without Josh to turn to I need to take matters into my own hands.

Chapter 11
Time flies

Reality is sneaking up on me. My next IUI treatment will be happening soon. I am not sure how I feel about it. Well, that's a lie. I will tell you exactly how I feel.

I feel confused now that Devon has popped into my life. I wonder if I can handle the possibility of heartache of it not working for a second time. July had been a hard month, a major disappointment. I want a baby, but I don't want it this way with the medical coldness of it all. It's too late to go back, this round is paid for, and things are now set in motion. If I walked away, I would be wasting a ton of money because there are no refunds.

I want to talk to someone about what is on my mind, but I can't talk to Josh, really, I can't, how would I start that conversation? I imagine it going like this, "Honey, I don't want to go through with this anymore because I am second guessing everything." When Josh starts questioning me, would he be able to see through my lies and see that there was someone else in the picture? I can't do that. I can't even talk to any of my girlfriends about this. I could only imagine the conversation, with me starting it off, "Hey, I don't think I want to have this baby anymore because I met this forty-two-year-old man online and want to fuck his brains out and I am seriously questioning whether I should stay married to Josh..." That would go just great if I revealed this secret to them.

Maybe one of my girlfriends would stand by me, right now Devon is still a secret, I haven't told a soul and I don't think that I ever will because the moment I tell, I know that it will raise worry in me on whether that friend would be able to keep her mouth shut. It's funny how things happen in hindsight.

Back in July, after I had found out that my first IUI attempt didn't work, in two separate conversations a family member and a friend told me that I should just try and find a stranger that would sleep with me, and then never talk to them again. I just can't believe this universe because right after everything failed, was when Devon walked into my life. It's too messed up, maybe this was meant to happen, I think I am starting to go crazy and with that thought my stomach starts to turn as I sit here at my desk ignoring the work email requests coming in, then my phone lights up with a message from Devon.

"Hey, just got into work, how is your day so far?"

"Oh, hey Devon, it's going good." Do I tell him? Should I keep this a secret, the fertility treatment? We have been talking for over a month now, I consider him a close friend even though we have never met. He is so far removed from my friends, family and where my life is. Would it hurt if I just unloaded this on him? No, I don't think so...I am going to explode with stress if I keep this bottled up.

I send another message, "Actually, I am starting to freak out a little."

Devon responds, "What's wrong Jordan." This will surely send him packing.

I gather my thoughts and mention, "I haven't told you everything about me. You have seen into my life, has the thought ever crossed your mind, seeing that I have been married for almost seven years that I don't have children?" I pose the question, hoping that he is gentle with his response; this is still raw for me.

Devon answers, "It has, and I did wonder but didn't want to ask. I knew that in time you would tell me. It's okay if you don't, I would understand and respect your wishes to keep it secret."

My fingers type as fast as they can and I follow up, "It is okay Devon, and I want to share this. I am healthy, but my husband isn't and long story short he will never father a child. This past July I went in for fertility treatment and it didn't work, my donor is actually from the United States. Anyway, it's been a really hard summer and now that I have had a bit of a break and regained my footing, I am going in again for a second try this fall."

Devon answers, "I hope and pray that it works this time for you. Every woman deserves the chance to become a mother." His response brings comfort. I don't regret opening up to him about this, his response makes me fall silent. He is mindful and respectful in this extremely sensitive topic.

I follow up, "It's just so hard, I just wish I had the chance to do it naturally; it would have been so much easier. To be honest, I don't think it will work this time either. I was stressed the last time and now this time, after knowing what it is, I just have a bad feeling that it won't work again."

Almost instantly Devon replies, "Jordan, if you need me on this level, I am here for you, please, I want you to know that I am not going anywhere."

I confess, "Devon, this is so messed up, but after it didn't work friends and family even suggested that I sleep with a stranger to make it work." I still can't even believe the words I type to him; it sends a chill up my spine that these people in my life have even suggested it and in the back of my mind, I wonder if I have a better chance that way, just to slut myself out.

He says, "That is a choice that only you could ever make. Sometimes you have to do things that are different."

I inquire, "Have you ever considered donating?"

"No, it never crossed my mind," he responds.

Taking a leap, I express my thoughts openly, considering I've shared everything else with him. "Devon, if I discovered that you were my donor, it would somehow alleviate the weight of this situation. The fact that my donor is a complete stranger adds a certain heaviness to it all."

"Jordan, you know I would send it to you if I could, but I don't think it would survive the journey. I would personally deliver it to you, if you catch my drift," he says, hinting at something.

A smile forms on my face, despite the oddity of this conversation. I reply, "I would accept it in a heartbeat, and if it worked, I would take care of the child. I wouldn't involve you in the upbringing or financial support. I am financially secure."

He contemplates for a moment before responding, "If we went through with this and it succeeded, and you became pregnant, would you stop talking to me?"

"No, that's not what I meant. I understand you were in a complicated situation before this, and I don't want to give the impression that I'm using you. It's something you see too often. I simply wouldn't want you to feel the way you did with the mother of your son," I clarify, hoping he understands.

Devon's quick response reassures me, "I get it. I just wouldn't want you to cut me out of your life. I know things would change if this worked, and you would have less time, but I don't want to lose what we have." Where did this guy come from? These words hold a deeper meaning now, transcending mere conversation. I find myself sinking further into the world we've created together. Sometimes, I wonder if he's only enduring everything, I throw at him to keep me as a friend, but deep down, I believe he wouldn't stoop that low. I trust him.

"I'll always be your friend, and I want to explore where this connection between us leads. It's crazy how we've never met in person, yet through our conversations, I'm inexplicably drawn to you," I admit honestly.

Devon changes the topic, asking, "What does your voice sound like? Do you have a northern accent?"

I'm puzzled by his question about a "northern accent," but I answer, tilting my head in confusion, "I don't have an accent. By the way, I came across a video of you on your Facebook timeline earlier. You sound more like you're from the south than Rochester."

He chuckles and asks, "Do you like the sound of my voice?"

"Yes, you have a sexy voice, my cowboy," I tease, feeling a blush rising.

Devon's response makes me blush even more, "Thank you. We should talk or maybe do a FaceTime or something."

"Sure, but we need to find a discreet way to do it. FaceTime requires dialing a phone number, and if my husband saw that on the bill—local calls and then a random number from Austin, Texas—he'd get suspicious," I explain.

"I understand. I'll look into it, we'll figure something out," he assures me.

I can't help but smile at the thought of seeing him and feeling closer to him through video chat. "I can't wait. It'll be like meeting you for the first time all over again."

"Yeah, I feel the same way," he responds.

I smirk playfully and say, "What if we get on video chat and you find out I'm actually some grandma?"

"Should I be worried? I think you've been honest with me. I've seen your world through Facebook and I'm confident that you are who you say you are," he reassures me, showing his perceptiveness.

He's not naïve, especially with Facebook's wealth of information. It's hard to maintain consistent lies when I have a profile with connections to my friends and family. "Yeah, I'm honest. I'm not a grandma."

"I didn't think so," he replies, his trust evident.

Our fast-forming friendship doesn't scare me in the least. It is hard to describe but it feels like Devon, and I had known each other in a past life. We click so well; the friendship is there as well as the mutual attraction and chemistry.

Devon continues, "My spouse will be leaving town next Friday we can arrange to chat or video after then. I will need to do some research; the last thing that I want is for you to get into trouble."

"Okay sounds like a plan and I can't wait. So um, I guess I will drop off for now and get some work done, talk to you later?" I ask.

"You bet!"

"Okay bye" He feels like my partner, and I add the hugs and kisses to see what he does with it.

"Hugs and kisses right back at you!" I smile, he always seems to like to have the last word. Here, I have him as a friend that I can write to, and he answers me almost right away.

Chapter 12
Forgetting About Troubles

My eyes open before my alarm goes off. Josh is good at waking early and without an alarm. I have no idea how he does it. I am someone that usually needs an alarm but this morning it must have been the gurgling of the coffee machine in the kitchen.

I rub my eyes open and find my way to the kitchen where Josh is making himself a waffle with egg and cheese.

He turns and sees me, asking, "Did I wake you?"

"No, I must have been ready to get up. How was your shift last night? I didn't hear you come in," I inquire.

"I got home just after midnight. I noticed you were already asleep, so I slept in the spare room," he explains.

"You didn't have to do that," I say, feeling grateful.

"It's okay, I was able to get some rest," he assures me.

With a cup of coffee in hand, I settle at the table, and he joins me with his breakfast. Curious, I ask, "Are you taking the day off?"

"I wish, but I have three meetings where I need to present my team's progress, and I also have a lunch meeting with some colleagues," he replies.

My gaze drops to my coffee cup. Josh knows I worry about him taking on so much, but I can't voice my concerns without upsetting him.

Seemingly aware of my thoughts, he says, "I have an evening off in the next few days. I can catch up on rest then." I nod, appreciating his consideration. He adds,

"We can leave at the usual time unless you'd like to go to work earlier."

I glance up, contemplating, "Actually, we'll need to take separate cars today. Unless you don't mind waiting an extra thirty minutes after work?"

He stops chewing and exclaims, "What do you mean, separate cars?"

"I have an appointment for a massage in the afternoon. It was prescribed to help me relax before the next procedure," I explain.

"What the fuck, Jordan? I work non-stop, and here you are spending money on massages?" he snaps.

"Josh, it's prescribed, and it's covered by insurance," I respond, trying to calm the situation.

"Not right away it isn't," he retorts.

"What does that matter? I pay upfront, and it will still be reimbursed. It's covered, and don't you want this next attempt to work? I'm doing my best to stay relaxed and healthy. The doctor prescribed this to help, and I won't turn down something that might be beneficial," I defend my decision.

He rolls his eyes and huffs," I'm not going to chase after the insurance to pay for this."

"I didn't ask you to," I assert.

"Jordan, I mean it. Don't let the paperwork sit around," he warns, his frustration evident.

"I'll take care of it."

Josh gives me a lingering look, as if contemplating something, though I'm unsure of what. Finally, he utters words that sting, "I can't believe how selfish and self-indulgent you are. This could have waited. I work so hard for our future, and you just throw it away."

"That's enough," I snap back, frustration bubbling within me. "Again, this is covered, and I'll take care of dealing with the insurance. I'm not selfish; I'm fucking stressed and worried that this next attempt won't work. I need a way to relax, and you certainly aren't helping. You're never here, and don't tell me your absence is for us. I never asked you to be gone all the time!" With those words, I storm away from the table, tossing my empty coffee mug into the sink. It shatters, the sound echoing my frustration. I retreat to the bedroom to get dressed for work.

Josh gives me space, and when it's time to leave, he says, "Look, I'm sorry. I'm just tired, and I don't want to deal with chasing after insurance money."

"I told you, I'll handle it," I reply, looking up into his blue eyes, bracing myself for another response that might require me to defend my choices. There's a moment of hesitation.

He nods and offers, "I'm okay with waiting the extra half-hour after work if you still want to carpool?"

I know he's trying, attempting to set things right in the morning, but I'm still annoyed. I let out a sigh and reluctantly agree, "Okay."

The drive to work is tense, filled mostly with small talk. He knows I'm still simmering with anger, and I'm doing my best to let it go. We touch upon his second job without either of us getting too upset about it. Josh reassures me that it's temporary, but for now, while he can manage, he wants to keep going. I don't argue. As we pull into the parking lot, I drop him off at his workplace.

He reaches over and kisses me, "I'm sorry about this morning. Have a good day and I hope the message helps."

I rest my forehead on his and murmur, "Thank you and have a good day and if you are tired, please tell me and we can talk about the second job." He nods and then slowly pulls himself out of the car to head into his office building.

When I arrive at my own office, I am mentally exhausted, though I remind myself that this will be a shorter day at work with the massage appointment in the afternoon.

As I get settled at my desk and soon find my groove and shake off what happened earlier. Lately my productivity has taken an upswing. At least here, I can focus on things that are engaging like being able to speak to Devon and keep my mind distracted and this week with the anticipation building with being able to see him, I have a bounce in my step, I'm all smiles and others seem to be taking notice.

I am at my computer plugging away at answering email requests when I receive a message from my secret southern man. He sends it to my work email. We had recently exchanged emails, engaging in a lighthearted conversation. In an effort to appear less absorbed in my phone, I prefer emailing instead of constant texting. So, when Devon's email arrives, I'm quick to respond.

"Hey Devon,

Things are going great. I'm really looking forward to seeing you on screen tomorrow!

-Jordan"

I hit the send button and anticipate his response. In the meantime, I attend to a work-related email, knowing it will take a few moments. True to form, Devon's reply arrives, but this time he has switched to text messaging.

Devon explains, "I'll have to make an early run to the airport to drop her off, but after 9:00 AM, I'm all yours. I think she's still going away for two weeks. When does Josh leave?"

I admire Devon's wife for her resilience. She had an accident while doing yard work earlier this week, twisting her ankle. For a while, our plans to video chat were uncertain, as we weren't sure if Sara would cancel her flight.

I respond, "I'm not sure when Josh leaves for work, but I'll likely be available by then. You can message me on Facebook, and if he's still with me, you'll know if I don't respond right away."

Devon assures me, "No worries. He comes first. I understand."

There's something about me that I dislike—I feel the need to offload what happened this morning onto Devon. I share every detail with him.

Devon responds, "My partner and I haven't had an argument in years."

How the hell do two people live together and not have an argument in years? I reply, hoping to encourage him to open up further, "That's incredible. It must be nice to have a relationship without arguments."

Devon explains, "There's nothing to argue about. We're not perfect people; we just get along. Like I said, we're roomies, but we love each other without all the complications."

It sounds like an emotionless relationship, but given my own circumstances, I think I would prefer that over the meaningless fights with Josh. I respond, "I constantly get grief about everything, even over something as trivial as dishes. And a few nights ago, our dog had an accident in his crate. I put the dog outside and took the crate downstairs to clean it. While I was doing that, Josh got mad at me for not giving the dog a bath first."

Devon expresses his opinion, "That's not right. I don't mean to overstep, but he has two hands, right? He could have done it too. He could wash the dishes and so on."

I elaborate further, "Josh eventually did it, but not without giving me a hard time. I had my reasons for doing things in the order I did. I put the dog outside so he could finish his business. Anyway, I know I'm not perfect either, but sometimes it feels like Josh fixates on the smallest things."

Devon provides me with the supportive words I need to hear. With Josh, I always feel like I'm somehow in the wrong, especially after he berates me. But with Devon, I feel supported. "Yeah, there are more important things to focus on," he says, shifting the conversation to a more positive tone. "I'm really looking forward to talking to you, whether it's through chat or video. You have no idea. And don't worry, I mean 'clean' in a completely innocent way, not the way you might be thinking," he adds with laughter.

I smile, feeling his enthusiasm shine through. It amuses me that he feels the need to clarify that he'll keep our conversations clean. Our chats have become intimate in a different sense. I respond, "I can't wait to talk to you for real. I hope we don't encounter any technical issues when setting it all up."

Devon leaned in, his eyes sparkling with anticipation as he wrote. "Are you nervous about meeting me? Be honest, no need to hold back. Personally, I'm buzzing with excitement to see you in person, beyond the confines of photos. Not that the photos aren't great; the camera truly adores you. Maybe it's the Canadian backdrop lending its magic to those shots. Silly thought, I know. But I can't contain my desire to finally meet you."

A smile formed on my lips as I responded, "Initially, I had some nerves, but now I'm counting down the minutes. It's unusual for me, but it feels like reuniting with a long-lost family member after months apart." Why does fate toy with our hearts? These emotions defy reason. I've tried to analyze and resist them, but my heart refuses to be swayed."

Before I could fully immerse myself in thoughts of our meeting, a text message from him brought me back to reality. "I feel like I'm about to meet an extraordinary person, truly."

My heart melted at his words. If he were here right now, the possibilities would be endless. "Likewise," I replied, knowing the night would feel long as we awaited our rendezvous. "I'll see you tomorrow, sending you virtual hugs and kisses."

He responded, his voice filled with longing, "I never want these feelings for you to fade away, even if we must remain friends, keeping it a secret. It's okay, but for now, in my mind, I think of you as mine. Alright, sending hugs and kisses back at you."

Oh, how his words made me melt, but I couldn't leave it at that. I needed clarity on tomorrow's plans to ensure we wouldn't get into trouble.

"Alright, Jordan, time to bring your head out of the clouds for a moment," I scolded myself. I needed to call Josh and confirm his departure time, even though the conversation we had earlier hadn't ended well, weighing on my heart.

After clicking send on my text to Josh about his work schedule for tomorrow, I dove into my emails. Frustration grew as I repeatedly checked my phone, hoping for a reply that never arrived. What's with him? What's the point of having a phone if he never checks his messages? I knew he wasn't purposely ignoring me; that's just not Josh. My guess was that his phone was tucked away in his bag.

As I answered another work email, I couldn't resist checking my phone one more time, only to be disappointed yet again. Resigned to my situation, I decided to call Josh on his work phone. He answered, his voice cautious. "Hello, Josh speaking."

"Hi, it's me. I wanted to know what time you're heading to work tomorrow," I inquired.

"Why?" he questioned.

Thinking quickly, I lied, "I was thinking of meeting up with my mom and sister during the day for a walk."

"Are you driving to your parents' house?" he probed.

I rolled my eyes, even though he couldn't see me. "Yes."

"Jordan, we can't afford gas. Can't you stay home?"

"Considering I'll be alone for the entire day; I'd prefer to spend it with my family. It's just a twenty-minute drive," I defended.

He sighed, as if my request weighed heavily on him. "Alright, but don't make it a habit."

I didn't want to engage in further discussion, so I quickly said, "Okay, well, I wanted to confirm your time so I can let them know when I'll be meeting them. What time are you leaving?"

"I'll be leaving the house at 9:00 AM."

"Okay, thanks. Talk to you later?"

Josh's voice softened as he replied, "I love you."

I couldn't fathom his actions. If he truly loved me, why did he question everything I did? In an effort to avoid further confrontation, I responded, "I love you too."

I hung up, feeling a mix of resentment and frustration toward him. I despised his behavior and sighed as I blankly stared at my work computer screen, trying to decompress. My thoughts then shifted back to Devon. Almost forgetting, I decided to send him an email to confirm the meeting times.

Chapter 13
A Devon and Jordan First

Saturday morning couldn't come sooner, and I hate to say it, but I was happy to see Josh leave for the day. There were no arguments or anything like that. I was just anxious to get to see and talk to Devon.

I have about thirty minutes from the agreed time to go online and talk to Devon and this strangely feels like a first date even though I'm not leaving the house.

I shower and am careful to pick my clothes. I don't want to be too done up, that it looks like I am over doing it for someone who is staying at home for the day, but I also don't want to come off as looking homely. I pick out a nice slim fitting short and a grey lace tank top, one that he complemented me on from a picture. I take time to blow out my hair and I put just a touch of makeup on, some brown eyeliner, natural shadow, and a bit of mascara. I give myself a final glance in the mirror before going downstairs, satisfied that I look good.

My computer finally started up, and as soon as Facebook loaded, messages from Devon flooded in. He greeted me with a simple "Good morning."

Excitement surged within me, and I quickly replied, "Why hello there!"

Devon asked, "How's your day going so far? It's sunny and bright here."

"That sounds wonderful," I replied. "Here, it's raining a bit and a little chilly. I might go for a jog later this evening." How I longed to live in a warmer climate. One day, when my novels sell, I'll buy that tropical island I've always dreamed of.

"The cooler weather is perfect for a jog," Devon replied. His ability to find the positive in every situation was endearing, and I found myself growing fonder of that aspect of him.

Without beating around the bush, I asked, "So, are you at home now?"

"I'm sitting in my home office," he answered.

I tried to play it cool as I replied, "Same here. Oh, and I must mention, he's gone to town for the day. He actually called me a couple of minutes ago to let me know he arrived safely."

"That's thoughtful of him to keep you informed," Devon remarked. "As for me, she's in the air somewhere over Tennessee right now."

"She must have needed a break from you!" I teased.

"Haha! I'm such a terrible person that everyone runs away," he chuckled. "She wanted to visit her daughter and family."

Curiosity sparked within me, and I inquired, "Where does her daughter live?"

"South Plainfield, New Jersey. But her daughter drove to Rochester last night."

"That's cool. I've always wanted to see the Jersey Shore," I confessed, letting my wanderlust shine through.

"It is nice there."

Eager for our long-awaited video call, I decided to be upfront and asked Devon, "So, how do I see you?"

I could tell that he had been searching while we were chatting because his response indicated it was on his mind. He explained, "Well, I've been looking around, but all I'm finding are video chat applications that require phone numbers. Facebook has a video button, but I'm not sure what it does. It would have been nice to see you, but I can't find one that ensures your privacy."

I typed out my random thought, "Don't we need to download another application for that?"

He replied, "I'm not sure, but there's CUNow for PC or Mac."

Feeling a bit confused, I gathered that he wanted me to check out CUNow. I responded, "Okay, let me switch my phone to airplane mode. That way, it'll be strictly data, I think."

Doubts started creeping in as I began to believe this video date might be a disappointment. We were still struggling to get off the ground. Suddenly, I noticed a missed call message and quickly informed him, "Ah man, I just missed a call from you."

He answered, "I'm switching to Chrome. You didn't think this would be easy, did you?" His jab made me smile, even amidst the frustrating process. Technology could be maddening when it didn't work as expected.

The failed attempts and text messages saying "It's ringing" or "I'm calling you" had a humorous element. Oh, and let's not forget, "Yes, I see that you're calling me, but I don't know how to answer the phone." After an hour of unsuccessful attempts, the call finally came through. I heard the ringing, and my heart skipped a beat because somehow, I knew this attempt would succeed. Answering the call, I felt it marked a new beginning, a long-awaited one.

Chapter 14
First Sight

For a couple of seconds, the screen is black, I say "Hello? Hello?" Like magic the video appears with the man in the photos that I so have a crush on. The feeling is amazing, and you know it is funny all the things that we end up taking for granted in our lives, like being able to talk through voice and see someone live. My friend has come to life before my eyes and he is all smiles on the other end, my handsome, masculine southern man. His eyes are happy and true. He has such beautiful, intelligent eyes, medium brown hair that is cut short and it has been flicked up in the front with a bit of gel; he has a goatee, trimmed short and a gorgeous complexion. He takes my breath away; he is beautiful, and I just can't shake the feeling that I knew him before. I see my own reflection, on the phone, how I look to him in the corner of the screen, my soft, silky brown hair, my tanned complexion, and my blue eyes looking back at me. It's distracting to see yourself as you appear to others, but when I look at myself, I see nothing but one happy girl, and nothing else matters in her world except for this moment in spending time with him. I hold on to this thought for as long as I can. I long to be closer to him, to touch him, and feel him in me, it's never enough for my little greedy soul.

His voice, friendly and warm with a Texan flavor, comes through the line, "Why hello there!" he exclaims, and then he can't help but gush, "You are so beautiful. I know I've said it before, but wow, Jordan."

I laugh, feeling a mix of flattery and awkwardness. "Thank you, you're handsome too," I manage to reply, though I feel a sudden loss for words. It's ironic how we talk endlessly through text, yet here I am, struck dumb. There's some feedback on the line, and Devon is quick to notice it. We continue typing to each other when the noise becomes too disruptive.

He points out, "There's a lot of noise on the line."

I respond by typing what I had intended to say to him through the video, "It's like there's a bird in your house or something."

He smiles and shakes his head, typing his response, "Nope, no birds, just me and two cats. Wow, that noise is bad, sorry. Well, at least the video quality is okay."

I suggest, "Maybe we could start the call over?"

"Okay," he agrees.

He initiates the call again, and I answer, but to our disappointment, the strange noise persists, as if a persistent bird won't stop chirping.

Devon explains, "If I turn down the sound, the weird noise goes away. I think it's the microphone causing it."

We are able to hear each other somewhat and again that weird bird noise is coming through between our chatter and it gets to the point where we have to use text, I tease him, my technical support guy on the other end to blame him for the noise. I say, "Oh its totally on your side."

He gives me a playful shrug on the camera and types, "I think so. I am trying to look at the microphone settings."

I watch him on my screen and can't take my eyes away from him. He smiles at me, and I can see that he is typing something. He asks, "So, am I okay looking?"

I am a little surprised that he even asks because I see myself with how I look through the camera to him and I am all googly eyed and smiles over my southern gentleman. I respond, "Of course!"

I see his eyes glance at the screen as he reads my answer, and he looks back at the camera and smiles. He types, "I want this bird to die."

"Me too, I hate birds."

Devon types, "Well I don't live in a jungle."

We are both entranced by the other. I see it in him as he sees it in me. I just lean forward on my desk to get a closer look at him and instinctively he does the same and when he does, I giggle.

I say, "Devon we talk so much in text and now look at us. We finally get this working and have nothing to say."

He laughs, "I know!" Our eyes catch each other staring at one another and we both laugh again.

"So, would you like a tour of my home?" I suggest, hoping to break the ice once again.

"Sure, I would like that," he agrees, his enthusiasm shining through.

I begin the virtual tour, taking him first to my office and then leading him through the different rooms in my finished basement. I explain that in my office, there are two "L" shaped sand-colored wood desks facing each other—one for me and the other for Josh. I delve into our respective work: my writing and assisting Josh with photo editing. Josh's hobby is photography, and his desk boasts three monitors. We recently renovated the basement, painting it a light grey-blue shade and installing oak flooring throughout most of the space. I maneuver the camera around the room so Devon can get a good view. I can't help but giggle nervously as I guide him to the next room. It feels awkward, but it's something I can manage at this moment.

I show him around the entrance of my home, the living room, and the kitchen, sharing the efforts we've put into making it a comfortable space. Displaying my home wasn't the initial purpose of our video chat, but right now, it's the only thing I feel at ease doing. I know it's not what he had in mind either because it's not what I had in mind. Suddenly, everything feels real and tangible, no longer confined to texts and still pictures.

Devon smiles back at me through the live video, his warmth evident. "You have a nice home," he comments, his smile radiating. There's a brief moment where we pause and simply gaze at each other. This is much more challenging than I had anticipated. It's a mix of excitement and nervousness, as if we were two people who had been locked away in solitude for years and are now seeing another person for the very first time.

Breaking the silence, I suggest, "Would you like to see my new car?"

"I would like that." he replies. I take him to the garage for a few minutes and then come in and head back downstairs to the office. The interference is becoming a little much, but we make do by typing messages when we can't make out what the other is saying. He is captivating and aside from the staring at each other we discuss our writing, where we get our ideas, how we work, it's a good conversation.

We have been talking for hours, but it feels like minutes, and he says to me, "I am afraid that I need to let you go. I am expecting a phone call soon." I know what it means; his spouse has likely arranged to call him once her plane has landed. I don't want him to get in trouble, so I don't put up a fight to keep him. He smiles, "It was so nice to actually see you today and we will do this again. I promise." With that he smiles and wave's goodbye to the camera and then my screen goes black. My heart already misses him. I sit there for a moment just thinking about it all and it makes me forget for a moment where I am.

Reality starts to set in, and I feel my stomach growling.

Chapter 15
After Intermission

It's now early in the afternoon and I have finished an awesome vegetarian sandwich. I am not a vegetarian; I just enjoy the taste of some of the food. I had put together avocado, cheese, lettuce, and tomato and for a sauce I mixed garlic hummus and mayo with a sprinkle of cilantro seasoning.

I will be alone for the entire afternoon because Josh is working a full day at his second job. He hasn't called, not that I expect him to. Working in a hardware store means that he is going to be with customers for the bulk of his day and he likely won't have a moment to call. In the back of my mind, I think about him and wonder if he will interrupt my afternoon with Devon.

I work on my writing downstairs, and it is not long before I notice that Devon is back online. Assuming his previous call has ended, I eagerly type, "Hey, so happy that I got to see you. Can I see you again? Hint hint!"

He responds with a smiley face, and my phone immediately alerts me of an incoming video call. Just like before, I quickly click accept. The screen remains dark for a moment, and then Devon appears.

He explains, "Sara has landed safe and sound, so all is good, and I have the afternoon to spend with you."

I notice that he's walking around his house while video chatting on his phone. It seems like he's trying to find a better reception because that peculiar bird noise has returned.

Playfully, I comment, "Do you have tin foil in the walls or something?"

Chuckling, he replies, "I was walking around to see if it got better. And no, I'm not a weirdo—no tin foil." His smile is infectious, and I can't help but giggle in response.

He explains via text, "I live in an older community where homes range from two hundred thousand to a million in price."

"No way!" I exclaim, surprised by the range of prices.

He explains, "It's just Texas. Are you sure that you are not just whistling at me?" He chuckles as I receive his latest text. I smile and shake my head no.

I mention, "It is hard to put price tags on things and get an idea because each city has a different economy."

He says, "I agree, the price doesn't matter it is the value of the area."

He gives me the tour of his home, like I did for him earlier and like me and Josh, Devon and Sara have done a bit of updating to their home. I am so jealous of his beautiful kitchen with the dark wood cabinets and stainless-steel appliances and his back yard is to die for. He opens the door, and it comes out onto this huge, covered porch that extends the full length of his house and his property backs onto a field. He explains that just down the hill is a river, but we can't see it because of the hill; it is all grass and sky. He returns inside and I see his living area, it has a brick fireplace. He takes me down a different hallway to where the bedrooms are. His master has this comfy looking four poster bed and for a second, I imagine myself there in it with him on top of me. He walks back down the hall and settles on a couch in his living room. He is all smiles.

"I would love to get up and leave," I type, expressing my admiration for his gorgeous surroundings.

He asks, "And go where?"

"Visit you," I reply with a smile.

He grins and types back, "That would be awesome."

Chuckling at the slight delay in our messages, I comment, "It isn't too bad between the typing and the video."

"My heart is beating fast. "You are so mesmerizing to me," he admits, seemingly just catching up to my previous comment. He quickly adds, "It works, and I don't want to get you in trouble."

I reassure him, "Yes, I'm being a big goof right now. I'm nervous too, but happy. It's like Christmas here." He nods in agreement, responding, "It's like a gift. This is awesome, and you do that for me with just seeing you." He mentions his cats meowing in the background and briefly steps away to address them.

After returning to his home office, he asks about the progress of my book. I know he's referring to the story I'm writing about our friendship, and I'm honest about my recent shift in focus due to our connection. "It's coming along; my word count is growing daily. The thing is, since I started writing about this after a couple of months of our conversations, I'm going off memory for the early parts," I explain.

He seems understanding and supportive of the creative project, as long as our identities remain concealed. I respond, "It's true, you have me every day, just not in person."

As our video chat continues, I can't help but feel grateful for this newfound friendship and the inspiration it has brought to my writing.

As I send my thoughts over, I catch Devon gazing at me, and he comments with a grin, "Okay, don't mind me. I'm just looking at you."

Smiling, I type back, "No, I don't mind. That's why we have video."

He compliments my hair length, and I playfully respond, "I like that you have hair!" Giggling, I find comfort in our light-hearted banter.

Unfortunately, the feedback on the line hampers our ability to hear each other clearly. I suggest typing instead, and he mentions that I have a northern accent. It's an amusing comment, given his southern background. I tease, "No, I don't! You're the one who talks funny."

He expresses his frustration with the interference, and I agree, "Yes, it sucks big time."

Devon then inquires about my character development in writing, asking if it is influenced by my work or the area where I live. I clarify that I draw inspiration from my life experiences and the people around me, shaping characters as representations of those I encounter.

He nods, showing his interest in learning more about me, and asks about my blue eyes. Playfully, I bring my eye close to the camera, asking, "Do they look blue?" He chuckles at my silliness.

Expressing my happiness about our video chat, I assure him, "Other than talking to you, I would be doing housework right now, so that doesn't matter. I prefer having you for company, and I willingly allow you to take up my time."

He smiles, feeling honored, and seems to be working on something on his computer. I give him a moment to respond, but my silly side kicks in, and I send a face with a tongue sticking out, playfully prompting him.

He shrugs, still smiling, and types back, "I am thinking of what to say." His chuckle shows that he's enjoying our playful exchange.

I can't help my poor southern man is trying so hard to be a gentleman. I just have this picture in my head of us on a real first date in person. This date wouldn't be going so good with both of our shyness but then again, I think we would be doing way more interesting stuff than just talking.

Devon asks, "What more would you like to know about me, like where I was born and such, stuff like that?" He laughs again.

In the little time that we have gotten to know one another, I have searched him out online just to make sure that he was who he said he was and not just someone feeding me lies to get close. I know those things about him, and I am not sure that he knows that I know. I feel sort of guilty for investigating but in my defense all that information was out there for me to find and after I did all that searching on him, I know that he is the real deal.

I feel guilty about admitting this but decide that it's best just to come clean. The worst that could happen would be that I scare him off but deep down I think he will understand the reasoning for my actions. I type, "I was creepy and searched out your biography and other online sources and stuff, so I know all of that." I watch his facial expression and try not to look at my image in the bottom corner of the screen but imagine that the look I have is somewhat shy, worried, and embarrassed with having just admitted to doing all of that.

I continue, "Creepy, right?"

He replies, "It just means that you are interested, right?" His expression reveals that it definitely surprises him, but I don't gather that he is too bothered.

I type, "I would be wasting my time if I wasn't interested, right?"

Devon asks, "Please talk, I love hearing your voice."

I ask Devon, "Did you finish that final chapter yet?"

Devon confesses, "No, but I am at the moment working on a sex scene between Alexis and Brad. She doesn't want to give in, and he is scared as hell."

Devon is a thriller and suspense writer and is just finishing a new series. He has been tackling the final scene for some time which tells me that he is a precise writer. He even wakes early every day to get a couple of hours of writing done before work each morning. I'm not like that. I write the moment an idea comes into my head and then go from there.

We are the opposites of one another when it comes to writing. I write sci-fi fantasy novels and am able to write out a story much more quickly because I don't need to do all of the fact checking that he does. I enjoy the benefits of being able to make stuff up, worlds, animals, people, it is fun and when I write, it somehow brings me back to that feeling of being a child. I can remember playing with friends at an incredibly young age and being able to imagine stuff as we played together in the backyard. We would imagine a scene and reenact them in our play time. That's what writing does for me; it is sort of a window into being a child all over again and allowing yourself to get lost in your imagination.

Going back to Devon's comment on where he was at with his progress. I say, "Does it really take that long?" He catches my jab at the sex scene and sees me giggle.

He explains, "Jordan you are silly. When talking, your lips move then voice comes in but I'm not complaining."

"Yes, it's the same here for me."

He types, "Sorry for being so goofy over you. You just have that effect on me. I want to reach through the phone and bite you!" He laughs.

I answer, "That's okay I'm feeling the same way."

He smiles, "Lucky me."

In an earlier conversation he had mentioned his timeline on when he thought he would have this project complete and I ask, "Why do you think it will take that long to edit?"

It caught him off guard and he takes a big inhale and exhale. I hear the breath leave his mouth and watch his shoulders rise and fall to the motion as he looks up to the ceiling and then back into the camera, "I'm not sure but you have to have a few rewrites."

I mention, "Let me explain my question a little bit. The sample that you gave, I only caught a couple of errors that's why I was wondering."

He says, "Thank you," I wrote 95% of it in two months. I am at about one hundred and nine thousand words, but it will probably get cut down to around the one hundred-thousand-word mark after the edits."

One of his cats jumps up onto his desk and walks across in front of him.

I smile and ask, "What's his name?"

Devon answers but I can't make out what he is saying and ask him to type it, but the thing is I don't think he can hear me either. So, I type, "Did you say that his name was Tiny?"

"It's Rocky. He is a polydactyl, he has hands."

"Oh, like an extra toe?"

"Yes"

I laugh; his affectionate orange tabby demands his attention by snuggling up to him on the desk. He has to pick his cat up to remove him.

Devon explains, "He talks a lot." He returns to talking to the camera, chatting about us, the situation that we have found ourselves in and the new affections that we have for one another. As he lays it all out for me to take in, I sort of go quiet with his honesty.

Devon types, "I think I am making you shy huh?"

No, it is more like speechless but in a good way because I feel the same. It's just an entirely different feeling when the person you care so deeply for tells you how they feel, and you know that you feel equally the same. I should feel like this for my husband. Instead, I type something stupid back to him, "I don't know, I am just reading my screen and trying to look at my phone at the same time."

He says, "Ok, I hope I was everything you imagined but that's hard to say without seeing me in person, but for me I am in heaven. Nobody's perfect but you are darn close to it!"

My cowboy is always full of compliments, I type, "I have gotten to know you over the course of a couple of months. I feel like I really have known you from somewhere else."

"Weird huh, I wish I was living up north or at least near the border."

I smile and type, "I wish that I could get through the screen and see you, like for real, that's all."

Devon says, "You and I both, well Jordan I am going to have to let you go for now."

Devon ends the video chat, and my screen goes black, but we still have the chat window open and keep the conversation going.

I say, "Okay, so did you want to talk again tomorrow around 2:00 PM? Are we doing 2:00 PM my time or yours?"

"Yours; okay don't get mad for me saying this but I am so fucking horny. I do think normal thoughts too. Wow I am in la la land."

"Okay poor guy."

"No, it is cool."

"Wish I was there to help you out. Josh denied me again this morning."

Devon types, "I will refrain, just love hearing your voice and loved seeing you. Darn, yeah you would get it from me, no denying. Sorry if I was shy and all googly eyed on screen."

"No that's okay, I was the same way. My cheeks hurt from smiling so much. Wow, I wish you were mine."

Devon admits, "Me too, but we have separate lives but wow oh wow Jordan you do it for me, you really have no idea, but glad you are my friend, and we can build on that."

I hold myself for a moment at the desk while reading the screen; this is so hard to want someone that you can't have. I simply type, "Yes, not fair!"

He continues, "I'd take you in my arms and caress you and kiss you and bring you down to the ground and take your breath away and watch you, but that's just dreaming, so I'll take what I can get."

I shrug, "We can take this one day at a time and see what this becomes. I really like you a lot."

"Exactly, but for now I am glad you are my friend, it may have to be only friends, no one knows."

Our messages are a little delayed and I write, "I wasn't looking to find a relationship like this I'm married but here we are. I still don't get it, but I think about you all the time. Wonder and imagine."

Devon says, "I feel the same, never was looking and you came along and my heart flips like crazy. If it is a secret love affair that turns into more, I am for it, hoping to get the secret meetings and enjoy your company and time trust me I can't stop thinking about you. It's driving me nuts and I can't do anything about it. I think you understand, God I'm dying to see you again but will soon."

I admit, "You know how I said earlier that I was denied again, well girls need to do the same. I had to this morning, thought about it being you."

Devon says, "I like that. It will happen, trust me it will. It has too, it's part of the story and my life now."

"You are a part of my life too. I can't get you out of my head."

"Then that's awesome. I never had a girl go nuts over me and I am a good-looking guy, not a fatso, just a few extra pounds that I am trying to get rid of that too. It is being used against me for denial of sex from Sara."

I respond, "I like everything that I see."

"That makes me happy. Sara cares and loves me, but she is fifteen years older and doesn't care for sex; the drive is gone. Not mine, it is alive and kicking and desiring that passion and I want it to be with you."

I still can't see a single thing wrong with Devon, and just flat out say, "So really, there is nothing wrong with you? You're smart, attractive and you seem to have no problems with erectile dysfunction." My statement is followed with the tongue out emoji.

"Nope, just a normal guy and from what I can see you are normal too and you are full of life and energy."

I continue, "No trouble with the law? I imagine that your work does background checks."

He responds, "No just a straight 'A' citizen and a forty-two-year-old male that writes and dreams about you. Well, I haven't written about you. I mean, I am an author."

A comma would have fixed what he had meant to say, but I knew that already even with the omission of the comma, I answer. "I got it."

Devon explains, "I will write about you, but will do that in our book. Imagine if we were together, this book would be real time and full of erotic stuff and not to mention an adventure leading up to it."

I say, "It will be and I'm not holding back. I sort of did with my first book because I had been gearing it for a

Young Adult crowd, but for this one I am telling it the way that I want."

He affirms, "Good! I am not joking when I say that I like you a lot and fallen for you hard, just know I have to keep the boundaries but when we talk there doesn't have to be. Be yourself; tell me whatever you need to and likewise from me."

I say, "Yes, it's just the feedback is a distraction and then I catch myself staring at you when I look at the screen and shy myself out."

Devon admits, "Me too, my eyes lit up many times when you stood up, sorry but they did, I was like, wow."

"It's a new bra that's all; holds me up!"

"There is more than just outside appearance, and I am being honored to see you and your inner side, loving every second, yeah it was a nice bra." I laugh.

He pauses for a moment, then says, "You don't mind if I wanted to kiss your whole body when we meet, do you? You have a nice upper half too that is awesome. Let's face it, you are a gorgeous girl and men should triple take when you walk by. So, I can imagine that your hubby knows that, if not, shame on him. I treat my partner to the best of my ability despite the no sex. Imagine having both from me."

I feel a twinge of pain at the reminder of Josh but tell Devon my thoughts; Devon is my friend and an outlet. "I think he does. He used to be so nice to me and now it's like, I look forward to not being with him. I enjoy going to camp without him to be with my family."

He declares, "That is wrong. I am so sorry, you have me in chats and video when we can and hopefully one day we can meet too, even if it were only a few hours, it would be like a lifetime for me. Just glad you are embracing this. I know I am saying things that may have an effect, not trying to, and just speaking the truth. I'll take you in secret and hope one day to have you normally that's all and if it takes a while then so be it, just hope that you want me if we both ever get in that spot of being single. I'm rambling now huh. I honestly have never been attracted to a woman like you before and it is like wow. I'm not a jerk, not an angry man. I have my quirks but know that I am loving. So, for now, like you said let's see where it goes, the first part is awesome as a friend my question, is what if it is a secret for a long time, will that make you fade away? I hope not but I would understand to. It's like I can't stop talking to you." He adds a smiley face.

I say, "I can't see myself going away, like I am borderline obsessive over you."

Devon says, "Just don't get in trouble and that goes for me too, as I am obsessed. I want you, desire you, wishing it were me when he does give in, you name it, and I'd try like every day if I could and let you know I was head over heels for you."

I sit here at my desk reading his words and catch myself glance up at a wedding photo hung over my desk and am reminded of reality. I type, "We wait and let this ride out and see where it goes. Before we started talking, I was already spending time away from him, you wouldn't be the cause if it were to happen."

Devon answers, "It's his loss; sorry, that was wrong of me."

"It's okay; I just know that he is not it anymore."

Devon says, "I so want to meet you, too bad you couldn't come for a week, I would definitely get you pregnant for sure."

"We will organize something and will need to keep it secret. We got to think with our heads and not with, well you know."

"Yes, I am doing that, don't mean to talk erotic to you, well let me let you go for a bit, call you at 2:00 PM tomorrow."

"Okay" I add a smiley face, "Talk to you later."

Chapter 16
Two Hearts Learning

The next day arrives, and I find myself in the same position as the day before. Josh is gone to work, and I am alone for the day. I go down to my computer to write and maybe, well hoping that I can chat up my Devon. I load everything up and sure enough he has beaten me to the punch.

This morning we are both in the same boat we have video chat up along with text messaging because of the feedback at times and even though we agreed to 2:00 PM to chat, excitement takes the lead.

Devon asks, "So do you have a personal website other than Twitter or Facebook?"

"No, I don't think I am ready for one just yet."

I already know that Devon has a few different websites floating around. He has written in a few genres and each website seems to represent a genre that he has done. He explains, "When you do, you will know if it is right for you or not. I have an older site and haven't done anything with it in a long time and need to get rid of it since I moved those books over to my promotional site."

"Yes, that makes sense. I think right now Amazon and Smashwords are doing a better job at exposure than I could ever do with getting my own website out there."

Devon inserts a random thought into our conversation, and I find myself tilting my head to the side for a second, wondering and then realize he is talking about the video chat. He says, "I just looked, it is a known issue with CUNow, there is no fix yet."

I choose to finish typing my previous thought and shrug to myself, Jordan he is a tech guy what do you expect? I type to him, "Everyone knows Amazon and so it's simple."

Devon agrees, "Then that's all that you need." Devon looks into the camera and says, "Tell me more about you."

I smile back and still I find myself a little shy and say, "What do you want to know about me?"

"What was it like for you growing up, what are your passions, where do you see yourself as an author?"

"I grew up in the suburbs, stayed in this area my entire life. Passions are you, I used to figure skate as a kid and a teen and competed in Canada and the United States sometimes."

Devon asks, "Did you ever check out my other site that had a sample of the writing on it? R. B. James, it is my other pen name. The book is not out for sale yet, but I want to put it on Smashwords eventually. By the way ice skating takes guts. You see you are a northern person. I can see you skating, skiing; I love sledding."

What a bummer I want to see this other website of his, but my stupid computer just doesn't want to load the page. Sadly, I say to him, "No I can't view the site it keeps asking me to download an additional application and when I go through the motions, I can't get it to work."

Devon replies, "Okay no worries."

I continue to tell him more, "What else? You know, I used to horseback ride in my teens. I would spend summers at a horse barn."

"There are many horse farms in Texas."

"I would work there in exchange for food, shelter, and free lessons. That is how I learned."

He says, "You seem like a very well-rounded person."

"I sound like a poor person, but my parents always had money."

"No, I understood. My parents did what they could do since my mom was divorced and remarried."

I explain, "I was never really good at school but trudged through it. I had a hard time caring about school. I was more interested in competition and horses."

Devon tells me, "My real dad is a retired cop. As for school, I wasn't an 'A' student, 'C, maybe a 'B' once in a while. In school I had long curly hair and many girls liking me; I don't have any pictures of my hair from back then. I was a part-time jock and part-time school paper editor."

He sounds like he always was an outgoing person; unlike me, I started off shy and it took a while for me to shed the shyness away, though it makes its appearances from time to time like for this video chatting, I'm trying to keep my shyness at bay. I say to him, "I would love to see you in one of those army pictures." I add a smiley face.

He continues, "Before I joined the Army, I applied for Naval Air Academy for F-14 School and got accepted only after I joined the army. You saw the movie Top Gun, right?"

"Yes, did you fly one of those?"

"No, wanted to, I flew AH-1 Cobra Attack Helicopter, two-seater; I was primary pilot and had a gunner in front of me sitting a little lower down. The movie 'Firebirds' shows them."

"That's so crazy, I just searched the images."

"Four years flying those bad boys. They were made for Vietnam, but I flew them in the Army before they were later phased out; still cool though."

"Yes very, like I said, you are the only helicopter pilot that I know."

"It was a long time ago, but part of my past."

I scroll through the images of these decked out flying machines and have to ask him, "In the images some are taking off from boats, did you do that, or did you just take off from the ground?"

"I only took off from the ground. My upbringing wasn't so much fun. Mom struggled to raise my brother and me. The brother you see on Facebook with kids is my half-brother. My mom moved us from New York to Texas when I was five."

He seems to have such a warm and caring soul and to get put into combat, I would think it would take a different kind of person to do. I ask, "Why did you join the army? I don't want to sound insensitive, but you could have died. How did you just decide that you would take a job knowing what could happen?"

"I wanted to serve my country, be the best of the best. I know not a really good answer. I hated living with my real dad and had to get away. He was controlling and mean."

Sometimes I feel like I put my foot in my mouth, and I don't want to make my questions sound as though I am placing some ill judgment of him and explain, "It's honorable, it's just I couldn't put myself in that mind frame. I would be too scared."

He explains, "It's a hard decision to die for someone else that you don't know. I wrote a song about military, well kind of but never sent it out and have also written some poems that got noticed, some were award winners."

Devon has more layers than meets the eye. Each one is intriguing. I say, "I saw some of your poems. I can be a little brat about things. I know there a lot of bad things going on overseas right now and I hate to say it, but I turn my head when it comes on. I know there are people out there doing what they need to but yes, I am a little brat and not the best person to be turning my back to that sort of stuff."

"No worries, it is understood."

I feel bad having just admitted that to a veteran. Wow, you really put your foot into your mouth. I explain, "It's fear really. I know that I have lived a sheltered life."

Devon says, "It's not for everyone."

"My family was good for keeping me safe and when I first started working, I learned that people can be very mean."

He says, "Yes people can be downright assholes. Are you close to your sister and brother?"

I explain, "Yes, I am close with both of them, although I talk to my sister more than my brother. I remember when I started working part-time as a cashier while in high school and wow, when the first customer started to yell at me it was a major shock. My parents would yell at me when I was a brat but this complete stranger that was the first time, I had seen anger like that."

Devon says, "People are strange, and it is obvious that whomever it was that yelled at you lacked personality and communication skills. Your sister doesn't know about us, does she?"

"Nobody does."

"Okay, I don't want you to get in trouble that's all, that's the last thing. If someone does ask, we are mutual friends as we are just with other desires they don't need to know."

"I know that if I tell a soul than I'll worry and get stressed, so know that my lips are sealed."

He replies, "Same here so don't worry about that. Like you said a while back, I was your guilty pleasure, well you are mine." I just smile at him, and he continues, "I can talk to you, laugh, giggle, talk shop, book stuff I mean."

I admit, "You know you are my perfect man." I type it just because it's still hard to hear, "Do you snore?"

Devon continues on his thought, "You take time out of your day to chat with me even if it is just a smiley face." He looks to his monitor and sees my question and answers, "Yes, but no vices, is that a deal breaker? I actually use a machine to try and cure it. What vices are you meaning? I don't smoke, I don't chew tobacco, I do drink occasionally, don't do drugs, I may have some habits."

I chuckle, "I am just trying to figure out how I am speaking to my perfect person. I'm trying to find a chink in the armor."

"Everyone has a dent in their armor, just depends on how you go about fixing it. I'm not perfect in any way but I'm lovable, caring and a down to earth guy, I know that's what my partner sees. I'm pinching myself to see if it is really real that a beautiful gal like you finds me interesting."

I ask him, "Do you like traveling? Do you enjoy resorts and stuff like that?"

Devon flips my own questions back on me, "Do you snore? I know most ladies don't. I do like to travel and find it very relaxing and mind lifting. So, yes love resorts, cruise ships, getaways."

Oh boy, the snoring question. He is being honest with me, so I will be honest with him, "I think I snore sometimes, but I'm told it's more like deep breathing, not an actual snore."

Devon continues, "I like private resorts, I'm active, well, I try to be."

I tell him, "I have been to Cuba and visited a resort there, but never been on a cruise ship. I would love to go at least once in my life."

Devon admits, "I like traveling and seeing the sites and history. Cruise ships are fun. I went on a seven-day seven night eastern Caribbean cruise and loved it."

"Ah man, I would love to go one day, just got to find someone that shares the same interests!"

Devon asks, "Is that a hint?"

Jordan, yes, I am talking to myself, you're a bad girl. I answer him, "Just saying" I have to add that smiley face to the end of that remark.

Devon shares, "They do have book cruises for authors. I guess there is more to life than just working and sometimes you have to get out and just do it. I would love to go to Venice or Florence."

"Me too, my aunt that owns the property where I camp, she did a tour of Eastern Europe, like she toured the castles and stuff. It was awesome seeing all her pictures from that trip. There are so many huge castles on the tops of these insane cliffs. It makes you wonder how the builders did it."

"That is fascinating stuff."

I admit, "I am also a huge Game of Thrones fan. I want to see Kings Landing."

"That would be cool to do, you should do that."

"I forget the name of the city that Kings Landing is filmed in, but wow. Maybe our book will give me that freedom? It's in Croatia, I think."

"There you go."

"Also just putting it out there, but sorry you are going to be my pilot."

"I'm a little rusty, but I can manage, like riding a bike."

"So, I guess it's like a license, it expires? Or could you go flying a helicopter tomorrow if you wanted to?"

Devon must have been looking up the city where they filmed Game of Thrones because his response is, "Dubrovnik, that's the city." He continues to answer my helicopter question, "Yes, it expires; I would have to get certified again. I wish I had kept up on it, could have made money flying peeps around."

I add, "Another place I would like to visit, I know that this sounds backwards since I hate the cold, but I would like to visit Iceland. They have natural hot springs there from the underground volcanos. I would go in naked because that's what the Icelanders do."

"That sounds like a cool place to visit. I know up north there are lots of caves that are historical, but in Texas where about twenty miles away from me there are caves and an actual hidden rain type forest. I would also love to go to Hawaii."

I smile and reply, "Oh me too."

Devon says, "Hell, I would love to go to Canada too."

I test him for some hidden meaning by wanting to visit my country. I ask, "You want to see the sites, right?"

I wait but I don't think he sees my question right away because he replies, "I used to go to Niagara Falls a lot." Then he sees and just gives me a "yep" for an answer, ah bummer.

I admit, "I have actually never been and it's so close by."

"You would love it, but you have to go on the maid of the mist."

"Yes, maybe I could get my sister to go with me or a girlfriend."

He says, "Take pictures. I love the pictures that you shared."

Devon changes topic, "My brother that has the four kids, he married a Canadian gal."

I ask him, "So what is it about us Canadian girls?"

I catch him smirk, and I am not sure if he meant for me to see it. He says, "I don't know, maybe just a magnet, I am drawn to you. I don't really talk to my brother's wife that much, but she is close with my partner."

"Ah I see, well same here, I am really drawn to you too."

He types even though I can see him, "Smiling big but you knew that. Well guess I better do something productive today, huh."

I have to tease him and ask, "Are you going to masturbate?"

"No silly" I see him laughing and I am busting a gut in my chair. He continues, "You can do that for me."

I say, "I may have to."

"Yeah, I think so. I'm not a masturbating continuously kind of guy."

I try to get our derailed conversation back on track, "Okay, so you are planning on doing something productive, okay got it!" I send him a wink face this time.

He expressed his gratitude, saying, "Thank you for sharing your time with me today. I am absolutely delighted!" Just as he finished his comment, the screen suddenly went dark. I observed an unusual flickering of light and became uncertain about what was happening—perhaps a poor connection, I speculated.

"Hello? Are you still there?" I inquired, peering at the dimly lit screen. Though it remained dark, I noticed faint glimpses of light. Had I lost connection with him? I strained to discern any recognizable sounds amidst the shuffling noises that reached my ears, but to no avail.

"I'm going to disconnect because I can neither see nor hear you," I announced through the video feed, reiterating my words in the text.

After a brief pause, he apologized, saying, "Sorry about that. My phone dropped the call. So, how much progress have you made with the writing?"

"I've managed to condense it to seventy-six hundred words," I replied.

"Excellent! Real-time conversations provide rich and captivating material for stories," he remarked.

"Yes, although I didn't record it, the memory remains vivid. You truly made my day."

"Yeah, I could stay here all night, but I will let you go for now." He beams a smile over.

I say, "Well I'll be online for a bit longer. Josh isn't home until a little later so right now I'm just trimming down our text for the story."

Devon sends me a wink face and types, "Have a good rest of the day. I know that I will. You can end the conversation today; I don't have to have the last word." He says it with a smile and it's only because I had teased him before about him always having to have the last word. I could probably keep him longer knowing that no matter what he will try to be the one to type the last remark.

"Okay maybe I can talk to you tomorrow, but I am not sure what the day will be like?"

Devon says, "Sounds good, sorry. I did it." I smile after reading his words; he just had to be the last one.

Chapter 17
Monday Massage

I woke up feeling unusually optimistic, despite it being Monday—the dreaded workday that usually brings me down. But today, my spirits were high. I eagerly prepared for the day, knowing I had a video chat planned with Devon later in the evening. Unfortunately, I had to wait until after work for our conversation to take place.

Another reason for my cheerful mood was the scheduled massage I had later in the day, promised a blissful afternoon of relaxation. Josh had left for work early, leaving the house empty when I woke up. After enjoying a satisfying breakfast, I dressed in a lovely pink dress with a flattering low V-cut, its length ending just above my knees. I styled my hair in a charmingly messy French twist and applied a touch of makeup before heading to the office.

The drive to work was quiet, and within an hour, I found myself at my desk, starting up all my computer applications. While waiting for everything to load, I placed my phone on the desk, only to be surprised by the absence of any messages from Devon. It was unusual since he often sent me a sweet "Hello" or something similar in the mornings.

With a shrug, I reassured myself that Devon must be preoccupied, and I should make the most of my time before heading to my appointment. Surprisingly, the morning flew by effortlessly, and soon the afternoon arrived, signaling it was time for my massage. I drove to the location and managed to find a parking spot on a nearby side street. Before stepping out of the car, I couldn't resist checking my phone one last time. To my surprise, there was still no message from Devon. It felt strange, and a twinge of concern washed over me. I hoped that everything was alright with him, but I realized texting him now would only make me late. I made up my mind to send him a message once I was back home after the massage if I hadn't heard from him by then.

This was my first time visiting this particular place for a massage, and a co-worker had highly recommended it. From the moment I stepped into the lobby, I could understand why. The entire space was adorned with pristine white marble flooring, even the front counter matched the elegance. Vibrant green plants dotted the area, adding a lively touch to the clean and well-lit space that was filled with the warm afternoon sun, its rays glistening off the polished marble.

The woman at the reception desk greeted me with a warm voice and a friendly smile. "Jordan?" she called out, and I nodded in confirmation.

"You have a massage scheduled with Stephan," she confirmed, and I acknowledged with a nod. Stepping out from behind the counter, she said, "Let me take your jacket, and please slip into these slippers." She handed me a pair of simple white slippers and graciously hung my coat.

"Follow me down this hallway. While you wait for Stephan, would you like something to drink?" she asked.

"A glass of water would be perfect, thank you," I replied, offering a grateful smile.

"Coming right up," she said before leaving me in a tranquil waiting area for a moment. The room featured four comfortable seats with plush cushions, and a serene waterfall gently trickled down the wall. With no windows, the space was enveloped in dim lighting, accompanied by the soft ambiance of calming music playing in the background.

I settled into one of the cozy seats, closing my eyes for a brief moment. Suddenly, I felt a gentle breeze as the receptionist returned, whispering, "Here you are," as she handed me the glass of water.

"Thank you," I murmured as I took a refreshing sip of the icy water. Closing my eyes, my thoughts wandered. I found myself contemplating both Josh and Devon, pondering my future and the choices I've made. I couldn't help but question if I worried too much and if my own thoughts were adding unnecessary stress to my life. Could I ever silence this inner voice that constantly clamored for answers? Society often deemed my actions as wrong, but in this one life we're given, should I deny myself new experiences and connections? As long as no one got hurt, what harm was there?

Suddenly, a deep and soothing voice interrupted my thoughts, calling out, "Jordan?" I startled, snapping back to reality, and opened my eyes to find a young, well-built man standing before me.

"Yes," I replied, slightly flustered.

"Hi, I'm Stephan. We have a one-hour massage scheduled for you today, correct?" he asked.

"Yes, that's right," I confirmed.

"If you could follow me to the room, please. I'll ask you to undress, leaving your underwear on, and then slip under the blanket. I'll step out momentarily," Stephan explained. He led me to the massage room, closed the door to grant me privacy, and I undressed before slipping beneath the covers of the massage table.

As I waited, I delved back into my contemplative thoughts. Deep down, I knew that what I was doing wasn't inherently wrong; it was society's judgment and the unfortunate truth that sometimes good things emerged from painful lies. Amidst my reflections, I heard a gentle tap on the door, and I beckoned, "Come in."

Stephen entered the room, his presence calming. "What brings you in for a massage?" he inquired.

"I was actually prescribed a massage by my doctor for stress relief, so this is a relaxation massage," I explained.

"Alright. Which areas would you like me to focus on? Your back, arms, legs, and head?" Stephen asked.

"That would be wonderful," I responded, a hint of anticipation in my voice.

He continued, "I can adjust the pressure to your preference. What level of intensity are you comfortable with?"

"Medium pressure will do," I replied, eager to experience his skilled touch.

Drawing back the blanket, Stephen's hands, strong, warm, and incredibly soothing, began their work. From the moment his hands made contact with my body, I felt a sense of surrender, as if I were melting into the table. Everything that had been racing through my mind moments ago took a backseat as I allowed myself to fully relax and drift away in the blissful sanctuary of the massage.

Chapter 18
Relaxed and Ready to Write

The drive home was a serene experience, my body feeling like a blissful ball of mush after Stephan's excellent massage. Despite returning to an empty house, I felt wonderful. After quickly satisfying my hunger with a bacon, egg, and cheese sandwich, I decided to dive into some of my ongoing writing projects. But before delving into my work, I couldn't resist sending Devon a text to let him know I was available for a chat.

I typed, "Hey Devon, I'm online and ready to chat whenever you're ready. Just give me a call."

A few moments passed, and I continued with my work, momentarily losing track of time. After twenty minutes, my anticipation grew, realizing I hadn't received anything from him. It was odd, but I brushed it off, assuming he must be caught up in something important.

An hour dragged by before finally, a text came through. "Hey Jordan, sorry for the delay, but I don't think it's a good idea to video chat," his message read.

My heart sank, and I hastily replied, "Why? What's wrong?"

"Nothing," he responds briefly.

"No, Devon, don't just brush it off like that. Something is clearly bothering you, and this is unlike you to dismiss it so easily," I press, a tinge of concern in my words.

Devon finally reveals, "Yesterday, during one of our video chats, just before we paused, I had you on video chat on my phone. At the same time, a call came through—it was Sara. She heard your voice."

My heart skips a beat, and I lean back in my office chair, feeling a sense of dread. "How much did she hear?" I ask anxiously.

"She didn't catch our entire conversation, just a word or two before our video chat dropped. But it was enough to make her suspicious," Devon explains.

A wave of worry washes over me. "What did you tell her?" I inquire.

"I denied knowing what she was talking about, claiming ignorance," Devon admits.

"Oh, Devon, you should have come up with an excuse like blaming it on the television or your computer," I lament.

"Regardless, she's now suspicious. She thinks I'm having an affair," Devon confesses.

I take a moment to gather my thoughts. "So, does she know about me?" I inquire, my voice tinged with concern.

"No, you're still a secret. Besides hearing a few words, I didn't divulge anything about you to Sara," Devon assures me.

I inquire, "So, is this why you've been silent all day?"

"Yes," he admits, his voice laden with resignation. "I won't deny it. The reality of the situation hit me hard, and it was too close of a call. I love Sara, and I've already been through a divorce once, losing a lot in the process. If I were to go through it again, I'd risk losing everything."

Feeling a heaviness in my heart, I leave my desk and make my way upstairs to the living room, switching to my phone to continue the conversation. I sense him distancing himself, and it crushes me. I gather the courage to mention, "Well, I don't understand why we can't find a way to move forward and be more cautious."

"Jordan, you know what we're doing isn't right," he confesses, his words are filled with remorse. "I feel terrible for coming between you and your husband."

"Devon, you're not the reason our relationship was already in a rough spot. It was difficult before you entered the picture, and you knew that," I argue.

He poses a question, he is heavy with doubt, "Do you understand that this is wrong?"

"Yes, I do," I admit, I am filled with a mix of defiance and vulnerability. "But I don't care. I have genuine feelings for you, and I'm not willing to simply let them go."

Jordan, I'm sorry, but I like to think of myself as an honest man, and what we're doing is wrong. I know you're intelligent and can see that too. We need to stop and go our separate ways," Devon states firmly.

My heart shatters into pieces, and I sink into a seat. A tear escapes and rolls down my cheek. I understand what's happening. He's right, but it feels so unfair. Throughout the entire summer, he has been more than just my secret lover; he has been my confidant, my best friend. I shared my deepest secrets with him, knowing he wouldn't betray my trust by revealing them to anyone. I can't bear losing all of that, not without him knowing how deeply I feel.

"What the fuck, Devon? You're breaking my heart and reducing me to tears. You're just going to toss everything away, our friendship, and me, like I'm some worthless piece of shit," I am filled with anguish.

"Jordan, you have no idea how terrible I feel," Devon confesses, he is heavy with emotion. "I've never felt so strongly for someone as I do for you. I was willing to run away with you. I wanted you desperately, and I still do, but this is wrong. We have our own lives, and we need to respect our spouses."

The weight of his words hangs heavily in the air, and I can't help but feel the immense pain of our impending separation.

"I don't understand why you want to cut me out completely. You were silent all day, and I can already feel you distancing yourself. It's breaking my heart. How can you just do that? Was everything you said about your relationship with your spouse a sick ploy to manipulate me into opening up? Please be honest with me," I implore, my hands are trembling from a mix of anger and hurt.

"Jordan, I can't keep apologizing," Devon responds, his words heavy with remorse. "Just know that this is crushing me inside. I feel sick to my stomach as I type this to you. Everything I said was honest. I wasn't playing games; it was genuinely me being real with you. This is for the best, trust me. Please don't take offense, but both you and I need some time to work on our relationships with our spouses."

I sink back into the recliner, closing my eyes for a brief moment, desperately hoping that this nightmare will end. He's not just my lover; he's my friend, and this pain cuts deeper than anything I've felt before. Another message from him pops up, urging me to say something, to confirm that I'm okay.

"Devon, I won't lie to you. I'm not okay," I reply, my body is trembling with emotion. "You're making me cry, and I don't have anything to say. No, I'm not okay."

"Please don't cry, and I can't keep repeating myself," he pleads. "Just let me know that you'll be alright."

Taking a moment to compose myself and wipe away my tears, I respond with a mixture of resignation and pain, "I need to cry and let it all out. I need time to process everything. Right now, I'm at home, and I'm truly hurt."

"He says, 'Jordan, you are my friend, know that, and believe me, I want to continue to remain friends. We both need to take a break here and cool it. You will always be my friend,'" I read his message, struggling to comprehend its meaning. What is he trying to say? I read it over and over, and it dawns on me that he's using the classic breakup line of "Let's be friends," which essentially translates to going our separate ways. The pain intensifies. How did I let myself fall for him? I sniffle, attempting to collect myself. You can't win this battle, Jordan. Devon has made his decision, and it's clear. I need to respond.

With a heavy heart, I type, "I will always consider you a friend too," and press enter, watching my message appear on the screen. He responds with a smiley face and adds, "Well, we will part ways then. Have a good night, and I hope that we can both move past this."

Reading those words sends a shiver down my spine. This is it. I've lost my friend. I send a final goodbye, typing, "Bye Devon, take care." Setting my phone down, I curl up into a little ball, wanting to hide from the world, to escape the pain. This feels like a twisted movie playing out, except it's my life. And right on cue, the telephone rings. Not my cell phone, but the home phone. I lift my head from the fetal position and glance at the caller ID. It's Josh.

Chapter 19
The Phone Call

The phone call made me tremble with intensity. Josh reached out to me in the midst of my raw emotions, leaving me curious about the reason for his timely call. Was it merely a gut instinct, or was there something more behind his perfectly timed connection?

I reached for the cordless phone, bracing myself as I answered, trying to maintain a sense of normalcy. "Hey babes!"

Curiosity got the better of Josh as he asked, "How did you know it was me?"

"Call display," I admitted, my voice tinged with lingering tears. Devon didn't deserve them, especially since he lacked the courage to confront me face to face through video chat.

"I should be home within the next hour or so. Just wrapping up a few things here, shouldn't be much longer," he assured me.

"Okay, sounds good," I replied, my voice tinged with a mix of relief and anticipation.

Concern seeped into Josh's tone as he probed, "Jordan, is something wrong? You seem upset."

I lie, "No, just tired that's all."

"Are you sure?" Josh questioned, sensing there was more beneath the surface.

I took a deep breath, composing myself before responding. "Yes, it's just been a long day at work. I came home, did some cleaning, worked on my book, and spent some time on social media."

His concern laced his words as he probed further. "You're not upset because I'm working late, are you? You know I'm doing this for us, to get ahead."

I reassured him, "Yes, I know, and no, I'm not upset. I just miss you, I guess."

With a hint of warmth in his voice, Josh suggested, "Well, I'll be home soon. Will you wait up for me?"

A soft smile formed as I replied, "I'll try my best, no promises."

Josh chuckled, breaking the tension. "Okay, well, see you in a bit. Are you sure everything is okay between us?"

My heart skipped a beat as I confessed, "Yes, I just miss you. I love you, and I'm anxious to see you soon."

"I love you too," he whispered.

I held the phone to my ear, lingering in the silence as I wondered how he could sense my sadness through the phone. After seven years together, it seemed like he had developed an uncanny ability to pick up on my emotions. I pondered what might have given away my true feelings, but the answer remained elusive.

Chapter 20
Aftermath of a Virtual Breakup

A whirlwind of thoughts raced through my mind, mainly revolving around the fact that Devon remained a secret from Josh. This virtual breakup was tearing me apart, and I desperately needed to snap out of it. I had to remind myself that I had never even met Devon in person. Our interactions were limited to a few video chats and endless text messages. How could I be so infatuated with a stranger? It was ridiculous, and I had to come to terms with it.

But my heart shattered as if it were a conventional breakup. The truth was this breakup with Devon was far from normal. Our relationship was anything but ordinary, especially considering I was married. I shouldn't be feeling this way, and yet the pain consumed me.

When Josh finally returned home, his suspicions from our phone call proved accurate. He could sense something was wrong, and despite my best efforts to hide it, he pressed on. He urged me to open up, relentlessly asking what was troubling me. I hadn't mentioned Devon to him before, but under Josh's persistent questioning, I finally confessed.

I poured my heart out, explaining that the summer apart had taken its toll on me. I questioned our relationship and whether I still loved him, because the little time we did have together felt excruciating. It was as if I had lost a battle, left with nothing but emptiness.

And then, the words spilled out uncontrollably. "Even the sex is emotionless. I mean I feel like we only do it for the sake of getting each other off and there is no passion. I don't feel connected to you when we are being intimate and it is like all we do, is do the deed just to do it and sometimes I feel like you don't even want to and it's always the same."

I laid bare my deepest concerns, bearing the raw truth of our stagnant physical connection.

Josh's eyes widened, resembling a deer caught in headlights. His expression turned numb, devoid of tears, yet it carried the weight of defeat. He looked away for a brief moment, gathering his composure. It was clear that he was skilled at concealing his emotions. In a wavering but steady voice, he spoke, "Jordan, I had no idea." There was a pause as he gathered his thoughts. "I don't want to force you to be with me. I don't want to be with someone who doesn't love me back. We can handle this without a fight, without involving lawyers. I don't want to fight with you, but I do want things to be fair. We can sell the house and divide our belongings evenly." He looked at me, waiting for a response.

Usually, I'm an emotional person, and a conversation like this would typically bring me to tears. Maybe it was because I had already shed tears for Devon, but in that moment, I simply looked back at Josh, feeling numb. I hadn't expected this discussion to unfold, and the breakup with Devon seemed to have triggered a cascade of events. "I would be okay with that. I don't want to fight either," I replied, my voice devoid of any strong emotion.

Josh elaborated, "Jordan, I don't want to upset you, but considering the circumstances, it's only fair that you don't proceed with your next IUI treatment. And I would ask that you repay my parents for the money they gifted you."

I nodded, my response mechanical. "Yes, that is fair. I would be okay with that." Inside, I was crumbling, feeling like a robot with no emotional warmth. I didn't know what I truly wanted anymore. Did I love Devon? It hardly mattered now. What mattered was whether I still loved Josh.

"Do you love me?" Josh asked, breaking the silence.

I hesitated, the pause stretching longer than it should have. I delved into my thoughts, questioning my own feelings. Did I love him? Finally, I spoke, "Josh, I loved the man I married. He was my best friend. But now, with all the constant bickering, the arguments over trivial things, it has taken its toll. It adds up, weighing on my mind, and I find myself dreading being in your presence. I don't want a divorce. I just want my friend back. I want the person I married." My words were honest, straight from the depths of my heart.

Josh took a deep breath and responded, "Jordan, I wish you had just talked to me."

Frustration tinged my voice as I explained, "Josh, every time I tried to bring something up or share my thoughts, it felt like you were always trying to argue and prove me wrong. It became exhausting, so I decided to save myself the headache and keep quiet." I turned the question back to him, mustering the courage to ask, "Do you even love me?"

Without hesitation, he replied, "I do. I love you." His next words wavered as he asked, "What do you want to do?"

It was a loaded question, and the weight fell squarely on my shoulders. In this moment, my heart continued to ache for a man who was miles away, someone I had never even touched. Devon still held a piece of my heart, even though I knew he didn't want me. It was realistic for him to end things, and he was right. Our connection was inherently flawed, and he had the wisdom to cool things off between us to avoid crossing any boundaries.

But now, I looked into the eyes of the man who had been by my side for years. Josh was the one here for me, caring for me, unlike Devon. Devon would never be the one. Did I truly desire this life? Did I want a life with josh? Could I simply walk away from him? The answer was clear—it was a resounding no.

"I want my friend back, the man I married. I don't want a divorce," I answered, my voice filled with determination.

"Okay," Josh whispered, leaning over to kiss my head. He held me in a tight embrace, and in that silent embrace, we understood that we had begun the process of working through our issues. In that moment, I could feel his love, and it was the first time in a long while.

"I'm going to sleep," Josh said calmly. "Is everything okay? Is there anything else we need to talk about?"

I shook my head. "No, I'm okay. I feel like a weight has been lifted."

I drifted off to sleep in Josh's arms. It was the first time in a while that I slept through the night, likely due to exhaustion from the emotional roller coaster these two men had put me through. It was time to let go of Devon and embrace the path ahead with Josh.

Chapter 21
Devon lets go?

As Devon read Jordan's last message, he couldn't deny the truth that lay before him. It was all on him—his feelings, his desires, everything. He had allowed Jordan to conquer his heart, and now they were both paying the price. If only he had stopped himself before things spiraled out of control. The pain in his stomach was raw, a constant reminder of the hurt he had caused.

Devon stepped out into the darkness, standing on his back porch, gazing at the starless sky of the hill country. The strong breeze failed to alleviate the ache in his heart for a woman he could never have. It had been foolish of him to hope for a future together. He tried to laugh away the threat of tears, realizing how complicated life had become. He had promised himself long ago that he would never stoop as low as his ex-wife, yet here he was, caught in a web of love, desire, and shame for Jordan.

Sara, his wife, was a good woman. Deep down, he knew she cared for him, and he had to fight to repair their relationship. He wanted to love her the way he loved Jordan. Even though he had never met Josh, he understood the pain he would inflict on Josh if he were to act on his own desires and pursue Jordan. His connection with Jordan was a dead end.

Devon paced back and forth, finally taking a seat on a step, overwhelmed by his love for Jordan and the pain he had caused her that night. He knew the wounds would heal, but he had to do what was right—stay true to his wife and strive to be an honest man. He had become the person he never wanted to be. Jordan was not his, and she never would be.

Chapter 22
Jordan's Fresh Start

The morning arrives, and the atmosphere between Josh and me feels different. It's as if he's acutely aware of my emotions and treads cautiously in his actions. The alarm jolts me awake, and without hesitation, I rise, no longer hitting the snooze button like I used to. I glance at Josh, who is already awake. I can tell by the change in his breathing, though I suspect he didn't sleep as soundly as I did. Who could blame him? I've essentially turned his world upside down.

I turn to him and ask, knowing the answer already, "Did you sleep okay?" It's a silly question, but I feel compelled to ask.

"No, it was a rough night," he replies with a yawn. "I'm going to take a shower." He wearily gets out of bed, discards his slept-in clothes into the hamper, and walks nakedly into the bathroom. His confident stride has been replaced by a heaviness in his step. I lie there, contemplating my actions. Oh, Jordan, what have you done to him, to us? I feel like the worst person in the world, bringing down such a self-assured man to this state of despair. It pains me to witness Josh's sadness, and it amplifies the guilt I feel for putting him through everything last night.

There's no future with Devon; I need to let him go. He made it abundantly clear that there is no life with him. I have Josh, a man who loves me right here. Devon will never utter those words, and I realize now that he was just using me. I was nothing more than a fleeting amusement to him. I pick up my phone and glance at the pictures

Devon sent me before. I should delete them; I'm only torturing myself, Jordan. But I can't bring myself to do it just yet. I still need to cling to the small trace of Devon that remains.

I leave the phone on the bedside table and go join Josh in the shower. He greets me with a tired smile, and we wash one another in the hot, renewing stream. We don't say much to each other. We know the others habits and are like two old souls reconnecting with what had once been lost.

After the suds float off each of our bodies, Josh asks, "So are you going to pee on a stick this morning?" He is referring to the ovulation test kit that I use to track the best time to do the IUI procedure.

"I thought you wanted us to forget it for now?" I look up at him through the stream of running water he says nothing, and I feel obliged to keep the silence away, "Well everything with the treatment is paid for already. I don't think we could get the money back. They made that clear on the receipt. I would like to use the attempt and try."

Josh looks down into my eyes, he is still hurt but I believe that he takes this as a sign of peace that I have not given up on him, and a simple, "Okay" escapes his mouth. He gets out of the shower to dry off and gets dressed for work and I follow shortly after. The pee stick was negative.

We decide to carpool today and the conversation on the drive in is formal, polite and courteous. It is like meeting someone for the first time all over again.

It is lighthearted and we talk about the things that have been going on in our lives, our work, commenting on the topics that are being brought up on the radio show that is playing. I can't remember the last time that we talked like this. We smile and giggle even and within the hour arrive at Josh's work and it's time to say good bye for the day.

Normally, it would be a hug and little kiss on the cheek but today Josh has given me a passionate kiss and a hug like it's the last time he will ever see me. Deep down I feel terrible for hurting him.

"I love you, Jordan."

I answer, "I love you too."

His eyes are on me, searching for the truth in my words and he asks, "On a scale of one through ten how do you feel about us?"

I respond with, "A ten, I feel better that we talked, and I know that we can get passed this; how about you?"

He is hesitant but answers with caution, "A four point five, are you sure that there is nothing else that we need to talk about?"

He must sense the sadness that I am feeling for Devon on top of everything else. I answer, "No, I mean I am a little rattled about last night. I wasn't planning to have that talk with you but it's over and out with and it's good that we did speak." Josh gives me a brave smile and one last hug and kiss, steps out of the car, and goes to work and now I am on my way to my own job.

This is it. I'm experiencing the emotions of a breakup while still having a husband fighting to save our marriage. I'm a mess, and Devon was right to end things. It was never right, and he was simply being sympathetic by playing the friend card. I need to let him go. I repeat those words to myself like a mantra, attempting to reason with my heart, even if it doesn't want to listen.

Jordan don't reach out to him. You have to let go. I sigh, realizing that I must stop torturing myself with thoughts of a situation that could never be. Okay, whatever happens, don't message him. It's time to move on.

I pull up to my workplace and step out of the car, determined to start a new chapter. I need to shift my focus and move past this. I will get my mind in the right place.

Chapter 23
Staying the Course

The workday commenced like any other, yet an ache in my heart lingered from recent events. Engrossed in my tasks, I mechanically maneuvered through the morning. Thoughts of Josh and Devon swirled in my mind, alternating their presence. Amidst the monotony, an email from my husband materialized in my inbox.

"Hi Jordan,

Just making sure that you are okay and that you are feeling better and making sure everything is okay between us.

-Josh"

His message served as a much-needed anchor, reminding me to stay focused and committed to my husband. He was the one meant for me, and this email reinforced that truth. Swiftly, I composed a response to Josh's message.

"Hey Josh,

Yes, everything is fine. I'm glad we had that conversation last night. I love you.

-Jordan"

Merely a moment passed before a second message arrived from Josh.

"Is there anything else, aside from what you mentioned last night, that you need me to do?

-Josh"

I knew it was time to be honest. I pondered for a brief moment, contemplating my response. After collecting my thoughts, I proceeded to compose another email from my office computer.

"Hey Josh,

Could you please lay off the homophobic comments? I mean, come on, my favorite talk show has a badass lesbian host. What does their preference have to do with anything?

And seriously, babe, ease up on the road rage. Yelling at bad drivers won't solve anything, plus they can't even hear you!

-Jordan"

I aimed to keep the message lighthearted and playful, not wanting to exacerbate the tension from the previous night. After a few minutes, Josh's reply popped up in my inbox.

"Hey Jordan,

Okay, I'll cool it with the 'homo' stuff, but those bad drivers will still be a challenge…

-Josh"

Last night tested the limits of our relationship. We had never been so close to calling it quits. I always imagined that if we ever reached the point of divorce, he would be one of those spouses who fought tooth and nail, trying to screw me over financially. But as we discussed it, he surprised me with his kindness and fairness. This morning, as the dust settled, I realized Josh's ability to maintain a sense of humor through it all. That's one of the things I love about him. I now understand the depth of his feelings. He loves me more than I had ever realized, and he's fighting for me to fall in love with him all over again.

I couldn't help but dwell on it—Devon's silent treatment for a whole day. What did he hope to achieve by ignoring me? Whatever his intentions were, it was a cowardly move, and I knew deep down that everything between us had been a lie. It hurt the most realizing that he was never truly a friend.

By mid-morning, I summoned the courage to do what I had been avoiding. I accessed my phone and deleted all of Devon's pictures. I also removed the CUNow video messaging app we used to connect with each other. It shattered my heart, but I had to take this step before I lost my sanity. They were gone now, erased from my life. After all, Josh deserved my love. We've been married for years, and I owe it to him.

Lunchtime arrived as a welcome relief, and I eagerly embraced the opportunity to escape the confines of the office for a walk. Swiveling my chair, I turned to face the computer screen, searching for my mouse to lock my workstation before leaving. That's when I noticed a new email had arrived. It was from Devon.

Chapter 24
Imagination or Reality

Pausing for a moment, I hesitate to open the new message from Devon. Why is he still reaching out to me? I feel my resolve wavering. Come on, Jordan, stick to your decision. Get out and take that walk.

As if escaping from Devon himself, I bolt out of the building, propelled by a need to distance myself. The early autumn sun warms my skin, accompanied by the familiar sounds of chirping crickets and lingering cicadas, still reminiscent of summer despite the impending change of leaves. Devon's presence feels unreal—I must be imagining things. He couldn't possibly be reaching out to me.

Following my usual route, I stroll down a quiet side street that leads to the city's Ornamental Gardens. Thoughts swirl in my mind. Should I confide in my sister or a close friend about this intricate love triangle I've entangled myself in? No, Jordan, don't be foolish and vulnerable. The moment you share with someone, the worry of it spreading and eventually reaching Josh will consume you. Judgment will follow, and that's not the kind of stress I need right now.

Walking along the garden paths, I observe tourists chatting, capturing memories with their cameras. They're easy to spot, always donning comfortable shoes, and at least one person in the group proudly sporting a backpack or a fanny pack. I watch them, their carefree smiles, and the delight they find in the garden's hidden wonders. Tourists always seem so unburdened here.

Entering the enchanting rose garden, my favorite sanctuary, I marvel at the vibrant blooms. This year, I proudly acquired my first climbing red rose bush, surpassing the beauty of the ones displayed here. As I approach the central bird bath, a photographer catches my attention. With unwavering patience, he captures close-up shots of the roses, attempting to immortalize a bee in its quest for nectar. I silently commend his dedication, noting the satisfying click of his camera. Perhaps I should bring my own camera next time.

Lunchtime comes and goes, providing a temporary respite from reality as I immerse myself in the bliss of the sun-kissed day. However, upon returning to my desk, the weight of what I've been avoiding settles in, beckoning from my inbox.

Alright, Jordan, enough with the teenage melodrama. Just read his message and be done with it. With a deep breath, I open the email, and this is what it says:

"Hey Jordan,

Just wanted to say hi and hope you're doing better today. Bet you didn't expect to hear from me, huh? Well, that's not how I roll. Anyway, just wanted to check in and send my greetings. Have a great day.

-Devon"

I reread his message, disbelief coursing through me. Is this real? What the hell is happening? Is he feeling sorry for me? I can't respond right now; I need some fresh air... again. My heart pounds in my throat, urging me to confront this situation. Dammit, Jordan, you can't keep running away. What should I do with this email? Should I reply? Come on, Jordan, this isn't high school. Of course, you should respond. Be polite; he's being polite too.

Perhaps it's an old message that I'm only seeing now? I can't shake off the feeling of disbelief, questioning whether my longing for his contact has driven me to conjure it in my mind. Regardless, I need to reread the email and check the date it was sent. Maybe it was a delayed message that somehow slipped through. Yes, that could be a rational explanation.

Examining the date, there's no mistake—it was sent today. There are no prior messages, just a simple email from him. I take a deep breath, feeling the weight of this unusual situation where I have messages from both Josh and Devon, the two men who hold a place in my heart.

Okay, Jordan, it's time to respond.

"Hey Devon,

I'm doing okay, although last night left me shaken. I won't lie, I feel sad about it, but I do understand.

How is your day going?

-Jordan"

Ending my email with a question, I hope to keep the conversation going. A few moments pass, and as expected, Devon responds.

"Hey Jordan,

It's going, actually. It's pretty hectic here with the new software launch, so I just wanted to say hi and let you know I have to go. Talk to you later.

-Devon"

Wow, that felt cold. What is he doing? He just essentially ended things with me, yet he's the first to reach out and say hello. At the same time, it feels like he doesn't want to hear from me. I've never felt so cut off. It's clear that I need to set my priorities straight.

Devon has made it abundantly clear that we've crossed a line and he wants no further involvement. His priority is his partner, and it's only logical that I prioritize my own relationship too. Jordan don't waste your time on this man. He's not here for you, and in truth, you've never even met him.

Staring at the two emails, one from Devon and the other from Josh, I feel a pang in my heart once again. I take a deep breath and delete Devon's message. Girl, you need to regain control of your emotions and make a genuine effort to rekindle your love for Josh.

The rest of my workday is spent attempting to focus as much as possible, pushing aside the overwhelming wave of emotions. Eventually, it's time to pick up Josh, and I must muster all my strength to avoid looking sad. I arrive at the roundabout in front of his building, and there he is, punctual as always. As he walks towards the car, our gazes meet, and I can sense his nervousness. He opens the passenger side door carefully, leaning in and asking, "Do you want me to drive?"

It's a question he rarely poses, as when I pick him up, he typically settles into the passenger seat and takes a nap during our hour-long journey home. Today, however, he's making an effort to mend our fractured relationship.

I reply, "It's okay, I can drive."

"Are you sure? I know I haven't been very sociable during these drives. It's not because I don't want to talk to you; it's just that I'm exhausted, and this is my only chance to rest between jobs."

"I understand," I say, offering him a polite smile.

"I still feel like something isn't quite right. Is there anything else you need to talk to me about?" His deep blue eyes search mine, seeking answers to an unknown question.

"Josh, I got everything off my chest last night. I am just emotionally drained from yesterday, that's all. There is nothing more to talk about. Everything is in the open and now we just have to get passed it." I say the words and know it's a lie. Could you just imagine me saying, yes Josh actually, I met someone online and I fell into some weird virtual relationship and my virtual boyfriend broke up with me just before we had the talk and now, I am just trying to get over that break up. Yes, that will just go so smoothly if I tell him what is really on my mind. I look at him for some sort of acceptance to the lie that I just fed him. He accepts it.

The conversation for the rest of the way home is awkward, but it needs to happen, and we need to make the effort. I need to make the effort. I am so used to driving in silence as he slept. With last night and our relationship in front and center and weighing on each of our minds, he is making the effort to talk. It's a light conversation, the weather, stuff we did at work, even just silly lighthearted jokes. I feel a little better as the air is filled with conversation and my mind is off of Devon for now. I feel myself slowly coming back to Josh, not by much but it's a start.

It's a quiet night for us with the exception to the fact that later on that night we reconnected and made love to one another, like we were brand new lovers. He is passionate, kissing, touching, feeling, and paying close attention to pleasuring me. I am so into it, we both are, hunger in our eyes, craving to go deeper, sweat beading on each of our bodies, his muscles are flexed with each loaded thrust as he drives me into the bed with force. I can't help myself and touch his defined pecks and arms as he pins me down and I draw him in to taste his lips and when I do I explode three times before he gets his. My muscles are tight, clenched around his hardness and after it's all done and he gets his own release, I relax; we both come to a slow and he rests on his forearms on either side of me. I needed it, we both did and for the first time in a long time I experience his hunger to have me.

Chapter 25
Polite Hello's

The next few days are the same. Devon is still giving polite hello's and when I return to the conversation and try to keep it going with normal topics, he says in more or less words that he is too busy to keep talking. He is nothing but mixed messages, maybe when he says "friends" he means it, I don't know. All I know is that my heart still wants him in a more than a friends' way. I mean even if we were to never meet, I do consider him one of my closest friends and all of this "too busy" stuff hurts, but for some reason I hang on to him even though I wish I wouldn't and wasn't so desperate.

I decide that it's best to just become immersed in my work and at the same time, try to relax. My IUI procedure is coming up soon and I don't need the sadness that Devon represents to haunt me and this second attempt.

Like a routine lunch arrives. I take a walk to my favorite spot in the gardens then back to work for the afternoon and before I know it, I am home, but tonight it's just me. Josh took the second car into work to his part-time job this evening.

I can't resist the urge and send a message to Devon. Jordan you are so weak. I write, "Hey Devon, hope that I am not bugging and just wanted to say hello and ask how was your day? What are you up to?"

Devon replies almost instantly, "You're not bothering. I just walked in the door. It was a long day. I'm doing okay; you? No shopping after work? That will be a distraction." At some point in our earlier chats before everything happened, I had told him that a store chain was opening up in town and that I couldn't wait to check out and today was opening day. I guess that he remembered and what is with the distraction comment? I guess he doesn't want me sending him messages. Well, I need this.

I reply, "No shopping for me today. I wanted to head home, and the drive into town is quite long. I just want to relax and take it easy tonight. I don't know why I'm sharing all this with you. Maybe it's because I have no one else to confide in, but here it goes." I proceed to recount the close call with the divorce conversation, delving into the details of our fight. I conclude by informing him that Josh and I are actively working on our marriage, and despite his hurt, I've noticed a positive change in his sensitivity since our talk and my newfound openness.

Devon responds, "Perhaps your openness will inspire him to become a better person, friend, and husband to you."

Feeling a sense of relief, I admit, "Opening up was difficult, but I do feel better now that everything is out in the open. It's like a weight has been lifted."

Devon shares, "I'm also trying my best on my end. Ending things wasn't an easy decision, but it was the right one for me. I believe that in time, you'll understand and genuinely wish us both well. Is it too challenging to remain friends? If it is, I'll understand. We both need to focus on our own relationships. I hope you won't be angry with me for saying that. I mean no disrespect; I'm just expressing my perspective honestly. I guess no matter how delicately I phrase it, the pain won't vanish. I apologize for that. Perhaps we can be friends as authors, but if even that proves too much, then yes, we should completely stop, and please know I don't say this to hurt anyone."

"I do understand. Everything is still fresh right now, so it will take time for me to bounce back. Given everything that has happened, it has revealed your true colors to me. We can still be friends. It's just that when people use that term, it's often out of politeness, and they usually want nothing to do with the person. Initially, I thought that was what you meant, but now I see that you genuinely want to be friends. I don't want to stop talking to you. Can I tell you something?"

Devon asks, "What is it?"

"This chat platform is really frustrating. There's a delay with these messages."

He agrees, "Yes, there is a delay, I apologize."

"You know, I only use this chat to talk to you. I wish we could switch to something else." We had to stop using Facebook because Devon's wife, Sara, was growing suspicious and had an account there. There was a risk she would discover our conversations, so when Devon drew the line, we had to switch platforms.

He says, "I agree. I haven't really used this platform before. I'm not sure if my 'true colors' being mentioned was a bad thing, but I believe it shows my commitment and dedication to my partner. Anyway, try not to feel lonely."

"When I mentioned 'true colors,' I meant that you're a decent person. You're doing what's right for both of us, and that means a lot to me. I have nothing but respect for you." I understand that he's subtly hinting that we should end the conversation.

"Alright, well, thanks for chatting with me. Talk to you later?"

"Yes, have a good night, Jordan."

Chapter 26
Devon's Commitments

Jordan's absence weighs heavily on Devon's mind as he settles into his cozy leather chair in his home office. His gaze drifts around the room, and he absentmindedly taps his fingers on the desk. Searching for a distraction, he spots a mini quadcopter at the edge of his desk and picks it up, examining it. Should he step outside for some fresh air or attend to the chores awaiting him in the house? Restless, he realizes he must refocus his attention on Sara.

His concentration shifts to the small flying machine in his hands; he's always had a soft spot for remote-control helicopters. Decision made; he decides to grab a quick bite to eat before heading out. It's been too long since he last flew his cherished machines. Perhaps he could invite a friend to join him.

Just as he's lost in these thoughts, the phone rings, jolting him back to reality. He answers, "Hello?"

"Dad."

"Hey, Bud! It's been a while since we last chatted." A smile spreads across Devon's face; conversations with his son are always treasured moments. His son lives a few hours away, near Dallas, with his mother.

"Yeah, sorry, Dad. I've been swamped with work."

Devon leans back in his chair. "That's okay. I'm glad you called, and remember, you can always reach out to me more often. I'm here for you."

"I know. Say, Dad, I wanted to ask you something. Would you mind if my girlfriend and I drove down to stay with you and Sara for a few days? She's interested in visiting the springs and exploring some of the hiking trails."

Devon's face lights up with a grin, and he responds, "Sure, just let me know when you're planning to come. Sara and I don't have any set plans for the next few weeks. By the way, since when do you have a girlfriend?"

His son lets out a sigh. "Since about a month ago. Why do you always get all weird whenever I start dating someone?"

Devon smirks, leaning forward and playfully replies, "Hey, I'm not getting weird. Your dad just has to ask because you never tell me anything."

"Well, I am seeing someone, and she's really nice. I want you and Sara to meet her."

Devon and his son continue their chat for a long time. They discuss his son's new relationship, remote control helicopters (his son even picked up a new laptop, sharing all its features with Devon), and Devon fills him in on his work and recent projects around the house. For the evening, his thoughts of Jordan take a break, as he fully immerses himself in the precious conversation with his son.

Chapter 27
A Funny State

Josh and I find ourselves in a strange state at the moment. We're both treading cautiously and being polite with each other. It's a bit awkward, but it's a nice start to the process of mending our relationship.

As morning arrives and the sun shines, we have the whole day ahead of us to spend together. Josh asks, "So, I don't need to go to work until this evening. What would you like to do?"

I suggest, "Maybe we could practice our photography and go out to snap some pictures?"

He gives me a mischievous look and replies, "Yes, we could do that, or we could do something else."

Curiosity piqued, I respond, "Like what?"

With a sly grin, he suggests, "Well, we could do 'it'." His playful tone reminds me of a sly fox.

Chuckling, I playfully scold him, "Josh, don't say it like that!"

He smirks and asks, "Is 'spanking the monkey' any better?"

His words catch me off guard, and I burst into laughter. Eventually, I regain my composure and reply, "How about we just say we can have sex? And yes, I would like that."

Our intimate encounter is passionate and filled with fiery desire. We embrace each other like two hungry animals unable to get enough, and afterwards, we both wear satisfied smiles. The rest of our day is spent leisurely, cuddling up on the couch to watch a movie. We remain in our pajamas all day, enjoying each other's company until it's time for Josh to leave.

After the movie ends, something triggers Josh to bring up a conversation he had with his sister earlier in the week. As the credits roll on the television screen, he explains, "Oh, I forgot to tell you, I was talking to Emma earlier this week. Don't get too excited yet because the plans aren't final, but she's considering a trip to the Dominican Republic in the New Year and has invited us to go with her."

To my surprise, Josh expresses an interest in going on the trip, despite not being a big fan of traveling. I raise a concern, saying, "Really? Do you want to go? And no offense to Emma, but I thought they were facing some financial troubles?"

Josh explains, "Yes, that's why it's still uncertain. I wanted to let you know just in case it becomes a possibility. I would like to spend some time with my sister and her family."

I respond, "Well, okay. I'm open to it if everything falls into place."

While the invitation from his sister is kind, deep down, I know we can't afford such a trip. Josh works tirelessly to pay off our debts and the costs of maintaining our home. I believe he didn't immediately decline his sister's offer because he sees it as his own gesture to win me back. However, as we discuss it further, we both come to the conclusion that we have to decline. While it would have been nice, spending more money on extravagant trips won't heal our relationship. We need to focus solely on each other without any distractions.

Josh prepares for work, and soon he's off for the evening. Left to my own devices, I retreat to my office to work on my book and keep myself occupied. As I fire up the computer and log into a couple of social media sites, I find myself engaging in a chat with Devon.

I send a text message, "Hey, how's everything today?"

Devon responds promptly, "Hey, what's new with you? Everything's going well here. Just got home and relaxing."

"Well, things are starting to look a little brighter on my side. I had a great day with Josh before he headed into work. How have you been?" I feel a mix of weirdness and a desire to share with Devon. After all, he's still my friend.

Devon replies, "That's awesome, Jordan. Embrace each other and cherish the moments. I'll still be your friend and thank you for that. I'm doing well. By the way, the new operating system is out for your phone, but the network is swamped. I heard there were a lot of calls today. Anyway, have a great night."

I let out a sigh. That's all I'm getting from him. Ah, Jordan, you can't seem to let go, can you? One moment it seems obvious, and the next, it's not. I find myself uncertain about what to think. Sometimes I feel like I'm being strung along, and just as I gather the strength to move on, he sends a message. His messages do seem sincere, but I know he currently has no distractions. He's home alone, his spouse is still away, and there's no reason for him to abruptly end our chat, but he does.

Well, Jordan, that's a sign. Just let him go.

Chapter 28
Mother Nature

After yesterday's brief conversation with Devon, I decided to make the most of the remaining hours of sunlight and tackle some yard work. I mowed the lawn, tended to my flower beds, and weeded the garden. As the sun began to set, I even took the initiative to wash the car. Staying busy was essential to keep my loneliness at bay, and besides, the yard was in need of some care.

Later that evening, Josh returned home. I was still awake in bed, but something was bothering me. My eye felt irritated, as if there was something scratching it, but I couldn't see what it was.

When Josh entered the bedroom, I turned to him and asked, "Josh, could you help me? I think there's something in my eye. Can you take a look?"

Concerned, he approached the bed and had me tilt my head into the light from the nightstand lamp. He carefully examined my tearing eye, his face close to mine, and I caught a whiff of the sweet aroma of cinnamon-flavored gum on his breath.

He spoke in a gentle voice, "I don't see anything. Your eye is watering, but I can't spot anything in it."

I inquired, "Do you see any signs of a sty starting on my eyelid?" I pointed to the area where the pain was.

His warm hands lightly caressed my face as he took a good thirty seconds to examine it. Eventually, he replied, "No, I don't see anything. Have you tried using eye drops?"

"No"

Josh heads to the bathroom to fetch the eye drops. He returns promptly to treat my eye, his touch gentle as he administers two cold drops. Instantly, I feel a soothing relief wash over me, and I let out a grateful sigh.

"Thanks," I express my gratitude.

He smiles and strips down to his boxer briefs before climbing into bed. We settle in for the night, hoping that the eye drops have done their magic.

However, when morning arrives, I wake up to even more pain and excessive tearing. It's a struggle to open my eyes, and the discomfort is giving me a pounding headache. I decide to make a brief appearance at work to attend to some urgent emails, but I can only manage so much with one functioning eye.

In the hallway, I coincidentally cross paths with my boss. She takes one look at my tearing eye and advises, "Jordan, your work can wait. Take care of yourself and get checked out. Eyes are important, and something is clearly wrong."

"Thank you," I respond gratefully, accepting the printouts I had been waiting for from the nearby printer before making my way back to my desk.

Before leaving for the doctor's appointment, I attempt to reach Josh by phone, but as expected, he doesn't answer. Mornings are usually busy for him, coordinating with his coworkers. He often leaves his cell phone in his bag when away from his desk. I leave him a message, informing him of my situation, and then gather my belongings and head to the doctor's office.

The one thing that I despise is going to see a doctor because you have to wait, especially if you don't have an appointment. I drive to the nearest walk-in clinic and waited a long time. I sat there and played with my phone, keeping the sore eye closed. Did I tell you how much I hate walk in clinics, they are full of sick people, and it is just gross to think that you touched the same door as them. You are breathing the same air as them, yuck, it makes my skin crawl. Finally, I am called in to see the doctor but to my disappointment he can't find anything. The handsome, young Australian Doctor knows that something is wrong and can't help, after flushing out my eye, laying me on the table to flash a light into my retina; he ended up referring me to a specialist.

With one eye open, I then drive ten minutes to the specialist's office and am greeted as soon as I open the door to the reception area by his staff, the doctor from the walk-in clinic must have called ahead for the referral because they know who I am before I had the chance to hand them my Health Card. The specialist explains, "Jordan we are going to put some drops in your eye. It will give you instant relief and we are going to wait for the drops to take effect. My assistant will call you back in so that we can see what's irritating your eye."

After the Specialist puts the drops in, I take a seat to wait. He was right, within moments my eye stops tearing, and the pain is gone. Whatever it is; is still in my eye but to my relief, I can no longer feel it. The room soon appears brighter as my retinas expand from the drops and within moments his assistant calls me back in.

In a dimly lit room, I find myself seated, surrounded by eye equipment. The specialist, a tall and slender man, enters the room, his bald head accentuated by a neat trim of light brown hair on the sides. A well-groomed beard adorns his face, and his own eyes look on with interest, highlighting his dedication to his craft. His genuine interest in my emergency is palpable as he approaches, ready to delve into the depths of my eye. With utmost care, he begins to explain, "Jordan, I can see it now, and I'll attempt to remove it."

Anxiety creeps into my voice as I reply, "Okay."

In a gentle tone, he instructs, "Remain still and do your best to keep your eyes open."

Equipped with what appears to be a blunt needle, he proceeds to pry open my eyelid. The sensation is uncomfortable, causing me to involuntarily flinch as he initiates a countdown, "I'll touch your eye in three, two, one…"

Withdrawing his instrument, he remarks, "You're quite the flincher. Let's give it another try. Stay perfectly still. Three, two, one…" This time, he succeeds in extracting the foreign object.

Examining the tiny intruder under a microscope, he triumphantly raises the blunt needle before his own eyes. "I've got it," he announces. Peering through the microscope, he confesses, "It's a minuscule piece of grass, no larger than the tip of a needle. Undoubtedly one of the tiniest things I've ever removed."

As I left the specialist's office, a wave of relief washed over me. The scratch on my eye would heal in about a week, and I felt grateful that the ordeal was finally behind me. Returning to the office momentarily, I realized I had carelessly left my computer on during the examination. I needed to inform my boss that I would be taking the rest of the day off to rest. I dialed Josh's number, as we had carpooled that day, only to discover that he had already received my message and obtained permission to leave early as well.

About to close my email, I noticed two messages from Devon. It struck me as odd since he seemed to be avoiding me lately. Unable to resist, I opened them and read the first, which had arrived just before 8:00 AM:

"Hey Jordan,

Thinking of you this morning and just wanted to say hello. Hope you have a wonderful day.

-Devon"

A pang of mixed emotions welled up inside me. Then, at around 10:30 AM, the second email from Devon appeared:

"Hi Jordan,

I interpret your silence as a clear sign that maintaining our friendship has become too difficult for you. This will be my final message, and I'll sever all ties from this point forward. I genuinely cherished the time we spent getting to know each other, and I sincerely wish you all the best.

-Devon"

My heart skipped a beat as I read his words, and a tear trickled down my cheek, different from the tears shed over a tiny blade of grass. With trembling fingers, I hit the reply button and began to type. It was just past noon, and I hoped that he hadn't gone so far as to block me.

Hi Devon,

I just read your messages now, as I had an unexpected emergency this morning that required a visit to the doctor. Don't worry, everything is okay now, and I'm heading home for the day. In short, I had a piece of grass in my eye, but the specialist successfully removed it. I'm left with a scratched retina and a headache, so I'll be taking it easy. I really hope you won't cut off all ties because you mean a lot to me as a friend.

I hope we can still keep in touch. I'm about to shut down my computer, but you can message me on my phone.

Take care,

Jordan

With a deep breath, I hit the send button, realizing that I've done all I can to address the situation. It's up to Devon now. I power off my computer and leave the office. Currently, I'm on my way home after picking up

Josh, who graciously takes over driving while I rest in the passenger seat.

My emotions are in turmoil, and I find solace in closing my eyes. Josh is concerned for my well-being, but he understands that I've had a tough day. The questions soon fade, and the rest of the drive is filled with quietness, accompanied only by the soft sound of pop music playing on the radio.

As we approach home, Josh unexpectedly turns into a store parking lot. Intrigued, I open my eyes and look at him quizzically.

"I just need to quickly grab something. I'll be right back," Josh explains.

"Okay," I reply, watching him walk into the store. Seizing the opportunity, I glance at my phone to check for any messages from Devon. To my surprise, there's a notification waiting for me.

He responds, "I hope you heal fast. Rest and get well."

A sense of relief washes over me, and I eagerly reply, "Thanks! My husband is driving me home because I'm relying on my left eye for now. He's just in the store picking up a few things while I message you. I can't help but feel like a clumsy goofball." After explaining the events of the morning, I continue, "By the way, I want you to know that I value our friendship immensely. I never wanted you to think I was giving you the cold shoulder. You mean a lot to me. Anyway, what a day it has been, and it's only the early afternoon."

Devon responds with a smiley face and says, "I was hoping we could still be friends, and I'm glad you feel the same way."

I confirm, "Absolutely! Why would I let go of someone who brings me happiness? Even though we've never met in person, I consider you one of my closest friends."

Devon replies, "You've made me smile, and I feel the same way."

"Okay, well I can see Josh walking back to the car; I have to drop off but am happy that we cleared everything up. Talk to you later."

Chapter 29
Eye Care

The next morning, I decide to call in sick for work. My eye still hurts, and I have a persistent headache. Josh, noticing my condition, leaves a little earlier than usual, giving me a gentle kiss goodbye.

In a raspy voice, I inquire, "Why are you leaving so early?"

"I'm going to stop by the coffee shop for an ice cappuccino and a bacon, egg, and cheese sandwich," he replies.

Squinting my eyes open, I catch a glimpse of Josh's shadowy figure. "I see. Well, have a good day. Love you," I say.

"Love you too. Feel better," he responds, his footsteps fading away as he walks across the hardwood floor, down the hall, and eventually locks the front door and closes the garage. With Josh gone for the day, I can focus on resting, which is exactly what I need. I fluff up my pillow and find comfort in the cool side. Settling myself in the middle of the spacious king-size bed, I quickly drift off to sleep.

When I finally open my eyes, the bedroom is bathed in sunshine streaming through the blinds of the two windows on either side of the bed. It's bright, and I wonder what time it is. I roll over and sneak a peek at the alarm clock. Oh, it's 11:30 AM! I can't believe I slept in so late, but I suppose my body needed the rest. Thank goodness I took the day off.

I get out of bed and head to the kitchen to make myself some breakfast, or rather, lunch given the time.

Well, regardless, since Josh had a bacon, egg, and cheese sandwich this morning, I decide to whip up my own homemade version. With my meal in hand, I settle on the couch in front of the television. Of course, I have my phone within reach because I'm eager to chat with my cowboy. Yesterday's conversation was enjoyable, and even with that little moment of panic when he thought I hadn't responded promptly, it just goes to show that he genuinely cares about talking to me.

I send him a message saying, "Hey there, hope you have a great day. Just wanted to let you know that if you sent anything to my work email, I didn't receive it. I took today off to rest my eye."

"Howdy! I'm just enjoying a not-so-healthy lunch. How's the eye?" Devon responds.

"It's still watery. They gave me this amazing pain-numbing drug, but it's starting to wear off. I can see out of it this morning, though. It's still tearing a bit. The hardest part yesterday was trying to stay still while the doctor flipped my eyelid and went in with a needle thing. By the way, are you still hungry?" I tease, adding an evil laugh.

Devon plays along and replies, "No comment."

I smile, deciding to switch the conversation topic. "I posted something on my webpage last night. I was worried my humor might offend, but this morning when I checked the post stats, it had almost two hundred unique views and no complaints."

"Nice," Devon responds.

"Oh man, when I first read the post, I couldn't help but giggle," I confess.

Devon asks, "Giggles from your own posts?"

"No, actually. I posted a link on my page to an article on funny text messages. None of them were my own, but I laughed at all of them. Here's the link," I explain, sending him the URL. However, it seems like he's a bit confused about the content.

He asks, "Which one is yours?"

I clarify, "I posted the link; it's an article on funny text messages. None of them are mine personally, but I found them all hilarious. Did you get it?"

"I did. They were funny," Devon replies.

I change the topic and say, "I think I'm going to take tomorrow off. It feels like I got the punch in the face I was wishing for. I should make better wishes. Yeah, I'm definitely staying home tomorrow." I vaguely remember mentioning to Devon that I needed a punch in the face during our awkward conversations. It's funny how the universe seems to deliver.

Devon replies, "I figured as much. I truly hope you feel better soon. Maybe your husband will take care of you if he isn't already. There's nothing better than being waited on."

His mention of Josh feels strange, and it stings a little. We're still in the process of healing our relationship, and despite the difficulties we're facing, his schedule remains unchanged, leaving me alone for long periods of time, which hurts. I answer Devon as honestly as I can, "Yeah, well, he's out until 11:00 PM again tonight. I'll look like a badass; people might think I was in a fight. Staying home for another day will spare me the curious looks."

Devon asks, "Did you take a picture for memories?"

His question brings a smile to my face. Maybe I should take a picture. I put my dishes in the dishwasher and retreat to the bedroom before responding. "Oh, you really want to see? Maybe I'll take a picture later. I think your lunch break is over, right? I'm going to try and lie down for a bit." The events of yesterday have taken a toll on me. It might not just be the painkillers; who knows?

All I know is that I need to rest my eye and alleviate this headache.

Devon answers, "Have a good rest. Take care."

I spend a couple more hours resting and when I wake up, I decide to move to the living room. I settle myself on the chocolate brown leather couch with a blanket draped over me and a couple of white furry couch pillows supporting my back. Taking it easy, I turn on the television and keep my phone in hand in case I get bored.

Suddenly, my screen flashes, and it's Devon again. I suppose he feels bad about yesterday, jumping to conclusions when I didn't respond immediately. It's unusual for him to reach out like this, but I appreciate the added interest.

Devon writes, "I hope your eye and head are better. Won't disturb you, just thought I would mention."

Ah, what a sweetheart. I smile and type back, "No worries, I'm all good now. I'm awake and soon I'll be at my desk, trying to be brave. I'll be working on installing my phone updates later. My vision is still a bit blurry, but that's to be expected." I add a smiley face.

Devon replies, "Well, hopefully, you'll be better tomorrow. Right now, I'm just sitting here watching the sky unfold. It's dark and fiery with storms from the hurricane, filling the night with electric bolts of sheer fear and massive booms. It echoes off the hills and valleys."

He paints an intriguing picture for me, and I respond, "That must be an incredible sight. Could you take a picture and post it, so I can, see?"

I wait for a few moments, expecting him to send me a photo, but I receive nothing. What's up with him? Playfully, I type, "Are you getting your thumb stuck on the camera? Remember, you have to press the button on the screen. Don't put your finger over the dark spot."

Devon quickly replies, "I haven't tried, but it's too dark to take pictures. It's a scary storm. The kind that makes the hair stand up on your arms after the lightning happens."

I take a moment before responding, and he follows up with an update on the pictures, "I just tried to take a photo. Anyway, it's coming out dark."

"Well, no biggie for the photos," I reply. "You're describing it well. I love those types of storms. When I was a kid, I used to stand on the deck at my grandparents' cottage and watch them pass over the lake."

I sense that our messages might be getting mixed up or arriving out of order. Or perhaps he's just now catching on to my playful comment about his thumb on the camera. He suddenly says, "Are you sure your thumb isn't sticky?" He adds a laugh out loud and continues, "Yeah, well, these storms would make you appreciate Mother Nature and seek shelter. I remember northern storms being just like you said."

I'm puzzled by his sticky comment. I have a suspicion about its meaning, but coming from the man who virtually broke up with me, it's an odd remark. Maybe it's a playful jab. Nonetheless, I need clarification, so I ask, "Ha, what's that supposed to mean?" Then I swiftly switch to my second thought, saying, "I miss that cottage. It's been years. I still dream of being there all the time. Anyway, I wish I were there to see the storm in real life."

Devon doesn't come out and directly explain but says, "You're a writer, use your imagination. I was just being funny, and it was out of line. Wow, that was loud. It shook the entire house. Anyway, I was just being a smart-ass friend." He ends his message with a smiley face.

I respond with a wink face and say, "I've got my eye on you! Anyway, I wanted to tell you that my new story is at eleven thousand words now."

"Wow, you're really cranking along," he replies.

"Yes, this story isn't hard to write. Everything is in my head, and I just need to get it on paper. It's fun, and I'm really enjoying the process," I explain happily.

Devon shares, "I did some more writing this morning and am getting closer. It's turning out to be more of a story than I thought, but it's all good though. I am going to plan out my query letters soon since I am nearing the finish line."

"That's awesome; I can't wait to read it!" I express my excitement. "What do you think your word count will cap off at?"

"Between one hundred and five thousand and one hundred and ten thousand. Right now, I'm at ninety-eight thousand words," Devon reveals.

"That is perfect. I've read somewhere, and I sort of agree, that anything under eighty thousand words leaves you wanting more as a reader. I aim for the one hundred-thousand-word mark with my own work," I share my perspective.

"Yeah, it seems to be a good range for thrillers, so I am sure after editing, it might drop a few but will stay close to that number," he comments.

Shifting the topic, I tell him, "You want to know something? My favorite reality show was on last night! I missed it. I am just waiting for it to load on TV on-demand."

Devon responds, "Guess I better settle down and do some writing myself tonight. Well, I'm sure I had something to do with that, huh." He refers to the television show I missed and adds a sad face.

I explain the reason for missing it, saying, "I still expect it to air on Thursdays! God, why do things need to change?"

"I will sign off and let you go. Have a good night," Devon says.

Feeling like he might have misunderstood my comment, I quickly clarify, "No, I would take a chat with a friend before stopping everything to watch a show."

"It's ok. I need to write anyway," he reassures me.

I let out a sigh, realizing that our conversations are improving over time, and I send him a final message, "Alright, take care and don't get wet."

Devon playfully responds, "So dedicated. Ha, no comment. LOL. I won't. Bye."

Unable to resist, I tease him, saying, "Your mind is going there; I know you. Anyway, cheers, have a good one."

True to form, he has the last word, saying, "Sorry, anyway, take care."

Chapter 30
Return to Work

I send a message to Devon, checking in on him, saying, "So, are you underwater today?"

He responds, "Hey there, yes, it is dark gray outside with massive rain pouring."

"Lucky you, I usually have the rain. Today it's sunny and warm autumn weather," I reply. He sends a smiley face and asks, "Are you feeling any better?"

"Yes, my headache is clearing up, and I wanted to say hello. I've got to drop off for a bit. Talk to you later." I pause as one of my coworkers peeks over my cubicle to ask if I'm going to the weekly staff meeting. Despite my disappointment, I confirm that I am. She informs me that the meeting is starting now.

I have a strong dislike for meetings as they often feel like a waste of time. They usually involve senior management highlighting their achievements and then piling more tasks on the already busy regular staff. The meeting finally ends just as the lunch hour begins. Seizing the opportunity, I decide to take advantage of the beautiful day and have lunch outside in the grassy field, bringing my phone with me. I message Devon, saying, "Got a moment? You know, it's funny how everyone I know with a smartphone is outraged about the changes in the new operating system release and looking for support, while I have my own direct line with you." It's nice to have him readily available. I add, "I just can't share him, that's all. Anyways, got to go. I'm meeting a friend."

One of my coworkers joins me in the grass for lunch, and afterward, we decide to take a walk and catch up.

Since I don't see her every day, my chat with Devon will have to be put on hold for now.

After lunch, I return to my desk and check my phone. Sure enough, there is a message from my sexy guy. Devon responds to my message, asking, "What's funny? Did you enjoy your company?"

I explain, "Yes, I always enjoy catching up with her. It's not funny if I have to explain it. Let me clarify, I just find it amusing that people are seeking help with their phones, and I can simply message you if I need assistance. I have connections." I send him a wink face and add, "I did manage to get the update working. The mail was a pain, but it's working now."

Devon jokes, "Ha! The bills in the mail to you for services rendered, lol. Just kidding. Have a great weekend."

Curious about his work, I ask, "Hey, are you working?"

He replies, "Yep, knee-deep in work."

Taking a playful jab at him, I write, "You know that you are a rude man. And by the way, regarding last night's comment, 'sticky'? Try 'slick and juicy'."

Devon responds, "Rude? Never! Ha, I'm not going there; I can't be hungry at the moment. Laughing. Okay, enough of that." He sends me an image of a little person with their hands in the air.

Feeling satisfied that I've piqued his interest, I reply, "Sticking tongue out at you! Alright, talk to you later!"

Devon responds to my previous message, saying, "Talk to you later. I had to delete my initial response. Wasn't going to go anywhere and not right after we set our friendship guidelines, but I'm sure you could guess what it might have been. Anyways, later."

Feeling satisfied with his response, I put my phone away and focus on my office work. Before I realize it, the day is over, and I find myself at home alone while Josh works late. I settle on the couch and decide to watch a movie that I know Josh wouldn't be interested in. It's about an author who writes an amazing story many years ago but loses it. In the present, someone discovers the manuscript hidden in antique furniture they purchased, and they publish it under their own name. It turns out to be a good movie, and as the credits roll, I notice my phone lighting up. I wasn't expecting another message since we had already talked earlier. It's from Devon.

He writes, "Are you trying to make me lose my concentration? Your comment earlier has stopped all my forward momentum. Thanks." He ends his message with a smiley face and a grumble.

I playfully respond, "A little frustrated, are we? Yeah, me too. I'll be good, I promise. I just finished watching that author movie you recommended. I really liked it, and just to set the record straight, it was you who started it."

Devon replies, "Yes, it was. I know, I know, blah, blah, blah. Laughing, well, there's nothing wrong with a few teases every now and then. No harm in it. That was a good movie."

Curious about his work situation, I ask, "Are you still at work?"

Devon answers, "Don't worry; I won't make it a habit. Yep, still at work." He is an hour behind me, but it seems like he's doing some overtime. It's almost 8:00 PM for me and 7:00 PM for him.

I inquire further, "What are you thinking about?"

He responds, "Nothing at the moment, my mind is fried. Too much work."

Feeling empathetic, I say, "Poor guy. Well, it's Friday. Why don't you sneak out?"

Devon chuckles and replies, "Not an option. The boss is still here, so I'm just acting like I'm working. Boohaah!"

I write, "Boooo!!! Well, hmm, okay. I've got to go release some tension; I mean bake some cookies." With Josh always being away, it's natural to have certain cravings.

Devon responds, "Yeah, I get the idea. Have a good baking session."

As a playful tease, I send him a message saying, "Bye, sticky fingers."

Chapter 31
Josh's Evening

It is another quiet night at the hardware store working in the tool rental department. He had received back a couple of returned tools and he rented a van out to a customer earlier in his shift and that was it. He walks the aisle looking to tidy up and straighten out the displays, but everything is as it should be.

He goes to the back and cleans off the returned tools. This job can be gross nonetheless it passes the time. He sprays the tools down and watches the brown soapy water disappear down the drain in the concrete floor.

He's lonely he knows it; he is sad he knows it and he misses Jordan. She says that she sees that he is trying to help the situation by working all the time but he feels like she doesn't appreciate what he is doing even though that she says she does.

No matter what, it never seems to be enough, and he is sacrificing all this time and effort for what, a tired body, tired soul, a lonely wife who seems somewhere else half the time he is with her? It is bullshit. All of it is bull.

He shuts off the water and lets the tools drip dry on the wet floor. It's bullshit that he is scheduled alone. Why couldn't they just schedule one other person so that he can at least have someone to talk to, to help pass the time?

He walks over to the counter where the cash register is and checks the time on the screen, ten more minutes until his shift is done. This is brutal.

He pulls his phone out of his pocket and unlocks his screen. He clears out a couple of junk emails but not a single message, not even from Jordan. It's like she doesn't even care that he is away, no check in, nothing. He wonders if he should even send a text to her and let her know that he is on his way home. He wonders for a moment if his text would come as a benefit to her and his thinking is that maybe a text would give her a warning and give her time to get rid of a lover if she is going against their marriage.

He shakes the thought out of his mind. Jordan can't be cheating; the phone bill doesn't have any strange numbers, there are no odd alerts of comings and goings from their home security system or are there are no unexplained costs being withdrawn from their bank account. There is no evidence for him to believe this idea. He lets the thought go and checks the time on his phone. It is time to head home.

Chapter 32
Office Buzz

My weekend flashes by without any significant events to report. It's pretty much the same routine as any other weekend when Josh is away, leaving me to my own devices. Returning to work after the weekend isn't exactly thrilling, and today the office is buzzing with activity. I try to resist chatting with Devon so I can focus on getting my work done.

You might not be aware, but Devon's job is actually a term position at one of the world's most powerful companies. There's an end date to his employment, and companies often hire term employees to test the waters before considering permanent roles. In Devon's case, they've opened his position for competition, and he's applied and completed two interviews.

My day at work is monotonous and not much fun. Every word I type about it feels like the sound of nails on a chalkboard. Let's fast forward to the end of the day when I finally get home. After making dinner, watching a movie, and settling in for the night, I text Devon to check on how things are going and to inquire about any news regarding his job application.

He responds, "Stuck in a traffic jam, and I haven't heard anything, so no news is maybe good news." He goes on to explain his day, "After work, I went to the chiropractor and then took a different route home due to an accident up ahead. It's been slow, and I still need to get an oil change before heading home. Fun stuff."

I reply, "Oh, that sounds quite unpleasant. Well, take it slow, I guess. I've never been to a chiropractor, and to be honest, I'm pretty scared to go. I've heard stories of people feeling worse after treatment. One of the girls in my office even threw up after getting her neck worked on."

Devon reassures me, "This chiropractor is a Nucca chiropractor, so they're better. My oil change isn't until 7:30 PM, and it's past the accident, so I stopped at a hamburger place to eat. It's been a while since I had fast food, so I can eat and chat for a bit." He adds one of his happy faces.

I comment on his busy day, "You're certainly keeping busy."

Devon responds, "Also, my fairly new car is slipping out of fourth gear when driving. I'm hoping it's not serious, so I'm taking it to the dealer."

As I hear the garage door opening, I realize that Josh is home. I'm surprised by how quickly the time has passed – I suppose the movie I watched and my conversation with Devon kept me quite occupied throughout the evening.

I message Devon, "Hey, Josh is just arriving now. I'll have to sign off soon."

He replies, "No worries, we can chat another time too. Well, have a great rest of the day. People are giving me odd looks as I type and talk out loud."

Josh enters the door, appearing tired and worn out. I put my phone away for the moment and go to greet him, asking, "Hey, how was your day?"

Josh hugs me and sighs, "It was dirty."

Confused, I inquire, "What do you mean?"

He huffs, "I got to work, and none of the tools that were returned were cleaned. I had to wash four augers – it was so damn gross. And the other guy there is completely useless. He just sat at the cash register the whole time."

Josh works part-time in a hardware store's tool rental department.

I gently say, "You know, you don't have to put yourself through this all the time."

My comment seems to strike a nerve unintentionally, and Josh snaps back, "You know I want to get ahead, and for that, yes, actually I do."

Sensing the tension, I try to defuse it, "Hey, I wasn't trying to start a fight, just saying."

It's evident that Josh is exhausted – his sudden change in mood makes it quite clear. I really dislike these moments when he's like this, so I decide to back off. He realizes he overreacted, sighs, and apologizes, "Look Jordan, I'm really sorry. I'm just tired, feeling dirty, and fed up with all the nonsense at that place."

Avoiding his gaze, I murmur, "It's fine. Why don't you take a shower? I'll meet you in bed."

"Okay." He gives me a kiss on the cheek before heading off. I return to the couch to continue my conversation with Devon.

A smile creeps onto my face as I read Devon's message about talking out loud. I type back, "I'd be looking at you too if I saw you talking to yourself. Oh, I have a few more minutes to chat. Josh is taking a shower now."

Devon goes on a tangent, "I look around, and everyone has smartphones. They're all products from my workplace."

I respond, "Well, I love my phone; it's practically an extension of my arm. By the way, I'm curious, if you could have any kind of car, what would you choose?"

"A BMW M series or a Mustang Boss, the latest model. Or maybe just a hummer limo with a driver. How about you?"

"I'd probably go for a sleek sports car like a Spider or a Ferrari."

He probes, aware of my writing project, "Character development?"

"Partly for that, and partly because I'm curious about your preferences."

Unexpectedly, he states, "Now I remember why I don't go to these places, the food sucks. Those cars are too high-end for my budget, but an Aston Martin would suit me just fine."

I add playfully, "That's a shame about the food. I'll send you a virtual taco or burrito if you want."

"You're so kind."

Returning to the vehicle topic, I jest, "Honestly, I want a helicopter, so I never have to deal with driving."

"I'll take the taco. Haha. Alright, off to the dealership. Oh joy."

I'm reluctant to let him go and try to stall for another moment, "I have a joke. Pete and Repeat were in a boat. Pete jumped out. Who was left?"

Devon playfully retorts, "Oh yeah? Nope, I'm not that gullible."

"No, silly, you're supposed to say Repeat!"

He counters, "I know you're trying to keep me here, bad girl!"

"That's me! Well, have a great rest of the night!"

"You too, Jordan. Have a fantastic night."

Chapter 33
Jordan's Day Off

This morning I have the day off and it is a laid back one for me. I need the time for myself to relax for the coming procedure. I manage an extra couple of hours of sleep and after feeling well rested I eventually get up, have breakfast, and go for a jog around the neighborhood. I should jog more often, I find even though I'm not overly athletic, a jog always makes me feel better. It lifts my spirits, not that I am sad its lonelier and I know that it sounds silly but after a jog, I feel more alert but relaxed and focused at the same time. Anyway, after the morning jog, I rinse off quickly in the shower, have lunch and eventually find my way down to my home office. The plan is to review the novel that I am working on and also it gives me the excuse to message my cowboy.

"Hey there, how's your day going?"

A quick response comes in, "Ever seen that video, the Monday song? Well, it kind of goes like this. Monday sucks, Monday sucks." He laughs and elaborates, "Just busy with work in general. Still no news on the job front."

It must be weighing heavily on him, waiting to hear about the job. To lighten the mood, I share my own updates, "Today's my day off, so I'm just chilling at home. Tomorrow is my big day."

There's no need for clarification; he understands what I'm referring to – the fertility treatment. His words come back soothingly, "I wish you the best success. Stay positive and believe. Don't stress too much, just breathe, and relax. Whatever the outcome, that's what it's meant to be. But know that I'm rooting for you."

"Thank you! The conversation with my boss tomorrow will be funny. I'm ovulating and need to visit the doctor."

He reassures, "I'm sure they'll give you the thumbs up."

I add a playful twist, "Last time I had to leave, the excuse was that I scratched my eyeball. She knows whenever something's up, it's important. Anyway, she'll probably have me rub her belly for good luck. She's nearly due herself."

Devon responds, "I thought you actually did scratch your eye. Did you lie to me? It's okay, I completely understand. P.S. I was being sarcastic when I said you lied to me." He adds a smiley face.

"No, I really did scratch my eye, silly. I couldn't make up a story as messed up as that one. My eye's all good now, and the swelling's completely gone."

Devon seems a bit puzzled by the news of the fertility treatment, as he mentions, "You know, you could've just told me you were going for treatment. But I get it, I don't have to know everything since we're just friends. It's all good. So, you get the results tomorrow?"

Before I can reply, he also comments on my eye injury, "That's good, glad to hear you're doing better. Eyes are delicate."

His comments take me a moment to process, but it's clear he cares. He wanted me to share this with him. So, I set things straight, "The procedure is tomorrow. They're injecting it, and then I wait almost two weeks to see if it worked – fun stuff."

He understands now, as he replies, "Oh, okay. Got it."

I elaborate, "I went for my last run this morning. Have to take it easy for the next two weeks."

He acknowledges, "Yeah, it might not be classified as fun, but it's an exciting step for you both, I agree."

I want to switch gears because thinking about it makes me anxious. I ask him, "So what's on the menu today, tacos?"

"Not sure, but maybe a tuna sub with sweet pickles and some onions. It keeps others way, ha ha ha ha."

I admit, "I had garlic pizza, and my breath smells amazing! Ha ha I think I'm starting to grow some chest hair from it."

"Ha ha braid it."

I send him an open mouth smiley face and say, "That's why I like talking to you so much, I just might do that."

I grasp the phone in my hands after tucking a loose strand of my medium brown hair behind my ear and ask, "How is your car?"

"They found nothing wrong, so all is well. I went with pulled pork."

"Oh, that is an awesome choice. If I were there, I would be stealing some off your plate, it's so good."

Devon's silly humor is coming out because he writes "They do have big portions. Everything is big in Texas."

"Wow Devon what was that supposed to mean? That stuff is easy to make. I have made it in a slow cooker. You add root beer and BBQ Sauce, and it makes a very flavor filled cut of meat."

Devon explains, "No, I wasn't being dirty." In a second thought to my pulled pork recipe he says, "Yeah, that's good stuff."

I say, "Yah I know! Well, all good, I can't go there right now with the dirty talk. I am just waiting for a repair man to arrive. He is late, they always are."

He growls and explains "My first bite landed on my shirt. Son of a... I'm good. I just have a hole in my lip I guess."

I giggle to myself as I type to him, "I'm sending you a virtual laundry stick. I know, not funny."

"I'm wearing a dark blue shirt so I'm good to go. I just used some ice on it. Such a dork I am."

I tease because I catch him using this saying a lot. As I understand, it's sort of like a cheer, I have no idea? Anyway, the word is Boohah or Booyah or Whooha. He explained that it was something he picked up when he was training in the army. I tease him, "Son of a boohaah? Was that the word you were going to use?"

Devon says, "Ha, it was nastier than that, so you're waiting on a repair man. What did you break?"

Just as his question pops up my doorbell rings and I head up and let the young man in. He must be just out of school.

The repair man says courteously, "Hello, I am here for the furnace cleaning."

"Yes, come on in." The young man removes his work boots.

I explain, "The furnace is just downstairs on the right."

He nods and asks, "Besides the cleaning did you need anything else done?"

I pause for a second glancing up and the thought comes to me, "Yes actually there is a furnace filter that is still in the plastic next to the furnace. I have no idea how to change it, could you do that for me?"

He smiles, "Absolutely."

I lead the way into the basement and point him to where the furnace is and decide to return to the office as it is still pretty close to where the furnace is.

I take a seat in my office chair and respond, "Oh it's actually just a furnace cleaning. He is here now making sure all is well as I work on my writing and talk to you here in the office. It is so cold today so I'm happy to get the heat on. I'm just hanging out while he does his thing."

"I bet. Well, I'm going to dive back into my list of work. Stay warm and have a great rest of the day. I bet, was referring to previous comment not the hanging out. As usual the texting is slow."

I have to read his explanation a couple of times. So, the, I bet comment was referring to the repair man making sure that all is well with the furnace. Okay I understand and then reply to him, "Okay my fingers are crossed for you hopefully some good news with the job status arrives soon. Thanks for talking to me."

Devon replies, "I enjoy talking to you and ditto in the fingers crossed for you too, bye."

What a sweetheart. I hope that this works out also, but somehow, I just have a feeling that it won't this time.

Chapter 34
The Day

Josh accompanies me to the procedure the next day. We are nervous as is to be expected, but unlike the first time we have learned what to expect and that makes this time a little less stressful. It has been a strange time for the two of us, spending so much time away from one another, not to mention the night when we almost separated for good. It still hurts to think about that time, and I wonder if this is going to work, will it bring us closer together? I look at Josh and know that he cares to see me happy. He wants this to work for us and in those still sad eyes of his, I do see a glimmer of hope and things seem to be getting better.

Anyway, those are just some of the thoughts that are weighing on my mind at the moment. The procedure happens just as the first, you already know what that entails and in no time, it is already done, and Josh and I return home. As the afternoon passes, my cowboy is nowhere to be heard from. I am feeling in sort of a weird mood, and I know that I can come across as overbearing with always wanting to chat. Devon has never said or even implied it, he has always welcomed my conversation, but sometimes I am too much even for me if that makes any sense at all. I decide that if I make a general post and put it out on the social media feed, that if he isn't busy, he will chat back to me. I type, "Come on! Say Something. I know you read this; sticking tongue out at you!"

Minutes later, I receive a text from my cowboy, a simple greeting, "Hey there. Pretty busy today and still in limbo for job status."

I'm convinced my broadcast message worked, so I reply, "Ah, thanks! So, I just have to tweet out to seventy-five hundred people to get your attention?" I add a smiley face to show my playful intent.

He clarifies, "No, why? I just wanted to say hello on my own. Didn't see the tweet; should I check it out?"

"No, it was just a generic message. I was curious to see who's reading." I'm not being entirely truthful – it was meant to grab his attention.

He counters, "Ha, I came around on my own doing so there!"

"Haha, well, your timing was perfect. Hey, if you need a fresh set of eyes for a resume read-through, I think I'm pretty good with that stuff. Let me know." He's mentioned that he might start passing out resumes if his current job doesn't pan out.

"That's what friends are for. I appreciate the offer. I think I'm good; it was done by a professional. Of course, that doesn't mean much, does it?"

"Wow, I've never had to go that route. I guess that gives you an edge. With government applications here, I'm always tweaking the resume to match the skill sets in the postings."

"Maybe my skills should speak louder than a well-written piece of paper."

"I agree. Here, they try to keep things 'fair' – I say that rolling my eyes. Not really fair with so many technical rules for job applications. And the processes take so long. I wouldn't be surprised if they weed out the perfect candidate on a technicality. People who screen applications tend to weed out candidates if their skills don't closely match the postings. I'm not sure if that's the case everywhere else?"

Devon confirms, "It's the same here. I think it's a global thing. Well, I better get back to work. Oh, by the way, I did some more writing this morning. Lord, the ending feels never-ending, but it's coming soon. I'm writing about smugglers' cove, with a mafia encounter near the end of the story."

"I'm so happy for you! Sounds like it's going to be epic. Will this be the final story in your series? Random thought, this banana is so good!" Yes, snacking and chatting all in one, why not!

"No, not the final. I'm coming up to the end of my first draft. Sorry, but I have to make sure this novel propels me forward soon. I'm thinking I'll have it wrapped up around Christmas. I know I'm a slowpoke. There's a sequel in the drafting stage too."

He misunderstands me a bit. I clarify, "No, I meant, is this the final story in the series? I think I remember you saying it was a continuation from the last?" And I reply to his slowpoke comment, "No, you're not slow. I imagine there's a lot of fact-checking."

I enjoy conversing with Devon, but sometimes social media platforms can be sluggish, and messages may get jumbled. I inform him that I sent him an email.

Devon clarifies, "This novel is a new genre that I decided to write. As for my other series, I'm working on the final installment, but the one I'm currently working on is a separate project. I have too many projects and not enough coffee and sugar to keep me going. I have to stay busy; I actually have fans bugging me for my books."

He notices my email mention and responds via the text chat, "I know this is slow, but it works better for me."

"That's pretty cool! Well, I haven't garnered any true fans yet. My social media analytics show that I have more male followers aged between thirty-five to forty-five, even though I wrote a young adult, sci-fi novel."

"Well, have a great afternoon and rest of the day. Take care."

"Okay, bye."

I understand that Devon is cutting the conversation short not because he's uninterested, but due to his work commitments. He's aiming to impress his employers for a permanent job, and I also need to focus on relaxing after the medical procedure earlier today.

I put my phone aside and decide to check in on Josh. The sounds of gunfire from the basement indicate he's playing one of his Xbox games. I head downstairs and snuggle up to him as he holds the game controller.

Josh relaxes with my presence and asks, "How are you feeling?"

"Good."

He playfully says, "You just got me killed."

I play along with a dramatic sigh, "Oh no, could you try again? I was really enjoying this movie."

I glance up at him and he smirks at my game-related comment. His games are so advanced that they often look like movies. I remember when I was younger, games were things like Mario Brothers and Legend of Zelda. Modern games are something I couldn't have imagined as a child.

Later in the evening, another message pops up from Devon.

He writes, "Sorry, I had to reboot my device because I lost the ability to reply. I think there's a bug with the operating system software on my phone."

I chuckle because ever since I upgraded my own phone's operating system, I've been encountering problems too. Since he works at the company, I took the liberty of emailing him about it. I reply, "I sent you an email with my own bug report; insert evil laughs!"

"I saw and will look into it."

"You better!" I add a wink emoji to emphasize my playful tone.

"Bite me! I will for sure look into getting it fixed." He smiles.

"Ha ha be careful, I bite hard." I chaff.

"Ha ha ha yeah I won't go there it will just get me all up in a tizzy." He comments.

I send a smile to him. The one thing about Devon is he can be very honest, and I know that he wants to play.

Devon continues, "I have to keep myself in check, sorry for the outburst."

I know that he is trying really hard to keep a boundary up between us and I will respect his gentle ask for us to keep the conversation tame. I focus back to what we were talking about earlier and say, "So, should I send the bill in the mail for my bug reporting services?"

"No, no, let's keep this at a nice friendly base level. It was me that made the remark, sorry for that." Devon mentions.

"I know where we stand and respect you for it; no worries, we are just teasing and there is nothing wrong with that." I send a smile his way.

"Exactly, because my mind was going to hell; I was thinking so dirty and figured that was so wrong. You don't want to know. You would be like, oh my god what an asshole." He adds in some laughs and continues, "So, I will be like I said I would be, but yeah you know where I stand and likewise. Thanks for not responding to that. I know it was wrong to even say. So don't be upset."

God, I want this man so badly. If we were in the same town, I know that I would be trying my hardest to get into bed with him and forget that I was married for that time. I answer, "You know how I feel about you. It's hard to ignore those feelings, hard to turn off, but I respect what you want with our friendship. So, if we ever meet, I won't jump you." I add a sticking tongue out face and continue, "I hope I didn't scare you." I click send and know full well that I am playing hard with his desire.

He sends me a smiling face before he replies, "Nope, it will take every fiber in my bones to resist and we would have to out of respect for my partner and yours, but if my hands were tied. I know stop. Anyway, just kidding, I better get back to work."

I mention, "I have over seventy-five hundred followers and only a few that have regular conversations with me, but it's completely different with you. You are the only one that I have let into my world."

"Is it my wonderful charm? Yeah right, I am honored. I have other author friends, but not really friends if you follow. I have four hundred and thirteen followers and only one chatting with me." Devon explains.

I send a smile his way before I say, "I find some authors tend to get jealous the moment you do well. If you do well, I just want a helicopter ride. I would lose my bananas for a helicopter, and you are still visiting my tropical island."

"I wish I could oblige; I don't own one." He comments.

"Maybe you will when your book hits the market. There's no harm in dreaming big. Hell, I do." I've actually got a whole plan in my head; I want a tropical island and a helicopter.

Devon responds, "Yes, indeed."

"Well, I'm over the moon that we got to talk today. I need to get some housework done before Josh gets home.

So, what's the ETA on my bug?" I add a silly face emoji to my message.

"I'm waiting for a response, not sure yet. Have a great evening."

"I have one more request – I'd like my bug named Jordan, okay?"

"I have to keep it low-key as they might not be thrilled about supporting unpaid contracts, haha."

"One more thing, just kidding. Alright, I'm logging off for now. Have a good one!"

Later in the evening, Devon follows up with me. He writes, "Install 8.0. It seems to resolve freezes and hangs. Also, have you reset the device power by holding the sleep and power button for ten seconds and when you see the brand logo, let go and it will power up. Okay, talk to you later."

After following his instructions, I reply to let him know, "Thank you, it's working better."

Chapter 35
Work Sucks

Things at work are kind of stupid to say the least. With this latest procedure, I have been careful with reducing my exercise to easier things like walking and such and I have basically refrained from doing strenuous things. I know that me being careful probably makes no difference but to me it's more peace of mind in knowing that I am doing everything that I can in order to make this work.

At work there has been an office clean up going on and basically one woman in the office is taking the lead in the task and that work involves lifting boxes full of paper and moving them to storage. She has asked me a couple of times for help and each time I have declined because I am playing it safe, seeing that I spent over one thousand dollars for the procedure but this woman can be a bit of a bitch and dense and doesn't seem to ever take no for an answer and I am not at the point where I want to make the announcement to the entire office to explain that I am going through fertility treatment.

So earlier today she had the nerve to come into my cubicle and tell me off for not helping and she did this when there was no one else around to hear her and to sum it all up, the conversation ended with me screaming at her to get out of my face.

It was bad and I don't feel that I need to explain my reasons to her. She was tasked with the office project, not me and I am not obligated to help. Anyway, that is my take on it and today the conversation with Devon picks up where we had left off. Devon writes, "How goes it today? My wife is staying another week in New York, due to finalizing the sale of land and her father got ill. Me, glad it is Friday and glad that we have each other to talk to."

I ask, "Does it have something to do with hearing my voice that one time?"

"Yeah, I'm also sure it is because of what we are going through personally too."

Devon had mentioned at one point that Sara's father is having some health issues and now I know that it was likely because of me that she is staying away. Devon denied any foul play and basically implied that she was hearing things and well her gut is telling her otherwise, I guess. I have never been on that side of the spectrum, but I guess it's her instincts kicking in and well, her intuition is right. We may not have touched each other but there is a bond between us and it's so hard to ignore and well, we can't. I still can't explain it as I write the words to paper. It's more than just lust or the excitement of being sneaky. I say, "I am sending you a virtual hug. I know that you will be able to fix it. You're a great guy and she will see that. Sometimes time away is good, sounds like she needs it."

"I know. My thing is I fell for you so damn fast. I had to honestly put myself in check and come back to reality. But you already knew that and the fact she sensed something. So now I am rebuilding my relationship as that is the right thing to do, just recapping that's all. We are good where you and I stand. I am just happy to have you as a close new friend. I have never fallen for a girl so fast in my life. I am still in love with my partner just was vulnerable I guess and loved the attention. I didn't use you so please don't think that. I normally don't have a beautiful gal take interest in me. So, to have you as a friend is like hell yah in my book." He adds a smile at the end of his text.

I write, "We are in the same boat except my husband isn't in tune with me. I know that you have control of this situation."

"I do. Well, he needs to dial in and embrace you." Before this gets deep Devon changes topic to both of our relief because I don't want to dwell on our reality. He asks, "Is it nice out there? I know this time of year is cooler."

"Yes, it's sunny and warm; I think it's in the low sixties according to your standard. The USA needs to upgrade to the metric system. It's so hard to explain weather, and what's up with one-dollar bills? They make me angry. The lowest bill should be a five-dollar bill. Oh yes, I also wish that Canadians could apply to be on American reality shows. There, got that off my chest!"

"Laughing over here, bitter much? Just joking, yeah well at least we don't call a dollar a loonie, laughing out loud. I'm just joking. I bet when you get heated it is a sight. A good sight, yep, mind went there, typical male."

"We have toonies also. It's a two-dollar coin and our money is colorful. All your bills look the same."

"I am actually laughing out loud; I just read that email you sent me this morning!"

His last comment is referring to the email I sent him about the argument with the co-worker from this morning. I don't regret standing my ground but regret that the situation got to that point. I write to him, "I think you would have left the room. I don't typically yell at people; it was really bad."

He says, "I just hope she gets what she has coming. Oh, I wanted to say that I did hide your photos and encrypted the file. I am not going to get rid of them."

I mention, "This isn't the first time with her. I did nothing wrong, I stood my ground, although I'm a girl, emotions come into play. I am just happy I didn't cry in front of the bully."

He asserts. "Never cry in front of them. It makes them feel stronger."

Our messages are starting to get a little mixed. I respond to his comment on my pictures, "Giggling over here, all good but I have to say that I got rid of yours." I insert a sad face and continue, "I was really upset when everything happened, and I did it in the heat of the moment. I regret deleting them but thought when it happened that you were going to break all ties."

He replies, "No worries. I completely understand. Besides, it is better that way. I should delete them, but I can't. I'm weak. Oh well."

I say, "When people generally say 'friends' it usually means that they are ending it and don't want to talk anymore. I thought that you were only talking to me at first to just lesson the blow. I know now that you really mean to keep our friendship."

Devon writes, "For my defense no. I was about to ruin years of relationships that's how strong you got around me. It was dangerous. I was entranced. I still am, but keeping it suppressed as that is the right thing for me to do and not pursue. It's nothing against you by any means."

I respond, "Keep them, the pictures. I wish I kept yours. We must have known each other in another life. I still want you. Anyway, hope I didn't scare you but it's true, can't help it."

Devon admits, "You make me weak in the knees and I have to keep myself in check, so that is why I only want to be friends as well as her catching on too. Trust me Jordan, I understand and know exactly what you are saying. So, I am just glad to have you as a friend. I know if we met, I would need a drug to demobilize me as I would be like let's go as I want to do you so bad. But again, glad we can understand each other."

I say, "I will just smell the cake, I won't eat it." I add a happy face.

He jokes, "As long as I can smell the cake too, boohaah, okay I think I need to refocus and tone it down."

I question, "I have heard of Viagra is there a drug to stay limp?"

He confirms, "Salt peter."

Out of surprise I write, "Laughing out loud, well I wish there was a drug for vagina dryness."

"Ha! Anyway, better change subject to keep my ground. I would love a picture of that, joking, no, good lord that was wrong. You are bad. It's easier to blame you at this second. I am glad that you put up with my stupid silliness. I think if I keep talking like that I will fall back into where I was before and can't do that. Well, have a good day, talk to you later."

"Okay, I'll be good, I was just saying." I let him go for the moment.

We have made it clear to each other and this is completely fine with me. Things seem to be where they were before, and we are getting comfortable again. I know and he knows that it is wrong, but we know that no harm will come about it. There is an international boundary between us. This is just a game of flirting and friendship but given the chance, I would fuck him.

The day progresses at a steady pace. I keep to my work and try not to pay attention to the office gossip because well, I am the gossip after I blew up at my co-worker because she was being an absolute bitch. She had the nerve to tell everyone that would listen to her chatter.

I am not like that. I don't need to defend myself or seek the approval of others to know that I stood my ground.

After a couple hours pass, I need a mental break and fall back to messaging Devon. I type, "Hey, you know what?"

"What?"

"I got my credit card bill, and the video chat didn't charge anything. The bill covered the dates we chatted, so I know that I wasn't charged."

Devon mentions, "That is great, so no alarm."

I write, "Nope, it was the perfect platform. So, your lunch is coming up, don't get anything juicy, no staining the shirt."

"I know you were concerned about the video chat."

Our messages are getting jumbled, but I'm undeterred and type, "Maybe you could grab a piece of stale bread or a taco."

Chuckling, Devon replies, "Ha, no comment on the taco. The Mexican food at work is pretty lackluster."

I express my concern, "Well, I was worried about your shirt."

Devon playfully dismisses it, "You're being silly."

I share, "For lunch, I had a veggie sandwich with a side of olives. It's strange; I used to dislike olives, but now I'm a fan of the green stuffed ones."

Devon responds with a touch of self-deprecation, "The only way my shirt could get stained – never mind, I almost messed up again. I can converse normally, I promise. How about I grab some lunch and let you enjoy your day? I wouldn't want to get myself into trouble once more. Yeah, I think it's best if I head out. Wishing you a fantastic day, my Canadian friend!"

I close with, "Okay well enjoy your lunch, don't stain your shirt and sending you a hump, I mean hug."

"You're a bad girl!"

We pause for a bit and later on in the day once I am home with Josh another message comes in from Devon. He writes, "Okay just have a side note and wanted to share. If your phone lags with the keyboard go into settings and under the drive turn off documents and data, then do a hard reset. Or reset all of the settings. Your keyboard should respond better."

I take a look and follow his instruction, "Thanks tech guy, all done!"

Devon admits, "Sorry, I know I need to leave you alone, but it was a good excuse to send one last chat today. Booyaah" Somewhere in the day I had mentioned that Josh had the evening off from his second job and as I read his final messages Josh has settled on the other recliner in the living room just steps from where I am sitting. Truthfully, I don't mind when Devon messages me, but for Devon he has asked for me to follow a set schedule for him as his spouse suspects and it is best to keep this friendship secret rather than non-existent.

I write to Devon, "I got to tell you something funny."

"Okay"

I admit, "My husband doesn't understand how I have become so tech savvy with my phone. I keep sharing your tips with him."

Devon replies, "Laughing, it's because you have a direct line to this handsome phone tech guy, virtual knee slap. Just tell him you are a smart cookie."

I send him a smile and say, "He is already having a hard time with my massage guy. You are still my secret."

Devon writes, "Good idea to keep me a secret and same here. Well good night."

I rest my phone down on the coffee table next to me and look at the television to see what's on. One of Josh's crime shows, and I glance over to see how Josh is doing, like if he is into the show. Josh glances back over and says, "Come up for air, have we?"

I say, "Yes, was just taking care of my social media."

Josh comments, "It looked like you were talking to someone."

I say, "Yah, just sending my hello messages to my new followers."

Chapter 36
Weekend Writing

Around mid-morning, Devon reaches out, saying, "Hi, have a wonderful Saturday."

At my desk, I respond, "Thanks! I'm here. What's on your agenda for today?"

Devon shares his plans, "I'll be doing some yard work, cleaning the house, and working on my writing. Sounds a bit dull, huh? What about you?"

"I'm in the process of transferring words to my story. I've hit just over twenty-four thousand words, and there's still much to go. Since I wrote at different times, I'm sorting out where events and conversations fit. I should probably mow the grass later, but I'm not exactly eager to do that," I admit.

Devon acknowledges, "Wow, your story seems to be making progress. The life of a writer—always weaving words. Mowing the grass might make for a good workout."

"Yeah, it sure does. I bought some burlap to wrap up my bush, but I'm not sure if I'll tackle that today. The weather's still fairly nice, and the rose bush grew another foot; it's over six feet now."

Devon shifts back to his writing, "Here, it's going to rain today, but I'll head outside soon to weed the rock yard. Started writing earlier, but now I'm diving into maritime jargon research for my story. Been up since 5:00 AM."

Noting the contrasting weather, I reply, "It's sunny here, always the opposite. It's odd that you don't have grass."

Devon stays on topic, saying, "I think this story might extend to around one hundred and ten thousand words, as needed and fitting. I'm not there yet, but it's coming."

I gently point out, "You keep saying 'maritime.' Your story is based in Victoria, B.C., right? 'Maritime' is for the east coast—PEI, Newfoundland, Labrador, and Nova Scotia."

Devon inquires, "Oh, is that not right?"

I clarify, "Your story takes place on the west coast—B.C. and Vancouver, Seattle too. I believe you're looking for conversations with the coast guard between the USA and Canada along the waters near the international boundary line."

Acknowledging the correction, he says, "Got it, thanks for pointing that out. It won't be credible if I use the wrong terminology."

I continue the conversation, sharing insights about the west coast, "On the west coast, a significant portion of the population is Asian, and it's a modern area with many affluent individuals. In the Maritime Provinces, you'll find small fishing towns with heavy accents, unlike in B.C., where the accent is more like the average North American."

Devon muses, "It's interesting, considering it's all Canada. The architecture and landscape give off a British and eastern coast vibe."

I agree, "You're right. Some of the older homes have that east coast feel, but overall, both coasts have a British influence in their architecture, given the time they were built."

Shifting gears, I ask him, "Getting excited for your trip? When you're on the island, you should visit Goldstream."

Devon responds with a playful suggestion, "I'll definitely make a trip there. Maybe you should enjoy the weather and ignore the lawn."

Still on the B.C. topic, I share, "It's so British there, everything screams it. But I have to say, it's one of the most beautiful places. I've been on B.C. Ferries, and the ride from the island to Vancouver is stunning. The water's calm, like a lake, and the ferry winds through islands with whales following beneath."

"That's what drew me to write my story around it. I've been to Nova Scotia and spent a whole summer there as a kid, but that's the other side of Canada."

Recalling my vacation pictures from a trip to B.C. stored on an old social media account, I find the link and share it with Devon, saying, "Here, I might look like a total goof in these pictures, but I wanted to show you my trip to B.C."

Devon responds, "Sure, let me check it out. The yard can wait a few more minutes. Oh, I can't see it. It seems I need to sign in and I don't have an account."

Disappointed, I think to myself before explaining, "Hmm, I thought it was set to public."

Devon suggests, "It might be an issue with the phone, who knows. I'd love to see them. Although I'm content with the pictures I already have of you. Less might be better. I copied the link to the browser, but it's asking me to sign in."

Recognizing his busy day ahead, I concede, "Ah, okay. They're nothing special, just a bunch of albums from years ago."

"Gotcha."

"I just wanted to share the B.C. trip with you, so you could get a feel for it for your book."

Devon reassures me, "I'm sure they were great photos."

While looking through the albums, I realize there are pictures where I'm not looking my best. I admit, "There are also the typical drunk party pictures, so don't judge me if you happen to see them later. I was young and foolish."

Devon jokes, "No worries. Well, now I'll have to look, just kidding. Guess I better create an account so I can see them."

I mentally facepalm at my own unnecessary revelation. Why did I mention that? Oh well, maybe he would have seen them eventually anyway. Trying to shift the focus, I talk about the trip, "You'll find pictures of B.C., Ontario, Winnipeg, Manitoba, cottage country in Quebec, and even up north past Sudbury. You've mentioned a few times that I have a northern accent, but I've never really thought of it. I think I sound like any average person from this continent. It's where you're from that has that distinctive warm southern accent."

Devon comments, "Nice, I've seen some on Facebook."

I can't help but wonder if he's looking at them right now. So, I ask, "Can you see them? I'm not an alcoholic, I swear."

He comments, "Yep, well you know what, I got them and am looking at them now. I know I said it before, but you really are a beautiful gal." He sends over a smile with his kind words and continues, "Is it the rainy season then? I recognize Victoria Harbor."

I reveal, "Those were taken in November. Here are some more." Now that I have the hang of my shared drive, I make some more albums shared for him and send through the links.

Devon compliments, "Very nice, thanks for sharing. Was this before or after your wedding? I don't have many pictures of me to share, only the ones you saw on Facebook."

I reply, "Laughing, I must be boring you with my photos. The China town photos were taken in Vancouver."

He writes, "I don't mind at all, besides its raining now so I got out of yard work."

I answer his question with regards to if they were taken before or after my wedding. I explain, "They were taken before. I had broken up with an ex and took off across the country to get away and ended up visiting my girlfriends who went to school out there at the time."

He says, "Well, from what you've seen in my photos, my weight tends to fluctuate too. I'm not particularly thin, but I'm fine with it. I'm working on improving that as well."

I send him more links to additional albums, then notice his previous message, "Here are more photos; these are taken north of Sudbury, about seven hours north of Ottawa."

Devon observes, "Lovely landscape photos. So, these are pretty far up north?"

Amused, I reply, "It's not quite in the Arctic Circle, but there aren't many cities north of it." I playfully stick my tongue out in a text, adding, "I think if you kept walking north, you might hit a city in Russia."

Devon responds, "I see, but I bet you get a lot of snow, haha. I had no idea it was that close to Russia."

Since there's a slight delay in our messages, I address his earlier comment about his weight, saying, "My weight has had its ups and downs over the years too." As for his Russia remark, I clarify, "Haha, it's not actually that close."

Our conversation continues with a lighthearted tone.

He explains, "Me too, for the weight but its human; you still are a hot girl then and now, just being honest okay, I will stop with that." He sends me a smile and continues, "Thank you for showing me your pictures."

I send him another link and explain, "This is at my mom and dad's."

"I bet Christmas is fun there."

"Yah it is, we go swimming on Christmas day." I smile.

"Inside or out; oh, that is right your mom and dad have an indoor pool."

I send him another link, "Here are some silly pictures of me being a goof."

Devon comments, "Looks like you were having a great time with friends, nothing wrong with that at all. You are far from being boring and that tells me you are human and not fake."

Sharing these old pictures with Devon brings back so many fond memories. I say, "Ten years goes by fast. Back then I could just get up and go where my heart wanted, nothing mattered. Those Christmas pictures with my two girlfriends, I can't remember what was funny, but I remember we laughed until we cried."

Devon admits, "Jordan, I can't wait to meet you. I am looking forward to the day that I can see you in person."

"Yes, that would be a great day; I'm looking forward to it." I send him a smile and say, "We probably would be speechless like the video chatting we did, smiling over here."

He says, "I saved a copy of that bikini picture of yours."

I sigh, "Really, it is not the one with the tadpole, geez!" Back on the topic of meeting him I say, "I would get over the shyness and talk to you. I like the sound of your voice." I explain.

Devon asks, "Do you not want me to save your pictures? Say so, and I can delete the copies."

I consider for a moment then say, "No, its fine with the pictures, they are just goofy that's all. I am just surprised that you saved some. It is all good. So, do you have any speedo shots? I just want you to know that I am actually laughing out loud as I type this to you. I doubt it. That's more of a European thing."

Devon asks, "What's a speedo?"

I explain, "It's a really tight underwear swimsuit guys wear, like what you see when guys swim in the Olympics. I can't picture you ever sporting a speedo. You mostly see older European guys in those. Guys from here generally wear swim shorts. God Devon, it's not funny if you have to explain." I send him a smile.

Devon says, "Well, I do wear bike shorts. I can give you some pictures of me wearing those."

I say, "I wear bike shorts so that my kitty doesn't show when I sport a short dress. Giggling, I guess I could use them to ride bikes. Yah that's the only thing that I don't like about bikes, those seats kill your ass. Anyway, I have a question for you."

"Okay"

I explain, "I knew a guy who would go on the really long bike tours. I asked him with the race what if he needed to pee than what, and he said that he would go while on the bike. Do you go on those long races or just the recreational stuff?"

"I do both, but I stop to pee like a human, not on myself. I once was propositioned by a cute girl to have sex with her on the fly on a recreational ride but didn't take her up on it. I pedaled faster."

What a weird thing to tell me but then again, I opened that can of worms with the pee question. "The stuff that comes into my head, like I need to pee every hour and now that I know; ladies in the Olympics must pee themselves."

He reveals "I did not know her but saw her several times before on the same roads."

I tell him, "Laughing over here, yah I just saw your comment above."

I put the phone down, I can hear my dog scratching at the door upstairs and go up to let him out to relieve himself. The dog is quick about it and within a moment I let him back inside and head back downstairs to the home office.

Devon explained while I was away for a few moments, "Yeah that is not cool, some stop and squat and some pee on bikes. Hey, I don't blame her, I would do me, laughing and I just joking by the way." There is a short pause in time when the messages are being received and then he says, "Now I am being stupid."

I take a seat and write, "Sorry about the pause had to let the dog out for a second, and well she had good taste, just saying."

He smiles and says, "Thank you."

Devon says, "Were your ears ringing this morning? Never mind, I'm joking. At least you let me be silly and talk stupid still."

I know him and know that his comment had a tone of truth in it. I focus in on it and test the waters because I think I know where he was going with it, I say, "If we ever bike ride together I won't ask, I wouldn't want you to pedal away and leave me in the dust."

Devon clarifies "I would pull you aside and well you know the rest. It would be like a friend helping a friend out. There would be no pedaling away. I don't know what would happen to be honest, but I have to say if it happened, I won't be upset that I broke my friend request, but you knew that. I won't keep talking about it, not fair to."

I smile, "I would be down for it, but I just wouldn't want what happened before to replay all over again. I would want to keep talking, you are my friend."

He confirms, "Exactly, I am still sorry I did that to you that's why it is good to be friends and not even go there, but I will forever have an image of you that you described to me, not letting that go and I respect you for saying that Jordan, we kept the lines open and you still want to be friends so with that said, going forward, I will not talk sexual or dirty to you and keep it friendly as that is best, but what I dream about is mine. Hell, that is all I got right now. I know poor me, but that is my deal. It is okay to be friends and have common grounds."

I admit, "I'm not letting go of it either. I am writing a book about it actually." I send him a smile.

Devon responds like a smart ass, "Really I had no idea." He smiles back and continues, "I'm not sure if you were being honest about describing yourself a few weeks back, but have no doubts to not think that, just glad that you did because it fuels my dreams. It's more than I deserved to be honest. So, I'm sure you need to do some writing and it looks like it has stopped raining for now. I think I better do some chores." He smiles and says more, "Yeah, I have to change subject, but glad that you said hi back to me today."

I say to him, "I was being honest. Why would I lie? What if we did meet and it was different than I described. You would be like, that's not what I pictured?"

"I was merely making a statement, didn't say that you lied, I'm glad that you told me how you look and what it does. I think that it's awesome and I didn't lie either about me, but I think guys focus on that more than a girl does, that is human male gender."

I state, "I have never lied to you, not once."

He answers, "Likewise, I have told you the truth and nothing but the truth. I know when she gets back, we will be arguing for the first time over what she thought she heard, that is my deal, but I made the choice to back off and salvage my relationship and I feel it was a good move for me. You did and still do have a powerful grip on me, and I have to keep in check and again thank you for understanding and allowing me to be a part of your life still as little as it is, I am thrilled!"

I say, "Ditto, I just, well seriously, I wonder if it was you here. I know that you know best between the two of us, and not trying to screw with your head, just not sure if I am ready for any major changes. I question the choices that I have made, the partner I chose. He loves me, but I don't think that I love him the same as he does me."

Devon says, "I completely understand and agree. You are married, trying to start a family and it is best to not go there, and for me to stay the course here."

I explain, "Look at my dilemma through friend eyes. I'm not trying to mess just saying that's all. Please don't be mad at me."

Devon says, "I have that same challenge and thoughts, oh know I am not mad at all. I respect your honesty but if you feel being a friend is dampening your relationship, then tell me. I know from my end if you were ever found out, I would be in a mess so by backing off and working on my own relationship, to me was the best thing. I was at the point of planning a split, running to you, and taking you away, but that was not realistic and throwing my relationship away was not a good move, so I had to opt out and her asking about it."

I say, "I think if we broke all ties, by the way, I don't want that. I don't think it would change anything with Josh, I don't think I love him."

He says, "I had to fight for what I had. That's how much power I let you have on me and shame on Josh for letting it get there. I love her, but not like I used to, but I am willing to fight for it again. I hope by saying that I haven't pissed you off. If I were single Jordan, I would be seeking you, but I'm not and seeking your friendship as that is all I can offer."

I explain, "Josh has been so nice to me, even bought fresh flowers, has been so kind and it breaks my heart because he is doing this and well my heart isn't there."

Devon confides, "I know, I hate the word friend as we all throw it around like it means nothing, but you do mean more to me. Josh is doing it because he sees that you are drifting away. His heart has to be in it and likewise."

I say, "It's hard, the mind thinks rationally, but you can't explain it to your heart."

He says, "I know so give it one hundred percent and if he doesn't then you know your path, and that is likewise for me. I have to try and not have any obstacles in my way. I refuse to give up our friendship. I will not do that sorry unless you say to. This went from a happy to sad conversation, sorry, let's not go there. I rather have you smile."

I admit, "I'll be good; I don't want you to cut me out." I love Devon, I know that I do and cherish the relationship that we have.

Devon says, "It's not you being bad it's my mind and that is bad, I am the one that needs to be good remember guys think with the wrong head but choosing you to be my friend was thinking with the right head, just don't hate me for dreaming about you. Besides, I'm the expert in my dreams and no one can see them or hear."

I say, "I think this story, when told, will catch. It's honest, true; readers aren't stupid they will pick up that there is a story behind the story."

He replies, "Yep, it's a classic Romeo and Juliet."

I ask, "What is your email address? I deleted it in my fit of anger."

Devon mentions, "Yeah, I got rid of emails and the other chat applications, except two photos and now one more. So, I have three photos of you that I am keeping."

I reveal, "Oh, and about the dreams it's the same here, you are in them, and we are at a country music concert." I stick my tongue out.

Devon says, "I had one about you this morning that is why I was up early. I am quite sure your book will be a best seller and a hit."

I complain, "All I have of you is your Twitter picture, and I noticed that you updated your Facebook image, no shades, I like!" He typically wears sunglasses in his photos.

He responds, "The black and white picture, Thanks! If you like I could gather some and place them on the sky drive and yes they all will be clean pictures nothing dirty as I know that offends you and not right."

What the hell is he talking about? I know we discussed it, and my issue was that I didn't want pictures taken that were identifiable. I just didn't want to deal with an accident of them getting out and having to deal with the embarrassment. I say, "I wish I could have been there this morning; I am smiling by the way. We are very dirty friends, ah well, we are who we are."

He says, "I only have two anyway that I took after our video chat, but I am going to delete them, feel silly having them besides not like you haven't seen one before. I think guys get off more seeing girl's parts over a girl seeing a guy's parts."

Our messages are coming in a bit jumbled. While he is on the subject of dirty photos, I am on the subject of the day which was sharing normal photos with him. I explain, "Yes that would be nice to have more photos of you, thank you for doing that. I know not everyone likes looking at photos; I'm an amateur photographer and love seeing them and get a glimpse into your world."

Devon promises, "I will do that this week and let you know, I can't guarantee lots of photos, but I can see what I have."

I have to read back and laugh. I say, "Oh wow what a delay, you're talking dirty photos, I'm talking trip photos, and then you are talking about sharing clean albums."

Devon says, "No worries, I know what you meant."

I write, "Yes, for this sky drive stuff, you should keep it clean because I think with me changing the permissions on my own albums; anyone can access the photos that I shared with you. Don't put your penis out there. I have a pretty good idea of what it looks like, and I am smiling just thinking about it."

Devon is quick to respond, "Laughing over here, no I won't, it's not like it is pretty like yours, so don't worry about that. Yep, not much to brag home to mom about, it is what it is, just not in action anymore, knee slapper!"

I go there, "I would imagine that it feels amazing."

There is a pause, and he says, "Um, yes ditto, you have no idea how much I'd like to feel you, okay, clearing throat, swelling up down there, thanks, laughing out loud. I must picture something gross now to come back to reality." He sends me a smile and continues, "Yeah this Twitter delay makes a good story you need to include it."

I suggest, to my cowboy with a hard on, "Play that song on you YouTube, 'What Does the Fox Say?' That will distract you if you need it."

Devon admits, "Laughing, maybe I don't want it to go down, joking. Anyway, I think it is time to part for now, don't you? I keep telling myself not to think that way, but there I go anyway, laughing. Bad friend I am, and no pun intended."

He is having a hard time. I say, "I am still working through my transfer of text. I'll be on for another thirty minutes I think, but if you have to go, I understand. We have been chatting for a while."

He explains, "I need to go or if I keep thinking this way, I am going to explode, so yeah I think it is best, at least you know you are the only gal I have ever chatted with that has made me do that just by chatting, so ha and you are the only girl outside my life that I have chatted with."

I let him know, "Wish I was there to take it. Okay I am there in spirit. Talk to you later."

Devon says, "Laughing, yes you were this morning, if I may say you had to be because I actually almost hit my face with it, too much information, I know but wow never happened before. At least I know I am still alive."

I send him a smile. I guess that means he is into me.

He continues, "You know even though we are friends, I am always going to think thoughts like that, oh well."

I say, "Me too, I think we can class each other as dirty friends."

He writes, "As stupid as it sounded, I was thinking about filming it with my phone and sending it to you, but you would have dropped me fast, but don't worry I won't, it was a moment thing. Now, I am talking stupid and really need to keep it clean and let you go so you can have a great rest of the day."

I say, "It would have been a tease, so don't. I already get soaked enough as it is."

He writes, "You don't know just how hot that is to me."

I say, "God, I'm soaked right now, and I am just trying to race through an edit, grumbles."

Devon replies, "Glad you get soaked thinking of this friend. Sorry, but I have to say this, yum okay, going to be good now I promise and let you go, geez thanks for image. At least tell me the color of panties you are wearing. No don't, that won't be good, sorry." He sends a smile then says, "You see I am a good friend, I helped you out, don't answer, that was rude to say."

I tell him, "If you were here, I would just say, fuck this friend crap, I would take you so fast, push you down and get on top and get mine because I am very greedy, and they are a pink/orange bit. Also want you to know that I wouldn't give you the chance to say no."

He types, "Oh lord, wow I am in la, la land, yeah I know we are friends but yeah if you were here, you would be eaten so much and that means my tongue and mouth on you, guess it didn't sound right. Okay, wow you see now I want a picture, dammit, I better go and rub one off sorry but true, but I know better, okay letting you go as I took it too far this time."

I admit, "I'm going to have to do the same. I'm here by myself today."

He tells, "I already started."

Chapter 37
Pushing Further

The next day proves to be the same conversations, we are pushing just a little further and more so than what it was before the entire Sara situation with her hearing my voice.

I write to my guy, "Hey there had to get my yard work done this morning before jumping onto the computer."

Devon replies, "Hey, that's ok. I have a busy day. I see it is nice weather up north. I was lazy all day yesterday. Can't be today, but glad you said hello." He adds a smile.

I ask, "What's your game plan for today? Josh is gone until 5:00 PM but already got my yard and the laundry done, so now it's writing. I do have questions about your pictures, but I'll pick your brain when you have time. So, tell me your cut off time, I don't want to interfere, I am like a moth to the flame here."

He mentions, "I have to get some yard work done and head out to get some groceries, I am good to chat until 2:00 PM your time. You are free to ask away and what does that mean, moth to the flame?"

I ask, "My question is your land, you said that your spouse was closing a sale, was that the land where you are in a photo with your arms spread out? For me, moth to flame means that I can't resist you, drawn to you, bad like a teenage crush."

He confirms, "Yep, that was up in Conesus Lake, New York and by the way I'm smiling, just happy that I have that effect on you."

I ask, "Was that like a second home for you?"

He explains, "Yep, well that was the plan. We never did end up building because things happen, jobs change and now I find myself here in Austin. So, what is it that you like so much about me?"

I admit, "Everything, it is the whole deal, looks, personality and charm."

Devon asks, "How is your book coming along?"

I say, "I still have a ton of words to copy over. It will probably round off at thirty thousand words today."

He confides, "I just want to apologize for the conversation yesterday. It was rude of me to make those comments."

I clarify, "Oh, I didn't mind yesterday with anything that you said, you're a tease, and the feelings are mutual." I decide to focus back on his photos. I love gazing at Devon's pictures, and he is just so handsome, confidant and yummy, I tell him, "Just saying, I know I'm being silly but there is some truth to the silliness, why do you have to be so hot?"

He says, "Oh silly, laughing over here. I wish I was hot. Why do you have to be so hot? I see your pictures and I get hard. I see your chats and I get drenched, so it is silly but yeah. There is nothing like having a wet spot almost show and I'm a guy. See now I am picturing you nude and doing things to tease me. Great, well I am chuckling over here. Anyway, I must refocus, or I will have to rub one off as we talk."

I write, "You are so far away. We lead different lives, and I can't even see you, like really see you in person, sighing. The day before our video chat, when you asked if I was nervous, I was excited and over the moon, like I was seeing someone that I hadn't seen in a long time."

Devon admits, "Me too, sorry about how it ended, but it had too at least for me. I won't go into that again, there is no need, we both know."

My heart hurts thinking about what had happened and I need to focus on the good parts of our conversation and go back to what we were talking about, "You're picturing me nude, giggling, do I have a baby frog in my hand?"

He confirms, "Nope, me in your hands, hey it's my image, and from what I can tell from the pictures I can guess at what you look like, and it is really driving me nuts right this second."

I question, "Do you think we will ever cross paths?"

He responds, "Okay, I will control my thoughts, but yeah, honestly, I don't know, wanting it to, one hundred percent yeah, but reality, I don't know. Even if it was a quick visit and we chatted for thirty minutes it would be nice, but hey, you get to chat me every now and then, so that is good. Anyway, you do have great pictures. When we video chatted, I thought for a second or two that when you stood up in the video you were going to flash, but I knew better. We had just met via camera and I don't do that stuff and knew that you didn't either, but when you did stand my heart stopped."

I blush, "Laughing over here so you're a boob guy? I don't have much going there, but I do have a butt and I do not lie.

He lets me know, "I am a crotch guy mostly, but yeah, love boobs and butt and well you got all three that are nicely defined, so yeah my eyes get glued. I shouldn't be saying that."

I glance at the bottom right corner of my screen and sigh, 2:00 PM has arrived. I ask him, "Should I let you get going?"

He admits, "Probably, but we can chat a bit longer, I will just refrain from saying stupid things that make the conversation heated."

I say, "Smiling, okay let's switch gears for a second. The wheels are turning in my head. Do you have an online payment account? The reason being, is I still feel that I may want to self-publish and cut the middle person out."

Devon confirms, "I do, it is the same as my email."

I take a look at some of his pictures, he always smiles with his mouth closed. I ask, "Hey you have teeth, right? I never see them; you smile with your mouth closed."

"Yes, I have my teeth, I'm not a redneck." He sends a smile to me when he makes the comment and continues, "I open my mouth when needed, laughing."

I admit, "Giggling, okay good to know for both; I am still thinking this one through with both going in together on this book. I just don't like the idea of my work sitting in a slush pile and what not if I do want to submit it to a publisher."

Devon asks, "What do you mean by slush pile?"

I explain, "Like, if I were to submit to a publisher, it would probably just sit there in a pile of other submissions for a long time."

He understands saying, "Ah, to avoid that you would use a query letter to attract them."

I look through some of the photos that he sent to me. There is one picture of him eating a pogo and I know American's call it something else and ask him as I am looking at the funny picture, "Do you guys' call pogoes something else?"

He tries to follow and asks. "Pogoes like a stick that you jump on."

I reply, "No like that giant battered wiener you were eating from one of your photos."

He writes, "Laughing over here, it is called a corn dog. Did it make you hot? I'm just playing with you, sorry."

I laugh to myself and say, "Oh, smiling here, okay they are called pogoes here."

He says, "You see, I say that I won't do that but then I do, grumbling at myself."

I look at another picture of his and say, "You look kind of annoyed with the person taking the picture."

He explains, "My son was snapping the picture. We were at a local fair that had RC jets and helicopters and planes and other things. It was actually cold out." One of Devon's hobbies, aside from writing is he loves remote-controlled helicopters and boats and such.

I suggests, "Ah I see you should have had a hot chocolate."

As we are chatting, I continue to share photos and he asks about them, "Are those your best friends in the pictures with you? Oh, by the way, I love hot chocolate and Quebec is a nice place."

I confirm. "Yah, I don't see them often, but when I do, it's a good time. We took the train to Quebec City for a Bachelorette party."

He comments, "That is cool. I think I saw some on Facebook a few weeks back."

I blurt, "One of my friends slept with the waiter in the photo, that's why you see the random photo there of him, too funny."

He asks, "It was the blonde girl, right? Laughing, here blondes have a reputation for being naughty. Man, I guess that I should have been your waiter. I was speaking to you, I meant."

I tell him, "Yah it was the one with the long blonde hair, giggling."

He comments, "No, not at all saying you are like that, but hey that would have been awesome."

I say, "You are being silly. How could you tell it was that friend of mine that had sex with him?"

He says, "She looked like she was looking for a piece of ass; you can see it in her eyes."

I say, "By the way you wouldn't need to wait on me, I'm right here. It would be like, let's do this now and talk later."

He confirms, "My thoughts exactly, I would tell you my name as we were engaged in doing it, if I could get it out fast enough. I had a dream that I went there and texted you, you came out and we went somewhere in the countryside, and we did it on the hood of the rental car. I know that I shouldn't be encouraging it but had to tell you."

I say, "It would make my year."

Devin agrees, "Yours and mine too, but thank goodness for washable hand towels, laughing."

I want to get into his fantasy and ask, "What type of rental car was it? If it's a hatch back, I'm out!"

He says, "I was thinking more of a BMW 3 series, and you are silly."

I demand, "Just take me back to the hotel and we would have the afternoon. I would take the day off work."

He has to go, "I guess I better get to work instead of thinking about how I want to have you and where. Well, a hotel would be better."

I mention, "We could in the shower, on the bed, no one to watch."

Devon says, "You are bad. You already know I want you to come so bad in my mouth. I can't stop thinking about how wet you get. I can imagine the hunger in your eyes, wow. That alone is hot as hell; too much again, huh?"

I let him know, "Well, you're in control of all of this my cowboy. You made it clear where you stand, but if ever we went there, I would be game."

He says, "Ditto, but I can dream about you, and no one can take that away."

I say, "Okay have a good afternoon, maybe chat tomorrow?"

Devon says, "Sure, just use email. Just saying one of these days you are going to have to show me your goods and I am going to explode for real. That was me thinking with the wrong brain. Anyway, my beautiful Canadian friend, have a wonderful day."

I assert, "You only get to see if you see in person, you know the rules."

He goes back to the idea, "Yep, I know that that is a dream that I am hoping one day comes true. Anyway, rules are in place for good reasons until then I have a sleeve that I imagine is you. Okay talk to you later."

"Have a great day." I end the chat with a smiley face.

I felt this coming; that he would return back to me, back to the way we had talked weeks before. He was feeling guilty for our unique situation, guilty at that fact that I am married and he has been in a relationship for over ten years. Almost two weeks he refrained entirely, and I was heartbroken. It was hard not to send him a message, but here and there I did, and he would always respond. It was just the fact of knowing that I was losing someone that I had become so close with that hurt. He made it clear to me that it was out of respect for each of our partners and it was the right thing to do, and I got it, it was hard for me to think with my mind because that was what my heart wanted, him, only him.

I knew at this point that Devon was letting his heart have what it needed. I allowed it, welcomed it, even craved it and before long we slipped into intense, hot, and heavy conversation. We are back to a good place, well if you call whatever this is.

I want Devon but I didn't want this, I have never had to live a lie that my reality is now. As I write this, I still don't love Josh the way that I used to, and I don't know what to do because right now what I want is not there. Sure, I know what Devon's feelings are for me, but he isn't ready to make a jump and as I think about it, am I? I hope we meet some day; I need to see him to know for sure. It's bad; I want to be with him to know if all of this is right. I want to kiss him, touch, and feel him inside of me. This isn't just about sharing a moment of passion with someone. We have connected on so many levels and it's scary and exciting all at once.

I wasn't seeking this, neither was he and here we are. I know that he is questioning his own life and so am I. He keeps reminding me that we can't just drop our lives and run to each other, yet he talks. I know that's what he wants. I see it, he cares and it's more than just a friend level. I know this is more than just a friendship. Friends don't check in everyday, flirt with one another, talk dirty and when conversations are had that turn serious, with Devon he always checks to see that I'm okay after the fact. He does that with me, and I do the same with him. He knows my feelings and knows that I am the weaker one with my own heart. I want him and know I can get away without Josh ever knowing.

Chapter 38
Josh's Thoughts

He sits at his desk while emails pile in. He is the go-to person at work. Others rely on him, count on him and he is always there to offer support. He knows it without being overly arrogant about it. He is liked and always a welcomed sight there. He feels acceptance at work but whenever he is home it's a different story.

Since it all happened Jordan seems to be saying all the right things to imply that their relationship is getting back on track. He sits at his desk wondering if he is worrying for nothing. It just feels like there is something more going on, like Jordan is holding back. He has known her for years and it feels like she no longer needs him.

A pondering voice calls him, "Josh?"

He startles out of thought and looks up at the inquirer, "Yes, what can I help you with?"

The co-worker says, "Wow buddy you were somewhere else."

Josh shakes the thoughts of Jordan away for the moment, "Yes, sorry I haven't been sleeping well."

The co-worker mentions, "Oh, sorry to hear; listen, I found out the lead in testing is calling for a meeting with all of us in the next ten minutes and wanted to give you the heads up."

"Ah thanks man." Josh smiles and squishes his worry to the back of his mind.

The co-worker starts to walk away as he says, "Hey no problem, see you in a few minutes."

Josh is alone for the moment and Jordan comes back to the forefront of his mind. She says that she loves him but he doesn't feel it at least whatever that is happening now is broken. She hugs him, kisses him, the chats are getting easier with each passing day, but it just seems empty. Is it him? Is it her? Maybe she needs time. Maybe he needs time. Maybe he needs to do something nice for her.

He sends her a text at work, "I am about to head into a meeting but wanted to let you know that I love you and can't wait to see you tonight." He clicks send. Texting Jordan feels weird. He never sends texts but feels like he should let her know that she is on his mind.

Chapter 39
Keeping it Secret

Devon's spouse has been out of town for weeks and has been angry with Devon ever since. She took the extra time to stay away. Devon reports that she is coming around. Sara had video chatted to him and he reported that she sounded happy, and I know that Devon is relieved that there will likely be no fighting and that things will return to normal for both of them soon.

Over the months our relationship, whatever you want to call this has continued in secret. We have both become experts in deception and I am about to have my wish.

Devon has just told me that he is taking his trip with his brother to British Columbia, but the change he has made, is he is taking an extra couple of days and a detour to Ottawa before returning home. He sends the details in an email, and I have to reread it. This is happening. We talked about it so many times, how we imagined it playing out and now we are following those plans. He is to visit during the week for two days and will pick me up by rental car at work and we will go to his hotel where we will enjoy each other, until I have to go pick up my husband and go home.

I had wished that it would come to this but never thought it would become a reality and now I am full of so many emotions. This is the boundary that we both are about to cross. This sick, intoxicating lust, love, I don't know, but I want it, need it, crave the excitement and adventure even though this is wrong in so many ways. To this day he is still my secret. I couldn't bear taking a chance in telling anyone and having them accidentally spill. Sometimes I have to pinch myself because I wonder, is he real or is he just some made up desire I wanted so badly.

Right now, I am at work, sitting at my desk and an email pops into my inbox, it's Devon.

Hey Jordan,

So, my vacation time is booked, and I will be in Ottawa come springtime. Right now, my brother and I are aiming for April or May and I will stop into Ottawa alone for a couple of days before returning home. I can't wait to see you Jordan, speak to you, feel you, touch you, and hear your voice. Are you having any second thoughts? I hope not, but please I want you to be honest with me. You know how I feel about you and know that whatever happens, I won't ever regret it.

-Devon

My heart skips a beat. I want to see him so badly just like the video chats we had done way back when. Everything will be different after this, and I wonder if my own path will become clearer after I see him or murkier? I respond to him.

Hey Devon,

This is going to be the longest winter ever, but I will wait. I am looking forward to it just like when we did the video chat and ditto on everything you said. I'm not having second thoughts. I want this and want you.

-Jordan

I click send and it's time for me to step away into a meeting. I will see him!

Chapter 40
Things are better

Things with Josh are better; I have learned how to balance my real and secret life. It was hard in the beginning because all I wanted to do was talk to Devon. I still do but realize that Devon will always be there and can wait and he has been the leader in helping me overcome the temptation to do so.

His partner and mine are oblivious to all of this even though we had a close call with Devon's spouse. We are passed that now and being the man that Devon is he has managed to smooth it over with his partner.

Devon is a quirky guy in a way because for one thing he has kept the secret which is me but at the same time stays loyal to his partner. Staying by her side and he has advised me to do the same with my husband. He wants the best of both worlds and so do I. We are the same creatures, loyal and dishonest at the same time. Well, whatever, I know this stuff is frowned upon by society but it's none of their business as to the choices I make in my own life.

Aside from the news of Devon's visit, the day is an average one, work was the same and the drive home with Josh is friendly and lighthearted. We stop for iced cappuccinos and before long we arrive home. After walking in the door, I realize that Josh is in a frisky mood tonight and like any good wife, I fulfill my roll and please him.

After stepping out of the shower, I find him sprawled out on the bed and I know what to do but tonight Devon is in my thoughts he is visiting soon, and I wonder what this will be like with him.

I carefully approach the bed, hair still wet from the shower, skin smelling of a mild fragranced soap, I climb up on top of him stare into his eyes and kiss him, a short one just to get a taste before going down.

His shaft is semi-hard, but my mouth soon changes that. I suck on him and grasp one hand around the base and the other caressing his boys with my warm soft, small hand. He grows in my mouth and his breathing becomes concentrated. Up and down, to the pace that he does me, gentle but deep, he touches the back of my throat and for some reason that always makes me so wet. I love the feeling of knowing that he enjoys me. I tease him, imagining he is Devon, and the thought soon becomes unbearable for me, I am soaked and need my own release. I climb on top of Josh, taking control and guide him inside. His hands are on my hips helping by steering me up and down, steady, and strong. I am in his grasp and can't go anywhere else until I get my release.

I go down for a kiss and catch a glimpse of the fire in his eye. I see his desire and close my eyes I want my imagination to take control. My breathing is heavy but quiet, I don't make noise. I want my release, oh man. Why am I having trouble?

Josh senses it and rolls us over and he starts to make love to me missionary. He knows what to do. I close my eyes, the tension is building fast, and he knows, he stays the course and as my muscles tighten up, he thrusts, moving in small circles and deep. It's coming, I let my voice out and the passion escape my lips as it pulses and leaves me. Josh knows, he can feel me throbbing but continues to make it last as long as it can. In a whisper of a breath, I tell him, "I got it." With a smile he keeps me in position beneath him and he changes pace, faster and with a force. Every now and then he draws near to smell my hair. Then a hand goes under me as he grabs, touching my hump and then moving to the more intimate spot. It excites him and his thrusts start to become uncontrolled, wild, and greedy and I feel his, it throbs for a moment. He is quiet and the only other thing that gives it away is his breathing, out of breath as it escapes him and as a joke he whispers in my ear, "I got mine."

I look up at Josh and smile, "Are you making fun of me?"

He repeats, "I got mine." and smiles, I know this kidding side of him and I just smirk as he pulls out. What a clown, he leaves the room to wash up and I lie there for a moment, wondering if Devon will feel different?

Chapter 41
His Song

Later in the evening, after dinner and just before getting ready to sleep, my phone's screen lights up, and I feel compelled to check it. It's his song. Devon has shared the lyrics to a song he wrote about a soldier heading off to war, with heartfelt words for his love, asking her to wait patiently for his return.

I read the lyrics a couple of times, attempting to imagine how it would sound as a song. I ask Devon, "Hey, I just read it. Is it more of a slow song? And do you have a specific set of notes you play it in?"

He responds, "I was aiming for a country style, kind of slow. Not sure about the exact notes. I actually have a pretty good singing voice."

I can't help but smile at his response and tell him, "I was hoping I'd get a video of you playing it. I'd love to hear you sing."

Devon replies, "Maybe someday once I gather up enough courage to record. Anyway, have a good night and sleep well."

I playfully retort, "Aw, you're such a tease! And boo, I'm not even feeling sleepy, so there!" Our lighthearted exchange continues.

Devon replies, "Okay, I just didn't know if my email woke you. I may be a Yankee but I'm a cowboy at heart. I still got time to make it big. Well lord willing."

"No, I'm wide awake." I send a smile to him and continue with a partial truth; I won't tell him about what I was doing earlier. I tell him, "Some girlfriends are trying to arrange a party, so I need to stay awake in order to stay in the loop."

Devon answers, "Cool gotcha. I'm just writing."

I say, "I think you will make it. I loved your writing before we became good friends. I remember reading your stuff that was posted online and was amazed, because you had originally really downplayed yourself."

Devon shares, "Well, thank you. I'm just trying to make my mark. I want my son to say, 'That was my dad,' when I leave this world. Hoping to leave a legacy for others to say they knew of me, the writer."

He shifts to acknowledge my previous comment about his writing, saying, "I know, as the author, you tend to downplay your work, hoping someone sees it in its genuine state. You do it too. I've seen that in your own writing. It's really good. Anyway, I'm going to get back to writing. Let's chat again soon." He includes a smile.

I respond, "It's a thought that can send shivers down your spine, but the truth is your work is immortal. Who knows how long it will live on in this digital world? You already have a legacy that will outlive any paper novel."

Smiling, I add, "I can definitely picture your books in print someday." Our conversation wraps up with a positive and encouraging note.

I let him go but not before I wish him a good night, "Have a good night, you wrote a beautiful song. I would love to hear it someday. Also, I'm getting shy, thank you for saying all that nice stuff about my writing; sending you a kiss and a hug."

Devon writes, "Thank you, goodnight."

Chapter 42
Jordan doesn't know

The next day, just before noon, I grab my purse from my desk drawer and head out to meet my friend. She's someone I used to work closely with, but she recently switched to a different sector within our department, so we no longer share the same office building.

I won't delve into the details of our lunch date, but it was a pleasant hour spent catching up with an old friend. We grabbed some ice cream from a nearby convenience store and strolled along one of the city's park trails. Even with her, I've refrained from mentioning Devon. There's a constant urge to share, but the potential consequences of anyone finding out are too significant to risk.

Upon returning from lunch, I waste no time in reconnecting with my favorite secret. I send him a text, saying, "Hello! What's new in your world? As for me, I'll be home alone tonight. Some of my girlfriends are making plans for an outdoor spa next week—hot pools, saunas, the works. Sadly, I can't commit yet." As I type, a hint of annoyance surfaces. It's frustrating that some of my friends can be inconsiderate at times. I can't really blame them since I never mentioned the procedure, but it still feels like they're judging me for not participating. Regardless, I know I made the right choice.

He replies, "I'm just going to be writing tonight as well as cleaning the guest room. I'm having friends from Dallas coming in Saturday afternoon. Sorry to hear that you are alone again, but you can ping me if you like, I will respond. Gosh it's too bad you are so far away. You know what we would be doing for an hour or so each visit." He adds in a smile and continues, "I know stop talking about it, but hey I am a friend so ping me, I will chat with you. There may be a delay as I will be busy too."

I write, "You are a tease. Save a horse ride a cowboy."

He teases, "Laughing over here, ride me hard and let loose."

I reply, "I will take you up on it. Yes, there is a bit of a delay in our messages. You know that I would come faster than a teenage boy."

Devon says, "I don't mind. I could use some sweet nectar. Yeah, you knew I like that."

I say, "It's a good thing that I'm a chick because I would be such a let down to a woman if I was a man."

He admits, "Ha, I would just wrap myself around your lips and hold you down until you convulsed. Chuckling, okay this conversation went south fast, laughing, sorry bad me."

I agree, "Yes, you are bad. It would be a treat, I never get that, would love you to do that to me."

He mentions, "Yes, I am bad. I almost asked you last week to drench a pair of your panties and send them to me, but I didn't. I was caught up in the moment. I know that was gross to say but I was under the influence and not thinking normally. I don't need a response." He adds in some laughs and continues; "Besides if that showed up, I am certain I would be in a whole lot of trouble, so don't, and just ignore me. How about I tone it down and ask how your day is going?"

I respond, "Good, I went for a walk in the park. I'm just reading through all your texts, giggling over here, what's with guys and panties?"

"Oh, just the mere thought of the scent that's all, pheromones, I was kidding. Okay, let's get passed my silly talk." He sends a smile.

I send him a wink and say, "I won't mail you anything, but you know that the real deal is here for you. I'll give you a rain check."

Devon says, "I'll take it. It won't expire right?"

I confirm, "Not for you, it won't expire."

Devon writes, "Excellent, I will use it I promise, but for now I'm honored to be able to speak to you and be silly with each other."

I say, "Sounds good my horny man."

Devon says, "A close friend with a side of pleasure."

I say. "Hey, I don't mind; you are the dirtiest talking guy that I know." I send him a wink.

He writes, "Yeah, sorry you just make me go nuts and out of control. I guess that makes me a dirty old man."

I ask as a joke, "What do they put in the water?"

He sighs, "If I only knew; what I really wanted to say you would be like oh my."

I smile, "Giggling over here, no it's cool. I love it and wouldn't have you any other way." Devon just sends me a smile and I urge him, "Just say it."

He mentions, "Laughing, something; as long as you don't get mad when it comes across; I won't tame it then. I'm sure it is words for your book."

I tell him, "Okay ready."

He writes, "The things I would love to do to you and where would be hot, but as time goes on, I will share but not now. I can barely move. I would love to have a laundry basket, a square one and have it suspended with a hole in the middle and have you sit in it, exposed, and place my tongue and spin you and have you explode. How is that?"

Feeling shocked I reply, "You tease so much. You have my full attention."

He admits, "Laughing, dirty man I am and then I would penetrate you and spin you and just come all inside you. So now you know my dirty mind and it's just a taste of what I like to do to you."

I comment, "Just saying the girls that appear to be good girls are always not."

Devon continues, "I don't just like missionary, I want to place your knees to your head and give it to you hard and slow, had enough yet. I think you are wild. That's just a sample from me."

I am soaked just thinking about everything he has described, "Mm, wow."

He says, "Hey what can I say, you could be all hot and sweaty from jogging and I would go down on you even then. I love munching. I'm not a gross guy I just love my pie and miss it so much. Anyway, lord I have to stop, or I will not be working anymore. There now you have some material for the book but know that it is all true."

I say, "Oh man, wow you're in Texas? Well, I think that I want a shower now, a cold one."

Devon laughs and says, "Aren't you glad I'm a friend with a filthy side?"

I tell him, "I love it and you always have me coming back for more. I have to admit that I'm totally taken up by you and I would want to live up to your fantasies."

He assures, "You already do, but you could give me a hint by wearing some tight jeans or pants without showing." He chuckles and continues to write, "Yeah from what I have already seen, I would love to taste you all over. I know I set the boundary, just saying, but at least you know that I would have."

I say, "Hmm, I thought you were taking the rain check?"

He writes, "I am I know we are friends, but I want to have you so bad. To experience you would be the best encounter I have ever had. Okay I think this soup is yucky. Broccoli and cauliflower creamed together; it looks like baby shit." He has got to be eating lunch now.

I say, "Okay, I'll be patient then because I want this. I'll take a protein injection though."

Devon agrees, "I want this too, but it will be just two friends having a pleasurable encounter, but yeah, you will get the full treatment from me."

Devon is on his lunch, and I decide to kid, "I don't want your soup it sounds gross." I send a face with its tongue out at him and then refer to his proposition and write, "Okay deal I'll have it."

Devon says, "Um yeah, I want to give you as much protein as you want; please drain me. Rest assured I'm rock-solid right now picturing you sucking me. I need to work but like the image."

I confirm, "I will, trust me." Devon sends me a smile and I continue, "I will drink it up and take all of it in, no wasting."

He replies, "Okay, wow what a lunch break. Um likewise." I send a smile to him, and he continues, "Okay, I know, no nude pictures but can I ave a close-up with clothing picture of it? That would be awesome. If you decide yes, let me know. I better concentrate on work and not you." He chuckles then writes, "Don't be upset I asked. If not it's okay too." He sends me a frown and continues, "I will understand."

I waver on the thought of if I should or not. I stare up at the office ceiling fan turning at its steady pace above my cubicle for a moment to think. I had told him before that I didn't feel comfortable doing it, because it was something private and it wasn't that I didn't want him to see me, it was just that if the images get into another person hands, like his spouse or accidently on the internet, it wouldn't be good. I think well, he did mention close-ups. I could do a close-up and not show my face? I write to him, "I'll work on something for you, but I want something in return."

He replies, "Okay, just tell me. I know, for me to stop asking huh."

I write, "I want you to share a picture that you are comfortable with."

"Okay, it doesn't matter to me because it is for you. Just tell me and I will do it. But I have to do it before Saturday."

"You are up first for sharing."

Devon writes, "I was comfortable since day one. I know it sounds weird, but I was."

I say, "I want you to surprise me."

He asks, "Okay, so tame or not tame? How about I give you a shot, hard but concealed. Or I can give you what I want to give you."

Maybe, it is my dirty side, but I was always curious especially after he described himself. I write, "Well, I am curious?" There is no mistake; I am completely distracted from my work. I sit in my office chair leaning forward, staring at my phone screen, waiting for Devon's response and bite my lip as I send the text.

He writes, "Ha, I knew you thought the same thing. Or, if you really want, it can be a Sunday school picture. Just tell me I want to share with you. This is not like me but hey you may not like who knows, so I don't know, but it likes you." He sends over a smile.

I say, "Send me what you want me to see."

Devon pleads, "Help me here. I don't want you to run. I want you to know what I have in hopes that you would like it, but I can be clean or not, anyway. Ok. I will think of something. Where would I send it to? I feel very naughty and it's your fault." He laughs.

I can't see over my cubicle wall, but I can hear my boss, she is on the move. I recognize the sound of her step, that steady, determined pace she has, like she is on a mission. My suspicions are confirmed when I hear the sound of her voice. One of my other co-workers has stopped her outside my cubicle to ask a question. I know that she is likely coming to see me and send a text to Devon, "We will talk later; I have people who keep visiting me. Sorry to leave this conversation hanging, but I want you to show me what you will. Anything is game."

Devon writes, "Okay where to? I will send one to start tonight and go from there. I'm excited to see whatever I can of you too, trust me."

My boss and the co-worker's conversation has ended, and I hear her steps, she is on the move, and I quickly write, "You can send it to my main email, where should I send to?"

He answers, "My home email is fine. I will make sure they are hidden and secure and only for my eyes don't worry."

I say, "Okay I'll do the same." Just as I click send, my suspicions were confirmed, and the boss enters my cubicle to give me some work to do. She doesn't notice as I tuck my phone into my lap which is covered by my keyboard tray.

While I am discussing work with my boss Devon sends a message, "Thank you for sharing. I know you may never have, but I so long to have you and this will provide me fantasies. Okay on that note, I will get back to work but ping me tonight if you get bored. I will respond."

After the boss leaves my cubicle, I respond, "Okay" and add a smile.

After work, I return home and am stuck trying to decide just how I am going to take selfies of my body without showing my face and I am also trying to figure out how I am going to be able to hold and aim the camera to snap something decent. After taking a shower I set up in the bedroom. I try all these different angles and find that it is harder than it looks, however I manage a close-up of myself by going on my hands and knees and holding the camera aimed down just below my chin to capture my breasts, stomach and thighs, he can see my sexy curves this way and I take one of my secret spot, close and it's just glistening.

I am nervous, but like him I do find myself wanting to share and finally happy with some of the shots I took I text him, "So before I change my mind, I will give you a look. It's a close-up; just make sure no one is looking over your shoulder."

Devon replies within seconds "Don't change your mind. I was looking forward to seeing. Boohoo, oh okay, smiling big."

While sitting on my bed with my phone in hand, I am having a bit of trouble with sending them and Devon's anticipation is starting to show. He writes, "Okay, where did you send to?"

"I'm sending them to your main email."

Devon answers in a heartbeat, "Okay I don't have anything yet. I checked junk folder too but nothing. Can you tell I am like a kid waiting for candy?"

I smile and respond, "Just sent them."

A few moments go by and then he writes, "Wow that is hot girl. Thank you, mine will be as good hopefully. My mouth is watering and I love that butt too."

I smile after reading his response and write back, "Wow, I was afraid it went to the wrong person. Giggling here, okay well I still don't get how men love these kinds of pictures. I think vaginas are ugly things. Do you want another?"

He disagrees, "Hell no, yours is yummy, trust me and yes can I have an open lip one, begging here or a wet one?" He sends a smiling face and continues, "I will send you some pictures of me tonight as well. I am hoping that you will like but if not just tell me nicely."

I let him know, "Okay sending another your way." I give him a close-up of what he asked for.

He writes, "Wow, I just want to nibble on you and play."

I ask, "Is it too close?"

He confirms, "No, not at all, it just makes me desire to touch and eat you. It's a perfect description in photo display." He sends me a gesture of him cheering, and I chuckle because the title I picked for the open lip shot was spread them.

I say to him, "See the things I do for you?"

He replies, "Yes, I am very happy and grateful that you honored me with a private part of you and love it. I will return the favor. Just hope that you like."

I say, "I'm sure that I will." I include a smiling face for him.

Devon says, "My tongue is wagging at your beautiful body."

I have to ask this, "When we were talking about these photos earlier; how much would you guess that I would let you see?"

Devon says, "I haven't seen one in quite some time, but I have to say yours beats what I have seen and had a wowser. Thank you so much. I will cherish those and look forward to having you for real. Feel free to send more after you get the return favor, laughing. Any chance of a chest shot, maybe later?"

My greedy cowboy, why not, I'm still naked. I tell him, "One coming up."

Devon says, "Nice, you are so fit and trim. I am trying to get there but I have some work to do, thank you, thank you, thank you." He changes his train of thought and asks, "You saw my pictures, and I'm, ok?"

I say to him, "Yes you're my handsome cowboy; so nice Canadian landscape, don't you think?"

He says, "Those are not tiny those are perfect." I had told him at some point that I thought my boobs were small and he continues to write, "Oh yeah, and I would love to travel the landscape."

"You should visit some time." I wink at him.

Devon writes, "Well at least now when I have my alone time, I am quite certain loads more will come out as you my dear are smoking."

My cowboy knows how to hand out his compliments; I smile and decide it's time to do some other things. I say to him, "Okay I'm going to get dressed; I will talk to you later and am glad that you liked them. I figured if the massage guy sees me, you should too."

He complains, "Okay, I'm so hard and sticky. Wow you are an awesome friend. Thank you, I will provide a few shots later. Damn, I am actually imagining your taste, thank you, thank you. I have forty minutes to go and an hour drive, but I will give you your shots then."

I admit to him, "I was sort of wet in one. I just showered and wanted to look clean."

He compliments, "All three were awesome. Perfect all around, that has to be in the book, the exchanging pictures you are very yummy, just saying."

Later in the evening Devon delivers as promised and, in an email, he writes,

Hey,

Okay, not that great, but I hope it is okay. I am sure I could use a grooming, but I showered. Laughing, well the camera is so, so.

-Devon

He has included three attachments and I download all of them and open them up one by one. I am just as bad as he is. The first image is a close-up of him hard as a rock. He is holding the base of his shaft and I see his big thick veined man. The second image is his shaft with his leg in the shot and I look and think wow, he downplayed himself because he is well endowed. The third image is a close-up of his shiny head that I just want to bite down on. Wow, I am wet just looking at him and seeing that he is hard for me.

As I finish being a pervert and close the email a second email comes in, its title, "something white".

Hey,

Okay, don't laugh, I talk out loud when looking at your pictures and then well you get the point.

-Devon

There is a movie attachment on this one. I hesitate for a second because I know what this is. Jordan, you want to see it. I open the video and it takes a moment to download and that moment is the longest feeling moment that I have ever sat through, come on, come on. Finally, it opens, and I see him rubbing himself. It's a close-up of his hand around himself, self-pleasuring and his voice in the video sends shivers up my spine because it's passionate and hungry. He says, "Jordan, I want you so bad." I can hear the sounds of his strokes. He continues in another breath, "Your pictures were lovely, tight, curvy, and beautiful;" His breaths become heavier, "oh I want to taste you. This one is for you." With that he breathes heavily and lets out a sigh as his rapid release pours out.

Wow, I wish I was there to feel that and have him release inside of me. I watch again and again because the combination of his lust and just the sound of his voice have my full attention and then I am startled with a text message from him.

He writes, "Hey Jordan, I sent you some stuff, I hope you like. I am not that huge but as you can see, I don't have a pencil dick, anyway."

I take a moment with answering him partly because I am still being a pervert and the other part is he has shared an intimate part of him that I love so much, and I want him to know that and not have it come off as sounding weird.

He sends another message, "I know that I am not that big, if you don't like just, please be nice about it."

I write, "I got them and love. That has got to be the thickest shaft I have ever seen."

"Thanks" He sends a smiley face.

"Sorry for the slow response. I have to admit that I had to look at your video a couple of times and by the way your man looks pretty large to me."

"I knew you wanted to see me just as bad as I wanted to see you. I am sure that you have seen bigger."

What the hell do I say to that? I write, "Devon you're not small, trust me."

He says, "I know that there are larger ones out there."

I admit, "I have seen a bit larger but anything too large is painful. You are perfect to me, would be a tight fit but I am sure that with how slick I can get, you would slide in."

He replies, "Laughing, you're a bad girl."

I send him a smiley face and say, "Well I need to go let off some steam, talk to you later?"

He says, "Yes, have fun."

Devon always uses the term, rubbing one off; well, I got to do the same because I am dripping with desire.

Chapter 43
Roll Over

The next morning, it's not long before my phone lights up with messages from my horny southern man. In fact, my alarm has just gone off. I role over in my bed towards the nightstand, pick up my phone that is sounding the wake up and turn it off. I look over my shoulder to see that I am alone in bed. Josh must be in the kitchen already. I decide it's safe to sneak a peek at some of the photos that Devon shared yesterday. Just as I close the last picture of Devon that I was looking at, I see a message pop up on my screen and he writes, "Good morning, I'm still gazing over the shared gift, very awesome. Have a great day!"

I message him within moments, "This morning, I did the same with what you shared." I send him a smile and continue, "I'm glad that you liked them."

He replies, "Yes indeed. Well, I'm off to get ready for work, talk to you later and thank God it's Friday."

I put the phone down and roll out of bed, get washed up and dressed. As I approach the main area of the house, I see that Josh is already in the living room eating his breakfast. We are taking separate cars again because he will be working later. I walk over and have a seat in the other recliner.

I say to Josh, "Good morning.

Josh is in a foul mood and answers, "Jordan why can't you help with breakfast or something? I am up immediately doing stuff for us while you're still in the bedroom deciding what to wear."

What is up with him? I haven't even seen him for two minutes today and he is already starting. I say, "It would be nice if we said good morning to each other."

Josh complains, "Come on Jordan, I do so much for us and the least you can do is help."

I defend myself, "Josh, what do you think I do while you work late? I have to do everything that needs to be done at home alone. The groceries, the laundry, keeping the house clean, give me a fucking break."

He snaps back at me, "I'm working a second job for us to get ahead; I just want some help that's all."

I am certain that he is going to argue forever so I give up and say, "Okay, you are right."

He can tell by my tone that it's not sincere and snaps back, "All I ask is that you wake up and help me."

"Okay Josh." I don't feel like putting any more effort into this discussion and go to the kitchen, get my lunch packed and things ready and head for the door.

As I approach the living room with my purse and lunch in hand, again Josh says, "Are you not going to sit down with me for a bit and watch some television?"

I don't wish to be in the same room with him let alone the house, I just want to leave. I say in a calm voice, "I don't like your crime shows and besides, I have a lot of stuff to do at work. See you tonight." I leave as quickly as I can, not bothering to hug or even kiss him. The asshole doesn't deserve it. Getting into my car is the escape that I need from him, and I head to the city.

About an hour after I get to work Devon sends me another message, "How's your day going? Mine is just about to start."

I respond, "It's going, I have been trying to get approval on spending twenty-three thousand dollars and the director is being a bit of a knob about signing off on it. Also, for lunch, I have an ice cream date with a girlfriend, her name is Hailey, I know her from high school and tomorrow, I'm going zip lining. I won't overdo it, just feel the need to swing from tree to tree."

Devon says, "Nice, I hope that you have a great outing. That sounds fun, be careful and enjoy."

I explain, "I've been before but not to the place where I'm going tomorrow so not sure if the lines go over any cliffs or anything."

Devon mentions, "Well, the most I did today for exercise was one hundred crunches. That sounds more fun, zipping across the trees."

I say, "You have got me beat on the exercise today, that is more than me. I just walked up the stairs at the office.

Devon explains, "Well, I have to work on my mid-section. You my dear, are slim. Hence not bearing it and showing, but I can see my abs start to form again and just need to reduce the other part." He adds his smile at the end. "Persistence will pay off."

I send a smile back to him and say, "We are our own worst critics. I have rolls, a butt and tiger stripes."

He assures, "Well, what you showed made me salivate so you are good. I didn't see anything wrong. Anyway, I can't think about you in that way today. I have to get some work done." He laughs and continues, "I just wanted to say hello. Hope that you have a great day and ice cream."

I reply, "Hey you too. Can I message you on your lunch? We won't be able to talk all weekend."

Devon is still caught up with the pictures of my naked body and close-ups of my kitty and says, "For some reason I am picturing the first picture moving back and forth and thinking I am staring up. Wow, I need to focus! Sure, send me a message later; I'm here until 6:00 PM."

I get some of my work done over the morning hours and then head out for lunch with my friend. After the lunch hour is done, I arrive back at the office, say hello to a couple of co-workers in the hallway on my way back to my cubicle and take a seat back at my desk. I take my phone out to check for messages and tuck my purse away in a desk drawer. I unlock my computer and glance at my phone simultaneously. I have a message from him, "Hey, I want to lick you, He, he, just a booster moment for ya."

I lean back in my office chair and respond, "Bad boy! I haven't laughed so hard in a while, high school girlfriends are the best, had a great lunch date. These past two weeks have been nuts and getting to catch up with an old high school friend was a nice break from day-to-day life."

He says, "That is cool. Hope you did and are having a blast."

I tell him what happened during my lunch and soon Devon ponders his own lunch plans, "I'm not sure what I am getting today."

I say, "My sandwich was on toasted waffle bread. It was so good."

"Waffle bread sounds good."

I tell him, "Don't get the shit soup."

He responds, "Laughing, nope, that was utterly gross. I will probably go with a salad. So are my pictures still in your email?"

I confirm, "Yes, I figured its best. They are protected with a password and well Josh has full control of our network at home, so I am certain he would find them if they were saved to my computer. Are mine still in your email?"

Devon replies, "My lunch is soon, ping then if you want and oh no made sure that your pictures were gone. I moved them onto a secure drive. Why do you have more pictures or perhaps a video to send?" He adds some laughs and continues, "Joking, it's too risky now that my partner is coming home tomorrow, but I would not turn them down!"

I say, "Well, I can look at you whenever I want with my email."

Devon says, "Love the ones I have, you are so yummy."

I comment, "You are one greedy guy."

He clarifies, "I was kidding. They are perfect. Right now, I want to bite you. That's how nice they are. I won't be greedy." He sends me a smiley face with a Pinocchio nose and continues to say, "Your man must enjoy they hell out of you."

I say, "Giggling over here, no biting my cat flaps."

He admits, "It would be more like sucking and tongue action and swallowing your come."

I admit, "Josh can be a little full of himself at times. He often tells me that he is hotter than me."

Devon says, "I've seen his pictures. Josh is a good-looking guy but you my dear ROCK. I would love to have you have me and be happy that you let me. Yeah, I went there. Okay refocus."

I smile and say, "Bad boy, you are making me wet."

He playfully replies, "Yum share, smiling, okay I will stop." He changes subjects, "Are you close to finding out if the procedure worked?"

I explain, "I should know if it worked by Tuesday or Wednesday, my period is due then, but my blood work is scheduled a couple days after that."

He says, "My fingers are crossed for you."

I take a breath and reply, "Thank you, apparently some women still get their period when they are pregnant."

Devon says, "I know once you become a mommy our chats will simmer down as well. Further then they will now. It's ok, I respect that. I still know how to get ahold of you, but if at any time you need me to back off from chatting too much it is ok. I need to simmer down a bit going forward but open to chatting."

Devon is probably right with the mommy stuff. He has been there and done that with his first wife and has fathered a son. I decide to keep the conversation lighthearted and ask, "So how is your salad?"

He confirms, "It's a chicken topped salad; it is good."

Just then I am knocked back to reality, my boss is at my desk, "Jordan?"

"Yes" I hide my phone.

She demands, "I need you to run the organization financial reports for me. I need a count of the dollars that will be spent for this quarter. Can you do that for me and have the reports ready in an hour?"

I look up with a smile and say, "Sure."

She smiles back and says, "Thank you Jordan." With that she rushes away. My guess is that she is off to her next meeting. I open up the reporting software and let the application run its course to pull the numbers from our database. As the software is doing its thing I explain the delay to Devon, "I had the boss with me, all good now. I forgot to tell you that I'll be on course downtown near parliament hill on Tuesday and Wednesday."

Devon says, "Okay, good to know. With Sara coming back I can only really chat weekdays during work. I have to have my fix of you for the week."

I say, "Me too." I glance up at my computer screen and watch as the report continues to run.

Devon explains, "The rebuilding of my relationship will begin tomorrow. Well, I have been trying already but

I won't stop chatting with you, I'm drawn to you. We just have to be friends and accept it. That's all. I'm happy for that and your naughty side but will long to hold you and embrace you for the encounter."

I say, "We will keep it going and not hurt anyone else in the process." I switch back to talking about my fertility treatment, "I don't think I am. I'm trying not to be negative. I just don't have that feeling that you get."

Devon says, "I am just hoping this time is a positive for you. That's what I want, to not hurt anyone in the process also, but if I can say this and it is true. A part of me is in love with you. I know sounds farfetched but it's true. That's what makes our friendship real. Just saying, please don't get upset for me saying it and not acting on it. You know my side and I can't. Not right under our circumstances as I need to give it my all with Sara. I am sure that you understand that, but at least you know my feelings."

All I can say to him is, "Me too but I think that you already knew, I'm sort of forward."

Devon answers, "I did, and do. I'm a lucky guy to have you as a friend. I know that word sucks but that's all I can give."

I love Devon and get what he is saying because I am in the same situation. I still love Josh. How can I be in love with two people? I can't think about this now and with this baby stuff on my mind it just adds to the equation.

I write, "Thanks Devon that means a lot to me."

He demands, "If I piss you off, tell me. I don't want to be a bad friend, only in bed with you." He laughs.

I kid, "My panties are in the mail."

He replies, "Yeah right, that would not be good, but I would sniff them and get off. I know it sounds gross but not really. The scent is what drives a man, but yeah don't send it would be bad."

I reply, "Laughing, just bugging, nothing is sent I don't want to get you in trouble."

Devon writes, "Phew, but I want you to know that when we meet those soaked panties are coming back with me and I will hide them. Course I would lick them clean and yeah, I will have to snap a picture of me halfway in you to remember. I know I talk sex with you all the time and I'm probably wearing it out but it's true I'm just drawn to you that way too. Ha went there again. I am so bad. Can't help it, I got to slap myself."

I say to my cowboy, "Giggling, well okay guess I'll pack a second pair then for when you visit."

He says, "Bingo. Okay let's change subject, I'm getting sticky again. I can't wait to watch you get yours right in front of me. Yeah, one last sex comment."

I say, "I'll give you a thong."

He admits, "I would try and hold on as long as I could before getting off in you."

What a guy. He wants to stop talking about it, but he can't. Okay I got to help him out because a picture that he sent comes to mind. It was of his underwear; he had a wet spot of his passion. I ask, "So when you go on the trip to British Columbia with your brother, do you have time penciled off to visit Gold Stream?"

Devon writes, "Not yet, I am trying to figure that all out. A thong, yes it just has to be totally soaked for my pleasure. Sorry for the underwear picture yesterday. I just had to show you what you did to me. I saw the first picture and I actually exploded a bit."

I chuckle and write, "When I told you that I was sending you a picture did you think that it was going to be a covered one?"

He explains, "Yes, I thought maybe a crotch picture showing your outline, but was happy when I saw your beautiful body and yes, it is not ugly it is very hot and yummy. You are a sexy gal. I'm sure your old boyfriends went crazy like I do over you. How could they not."

I say, "Thanks, my hot man." I tell him, "By the way I thought the dirty laundry picture was hilarious you are one bad boy."

He admits, "Blushing, I would have loved to give you a front shot of me but could not think of a way. Sorry and ain't I? How's that for bad English too. I have to ask if you were to get off when being eaten, do you come a lot, just curious. That is what I am hoping to actually get a mouth full. Well, you said to be myself so I am." He sends me a smile.

I detail, "You would get a mouth full; I think. I hope that you visit sooner like if this fertility treatment works, and I am pregnant than there are no issues with explaining."

He assures, "I will try. If I do and you are, I still want to have you."

I explain, "That way we have free rein, and we can do whatever."

Devon agrees, "Yes, I will try my best to come earlier. I don't want to wear any protection. I want to feel you naturally. Besides, it will probably be the next time I get laid anyhow but it will be so damn worth it." Devon continues on another thought, "Well, I will see if I can come earlier and if I can change my flight. How do you get any work done with a horny guy like me pinging you every minute? Guess I better ease back."

He is right, well I did get that report finished on time. It was sitting in my bosses' inbox when she returned from whatever meeting she was at. My day is almost done, and

I explain to him, "I have a few minutes left so I'm just doing odd jobs."

Devon says, "I'm here until 6:00 PM so ping me when you want and if not have a wonderful weekend. Are you alone tonight? I still have to work on finishing the home clean up, but you can ping me if you like."

I explain, "Josh actually booked the weekend off, including Monday, so I'm afraid that this may be goodbye until Tuesday. For Tuesday and Wednesday, my messages may only be a few because I'm downtown on course."

He replies, "Alright, no worries have a great rest of the day and time with your hubby. Chat next week. Take care."

"Bye!" I send him a line of kisses and hugs, and say, "Over the top?"

He says, "Love it and ditto."

Chapter 44
A Mix of Things

The weekend was a mix of so many things. Josh and I had to clear the air before the weekend started. I apologized for rushing out of the house the morning before and he asked that I be patient with him. This marriage is a struggle, but we are both fighters and besides why let a fight ruin a weekend especially one that is full of plans.

Josh and I had gone out zip lining and the experience was nothing short of amazing. This zip lining place was at a ski resort close to Montreal and the views were priceless. Fall is beautiful in Canada the vibrant colors of the leaves, the breathtaking mountains and there is that crisp smell of the season that I can't quite describe, it's almost like a sweet smell mixed with a faint smell of burning firewood, mixed with the smell of the rain. Josh and I took our time on the zip lining course and we were true partners in that time. For the few hours that we spent together, it was as though we were in the first months of our relationship. Conversations were easy and we did a lot of laughing together. Even after the zip lining course we decided to tour the nearby French resort town. The streets were a sea of tourists and locals. There were lots of high-end cars driving up and down Main Street and everyone seemed well dressed, like they came from a fall fashion shoot. I am sure it has something to do with being close to Montreal.

I always found that the culture of Montreal is fashion savvy. By the end of the weekend the disappointment of finding out that the procedure didn't work became my reality. I learned that despite our ups and downs, that I have Josh in my corner. This is bearing hard on him too and he asked me again if I wanted to divorce, so that I could find someone who can father children. It breaks my heart that he can't but in the same breath I can't walk away from this marriage. I love him and told him that we would try again. I took the discovery a little more easily; I cried but was able to pick myself up soon after. I learned with the first failed attempt that being upset about it won't help matters and that I just need to think about the next try.

It is Monday and both Josh and I took the extra day off, but it doesn't stop me from my desire. I write to Devon. I have a lot on my mind, and he is the only one that I can really confide in that is far enough removed from the rest of the people in my life. I say, "Hey hope that you had a great weekend. I just wanted to say hello. Mine was good, this morning I learned that I'm not. I'm okay; I didn't get my hopes up. I think that helped."

Devon responds, "Hello, thanks for saying howdy. Yes, it was ok. It's cold out like your cold." He sees the second part of my message and writes, "Oh no, I am so sorry. I was hoping for good results. Do you think your body isn't letting this happen? Just pondering, I do feel for you and again I am sorry to hear that."

I say, "I'm not sure? These doctors time everything and they know that I have a ton of healthy eggs before the procedure. They count your eggs; they hope for at least thirteen. When they checked me, I had like thirty-three ready to go."

He says, "I don't know." He adds a frown.

I write, "I think the mind has something to do with it. I don't think I was ready. Anyway, were you able to work things through with Sara, are things good?"

He admits, "That is a work in progress, but working towards the better. We had problems prior to us meeting so it just added to it and still trying to work at it."

Josh hollers for me from the front door looking for help and I send a final message for now, "I got to drop off for a bit, Josh needs help hooking up the trailer, anyway I'll leave you be."

Devon says, "Have a great day."

Josh and I manage to hook up the trailer and we make a trip to town to do some shopping. Josh is picking up this monstrous toolbox. That's why the trailer was needed and well I have the green light to shop for myself since I have been Josh's helper today and the shopping eases the disappointment with the failed pregnancy result.

Once we return home from an afternoon of shopping, Josh goes down to our basement entertainment room and loads up a game on the Xbox and I am left upstairs to my own devices. I am just itching to talk to my cowboy and send him a message, "Hey how was your lunch? I ended up going shopping earlier."

He explains, "Lunch was quiet, I just had a sandwich. Shopping, whatcha buy?"

I say, "Some skinny jeans, darker blue denim and a top, the sleeves have thumb holes so you can wear them over your hands."

Devon says, "Cool, how was the zip lining?"

I reply, "Zip lining was amazing some of the lines were over five hundred feet long and forty to fifty feet up in the air. There were ones that really played with your mind. Like for some you had to walk across a rope forty feet up. I felt like an acrobat. I have to admit that I feel so blah today, had my cry and I just dread having to tell my parents that it didn't work again."

Devon says, "It is ok, don't be hard on yourself. Maybe next time that you try with the doctor it may work. I am sure they will understand and comfort you too."

I confess, "I'm handling it better this round, I think." I rest my cheek on the side of the couch and look outside the window as a way to sooth myself while I explain it to Devon.

He says, "That's good. I wish it would have happened. You are still young. It can still. Just have to keep trying of course when you can."

I accept his kind words and am sort of at a loss of words on what to say next and end up distracting myself with chores. I empty the dish washer, put away the clean dishes, and sweep the kitchen.

I distract myself well enough that twenty minutes have gone by and another message from Devon comes in, "Did you fall asleep on me? Just kidding, just looked at phone the workflow is a lot right now. Anyway, have a great night."

I see Devon's message flash on my screen and head back to the living room and take a seat on the couch in front of the window and reply, "I'm back. I had to step away for a bit. Are your visitors from Dallas still hanging out at your place?"

Devon explains, "No they ended up canceling on us. I was kidding, I knew from last week you would not be on much today and most of the week. My partner came home sick anyway. So that stress is there too. I tried to comfort her but get the, 'leave me alone,' so I have sort of backed off until she gets better. I'm just trying to be supportive."

I say, "Hey, I got something to cheer you up, I think. Want to hear something silly?"

He replies, "Sure"

I explain, "So, this morning Josh made us some homemade ice cappuccinos and put a couple of straws in them. I start drinking mine and something is wrong. I'm sucking through the straw and all I'm getting is air. Josh asks what's wrong because at this point, I'm looking at my drink. I tell him that my straw has a hole in it can you get me another one? He just looks at me and is like, 'what?' Laughing, I had to explain there was a second hole on the side of the straw. I know not funny, you kind of had to be here."

Devon says, "Ha, I would have taken some of the drink and then take the straw, faced him and blew, chuckling, I get it."

I admit to him, "Last night he was being such an ass. Josh videotaped me mouthing words to the song, 'What Does the Fox Say?,' and posted it on YouTube. I made him take it down."

He mentions, "I'm laughing over here, too funny."

I explain, "I think he still has me up on YouTube somewhere getting shocked by a bark collar. God, the stuff that goes on here, you have no idea. So, tonight are you going to pick up some flowers or anything for her? Maybe that will cheer her up?"

Devon says, "Hey sounds like you two have fun with one another. Joking and pranks, which is good, keeps the relationship alive."

I tell Devon, "It's still shaky at times this morning he asked me again if I want a divorce so that I could find another that I could start a family with. I'm pretty bummed; I can't allow myself to dwell on it."

He writes, "I think he feels bad for not being able to give you what you both want."

I say, "I know that my parents and his are ready to help for another round but with Christmas not far, I can't take their money."

He says, "So, don't. Think positive and tell him how you feel. I am sure he loves you and would if he could, but again that is your choice like me to stay and work it out."

I write, "I'm going to have to wait a bit. I'll just feel guilty with getting a handout."

He says, "If they are willing to help it doesn't make you a lesser person. I hear you, me too so I try and do it myself but please don't let our friendship steer you in any way okay, please? I value you and want you to succeed in your marriage, but you have me as a good trustworthy friend. I hope that makes sense and I am not talking gibberish."

I type, "I think I am going to open a separate account and transfer some savings bonds over eventually and go in after Christmas and try without any pressure."

Devon says, "There you go. That is a good approach. You have your head on straight and you are a smart girl. I can tell that in just the few months of chatting."

I send him a smile in response to his compliment and say, "Yes it makes sense, what you are saying. Nothing has changed for me over the weekend that would change my mind or do the jump now and act later bit."

Devon says, "For me too, as much as my partner and I differ. I am not a quitter and opposites attract so it is in my best interest to give it my all despite the personal stuff you know about me. I'm just glad I can chat to you but if it gets to be too much just tell me. I realize we will have to scale back chatting but I'm good with it. I have to say that you both are more active than us. Sara and I do stuff but can't all the time because of her bad knees. I still love her though and care to make it work or die trying. We have split-up at times over the years and came back so it is not like we hate one another."

I tell him, "You are never too much. Sometimes I think I am too much. I never talked so much to one person." I add in a smile.

He wraps up, "Anyway, enough of that stuff. This chat wasn't about me this was about comforting you. Here is a virtual hug coming your way."

I tell him, "I still can't wait to see you and by the way I am keeping the photos and video. Yes, I am greedy over here and I like hearing what goes on in your world. Our friendship can't always be about one person."

He writes, "Ha, no worries, I used your photos for self-pleasure this morning. Such a nice shot can't complain here. I tried to lighten the pictures and make them clearer but still awesome shots. I'm not deleting at all."

I explain, "Laughing oh my god, I should have figured that a tech guy would do that."

He says, "Hey can't waste a perfect photo to being dark when I have tools to make it reveal itself."

I write, "I want you in me, no glove, no pulling out before, I want the real deal."

Devon texts, "Good because I want to be deep in you when I explode. I've been told it pulsates afterwards. It's true I can feel it too. Well, I did."

I warn, "Just know that I'm not on pills or anything and I don't care to be cautious, and I know that you have told me you are healthy, and I am putting a huge trust on you. I vibrate when I get mine."

He compliments, "Pussycat; nice; I am drug free and disease free, so I am putting my trust in you too. What will you say if you get pregnant?"

I say, "If you get me knocked up, I will just be thankful for your gift."

Devon says, "Well I am hoping to at least come three times for you. At least you know I gave you both sides and emptied out." He adds a smiley face and continues, "Of course a break after second and then again and we already talked about me not being involved and allowing you both to have a family but knowing I was able to help would be my friend gift to you."

I agree and say, "Yes, I wouldn't put that on you. I know that you have your own family."

Devon says, "Okay, well I can't wait to have you Jordan, really I need this to happen to make me feel alive again."

"If it worked and you were curious on what the baby looked like and what they were like, I would let you see in. I wouldn't cut you out."

Devon sends me a smile and replies, "Thanks, just trying alone would be awesome."

I admit, "I would be curious myself if I was donating my eggs, just to hear about their personality like if they were like me."

He says, "Exactly, you know what's going to happen we are going to meet and within seconds my hands will be feeling all over you and wanting to rip your clothes off."

I don't know how long I have been sitting on the couch and chatting with Devon, but I hear signs of life coming from downstairs. Josh must be finished playing with his Xbox as I can hear the sound of the footrest to recliner couch in the basement, click closed and the faint noise of Josh's step. I say to Devon, "Anyway I'll let you get back to work. Josh is done playing his video games."

Devon says, "I can't wait to suck on your boobs. They are yummy too; just want to see you smile. Anyway, talk to you later."

I respond, "Easy tiger, talk to you later, will likely tomorrow, have a good night."

Chapter 45
Josh's Routine

Josh is a creature of routine; he tends to follow the same pattern day in and day out and this is not being said in a negative light. He sticks with the things that he loves and today is no different.

He joins a couple of friends in the cafeteria at work. As usual he is the last one to join the table and his lunchtime companions don't seem to mind because it is often this way. Josh tries to finish up the tasks that he can before breaking for lunch but often his completion of things end up creeping into his lunch hour. He takes a seat at the table.

"Hey Josh" Bob says.

Josh says, "Hey how is everyone?"

"Good, well this pizza is a little dry but other than that things couldn't be better." Jasmine explains.

Josh glances at her half-eaten slice and decides, "It looks like they kept that one under the heat lamps a little too long."

Jasmine says, "I should have gotten a sandwich. Maybe I'll do that tomorrow."

Josh says, "As I was walking up, it looked like you two were in the middle of something good."

Jasmine giggles, "Not what you think. No gossip today."

Bob shakes his head, "The gossip around here is tiring. All you hear about are things like so and so got a promotion or such and such is jealous, or someone fell asleep in a meeting or that woman in marketing is having relations with that guy in accounting, like who even cares is what I think." He crosses his arms and looks to everyone for agreement.

Josh agrees, "Yah I am with you. I have got too much of my own stuff going on than to worry about others."

Jasmine blurts out, "It's what keeps this place interesting. I don't mind hearing a little gossip."

Bob says to Jasmine, "We can agree to disagree on that." He looks at Josh and asks, "What is that supposed to mean?"

Josh sighs, "Oh it's nothing. I have been just so busy with work and this part-time job that I have no time for anything else." Josh isn't the kind of man to talk about his personal life and he feels that even admitting this to his friends is cutting it a little close to the real issues that he is facing.

Bob says, "I forgot that you were still doing that. No wonder you look so tired."

Jasmine asks, "How does your wife feel about you working so much?"

Josh says, "She is okay with it." A lie will hopefully put her questioning to rest.

Jasmine admits, "If I was your wife, I would want you home after your regular job here. That's just my take on it Josh, she must miss you."

Josh nods, "She misses me but knows it is temporary."

Bob asks, "How long are you keeping this part-time work up?"

Josh holds in a sigh and refrains from rolling his eyes, "I am not sure, yet I am just trying to save up for a few things and once I have enough, I'll look to quitting."

Bob leaves it at that and says, "A man with a plan, that's a good thing." He stands, taking his empty food tray in his hand, "I got to get back to the grind. See you guys later."

Jasmine and Josh say bye. Josh likes Jasmine as a friend but hates that she can be a little nosy at times. If Josh were single, Jasmine would not be the kind of person he would date. She is attractive and smart, but he finds her a little over the top sometimes.

Jasmine giggles, "A man with a plan, that's a way of putting it."

"What are you trying to say?"

She asks, "Josh, what are you saving for, another laptop, drone or a camera?"

He knows that Jasmine participates in the office gossip and will not tell her anything more. He lies, "Yah something like that. I am undecided what to get. Well Jasmine I need to head back and prepare for a 1:30 PM meeting. See you later."

She laughs, "Go figure all that overtime for some toys. Talk to you later."

Josh lets it go. Jasmine has no clue that he is working overtime to pay for the attempts at starting a family. The failed attempts, it's frustrating that it is not working, and he has to keep this part of him private or he will lose himself.

Chapter 46
Devon's Day

Devon returns home, utterly drained from a grueling day at work. His attempts to chat with Jordan didn't yield much success; the impending launch demanded his full attention. Not to mention, the drive back was a nightmare due to a highway accident that extended his journey.

As he turns onto his street, the warm Austin hill country air fills the car, carrying the tantalizing aroma of BBQ dinners being prepared nearby. He wonders if Sara decided to use the BBQ tonight—his appetite craves a juicy burger. Finally, he arrives home, the long day's chaos behind him. He parks the car, turns off the ignition, and steps out. The feeling of home envelops him as he approaches the front door.

Unlocking the door, he steps inside to find Sara in the kitchen. He greets her, "Hey, honey, how was your day?" Slipping off his shoes, he heads over to the kitchen island, seating himself on one of the stools.

But her reception surprises him. She glares at him and demands, "Where were you?"

A bit taken aback by her unwelcoming tone, Devon explains, "I was at work. I had to stay late to assist with the upcoming launch, and on the way home, there was an accident."

She retrieves a plate from the fridge, her actions clipped and tense. Slamming the fridge door shut, she sets the plate on the counter in front of him.

He tries to understand, asking, "Sara, what's going on?"

With an air of skepticism, she retorts, "How convenient."

Sighing, Devon replies, "Sara, what's bothering you? I've been working all day, came home, and have been nothing but friendly. What's with this reception?"

She huffs, "Seriously, Devon? Do you think I'm that naïve?"

Confused, Devon responds, "I have no idea what you're implying."

Tension hangs heavy in the air as their conversation takes an unexpected turn.

She comes around the counter so that she is face to face with him, points a finger at him and says, "You are having an affair. I know it. I can feel it in my bones."

Devon knows he has kept things with Jordan well-hidden and besides it's not even at that point where they have met. He shakes his head, "Sara I'm not having an affair."

She slaps him across the face so hard that it causes Devon's cheeks to flush where her hand met his skin. She says, "How dare you lie to me. I can smell her perfume."

Devon shakes his head; he is a gentleman and doesn't react to her slap. What is she talking about? He hasn't been in contact with anyone today and then he realizes, saying, "Sara, I am not lying to you. I opened up a new bottle of cologne this morning. The one you got me last Christmas. I promise and if you don't believe me, I can go get it and show you."

She holds his gaze for a moment, searching for truth. She hates this feeling she has right now. The anger, the insecurity and lack of trust she feels. She prides herself on being a strong woman but right now she feels weak for feeling this way and it angers her more. She nods and follows Devon to the bathroom for him to show her the cologne. When he sprays the air, she realizes she was wrong. Her emotions are out of whack, her husband has proved his innocence, yet her heart is telling her otherwise and she doesn't know why.

Devon asks, "Do you believe me now?"

Sara hates being wrong but is relieved and sad for having doubted him. Tears start to roll down her cheeks. She hates feeling vulnerable and says in a cracked voice, "I am sorry. I don't know what has gotten into me."

Devon takes her in his arms and holds her. He knows her instincts are kicking in and knows that his wife senses his heart wants another. He looks down at Sara in his arms as her shoulders rise and fall from her sobs. All he can do is hold her. He feels pity for her. He loves Sara but it is not the same anymore.

Chapter 47
Jordan's Fire

Devon is my fire, and I try to please him in the way that I can, and it is not because I have to but because I want to. After sharing our intimate photos with one another and even him sharing a video of him self-pleasuring he hinted at me sharing my own video and I had sort of put it off for a bit but one evening after work while Josh was working late, I decided to deliver the goods.

After taking a shower, I lie down in the bed and set up my phone so that it's focused on my intimate parts. I go to work with rubbing my warm wet spot. It swells and becomes sensitive as I touch and feel my insides as they start to quiver.

I am so nervous, wanting him to see just like the photos but this is now something more. I explode and I let out a holler as my girl vibrates and I take a moment to enjoy the release before stopping the video recording.

As I lie on the bed, I review the recording and start to laugh, oh my god I can't believe I just recorded this and wow so that's what it looks like up close. Jordan wow okay so you have a video do you send it to him?

I watch the video a second, third and fourth time and get brave enough to send Devon a message.

I write to him, "Hey, so I am going to send you something in a few minutes, but you have to open it when no one is looking." I click send and I am not sure why my heart is beating so hard, besides Devon has already shared a video of himself.

Within moments he responds, "Hey, I am just wrapping up on a few things before I head home, I will take a look at it later tonight." He adds a happy face at the end of his comment.

I read it and don't think he knows that I fulfilled his request. I push, "Okay just know when you view it that all of it happened to the thought of you."

He replies, "Jordan, I am growling over here, okay I am going to look now."

I send it and smile as I laze on the bed and wait for him to give some sort of acknowledgement. Minutes turn into ten minutes and then he replies, "Damn girl that is hot. I actually had to go out to my car and take care of business. You have me in la la land. Thank you, thank you. So happy that you shared and like I said with your photos, I will keep this safe."

I respond to him, "Glad that you liked. Have a good night mister!"

Devon says, "You too, wow I love it!"

I went on to send him more over the months prior to our encounter. Self-pleasuring isn't something that I need to do often but for Devon I made some more videos for him, and he always returned the favor. It's a different feeling, to record yourself even if your face isn't in the picture, it's almost like I always had a bit of stage fright but at the same time it was a thrill to do and fun to be able to share with my cowboy.

Chapter 48
A Gentleman

I am not sure when this conversation happened or where I was, but I know that I was alone and so was Devon. I can tell that we have lived in different worlds, and we have been raised differently. Let me explain, there is nothing wrong with the way that he is, all I am saying is that I think that with the both of us there are some small international differences in our outlooks on life and for him the man that he is, I find that he shows more characteristics of a gentleman than I am used to. In subtle ways he shows me that he is a caring, southern gentleman and also a man that takes care of everything and everyone in his life. I know that he doesn't like the feelings he has for me being in the situation that we are in but at the same time he can't deny them. He wants to be a good husband but the carnal instinct in him wants me too and he can't deny himself.

I feel as his friend that I need to give him the courtesy of letting him lead and allowing myself to follow without interfering, which I'm not used to. I am used to more of a partnership, I think in a perfect world if Devon and I could be together I am not saying that we wouldn't be partners, we would but I think with Devon the added thing with him is he brings in the charm and chivalry and takes the lead in the "dance."

Anyway, Devon every now and then brings up our situation just to make sure that nothing has changed in thinking, he wants our two lives that we lead with our own partners and each other to remain separate and not interfere with the other and this conversation was one of those.

Devon says, "You are more than a sex object. You are human, a friend, and fellow author. I do see you normal too, not what's under your clothes all the time. I just think what's under is so damn hot. I had to send a last remark, chuckling here."

I say, "It is all good I'm flattered, and I know that you drop the word, friends all the time but I know it's more than that, more like secret lovers who care deeply for each other."

Devon says, "Yes, but it keeps the reality in check that's all. I know you love Josh as I love Sara but we both have a love for one another too secretly and it has to stay that way for me. I know you hate hearing me say that and I do not want to hurt you. You already know where I stand and that is cool that you still want to be involved in my secret life."

I explain, "I do want to keep you secret. I'm greedy and we keep a secret, and I don't mind."

Devon asks, "I hope that you are not mad about what I said. Do you think it is possible to love two people at the same time? Is that even fair to the other party? I do, it's a first for me but I do."

I explain, "I have no regrets about anything we have done. I think that this was meant to be exactly as how we set it out. I think it is possible because I'm living it right now. Fair to the other party, well I try to put myself in the others shoes. I don't want to hurt him, but I know he would fall apart. I saw it the night I had the talk with him, Josh is trying."

Devon says, "I hear you and that's good. You have to let him try, but know it must remain hidden and never found out that's all and if you ever decide that you don't want to do this anymore then tell me. I will still be a friend. You know what I mean?"

I confirm, "Yes, I think so."

Devon says, "But like I said I am trying to rebuild my life too with my partner and don't want you to be mad I am and like you said we are a secret hidden guilty pleasure for one another. Anyway, I want you to smile today and not think about that stuff."

I tell him, "It's like Josh is courting me all over again, with the dates, and flowers and stuff."

He says, "That is awesome. Anyway, my secret lover it must be your lunch time huh? You should be outside smelling the flowers and air instead of talking to me."

I sort of get mixed signals and need to be direct with him, so I ask, "Do you want this to end? Or are you hashing this all out because you fear that I will toss my life away?"

He explains, "I don't want you to toss your life away. We both have lives before meeting and still need to work at them too. I think I am confusing you, sorry. No, I don't want this to end, I like our chats. We have talked about this over and over before, no need to cross the same water. We know where we stand."

I say, "Yes I know, I'm not giving up on Josh but I'm not giving up on you either and it would honestly break my heart if you and Sara split. I know that it sounds weird coming from the girl who is stealing your affections but it's true my heart would stop if that happened."

He writes, "Sara would be devastated, and I would lose lots. So, thank you for understanding that means a lot but we both know an encounter will happen as that is destiny I believe. Anyway, talk later?"

I reply, "Sure"

Chapter 49
About Earlier

This conversation was received not long after the previous one.

Devon writes, "About earlier I want you to know if it gets to the point of causing either of us to cause a split, we will have to stop completely. So, let's not get to that point and just enjoy what we have now. It's fueling a book and making me feel young again. I have to have you at least once in my life. It would be a shame not to. I can't wait to feel your heartbeat on my chest and feel your body in rhythm with mine. I love seeing you up close imagining being there feeling the heat, smelling your scent, and tasting you. Yep, you just drive me nuts. I want to give you another video soon but have to be discreet about it. It will have to be no speaking."

I read his message, he is trying to be cautious and let me know where his heart is in the same breath. I chuckle before responding, "I'm surprised you're not some kind of player, I am putty in your hands. You say all the right things."

He admits, "I am just a normal guy who is hooked on a beautiful Canadian bombshell."

I send him a smile and reply, "Thanks you know that I love to see my entire stallion."

He says, "Will try, it will be a coming video too. By the way, I loved the tiny lips and yes you look very tight. That is hot as hell. Yeah, back to talking sex. Sorry."

I say, "Thanks babes, they all must be tight for you. I'm not lying when I said that you are the thickest, I have seen."

Devon says, "I'm glad that you like. I know last time I had some, she said that it hurt and there are others who have said the same. Hey, I need the love too. So, I guess it scares you? It will give you more than enough juice you seek, but I'm sure it will be tight at first, just take me slow."

I say, "I'll be slick so it should help."

He explains, "I do want to put all of it in you and feel your insides. Want to see your eyes and face. Lord knows mine will be open and closed just from the feeling. I should have a sex call number. I could get someone off by chatting to them while thinking about you."

I tell him, "You can give me all your length. You are about the same length as Josh. We take it slow that's all. I want this."

Devon says, "I'm a bad boy. Please do me for punishment." He chuckles.

I say, "I'll grab your ass and pull you in. If you were bad, you wouldn't be getting any!" I have to change topic because I am slick. I ask, "I have a question about your office. I'm changing subject. I know you took care to hide me. I just want to know if your desk, does your computer screen face the door? I am just curious if there is a chance of you being snuck up on."

Devon explains, "It faces the back wall so no for at home but at work, yes it faces out, so I just hide you and the sound is off. I only use my personal phone with you and at home I use my personal computer. There is a chance, but I am cautious."

I ask to clarify, "So at home you can't be snuck up on, right?"

He confirms, "I could be, but I would hear her. I only view your stuff when it is clear to. Like in the morning I can watch videos and not worry as she is across the other side of the house sleeping, if the video had screaming then yes, laughing!"

I explain, "Well, I'm not a screamer, I make noise when I release, not a full out moan, well you already know anyway." I send him a wink and continue on another thought. A work friend stops by my desk to share her lunch and I say to him, "People at work are awesome. I just got some fries given to me."

Devon says, "I don't expect you to scream at all, just bc normal and that was nice on the fries. I can imagine your breathing and facial remarks as you orgasm, so I'm good." He changes topic, "So for the book. Where are you in the storyline?"

I explain, "I am at the point where you have come back to me. You let your guard down and we are back to our natural tendencies. When I last checked, it was at fifty-one thousand words."

Devon says, "Okay, cool! Ha, you reeled me back in hook line and sinker, didn't you?"

I admit where I believe the change happened and say, "It was the night of the thunderstorm. That's when I knew that your 'breakup' was just a smoky mirror. I knew that you wanted it back to the way it was."

Devon admits, "I was really thinking of a way at the time to leave and that was wrong, so I had to set some ground rules and let you know that I need to work on my side of the fence too. But yeah, you got to me in a big way. When I saw you on video chat for the first time, I froze in awe of your beauty and fell for you fast. It was dangerous, just saying. I wanted you then and got excited every time that you stood up, hoping to get a glimpse of you."

I mention, "I had a feeling all along. People don't go from red hot to ice cold, I had a hunch." I smile and continue, "Anyway that's where I am at in the book."

Devon says, "Your voice is a drug to me, and your eyes are like kisses and your smile is like a stamp of approval for whatever."

I say, "My author guy." I send him a smile.

He says, "Just because I am smooth with words doesn't mean I don't mean it. Anyway, I better work today. I was useless yesterday. Laughing here, well I am going to drop off for a bit and p.s. that's why it is so important to keep this at a friend level and other parts secret. It would be different if we both were single and not because of split-ups. I would court you in hopes that you would like me but value you deeply now for what it is."

I tell him, "You would not have to court me; I would already be yours. Well have a great day."

Chapter 50
Weekends at Camp

It's been a while since those weekends up at camp with my mom, dad, and the extended family. I find that the summer is an easier time to be with others such as friends and family. Typically, everyone tends to take vacation to unwind and enjoy the few months of warm weather that we get here in Ottawa. I took time off in the summer, but as soon as September came into full swing the weekends up at camp soon wrapped up and my parents closed their camper for the season.

My parents' home isn't far from where Josh and I live, so distance isn't an excuse for me not visiting them. The truth is that I've become consumed by thoughts of Devon and our story. Every moment I have while Josh is at work becomes an opportunity to talk to Devon. I'm aware it's no excuse.

In the evening, when I'm alone after work, I receive a text from my dad. "Hey kiddo, should mom and I worry? Are you still alive?"

I hear the buzz of my phone, assuming it's a message from Devon. When I pick it up and see my dad's message, I chuckle to myself. Yes, I've been neglecting my social responsibilities with my parents. I deserve that. I text my dad back, "Hey Dad, yep, I'm alive. Just been busy with work. How are you and Mom doing?"

"We're good. Your mom actually got an acting position for a few months. She's filling in while her boss takes time off for training. It means higher pay for her."

Impressed, I reply, "Wow, that's great. She must be happy."

"She's happy."

Curious, I ask, "And what about you? How's your work going?"

"I have a business trip to Toronto next week, but other than that, it's pretty much the same old."

"That's good. Toronto should be fun."

Dad sends me a smile and then adds, "Hey, listen, kiddo, is Josh around?"

"No, why? What's going on?"

"Oh, I just wanted to talk to him about my home network. I'm thinking of making some changes and wanted to see if he could help. It's not a big deal, but I also wanted to try something with our phones, if you're up for it. I have this FaceTime app that I've never used, and I wanted to give it a test."

"Sure, I have it too and haven't really used it. Want to try a FaceTime call?"

"Yes, just give me a minute."

As I wait, I'm reminded of the need to balance my connections with those around me, both in-person and virtually.

My dad's image appears on the screen. He smiles, "Hey kiddo, don't you think this is so much better than texting?"

I grin, "Absolutely. Good thing I wasn't on the toilet taking this call."

"Jordan, you're such a dork! You're your mother's daughter. Anyway, now that I'm speaking to you face to face, your mom and I were wondering if you and Josh would like to come over for dinner sometime this week?"

I smirk, "So you can put Josh to work setting up your home network?"

Dad chuckles, "That's part of it, and also because we haven't seen you guys in a while."

"Sure, let me check Josh's schedule and find a night that works for us. I'll get back to you."

"Great."

"Where's Mom?"

"Oh, she went into town to pick up a few things. She'll be back later, but she wanted me to go ahead and invite you."

"Got it. Can I ask you something?"

"Of course, kiddo. What's on your mind?

"This FaceTime call—is it using your email address to call me?"

"Yep," Dad confirms, going into an explanation of how it works. Before we know it, an hour has passed, and we eventually say goodnight. It's funny how things like catching up with your parents can sometimes slip through the cracks. Well, I'll be seeing them soon, and Josh doesn't mind helping them with technical matters. Speaking of technical stuff, I'll have to mention FaceTime to Devon.

Chapter 51
Bloodwork

The fertility clinic insists on bloodwork even with a heavy period. I knew that I wasn't, I had talked to my mom, and she never got her period while pregnant and being her daughter, I imagine that I wouldn't either. Nonetheless I still went in to have bloodwork taken and the result was as expected.

It is not an easy process of being given the news of failure. You always hurt and then wonder if it is meant to be anyway a few days after the nurse's call, conversations start to return to a happier level. All I can do is continue to do the things that make and keep me happy. I know that if I ever stopped, I would probably sink into depression and I can't do that, not to myself, Josh, or Devon. I refuse to lose myself and instead focus on my work and now in this moment as I tell you my story, I wonder how my friendly cowboy is doing, so I decide to reach out to my friend.

I ask in a text, "Hey, how's your book coming along? Finished yet?"

"Hi there, how are you? The book is in revision now. How was your weekend?"

"It was good. Enjoying my day off, but it's raining, so I'm stuck indoors. I missed talking to you over the weekend. I got a new yard toy, and my arms are a bit sore from carrying it around. My wrists and the insides of my elbows ache. I didn't know there were muscles there."

Devon responds, "Sorry, wasn't trying to avoid talking. I was driving around all weekend. I even went to the San Antonio River. What yard toy did you get?"

"No worries, I understand you had company, and I didn't want to intrude. All good. Yes, I got a leaf blower that also vacuums and mulches. We have a huge maple tree in the backyard, so it's better than raking. It has a strap, but it still gets kind of heavy to carry around."

He says, "Oh my, I can imagine. I have company here all week, but I'm glad I can still chat with you during the day. Sounds like you handle most of the yard work."

I reply, "Yep, I mow the grass, vacuum leaves, and take care of the flower beds. Josh occasionally takes out the weed whacker because I'm afraid of it. He usually handles snow removal in winter, but this past winter, I had to learn how to use the snow blower. One time during a snowstorm, I was pulling so hard on the cord and couldn't get it started. I eventually gave up and just lay down in the snow. A neighbor saw me and came over to teach me how to use it."

Devon has been reserved about his job lately, and I sense he's ready to share now. He writes, "Understood. By the way, I heard a rumor that even though I'm doing well, I won't be getting the job. Seems like favoritism is at play."

Changing the topic back, he asks, "That's not good. Do you have a plow on a truck or a four-wheeler?"

I respond to his job news, "Ouch, really? How would anyone even know that?" Then, on the snow removal conversation, I reply, "No, just a gas-powered snow blower. It's a big machine and guides itself, so I don't have to push it."

Devon remarks, "Ah, I remember those snowstorm struggles. Be careful." Returning to the job discussion, he says, "There are rumors, and it seems true. It's disappointing. I'll still stay on as contract to hire."

I ask, "When will you know officially if you got it? Are they extending your contract at least?"

"Not sure about both. That's life. But I should know soon."

"I've got my fingers crossed for you."

"Thank you." Our conversation takes on a supportive tone, acknowledging both his job situation and my everyday experiences.

I say, "I did a fair bit of writing on the weekend and did some creeping too. I admit that I visited one of your websites and saw the photo section. You are such a hottie."

Devon explains, "I am still working hard and maybe down the road it will happen." He sees my latest comment and replies, "My old site? Thanks for the compliments, smiling here."

I say, "Something good will come out of it, you are a smart guy. I wish I lived down there because there are so many cool companies to work for."

Devon says, "There are. Yes, I'm confident."

I explain, "My work is secure but it's pretty dry stuff. I spend tax dollars and then write reports on what the money is being used for. It is so lame."

He says, "No, that is needed; it's not lame at all."

I complain, "Some of my family thinks that government workers are lazy asses, so I actually leave government off my online profiles."

Devon says, "Government jobs are awesome. I don't blame you. I know that you are not lazy."

I change subject, "My eight-pound Maltese just jumped on my stomach and tried to steal some kisses. God, he has some horrible breath. I'm seriously debating on buying some of those fresh breath tabs for him."

Devon writes, "That is funny. Well, my breath is fine. Can I jump on you?"

I ask, "Are your toenails clipped? I don't want to get scratched. Oh, and you must be an amazing kisser. I have sort of forgotten what it's like. It's been so long since I was with someone that enjoyed a good kiss, silly hunh?"

Devon says, "Yes I am groomed. I love to kiss, and I don't get enough of that either. I would prefer you to leap into my arms and wrap your legs around me but don't be shocked if you get a poke, laughing. You should just go up to him and take the kiss, but you should not have to."

I send him a smile before answering, "I would do that to you. If I were wearing a dress, I would have a bit of a hard time with leaping." I switch to talking about the first book that he wrote and published. He has a few published books and one that as you already know, is in revision. I reveal, "So, I finished your first book and for real, Tim is dead? I don't get why Alana did that? I had to read it twice. Like, I know that the title of the book implies that Tim died but I thought that the title was referring to Tim's dad not him."

Devon chuckles and says, "That's why there is a sequel. It's a cliff hanger." He goes back to talking about the other stuff, "Yes, I am hoping you would wear a dress when we meet for selfish reasons but hey easy access."

I ask more about his book, "So the guy in black was the brother of Remy that all gets resolved in the end, Remy dies and then Alana just shoots Tim?" I remark to his dress comment, "Sure, I'll wear a dress for you. I'm giggling there won't be easy access if I wear spandex."

Devon explains, "Ah, not exactly, but somewhat right. What? Do I have to bite through them? Laughing over here girl."

I say, "Okay tell me, without giving away the second book."

Devon tells, "Tim survives but Alana; well, that's a different story."

I assure, "Okay I'm following. To answer your question, spandex, I wear them as undies to keep stuff tight, booty won't bounce."

Devon says, "The twist in the series comes next in the second book. Nice booty by the way. I can't wait to feel it."

I ask, "Okay so will I find out why Alana shot him in book two? I don't see her motivation behind it."

He explains, "Yes. Ha you are trying, laughing over here. The book is better and more detailed. I am sorry that it confused you. I feel awful that it did. That makes me wonder about my five-star reviews on Amazon. I wonder if they just lied because I was a new author. On another note, I love your new video. Yes, I said that already but loved seeing you get off and actually watching it explode. Yes, I said it and smiling over here."

I answer about his book, "Yes, I appreciated the story second time reading through. I know why I got lost. There were a lot of layers, and the story was fast moving. The scenes, like the one where Tim was contained and Alana came through the ceiling to rescue him and then they get a helicopter ride out but then the next chapter Tim is getting punched in the face, I was like what? But then I realized that you were just moving it ahead. So, if I honestly didn't know you how would I rate your first? I think if it were a full-length novel, it would have been a five-star hands down because I think more words would have been able to guide the reader a little more. I liked the story, the twists, but wanted to know more about Tim and had to read it twice to get a grasp of the story. So, my rating would be a three star, you compensated in the end because I was like what is with Alana shooting Tim and because of that I want to get into the second book."

Devon writes a simple, "Cool"

I have no clue if he took my feedback well or not and say, "You have free rein to be hard on me when you give me a review. Those comments were me being brutally honest with you. It's hard to critic the work of the people that you know."

Devon says, "And I appreciate it. The second book is three hundred and sixteen pages but probably less or more in e-book form."

I think I hurt his feelings and offer, "I feel like I should send you some kisses. Geez, well because I purchase through kobo, I'm not even sure I can publish a review. Well, I think I can if you are on Goodreads. Do you want me to put up a three star or just leave it?"

Devon says, "It is okay, you don't have too. Knowing is all I need."

I sense he is hurt and try not to make it worse and mention, "For your second book, I'm going to purchase it through my kindle app so a review can be put on biggest book retailer site. Okay, well if you change your mind, I don't mind doing that for you. I know that a review shines light on a book no matter if it's good or bad, and really you did get me in the end because I am going to purchase the second and that was even if I didn't know you."

He replies, "Okay, as long as it is no trouble then I welcome it. I do appreciate your feedback really. I was young when I wrote it. But have since then grown up." He sends me a smile.

I explain, "I'll send you a draft first to make sure that you are comfortable with it. If it makes you feel better, I gave a recent best-selling series a three-star review and that author sleeps with bags of money from all her book sales. I did finish her series because I wanted to, and you know that you were still older than me when you wrote it. Anyways, my sexy guy, you told me that my first book has lesbian tendencies in it."

Devon says, "Yes, but I was hotter then too and well your book was leaning that way or maybe I was making it lean that way. I am laughing over here."

I say, "Oh, you are still really hot. That's the thing with guys they get sexier with age. Women they just become old farts. Well, the girls in my book do like to swim naked and bathe together, so I see it. I do think women are beautiful creatures. I'm not a lesbian but it would be neat to kiss a girl just to see. I imagine women in general are good kissers with their flavored Chap Stick."

He replies, "Laughing over here, thank you, you are amazingly hot yourself. Really you are. I get all caught up in gazing at you and no don't ever kiss a girl because you won't want me anymore. Whatever you do, just don't go down on her because you will be hooked."

I admit, "I couldn't go further than a kiss, just not my thing. It would be more curiosity than actual attraction to women."

He says, "Cool, well it's not like I would have a say in stopping you."

I comment, "You are silly."

Devon says, "I am just glad there is a girl out there that actually wants me to be sexual with them and still be friends. I'm happy as hell."

I say, "I like dick way too much to change teams. I'm just happy that I have you. My southern gentleman and dirty man all wrapped into one hot package."

Devon says, "I would have never known as I wasn't seeking that. Yes, I am sometimes too dirty but that is because you are so damn hot and yummy all over. I am just saying that Josh should be happy as hell to have you."

I ask, "So tell me of the two videos, rate the first and rate the second."

Devon explains, "The first one was nice hearing the noise and seeing, very intriguing and the second seeing you up close and glistening and moving and hearing your voice I actually got off hearing your voice and the ending, I was spilled over, loved it. I rate a three for the first and a five for the last."

I explain, "I think Josh wants to stay with me; he shows it in odd ways. The leaf blower was his gift to me. I would have liked a piece of jewelry, but nothing says I love you like a leaf blower."

Devon explains, "The video made me want to spread your legs and suck. On Josh, that is great, maybe it will happen at Christmas from him."

I send him a smile and say, "I thought that you would like that second one way better. I was wishing that you were in me while I was doing that. On Josh, I'm not sure what he will do for me, honestly the last piece of jewelry he got for me was my wedding rings and that was years ago."

Devon says, "Oh trust me you have such beautiful lips and form. That's some good eating."

I say, "Thanks for the compliments. On Josh, his gifts are things like, an elliptical machine, cameras, computers, leaf blowers; he bought a lawn mower and said it was my gift."

Devon's says, "Ha. go buy it and hand him the receipt and say thank you."

I agree, "Laughing over here, yes I should. My favorite jewelry store is in the United States. I could always shop online."

Devon says, "You should buy him a hammer and nails and see if he likes it." He chuckles.

I type, "Oh, Devon you have no idea. He would like that. You should see all the power tools in our garage. I'll tell you this, one year I purchased for his birthday a bottle of Ralf Lauren Cologne, like really nice stuff and he hated it. He admitted to liking the smell, but he told me that he rather have a practical gift. I think that's why I get things like leaf blowers."

Devon says, "Damn that would have been nice. That is great cologne."

I say, "I should give him a gift certificate to see my massage guy, Stephan."

Devon says, "Everyone is different."

I ask, "What type of cologne do you wear?"

He says, "I wear Stetson by Tim McGraw. Lately, it's been my own scent in the morning when I have my alone time thinking of you. I was being silly again." He sends a smile.

I mention, "I know Tim McGraw but didn't know that he had cologne. I like my Calvin Klein, cK one is my favorite and I have some Bath and Body Works."

He says, "Nice"

I ask about his self-pleasuring, "Did you do that this morning?"

Devon confirms, "Every morning, this time in the shower, yes I am building up my hand muscles; knee slap, sorry, I just can't help it."

I mention, "Wow I wish I could do my own in the shower. I would be smiling every day. So, before you knew me, were you doing it every day?"

Devon says, "I must sound like a compulsive person to jerk off as much as I do now. I never did it this much. It used to be every now and then. I swear that you could have had at least an entire glass full by now from me."

I reveal, "I love that you do that to the thought of me. We would be a good match; I wouldn't say no ever. It's usually the guy that wants it more but it's always me that wants it. I know it sounds backwards eh."

Devon explains, "I want it more than her, but I have learned to live without it. So don't be surprised if I am very into it when we do. I am going to be smiling."

I reply, "I wouldn't have it any other way."

He asks, "So do you like to have sex just in bedroom or all over the house?"

I say, "God I am going to sound vanilla; I have done it in the living room, in the car, on the beach, in the woods, in the shower but prefer the bed because of comfort. I also did it in a basement while a party was going on upstairs."

Devon says, "No that is cool, I'm just seeing how kinky you are. My phone battery is exactly 69% left, that's a nice number."

I comment, "I don't sound kinky at all. What about you?"

Devon explains, "On top of live ammo, backseat of a car, train, high school backstage, woods, couch, kitchen, living room, neighbor's house who were at my party. I was younger. I got laid once in Kuwait by a hot army girl and you are the first, I understand that you like to give head and that rocks girl. All around you rock."

I admit, "You are kinkier than me and you also said that you got a blow job at work."

Devon says, "Just thinking about you, I get sticky down there. Geez I am such an easy guy. Yes, but you girls are rare. I meant you openly admit to liking it instead of, oh this is just part of the deal. I would love to see your face when you are doing that and get your mouth full. Really, that would make me blow out more."

I explain, "I get off on it knowing that I'm pleasuring, and I love it and the control that I have. They stay so still. The only thing that I'm not a fan of is anal. I have gotten mine from back door, but I don't like the feeling of needing a shower after."

Devon explains, "I don't say that in any way to downgrade you. I just love how you like doing that. Even though your ass rocks, I won't be rocking it, just the front."

I say, "I thought it was normal to like doing that. Guys seem to talk about it all the time, blow jobs."

Devon says, "Well, if you never did that it is okay too. It's just a nice feeling but not as good as the real deal but really awesome though."

I confirm, "I'll give you one, I promise, and it will be fun. I want a taste."

Devon says, "Well it's not a requirement just saying. That is what I wanted to hear and likewise."

I reply, "I want to, not just for you it's for my own greedy pleasure too."

He says, "That's my kind of gal."

I send him a smile with his response and then switch gear, "So in my book you are meeting me in a Lincoln mkx. I'm just looking at rental car options."

Devon says, "Nice there is lots of room in those. So, I finally arrived. So how long do you think the book will be?"

I mention, "I'm going to hit the hundred-thousand-word mark. I'm nearing fifty-seven thousand words now. Oh, and I think that I have the titles to book two and three. Book one will for sure be called 'International Boundaries' the second will be called, 'Boundary Line' and the third will be, 'Changing Lines' I'm not totally decided, or it could also be called, 'Crossed lines.' I'm not sure yet."

He assures, "I do like. Well, I think I sparked some writing for you." He sends a smile and continues, "I know you are married, and I am too but I have fallen for you secretly and want to be with you and offer you a gift.

Anyway, wow we talked a long time. Laughing over here I can't believe how much we talk."

I say, "You have sparked some writing for me. I believe that I am truly on to a great story, one never told like this. I'm going to have to drop off soon to make dinner. When you start going through dates you need to give me about a month's notice. The reality is that I think I will still need to place a sperm order to make it look legit and plan for a procedure. I have been running this through my head and the reality is I think that I need a solid cover in order to pull this off. Ideally, I would want you to visit during my fertile week then after having you I would go in for the procedure. I have a better chance with you than with frozen sperm."

Devon explains, "Okay, if it looks like it can't happen just let me know. I do not want to expose us as that would be bad, but I will keep you posted, and I understand and agree with you. Well, go make dinner. I'm quite soaked and need to clean up. Yes, just thinking of you and it happens."

I comment, "I think it will be easy for us to meet, there are no problems there. It only becomes difficult on the, what if you get me pregnant factor. I think Josh will go digging through finances and I need a transaction to show that I went in for treatment."

He answers, "I understand and agree. It will all work out. Timing is everything and the availability too."

I write, "Okay well talk to you later and love you! Yay I can say it now."

Devon replies, "Love you too, have a great night."

The planning and timing are weighing on our minds, but our conversations are not all about it. Today the discussion is everything but that, which is fine with me.

Like clockwork by mid-morning, I receive a message from Devon. He writes, "Hello I hope that you are having a great day. You don't need to make another video silly. I have just been under the weather and am feeling better today."

I reply, "Good morning cowboy. I am glad you are back to yourself. Ah shucks, I was looking forward to making another video for you. I am alone this evening. I mixed up my schedule yesterday."

He doesn't answer right away. The reality is I know that he has been off work for a few days with being sick so my guess is if it's anything like my work, he must be sifting through hundreds of emails. I wait a couple of hours and get some of my own work done. I check my phone periodically during the day, there is no reply and before long it's time to go home. After getting settled down for the evening I finally try to get his attention and say, "Hey smelly! Don't tell me you are working. Anyway, I got some office gossip. The lady I got in a fight with a while back, we both apologized to one another and are on speaking terms. So, she told me that her sixteen-year-old daughter and her daughter's twenty-five-year-old boyfriend are now engaged. She is so pissed, but the thing here is you need parental consent for anyone who is less than eighteen years of age, so my co-worker hasn't consented. You got to wonder from a guys view on things, like what would you do if your son out of nowhere said, 'Hey Dad I'm engaged,' would you be mad or giving him a pat on the back?"

I get a quick response from Devon, "Well, I would be shocked and confused maybe happy I guess, but not sure."

I comment, "Yes, that is a tough call, sixteen is still a kid and the age difference between sixteen and twenty-five, she's still underage. You know with yours now in his twenties it will come maybe sooner than you think. My parents got all funny. I was engaged at twenty-three and they were like, 'you can wait you know' and I said, 'Well weren't you two married at twenty-three and twenty-four?' I had to laugh at them because that discussion never came up again. Oh and P.S. you are old; laughing over here!"

He replies, "Ha, are you calling me old?"

I tease, "Laughing over here, I'm just trying to get a rise out of you. You are my sexy guy but P.S. you will always be older than me." I send him a smile.

He comes back with, "Yeah, yeah, but this old guy can rock your world. Booyaah!"

I say, "Yes, I bet, bad boy. I am tempted to ask you to mail me a toy of yourself, so that I can play."

He replies, "Laughing, it would be hard to do now."

I suggest, "Maybe send it with Santa. Smiling, well those three weeks while Sara was away would have been perfect to do that, Ah well."

Je ponders, "I may have a chance in January, all is not lost."

I say, "That would be so hot." I send him a smile and he smiles back. I suggest, "Maybe we could do a trade just link what you want me to order for my own kit and I'll do the same for you or something."

He says, "That would be great. I am not sure how I would get yours and not get busted. That would be bad. The one I have now, only I know about it."

I say, "We have time to think about it, I guess. I would send you that and some thongs. They are small so they would fit well. There, I feel much better. Guess what I did? And don't say I took a laxative."

Devon says, "Chuckling here, what did you do?"

I admit, "I played with myself to the thought of you, recorded it and saved it to my email for a rainy day for when you are hungry."

He types, "Oh, I'm hungry; I just didn't want to make you feel like you had to provide that's all."

I admit, "I love doing these things for you, the shyness is gone with me, and I get off faster knowing that your eyes will see. Want me to send to your personal email?"

He describes, "Of course, I am tapping my fingertips being greedy." He sends me a smile.

I tease, "You will need a headset, it's sent."

He comments, "Thanks. Hmm last time you tricked me and made me go outside and I viewed a nice greeting video. Are you playing with me again?" He chuckles.

I say to him because he is likely watching it now, "I bet you're wishing to smell those little fingers of mine. They smell pretty amazing. I was so wet it was dripping."

Devon says, "I want to smell and suck your fingers, bad girl. I wanna gulp you."

I explain, "The video was longer. I had to cut it down, told you that I'm wishing this is you, deep inside me with your large hard man. I want you."

He confides, "I like that."

I say, "If I had a toy of you, I would show you just how much I enjoy your man on video and send it to you. I would lick it and suck it just to show you what I can do."

He asks, "Are you trying to get me aroused?"

I know him well enough and tell him, "If you watched, you already are hard as a rock and wanting me."

He replies, "Haven't yet, I am still working, but I will soon."

I complain, "By the way, you are a bad boy for saying earlier that I play games with you! I am so hungry for it, nothing I want more than to have you."

He sends me a smile and says, "I was being silly."

It's getting around to that time of the day when he is about to leave for home. I say, "So I bet you're packing up? You're going to have to let me know if you liked it."

Devon says, "I will thank you for the video. How could I not like it?"

I explain, "It's short that's all, I have limits when sending. I will be dreaming of riding you tonight. You should write a book on how to make women want to jump you. God, I am so not used to not getting what I want."

He watched it because he says, "So yummy, I would lick you until you exploded and then some. Wow dreaming of the taste."

I say, "You are such a tease. I need you to know my pussy wants you so much."

He writes, "How can your husband not want to dive into you and eat you? God, I want to drain you."

I say, "I think some take for granted the things that they have, such as life and ditto, I would drain you and you would beg me to stop."

He sends me a smile and says, "Well my friend have a great night. Chat tomorrow."

I reply, "Night sexy, living life on the edge eh, you shouldn't text and drive!" I send him a hug and kiss.

Chapter 53
Anything but Normal

It is a new day, and my morning is anything but normal, I get into work and am immediately swamped with a tight deadline that is due at the end of the day and not to mention I have to work with three other co-workers to meet that deadline, so work has involved a lot of running around, ensuring who is doing what and double checking the information that is being produced with our group.

Lunch soon approaches to my relief; I need the break and to add to it I am meeting a couple of high school girlfriends at a restaurant that I haven't seen in a while which means that lunch will be time well spent in catching up.

I check my phone before I leave but I guess Devon is having a busy day also because no messages have come in. I trust that I'll likely get a message around 2:00 PM my time. He is an hour behind me, and he takes his lunch at 1:00 PM his time. As for Josh, he isn't one who messages during work. The only time he messages me is when it's something important or if we are making plans outside of our regular routine, so there aren't any messages from him either.

The drive to the restaurant is five minutes and to my surprise my two girlfriends are already in the lobby, waiting for me, I say, "Hey guys!"

Hailey and Ophelia in unison say, "Hey Jordan!"

"Were you guys waiting long?" I ask.

Hailey explains, "We both just got here a minute before."

Ophelia adds, "Great timing!"

The server meets us, and we are seated, orders are soon placed and in no time, we are all eating. Hailey and I talk about our husbands and Ophelia talks about her boyfriend. They recently moved in together, so life for Ophelia has taken a dramatic change. She used to be a super laid-back person; some would say too laid back as in lazy. Ophelia used to be late for any plans that were made and now with her boyfriend she explains that he has positively impacted her in that department as she feels the need to meet commitments and be more active and she says it all with a smile and giddiness that she can hardly contain. It is cute to see her so happy.

As Ophelia shares all of this news and her feelings, I just ponder to myself, wishing that I could be happy with just Josh and not be drawn to another. I am happy for Ophelia and her commitment and love for her boyfriend. That head over heals, falling in love feeling is what I should feel for Josh. I shouldn't divide my heart between Devon and Josh, like I do now.

Hailey interrupts my brief daydreaming and jumps in saying, "Ophelia that is fantastic!" I smile to show my approval.

Ophelia says in a squeal, "I know, and I truly think that he is the one!"

I say, "Your instincts are usually right when it comes to stuff like that. When I met Josh, I knew from the beginning."

Hailey says, "Yes that was the same for me also. You just know it in your heart."

With having such a great time, the lunch hour feels like it was only ten minutes and we all have to get back to work. The server returns with our bills, and we are soon all saying our goodbyes.

Hailey, having made the lunch plans says, "This was so great we have to do this again sometime."

I answer, "Yes, agreed, well take care you two and hope to see you guys again soon."

Ophelia says, "Yes okay, bye Jordan."

Hailey says, "Bye, take care."

We all wave to one another and go our separate ways in the parking lot to our cars. When I get into mine, I have the urge to look at my phone and sure enough there is a message waiting for me.

Devon says, "Hi there, I wasn't texting while driving. I was stopped. How are you today?"

I reply, "Hey, I'm good, just came back from a lunch date with two girlfriends I went to high school with and haven't seen them in a while. It was nice to catch up. You would be so disappointed with me, I went to a Texas grill and wanted to order a burrito, but I was worried about the size, so I ordered a salad. Anyway, just changing thoughts, I have to ask you something tech guy. I noticed with FaceTime that I can program my email address, so I did and now I want to know, if I'm on Wi-Fi anyone can call me through email?"

Devon replies, "Yes"

I say, "Wow! Okay that is so awesome thanks tech support guy. So, anyone outside of the country can call me?"

He mentions, "Yes, but data charges again if using phone. You would have to check to see."

I reply, "I saw the fine print on the support page. I think as long as my phone is on Wi-Fi, I'm good."

Devon replies, "Yes, you are right." He sends me a smile.

"I sort of found this all out by accident. I was calling my dad the other day and hanging up on him and Dad finally video called me back. Anyway, it's too awesome.

I thought FaceTime used telephone numbers. It is so cool to see that it uses email."

Devon sends me a smile and says, "My work just rocks. Oh, and by the way I got the job, they hired me as a permanent employee."

I say, "Wow Devon congratulations and yes your work does rock and may I add their employees are way hot."

He answers, "Thank You!"

I explain, "Well, I hate to do this now after just hearing the great news, but I got to drop off so that I can drive back to work, wish I could keep talking to you, maybe in an hour I hope, if not have a great weekend. I'm alone tomorrow."

He says, "Okay, well I promised Sara I would do things with her tomorrow but have a great day and weekend if I don't hear from you."

I am still in the parking lot of the Texan restaurant; sheesh I am going to be late going back to work.

Chapter 54
Before November Turned

Before November turned to December Josh and I had a couple of dinners at my mom and dad's home and Josh helped my dad get his home network up. December was soon upon us, and it was busy for both Devon and me. We kept chatting throughout but refrained a little more since we needed to focus more on our families during this time. Devon's holiday season, kicked off with Sara's children and grandchildren visiting Devon and Sara's home for the American Thanksgiving and for my own Josh and I started to think about gifts, and we were often shopping after work or going to friends' holiday parties. Come Christmas Devon's son visited him for that week while Josh and I took that week off to visit with Josh's family up north.

After the holiday season was over and January was upon us things soon returned to our regular daily chats and there isn't much to it than that. We got to video chat again in January one evening while Josh was working late, and Sara decided to go visit her sick dad in Rochester. If you are wondering he never made that toy of himself for me, and I didn't mail him my panties. Those were sort of heat of the moment conversations. Getting to see him was always like a breath of fresh air and an hour of video chatting always felt like moments when talking to him.

By mid-March planning was ongoing while each of our own relationships improved. The nice thing about Devon and my situation was there weren't any jealousy issues we wanted each other to succeed in their own relationship so that we could continue our own in secret without any suspicions or interference in our lives.

Josh is my friend, my partner but the depth of the situation is a future of creating a family with him is non-existent but with Devon it's possible, he can give me that but on the flip side he can't commit to being a companion and that's where the two of them complete the puzzle. They complement each other and Devon is also my best friend but on a different level, he is full of ambition, and we have so much in common. We can talk forever whereas Josh has more differences, sort of like the rule of opposites attract. Well, we aren't complete opposites, but our personalities can be pretty different at times, but they complement each other.

Devon has made it clear that he wishes for the encounter to be natural, no protection, he wants to give me what I seek and for me if this does work and I end up with child I need a plausible story. For starters I have opened a separate account. Josh and my accounts are joint, so I needed a separate one to come up with a believable story which is that I made a transaction on my own in secret to rid any added stress from others knowing. The money is coming from one of my own savings bonds so it's as simple as a transaction in and transaction out. I know it's not a perfect story but it's the only one I can come up with right now. If by chance Josh finds out about this account sooner, I will just excuse it as something I created to track my own sales with my book. For the doctors, if this ends up working, I will just act as though it just worked with the procedure for Josh and me, just a normal pregnancy. Only Devon and I would know the truth.

This is all we have, and I need this, we both do. We have brought the other to life, this is exciting, and we both get something out of this coming together. Me a chance of a lifetime and to feel desired and him to connect with another intimately because his own spouse has not with him in years which is sad because when it all comes down to that, it's a form of love and to feel desired on that level any person needs that intimacy, love and desire from another and I can give that to him. If I weren't married and he wasn't in a long-term relationship I would seek him, crave him for my own and love him to my heart's desire. I do now but need to keep a boundary as my marriage is to Josh.

One quiet evening while Josh is away at work, I receive the message from Devon.

He starts with, "Hey Jordan do you have a moment, can you talk?"

I answer back, thinking that this is just another one of our many conversations, "Hey sexy, I'm alone tonight, I can talk. What's up?"

He types, "I can visit you."

Chapter 55
Take a Deep Breath

I sit back in my recliner and take a deep breath, "Don't leave me hanging Dev, when will it be?"

He responds, "Once I purchase the plane ticket there is no going back."

I answer, "Yes, I understand. I want you, please tell me when."

Devon explains, "Next week, I am going to book the ticket now if that works for you. Does that work for you?"

There is no going back, I know this and if everything works out then everyone will have what they want. My plan needs to be fool proof. Can I do this? Wait, I need this to be believable I just can't have an encounter with him and if it works, Josh won't buy into the fact that I went in for IUI treatment on my own, Jordan wake up. A week, can I do this? No, I can't, I need to have a real transaction happen and the sperm needs to be purchased before day one of my cycle which I'm due next week.

I answer him and my heart hurts with the disappointment, "Devon, I can't do it for next week, before you say anything please here me out, it's not that I have cold feet it's just the timing needs to work, let me explain." I repeat my thoughts to him, I need to set up an IUI treatment for the month he visits, his encounter and my treatment have to happen around the same time, it's a no brainer, less likely to arise suspicion with a mysterious pregnancy and it gives me a good chance to get pregnant if he visits me during my fertile week.

Devon says, "Okay I understand so when should I book this trip?"

I pause, "My period is due in a week. I can place the order now for my treatment and then we count the days, you should come down for the ninth that would be one to two days before I would go for treatment. Could you do that for me?"

Devon says, "It will be hard for me to pull off, but I should be able to manage."

I ask, "Why next week, what is going on?"

He explains, "Sara just mentioned that she would be out of town." He answers.

I ask, "Did you already book the time off for next week?"

Devon says, "Yes and no, my work has me marked down for taking time off for the spring, but I haven't confirmed exact dates, I'll make sure that the ninth and tenth are for you and my brother is pretty flexible and the change won't interfere."

I take a breath, relieved that this is falling into place, "Okay thank you Devon, you have no idea how much this means to me."

My perfect man is coming to see me and give me his gift so willingly, lovingly, my friend, and I think my soulmate although we both know it will never be. A modern-day Romeo and Juliet tale of a love that can never truly be, he is giving me as much as he can, and I will take it willingly and be so happy if it works. I hope to have his babies; he is so incredibly smart, handsome and he is my friend. We are a good match and I know that if this worked, we would make a beautiful baby.

A few moments pass and then a response from Devon comes through, "Okay Jordan, my flight is booked and now the countdown begins. I wish it could have been next week, but I will wait a little longer, it will be so worth it."

I smile and my heart still hasn't gotten used to it, I am nervous, excited, and happy all at once, "Thank you."

He says, "Anything for you my dear, well, I am going to go for now, I got to call my brother as he is going to be with me on the start of my trip, but he won't be with me when I come to see you."

I says, "Okay Devon talk to you soon, xoxo."

"Right back at you" he replies.

My mind is working at a mile a minute, okay focus Jordan, focus. I have to tell Josh about my next attempt so that this doesn't have a chance at becoming weird. Yes, that is my next move. No wait, what if he says no? Oh god, would he say no? What if I called and placed my sperm order now? It's not like they do refunds and besides its coming from my own funds that I set aside for this. What do I do?

I get up off the recliner and start pacing the room, do I, do it? If I wait to tell Josh he may ask me to hold off then what? That would mean that my plans with Devon would be completely screwed, well not completely the encounter could still happen but if he asks me to wait for a longer amount of time and Devon's seed works then Josh will know that something was up.

This is a no brainer; I know my husband he will be a little pissed off that I made the order without talking to him, but I can't risk anymore risks and especially when plans are already being set in stone. I decide and then instantly go downstairs to my office to place the order. I send the request to the Sperm Bank and call to confirm that my order has been received. All is good and I put the phone down.

The order is placed.

Chapter 56
Telling Josh

I exhale, one more plan set in motion and falling into place. Now I get to face the music and tell Josh. I doubt that this will go well. I actually dread it.

A couple hours go by, and he is home. From how he looks he appears to be in a decent mood, I will let him get settled. I look down at my hands, they are shaking so I just put them in my pocket and hope that he doesn't notice.

Josh asks as he hangs his jacket in the closet, "So how was your day? Anything exciting that you want to talk about?"

It is funny the choice of words that he uses, if only he knew what I was about to offload onto him. It is hard to maintain a poker face with things that come as a surprise, and I don't mean to but end up giving him a look that raises concern in him.

He walks over to me, "Jordan, what's up?" He is halfway in the living area, steps from the front door and he walks over and places his hands on my shoulders and gives them a gentle rub.

I do my best to stop shaking and I smile and look up into his clear blue eyes. "Josh I, placed the order." It has been months since our second attempt. What I was expecting from him didn't happen at all.

He takes a moment, swallows before opening his mouth, "The order? You are going to try for your next cycle?" I nod yes and he continues, "Wow Jordan that is news."

His response seems to be good, and I ask, "Are you okay with that? I can't really cancel the order now."

He smiles, "Yes I am fine with it. I know the drill."

"Can I ask a favor of you?" I look into his eyes.

Josh says, "Sure"

I explain, "I want this to work, and I ask that for this time we keep this attempt between us and also one more thing. I want to be as stress free as possible and ask that for the week that my ovulation starts, I want to keep that week opened and not have to worry about people visiting." Josh's family visits from up north regularly and he will almost always jump on the defense when I ask of something that appears to be against their favor. I start to see what I perceive as the beginning of a disagreement building in him and I continue, "I only ask of this because I really want to keep this secret. It is important to me and having visitors during that time, it will be difficult to hide it from them." I see the tension in his shoulder start to relax.

To my relief he gives in, "Okay, you know my parents like to visit around that time, I will make sure that they come after it is all said and done."

I smile, part relieved that this went all too well and partly because this plan is working itself out. I say, "Thanks Josh, I only ask for that week, and any other time they are welcome to visit. So, it will be the week that falls on the ninth, I need that week free for us."

"Okay sounds good." He replies with a smile.

I look up at him and ask, "What?"

He gazes down at me and says, "You look happy, it's been a while."

I say, "I feel happy." I am happy that this fertility stuff is falling into place and that Josh, and I seem to be in a good place and that I will get to meet my southern gentleman.

Chapter 57
Devon the Creative Mind

Before Jordan had come into Devon's world, he had been busy writing a new book. Jordan had read his sample on Wattpad, but truth be told Devon's story plot was complete and just a matter for him to finish and get the words to paper. Devon is the creative mind behind his story telling however for this new story his brother Shane assisted him with editing and in helping Devon close up the story gaps. Shane is someone that Devon can bounce ideas off of and to make a long story short Devon wants Shane to go on a trip with him to B. C. so that they can get a better idea of the lay of the land since part of his story is based there.

Devon has been thinking about this trip up north to Canada's west coast for a long time and now even more so after having met Jordan online. Devon has been thinking of ways to use his trip as a way to meet Jordan.

Sara and Devon have been having problems and to get away from facing her problems Sara has needed to give herself space. She heads out to do some groceries and other shopping leaving her husband at home.

Devon's take on the matter is it is what it is. He tries with her but it's never enough and he just doesn't care to go chasing after her even though he knows that's what she wants. He lets her go and besides, it allows him time at home to relax and catch up on his hobbies.

Jordan had chatted with him for a bit but had to drop off and now he finds himself at a standstill. He finished another chapter to the series and even spent some time on

YouTube browsing through some remote-control helicopter videos. He has seen most of them.

He looks at his watch, ten to noon, his stomach is rumbling. Devon heads to the kitchen opens the fridge and pulls out some food to make a sandwich. He places the ingredients on the kitchen island then opens a cupboard and pulls out a loaf of bread.

Sara used to love cooking and have him taste her dishes and now there is not a homemade dessert or meal to be had. He works all day during the week while she stays at home, doing what he has no idea. Sara doesn't have any hobbies that he knows of. She never talks about her day or who she saw or what she did. He has concluded that all she does is sit at home, watch television, and litter her social media feed with opinionated posts about random crap. He concludes this because he sees her posts but ignores them most of the time. He has no reason to bother with those sorts of things.

He tops his sandwich and the phone rings.

He picks up the cordless, "Hello?"

A familiar voice says, "Baby brother"

Devon smiles, "Hey Shane, what's happening?"

Shane explains, "I thought I'd give you a call since you sent me an email asking to book time off."

Devon chuckles, "Yes I was meaning to call you today about that. So did you get it off?"

Shane huffs into the phone, "What do you take me for of course I got it off."

Devon asks, "What days?"

Shane confirms, "I took off the entire week, you?"

Devon replies, "I got the week off too and I took a few days off the following week."

Shane questions, "Why didn't you say anything? I could have booked more time."

Devon walks around the island to the stools, takes a seat with his plate of food and assures, "No, it's okay Shane I needed a little more time I wanted to scope out Ottawa to see the sites."

Shane asks, "Aren't we going to B.C.?"

Devon elaborates, "Yes, but I will also be headed to Ottawa for a couple days before returning home."

Shane questions, "Why, Ottawa isn't even mentioned in our book."

Devon says, "No but I think in our sequel I may want to set a few scenes in Ottawa."

There is a moment of pause and then Shane says, "You know Sara has been talking to Kim a lot and has said things."

Kim is Shane's wife. Devon should have known that Sara would tell others about their personal issues and the fact that it has his brother asking means that it has to be pretty bad. Devon sighs, "I am sure that she has, and I am sorry that you had to hear about it."

Shane admits, "Kim said that Sara is happy that I am going with you because she suspects you are having an affair or something. I told Kim that it's not your style especially with your ex-wife doing that to you." Devon wasn't expecting Shane to continue on this topic and remains quiet. Shane feels obligated to fill the silence and continues, "Should I be worried that you are going to Ottawa? Are you meeting someone there?"

Devon replies, "What? No, Jesus' man"

Shane laughs, "Hey I just wanted to ask because that's what I hear from Kim."

Devon confides, "Sara and I are having a rough patch but it's not like that. I just need some time to myself before heading back home."

With understanding Shane offers, "I get that."

Devon says, "I'll talk to Sara about what she has been saying to Kim."

Shane interrupts, "No, don't. Kim promised to keep it secret and if you mention it Sara will know that Kim told me."

Devon rolls his eyes, "Okay I won't mention Kim. I'll talk to her though and hopefully that will put the rumors to rest."

Shane says, "Thanks, well I am excited about B.C. It has been too long since I have seen you."

Devon forces a smile to get past his worry and agrees, "I know."

Shane says, "Well little brother, I have to drop off. Kim wants me to drop her off at Yoga."

"Bye" Devon sets the cordless down. He hates that Sara talks to others about things that should remain private.

Chapter 58
Anxious for Something

Time passes by slowly whenever you are anxious for something, at least it does for me. It helps that Devon and I chat every day and I always look forward to hearing from him. Soon enough I call the nurse to report day one of my cycle.

The two men in my life are both excited. My relationship with Josh right now has never been stronger. With Devon and me, even though we are countries apart I feel close to him in so many ways.

Days have passed since my day one, it is almost bedtime, and I am just lying in our king-size bed with Josh at my side. We both have our reading lamps on. He is just on his phone browsing the local flyers that are emailed to him and I have my e-reader on reading the latest book to a fantasy series.

Josh asks, "So you must be getting close now to going in, when are you starting those pee tests?"

I honestly forgot about them, the things that slip my mind. At least I can rely on Josh to remind me and thank God I still have a lot left over from the purchase for my second attempt. Those test kits are expensive. I pretend to not be surprised that he asked about them and pretend that I didn't forget, "I am going to start testing tomorrow morning."

Josh asks, "Do you have enough for this round, if not we can stop and pick some up tomorrow when we are in town?"

I reply, "I should have enough." I put my e-reader down and snuggle up to him, resting my head on his pillow and steal a peek of what he is looking at on his phone, a flyer for some power tool sale going on this week, go figure.

Josh gives me a kiss on the cheek and says, "I am going to turn over and go to bed. Did you want to cuddle or are you reading a bit longer?"

I shuffle over to my own pillow, "I am going to read for a bit."

With a smile Josh says, "Okay well don't be waking me up in thirty minutes because you want to be cuddled." He winks at me as he gives a playful warning.

I roll my eyes, "Yes Josh."

Chapter 59
At Work Early

The drive into work isn't bad, and I find myself at work a few minutes early. I turn on my computer; make a brief stop by the water cooler to fill a glass of water to sip at my desk and say a polite good morning to another co-worker who is in early. I load up my desktop applications, there is a weird feeling that has come over me and I feel compelled to check my phone.

Sure, enough there is a message from Devon that reads, "I am here." sent two minutes ago.

What? Oh my, I wasn't expecting him to arrive until later on in the week. Is that what that means, or does he just mean that he is here as in, here online? I respond back, "What do you mean by here?"

A response comes in within seconds, "I am parked out front; you said building one, right?" I am starting to freak out, what do I do? Jordan don't waste time go down and see him.

I thought that our first encounter, well I pictured what I would have worn being my favorite black pencil dress with large waste belt, short sleeve, and a V-shaped neckline. Today I'm just wearing a pair of skinny jeans and a simple cotton shirt with a dress scarf. Wow, first impressions oh well alright now to not waste time I leave my office and run down the hall, down the stairs to the front doors. I see him pulled up at the bottom step in a white Lincoln mkx. I smile to myself because he remembered that detail when I was telling him about my writing. He has the window down and is all smiles with a spark in those smart brown eyes of approval and desire. I skip down the steps to his window and as I approach, I say practically out of breath, "I wasn't expecting you today."

He tips his head to nod, "I know, Jordan come here."

I draw closer and know what he wants and without a care of who may be watching I go in to taste his lips. He has had some sort of mint; his taste is fresh, clean, and warm. It's a gentle slow kiss like he has slowed time for us to enjoy. My eyes close and then at the same time I pull away as we finish. I must have a foolish smirk on my face but whatever, who cares. He glances into my eyes and asks, "Are you coming?"

I giggle, "Oh boy you distract me, yes of course give me a few minutes. I need to pack up my things and I'll be right out to move my car." For today I am going to just say that something has come up and take the day off. I say goodbye to the one other person in the office, grab my things and head back out to Devon and my car. To not draw any attention, I just move my car to one of the other parking lots at the building complex and then I take a breath and get inside the Lincoln to see my Devon.

The vehicle is idling, and he is all smiles, his eyes already have a fire within them like he is already undressing me. Just like the video chat, months before, we are speechless only this time it's in person and that boundary is no longer. Devon doesn't waste time; he knows that I want him, and he leans toward me and goes in for another kiss this time his one hand rests on my inner thigh and the other on my cheek almost to warn me to stay put and have him.

We have said few words and are locked in; his tongue is warm and gentle as it willingly tastes me. Gentle but in full control he leads this, and his hand runs up my thigh, it doesn't have to go far to reach my most intimate area. He draws back at his discovery, "You're already wet Jordan."

I smile, "That is what you do to me. Shall we go somewhere more comfortable and private?"

He takes a breath knowing that this much anticipated meet will soon get to what we have been waiting for, for what seems like forever. He answers, "I think that is a good idea." He takes my hand and shows me, he is rock hard.

I smile, "I will have that."

He chuckles, "Oh you will my dear." He is confidant. He drives the Lincoln out of the parking lot. His hotel isn't far; it's near the airport, one of the nicer hotel chains.

It's funny, I say this over and over again in that we talk nonstop via text but get us together and we are quiet and constantly gazing at each other. I decide to get the conversation started, "So tell me; am I what you expected?"

He gives me a teasing eye and responds, "You are way more beautiful in person than in any picture." His eyes then glance forward on the road, "What about me, what do you think?"

I giggle, "Look at me, I'm having a hard time talking, you are my cowboy, and it is amazing to actually see you. You are my sexy." He smiles and nods while staring forward and driving. Devon is attractive, and it's even more so in person, those brown eyes that I am always talking about, pictures are one thing but seeing them in person, I can get lost in them. They are warm, loving, and caring. He has smooth youthful skin, the way that he trims his facial hair, his short, thick brown hair, and the scent of his fresh cologne, he does it for me. He has a nice body, strong but not over the top, and that personality and charm that goes along with it just makes me putty in his hands.

I change topics, "Tell me, how was the trip?" I know that Ottawa for him is his last stop before home. He had spent some time out in B.C. with his brother, even texted me a few times while on vacation, which is why I am a little surprised that he is here today. He has taken a detour to Ottawa, solo and just to see me.

His eyes glow and I assume it was reminiscent of the new fond memories he made with his brother, "It was great. I got to see all of the sites that I had set out to visit and see my brother whom I hadn't seen in a while."

I ask, "How is he?"

"He is good." He chuckles.

"What?" I ask. I feel like he is holding back.

Devon admits, "Oh, he really wanted to come with me to Ottawa that is all."

"How did you convince him not to come?" I ask.

He explains, "I said that it's going to be a short stop to check out the scenery and the layout."

"And he was good with that?" I ask.

He glances at me with all of my questions, "He accepted it, wasn't happy but he could see that I needed time to myself."

I smile back, "Time to yourself, well that is hardly the case." I run my hand up his leg and find that he is still rock solid.

I compliment, "Wow Devon, he hasn't relaxed.

He says, "Not with you here."

We pull into the hotel parking lot, and he pulls into a parking spot and turns off the car. My heart is thudding in anticipation, and he removes his seat belt and leans in for another kiss. He is smooth and sends a chill down my spine. I don't wish for this to end but I pull away, out of breath, "Devon let's go inside."

"I want you here and now." He holds my face in his hands as he makes the demand.

I complain, "It's thirty seconds to the room and a day of no interruption. Here we are likely to be interrupted."

He weighs my point. "Okay, for you I will do that but for the record I wanted to take you here and now."

I give him a peck on the lips, "Show me your room sexy."

We go through a side entrance down the hall to the lobby elevator and take the ride up to the fourteenth floor. Devon wastes no time; we have the elevator to ourselves, and he has backed me into a corner pulled my leg up so that he can be as close as we can and are locked in embrace. This is it Jordan I think, there is no going back after crossing this line. In no time the elevator signals that we are on his floor, and he ends our kiss, gives me his arm, and leads me to his room.

Chapter 60
Long Forgotten

In this moment, the stresses are long forgotten, and I had made a promise that I would be his. I was his; I had forgotten my entire life and only known him for this time, which was all that mattered.

He closes and locks the door. I find my way over to a king-sized bed and start to remove my clothes.

A command startles me. He walks over to me staring down into my eyes; taking my hand away from the button of my skinny jeans, "Allow me."

"Okay" I breathe. He slides my pants down and I step out of them, and he kneels down so that he is at eye level with my crotch with my panties still on, he sticks his nose in to take in all my scent. I stay still for him, "My god Jordan, your smell is just as I thought." He grabs them and pulls them down, I am soaked. He looks up at me, "You want me."

"Yes" I whisper, and he takes a taste, it's gentle at first and then he puts a hand on my butt and pulls me in as he clamps down with his entire mouth, sucking and tasting and I feel my legs start to go weak.

He teases, "Having trouble, are we?"

I nod, "It's been years since I had that." I answer out of breath.

He grins at me, and his lips are glistening from my juices. My panties are now at my ankles and as I step out of them. He grabs and holds them up, "You know these are staying with me?"

I smile, "Kinky man."

He asserts, "You know it, get on the bed."

I sit down and he removes the rest of my clothes and I help him out of his. His dick looks amazing and thick, he is rock hard. I go for a touch, it's hot.

Je orders, "Not yet Jordan." He removes my hand from him and then guides me to lie back down. I think he is about to enter me but to my surprise he starts with going down on me.

He pins me down and goes at me strong and intense. His mouth over my opening, licking. I feel his tongue go in deep, tasting and making me squirm, and I try to stay still but he makes me quiver with each movement. He licks my opening circling it and nibbling. He stops for a second holding me in his teeth and I am nothing but tense and he let's go and then moves up my body giving me kisses and resting his at the opening. He has brought me to the edge and being greedy I push up against him, wishing that he would enter.

He isn't going for it, and I let out a breath and realize my hands are free and I try to reach for him to guide him in, but Devon just laughs saying, "No Jordan not yet." I look at him with such desire and some disappointment that he isn't letting me have my way. He whispers, "Let me kiss you." His kiss is warm, loving and he has the scent and taste of me on his lips, it's a sweet sensation and it's for a moment. I feel him at my opening and want him to enter and he knows it. "Jordan, you are going to let go in my mouth and then I promise you can have me." He goes back down, and he holds me in place as his tongue moves over my soft wet, sensitive area. I close my eyes to the sensations of my lover and let it go, moaning to the pulses that he has caused in my entire body. It's intense and his mouth is still there, sucking and taking in all of my juices. Devon is gentle as I release but doesn't let up and towards the end of it, he is causing more quivers through my body. I glance down at him and find that his eyes are on me, watching the effect of what he has just caused. He takes one final, but strong lick and I gasp.

"You react so well." He smiles and I smirk at him.

"Can I have you now?" I whisper to him almost out of breath.

He moves back up my body and this time he gives me what I want. He is slow and controlled as he enters. He is like no other that I have experienced. He moves in deeper and mindful of me, hc knows that it's a lot for me to take but I am slippery as hell, so it helps. He is rock hard and warm, and I look at his face and he is the one that is now concentrating, his eyes are closed for the moment and his breaths are deep and slow as he moves in and then presses against my pubic bone when he opens his eyes again, a smile crosses his lips.

He says, "Jordan, you feel way better than I have ever imagined." I press into his force and crave my second so bad. I wrap my arms around him feeling his skin and his warmth. Feeling like he is at home inside me, it's so good and I watch beneath him, looking up at his face and seeing his concentration as he starts to move to his rhythm, concentrating on making it last for as long as he can.

His brown eyes open momentarily; they are full of passion and desire as he thrusts deep inside me.

He asks, "How do I feel?" As he slows for a moment, changing pace a thrusting deeper as he goes.

I say breathlessly, "Amazing" there are no other words for this, to crave someone so bad and wait for so long, its ecstasy to have what you have been longing for.

He smiles but never stops his motion and takes a couple of strands of my brown hair and pushes them back out of my face he goes in for another kiss and that's when I explode with him in me. I let out a holler this one even more intense then the last and I can feel my throbs contracting around his shaft. He closes his eyes for a moment, and I see his smile. He slows his rhythm so that he can hold on for that much longer. He enjoys the sensation of me getting off with him inside.

I feel the flood of my passion, the wetness and know that the scent that it brings is driving him even more. He says, "Bad girl, I was trying to make you last a little longer than that. You know what happens now right?"

I know, "You're going back down on me?"

Je growls, "You know it." The feeling of him pulling out makes me sad for just a moment as I want him to stay there but it dissipates as that hungry mouth of his is back on my swollen parts. He laps up all of my juices like some kind of hungry animal and without saying a word he moves my legs up so that my knees are close to my shoulders making my pelvis raise slightly and he enters me again.

This leaves me to stay still and not even try to push back against him but that is okay because his gentleness in the beginning is starting to fade. He knows I want him hard without me saying a word. His motion is stronger and faster, and I know he is working on his.

He says, "You want this?"

I know what he is talking about and in a breath, I answer, "Yes"

He looks at me with intensity that no man has ever looked at me in that way before, "This is my gift to you." He thrusts deep and I whimper with the slight cramp of pain that feels good all at once and I feel him start to pulsate. He holds himself deep in me and empties his passion, filling me up with his love. His throbs last for a moment and see his bliss. He wanted this for so long and now we both have given the other something priceless.

He lets my legs go back to a natural position and I lay there with him still in me and run my fingers through his damp short, thick hair and we lock eyes. He says, "I have never made love to such a beautiful woman." Before I can say a word, his lips are on mine, and I melt into him, my southern man.

Chapter 61
Never Enough

He says, "I have never felt this strongly for another." Again, his lips are soon on mine, and I can never have enough of him.

It is funny how life deals you with the strangest twists, you wish for something and expect it to play out a certain way but then you are given something completely different and unexpected.

Laying here in this hotel room with someone that I have only truly met just a couple of hours before and it feels like it was always supposed to be. This was supposed to happen, and I don't feel a sliver of guilt about it. Time has stood still in this meet, and this is outside and separate to each of our lives. I have not spoken a thing about him, and he has not of me we are just two friends that are granting each other a wish.

I lay there on the bed and Devon got under the sheets with me and I cuddled up to his warm body.

He spots me in thought, and I know before he even asks, "You are deep in thought" he says.

I apologize, "Yes, sorry just thinking about how natural you and I are together."

"That is a good thing, right?" He leans over and watches me with kind regard. Those confident brown eyes make me melt.

I smile, "it is." I give him a kiss, which I intended to be just a little peck except Devon has put his hand behind my head and turns it into something more intimate.

He is just as I had thought, a man who knows his entitlement and with all the confidence in the world takes what he pleases and that is totally okay with me. I lean into him and then guide my hand under the sheets to find that he is standing tall yet again. I pull away at my discovery with a smirk and he chuckles knowing full well what I am thinking.

He speaks. "I am just that easy. That is what you do to me." He explains it with a sort of whatever shrug.

I know what I am going to do next and know that he will enjoy every moment I go in for another kiss on his warm lips and say to him, "I want you to guide me." The sort of light mood that he was in turns to passion and fire. He says nothing and I draw the sheets down to his mid-calf, turn around so that I am nestled up to his side, my back to him and go in for a taste of his rock-hard sex. He is so responsive to my lips, my tongue, and my touch that it surprises me.

I hear him let out a breathless sigh, "Gentler please." I relax my mouth a little more and allow him to touch the back of my throat. He has said to me before that he doesn't think his size is anything to brag about, however I beg to differ its large enough that my jaw feels the pressure of keeping my mouth that opened but it's not enough to make me wish to stop because my own greed is starting to take over. Being able to give pleasure in this way is something that I get off to.

I move up and down his shaft at a steady medium pace and can start to taste his pre-cum juices on my tongue. It's sweet and I know his release is not far away, so I slow for a moment and concentrate on his head and tip and lick his love up while cupping a hand on his forbidden. I take a moment and look back at him. I know that he is on the edge of exploding. He opens his eyes to see why I have slowed, and I smile at him.

"What?" He asks.

I joke, "It doesn't take much to put you on edge."

He sighs, "Only you do this to me."

I ask, "Would you like to come in my mouth, or would you like to be inside me?" I smile as I say this while massaging his hardness.

He demands, "Get on top" to my surprise I thought it would have been the other and I have no objection. He helps me sit on top of him and grabs my hips pulling me down so that I can feel his size. I close my eyes to the amount of pleasure this causes, and I can't help but start to rock my hips back and forth and up and down. He is holding his own release in so that I can get mine first I can tell because as I am moving to my rhythm, he is guiding my hips and forcing me to slow which I do because I know that's what he wants. I move up and down and with the tension building in me I try to ignore it and lean in for a kiss which he gives me.

He whispers in my ear, "Explode on me." It sends a shiver down my spine and makes my insides quiver so much that I let go and moan while I throb with his stiff shaft deep inside. I collapse into his arms, naked and warm and he carefully turns me on my side, spooning me and enters my slick opening from behind. I can feel his breath in my hair and has a hand on my breast feeling as he pushes into me, and his release follows, and he pumps it deep inside.

I feel the firmness in his hands as he holds me in place, making sure that I receive all his studs and when he relaxes, I roll to face him, we are both smiles.

I say playfully, "We are making good time." We are a couple hours into this visit and have already done so much.

He confides, "If this was the only time, I got to have with you on this trip, I would still be leaving happy."

I admit, "I am so happy that we found each other." I go in for another kiss and he gives me his love so freely.

It's hard for us to keep our hands off each other and we don't even bother to restrict ourselves because we know that there is a time limit to this meet. We are both greedy and touch, kiss, and explore one another.

We take this time to rest up from this morning's activity and with the afternoon still ahead of us I ask, "What would you like to do?" We are still lying on the bed with the sheets to cover ourselves and Devon is running his finger up and down my arm. It tickles and I smile at his touch.

He answers, "Well we could take a shower together and then go get something to eat?"

I make a silly face at him, "Why do you say it like that?"

He smirks, "I could lie with you here for the rest of the day and that would be fine with me."

I answer, "Whatever we decide on either way, we will be together for the time that we have."

This time he leans in and gives a gentle kiss on my forehead and says, "Well then my dear, let's shower and go out on a little date."

Our shower, I could say was a little longer than anticipated and Devon insists on washing my body from head to toe but again that causes him to go rock hard. This guy is just that horny, wow! I can't have him sexually frustrated out in public, so I do for him what he had talked about for months and I take him in my mouth in the shower. It's quick but powerful and like the overcharged man that he is he explodes, and I make sure that he is deep in my mouth when he does. His warm love coats the back of my throat. He is mildly sweet, and I swallow and lick his tip clean. His moans tell me that he is feeling good now and I ask, "So how was I?"

"Jordan, everything was a ten." He sighs with a sense of relief in his voice. He helps me to my feet then asks, "How was I?"

I chuckle, "Ten, it was incredible, you cowboys know how to satisfy."

"We aim to please." He winks at me with those doe eyes of his.

I am clean as can be at this point and we finish up with soaping him up and rinsing him off. We go through our rituals of getting ready, which is kind of funny because technically this is our first date, yet we have already fucked each other's brains out.

We both seem to be ready around the same time and he gives me a nod and extends his arm for me to take and with that we leave the hotel room for an adventure.

Chapter 62
Love Burgers

We are both in the rental car, Devon in the driver's seat and me in the passenger.

I ask him, "So what were you hungry for?"

He smirks, saying, "Are you asking, besides you?" I sense cheesiness in his voice.

I laugh, "Yes Devon, my god. So, were you thinking, fast food, a deli, a restaurant?"

He smiles, "Your decision, tell me where to drive."

I smile, ah man I can be the most indecisive person at times I think for a moment, where can I take him that is authentic and where I will not be recognized. I have a restaurant downtown in mind and reply, "A restaurant, do you like burgers?"

He nods, "love burgers"

I say, "Okay this place is not your typical burger place. They have some unique recipes, should be fun."

He nods and says, "Sounds great Jordan okay tell me where to go."

I instruct, "Okay turn right now." I can tell that he loves to drive, and I feel safe with him in the driver's seat. He is calm and in control and that says a lot with him being in a city that he isn't familiar with.

I steal glances of him and get caught, he chuckles, "What is it girl?"

"This is just surreal." I explain with a smile.

He looks at me, "Trust me, I know how you feel." Changing subjects he asks, "Where is it?"

I look ahead and say, "Oh, the place is just coming up on the right. There is a spot right there." He pulls in and I take my seatbelt off and go to try the door and he distracts me with his hand on my arm, I turn to see, and he leans in for another kiss.

He is getting in as much as possible and he says, "Allow me." I give him a sideways glance but then realize as he comes around and opens the car door.

I blush at his chivalry, "You are so kind to me my cowboy."

He gives me his arm, "Only for the one that I love. So, is that the place, there?"

I follow his gaze and confirm, "It is."

He replies, "I can already see that you have great taste."

We enter, the greeter gives us a look of knowing the people standing before her are an item. Geez, I try to hide my worry, I think I picked a place where I wouldn't get spotted by people that I know and to think that if I were to be spotted, I was going to introduce Devon as a co-worker or an old friend, yah right Jordan that would go over well.

The greeter says her welcome and leads us to a table for two, before she leaves, she asks, "What can I get you two to drink?"

Devon answers for the both of us, "Two Long Island Iced Teas."

The server smiles, "Okay great, I'll be back soon with your drinks and to take your order." Devon gives the server that confidant smile of his as she has put the order to memory and departs.

Devon turns his attention back on me and asks, "So, tell me, what is the best thing about being able to see me in person?"

I gush, "Everything, your looks, voice, scent, your touch; I love all of it." I explain, leaning forward in my seat.

He smiles, "I have to say that it's ditto for me too. So, what's so authentic about this place?"

My gaze goes to our table setting and I suggest, "Open the menu."

He sets the menu down on the table before him, opening it and starts to read through, "Mac and cheese on a burger; peanut butter on another? Oh wow, okay I see how this is going to be an interesting meal."

I explain, "I know that it sounds weird, but they are really great combinations. You have to be honest and tell me once you taste the food, if you do like it."

"I will, I promise." He answers.

The server returns with our drinks and asks for the order and again Devon orders for the both of us, two mac and cheeseburgers. She collects the menus and departs for the kitchen.

I say, "So, I hadn't thought to ask and now I am curious. So, I know that you were in BC with your brother to get a lay of the land for your book and you made up this trip to the capital for more book research. But answer me this, I know you said that your book is now in the reviewing stage. Does that mean that any findings from your trip to BC could be added or are you preparing for a sequel?"

He smiles in response to my question, enjoying the fact that I take interest in his other passion and answers, "Review is never final, so with this trip, I did notice some minor things that I will include."

I lean forward, "Like what?"

He gives me a dark glance, clears his throat, and says so that only I can hear, "Like what it feels like to be inside such a hot woman."

I lean back in my seat and admit, "Ha, I didn't know you were writing erotica?"

He shrugs saying, "I'm not, every book needs a bit of fire to it and let me ask, how is your writing coming?" He smirks and takes a sip of his drink.

I chuckle; he knows full well that he and I, whatever this is that we have is fueling a love story. I look at his hand that is now holding mine on the table looking at the sheer size of his in comparison to my own then look up at him, "Oh, I think you know how it's coming."

He suggests, "You know we can create some more moments for your book."

I know that he has a very dirty side. I wonder what goes through his head, whatever it is it's always for pleasure, so I am curious what he has in store. I answer him, "I hope we do."

He says, "Jordan, come sit with me." He motions me to him.

II cautiously ask, "Devon what are you up to?" He makes a glance and I know he wants me to sit on his lap. I'm not used to public affection, but fair game he warned me that this was something that he enjoyed doing. I sit on him and know, he whispers in my ear, "I had you all morning and I want more." His hardness is pushing up against me.

He is ready for more and we are at the restaurant. I feel a little self-conscious with me sitting on him. I give him a kiss on the cheek and try to get up to return to my seat, but he holds me on him.

I complain, "Devon?"

He grumbles, "I can't help myself."

I whisper in his ear, "You are a horn ball. I promise one more go, but after we eat."

I try to get up to move back to my seat, but he holds me in place, I give him a friendly but serious glance, trying to show him that I mean business.

He asks, "Uncomfortable, are we?"

I murmur, "A little, you know I prefer my privacy."

He says, "I know my hottie. I won't have you feel that way, but there is one more thing that I want?" He closes his eyes and puckers his lips, and it makes me giggle and I give him another intimate moment before returning back to my spot.

Just as I take my seat our food arrives. It's funny how we are together. We both know with sitting across from each other that this day is still not over. We finish and he insists on paying when the bill comes.

I say, "Devon let me get this, it's the least I can do for everything that you have done."

The southern gentlemen in him won't hear it, "Jordan, I would take it as an insult if you didn't accept my gratitude." The alpha male is shining through those brown eyes of his and I know not to object and accept.

Looking up at him I answer, "Thank you."

He smiles back, "You're welcome. Let's get you back to your car, but I have one more thing planned before this day is done."

I give him the "what" look, and he just gives me that mysterious sideways glance and opens the passenger side door for me. I know Devon wants another go but what, God I hope he's not thinking some form of public display especially in the middle of the afternoon. We start driving but we aren't going in the direction that we came.

I ask, "Do you know where you are driving?"

He asks, "Show me that forest where you walk on your lunch breaks, there is a place to park there right?"

I explain, "There is, okay take a right here." The drive this time is a little quieter; I guess we are both digesting our late meal. I jump in, "It's a left here", and he brings the car to a slow and turns into the gravel driveway to the forest trails. He brings the car to a stop and turns it off.

He smirks at me, "You know that this morning was just not enough for me."

I admit, "I knew that when I sat on your lap."

He says, "Then you know what I want." He has spent money making the trip to see me and I need and want to show my gratitude for all that he has done.

I smile and say, "I know what you want."

I remove my seat belt and lean over to get closer to him and unbutton his pant and unzip to let his hard on, free for me to play with. It stands tall and the tip is a shade of purple from all the blood pumping in it. I lean down into his lap to put my lips to his member and it's warm, smooth, and already starting to leak in anticipation. My mouth moves down his shaft slowly and he lets out a gasp, "Oh that feels wonderful." I continue to do what he likes. I swallow his early excitement and continue to work on pleasuring him, allowing him to touch the back of my throat. I can feel his pelvis start to thrust into my mouth. He is getting closer. His breathing is heavy, not controlled and I know this is going to be a strong release. I start to slow but it drives him nuts and he puts his hand on the back of my head for me to take him deeper. Men often forget that we all have gag reflexes and before this turns bad, I put a hand on the base of his shaft to prevent him from forcing me to gag. I say nothing, he is in the moment and I hope for this to be good for him. He is too long to fit in my mouth completely and I make up for it by continuing to let his head deep into my mouth and stroke the base of his shaft with my small light hand, to the rhythm of my mouth.

He is losing control and his fingers run through my hair as he pushes his pelvis for me to take him. There is no way I can go anywhere as he grips my head. I don't mind, it makes me wet knowing that he likes it that much. He orders, "You will swallow." He pulses his hot lava to the back of my throat, and I do as I am told; I have to, and I want to for him. I'm gentle and close my lips around him as he gives me all. It's warm, and amazing that he is able to come so much at the thought of me. His sighs tell me he is happy, and I have swallowed a few times. I don't want to end it for him he will need to do that and say when to stop, seeing he has a firm grip of me. His hand relaxes and allows me to sit up but before I do, I run his length deep into my mouth and then end it with a kiss on his tip.

I sit up and he is the most relaxed man I have ever seen. "God Jordan, you know how to please this cowboy." This time it's me leaning in to take a kiss from him. He approves of all of it and shows me with his affection in wrapping his protecting arms around me and tasting my succulent lips.

I whisper to him, "You know that I don't want to leave but I must get back to my car."

He nods, "I know Jordan."

I ask, "What are you going to do later tonight?" I run my fingers through his short brown hair and tracing his features with my fingertips.

He grins, "That my dear is a surprise."

I smile and touch my fingers to his lips and say, I nod and reply, "Then I will anxiously wait until then."

The drive back to my car feels like seconds, I love this man so much more after seeing him in person. It makes me sad to part ways. We quietly roll up to my car and know that it's time.

Devon is the first to say, "We have tomorrow, go and be with your husband, I will be here for you tomorrow morning."

I smile and ask, "Promise?"

He nods, "Of course, silly, I wouldn't have made the journey all this way."

We embrace one last time, I hold him and feel his heartbeat, his warmth, his soul, and he is the bigger person and holds me at arm's length, he reminds, "You are going to be late if you don't go. Have a good night my hottie."

I put on a brave smile and get out of his rental car looking over my shoulder. He is waiting like a gentleman to make sure that I return to my car okay. I get into my own car, start the engine and smell myself; I think that I smell like Devon and so I take one sanitary wipe in the back seat and bring it forward so that I can mask his smell. Devon is still waiting for me so rather than wipe myself down here I'll just do it on the drive to pick up Josh. I pull out of my spot, wave goodbye to Devon, he blows me a kiss. I make the trip to Josh.

Chapter 63
The Good Thing

I pull up to Josh's work and to be honest I am a little worried that he will pick up on something. The good thing is I am a few minutes early so I park in front. I check myself in the mirror, no marks or messed up makeup. I now smell like sanitation wipes because that is all I had in the car to wipe off with, which is okay, I rather that than the scent of Devon, although if I didn't need to worry about Josh, I wouldn't want to get rid of Devon's amazing scent. Oh well, I keep telling myself that I still have tomorrow with him, my secret love.

There he is. Josh is walking out of the building, and he looks to be in a good mood, I smile at him, and he returns the smile and comes up to the car.

He opens the passenger side door and takes a seat next to me, tossing his bag over the seat so that it lands in the back. He says, "Hey Jordan, what's up?"

I smile, shrug, and say, "Not much, had a productive day got a lot done."

Josh says, "That's good, do you mind if I take a nap on the way home?"

I say, "I don't mind driving." It's a good thing that he wants to nap which means I don't need to tell him a string of lies about my day. I hear the creek of his seat as he tilts it back so that he can rest.

As we start driving, I don't get off Scott free Josh grumbles, "Why does it smell like sanitation wipes?"

I explain, "Oh, my makeup was running in my eyes, so I wiped my face off." Well more than just my face, but this cover should suffice.

Josh complains, "Holy it's burning my nostrils."

I murmur, "Sorry love." I shrug and peek over at him. He seems to take no more notice, which to my relief makes me relax a bit more. The last thing that I need is to feel nervous and have this all go to hell.

He mumbles, "Maybe take a shower when you get home." He reclines his seat back a bit more and covers his face with his baseball hat and starts his nap.

Well, yes, I need to shower. Surely if I don't, Devon's scent is likely still on other parts of my body and I don't wish for Josh to pick up on it.

The night goes by easily, I shower get changed and wonder if this transaction with Devon will work. Devon is confident that it will, and I am hoping for the same. I find myself wondering about him, and what he is doing in this moment.

Chapter 64
Ready for Devon

Today I am ready for my Devon and pick out that simple black dress for him that hugs me in all the right places and shows off all of my sexy curves. Devon has said to me before that his wish is to see me in a dress and I won't let him down.

I meet Josh in the kitchen for breakfast, he says, "Hey good morning sleepy head, come to join me, have you?"

I yawn, "Yep" I go over and give him a hug and kiss.

Josh comments, "Who are you trying to impress today?" He looks me up and down taking notice that I have dressed up.

I explain, "Oh, my boss mentioned that a client may be visiting early this afternoon so I thought it would be best and dress to impress."

He nods saying, "I see, I see" I have to admit that even after seven years of marriage it's still a nice feeling that your husband takes notice. I smile to myself; I must look hot and that is the look that I am going for to see Devon today and that is even if my dress is off for the majority of the day.

I help out with what is left to put together for breakfast and sit down with Josh for a bit before heading into work.

Between bites Josh mentions, "I forgot to tell you, I checked my schedule yesterday and my second job has called me in to work this evening so we will both be taking cars to town."

Oh, this is amazing, I am internally jumping for joy, but I can't share my joy in this moment. I need to act bummed because this means that he is working late.

I glance at him and ask, "What time do you expect to be home?"

He says, "It will be either 9:30 PM or 10:00 PM at the latest."

I nod and reply, "Okay, just curious."

Josh asks, "Is something wrong?"

I shake my head and answer, "No, I know that this happens, no worries. I will try to wait up for you."

His blue eyes meet mine, "Something tells me you will be asleep by the time I get home."

I smirk to myself, yes who knows with everything that Devon wants to do; maybe I will be tuckered out. I try to say with a straight face, "I will try my best to stay up for you, no promises."

Josh gives me one of those sideways glances, "I saw that smirk and doubt you will even try to stay awake."

I giggle, "Oh babes I will do my best, no promises."

We finish our meals together, pack our bags and head our separate ways to work; well for me it's to meet Devon for day two of amazing sex. Somewhere during that time, I email my boss telling her that I am sick and won't be in.

The drive in is an easy one, no traffic and when I arrive in my work parking lot where I had parked the day before I see Devon already parked and waiting for me in his rental. We exchange smiles and I leave my car to get into his.

I walk over to the passenger side and hop in and say, "Good morning honey, did you miss me last night."

Devon explains, "Like you would not believe my beautiful Canadian girl." He leans in for a kiss and while our lips are locked, he takes a hand and runs it up my dress and at his touch I put my hand over his wondering one and guide it further to my wetness.

He pulls away just a bit, smiles, and says, "I really like your dress, let's take a drive to that abandoned parking lot over there and see what we can do."

The office building next to mine is no longer in use. It is in the early stages of demolition. The building is barricaded off with fence but the parking lot remains opened and in use. It is a perfect spot to do stuff and not worry.

Devon pulls in and parks the car and I know what I want, I'm hungry and so is he. I feel for his hard man and bring him out of his pants. It's waiting for me to just hop on top.

I give him a lick and am about to go over to his side to get on top when he says no.

I give him a pouty sideways glance and he explains, "I have something else in mind."

Before I can say anything, he gets out of the car, walks around to my side, and opens the door and says, "Get out of the car." A little confused I get out.

"Turn around." He orders. Slowly I turn so that I am facing the passenger seat, my door is still open. He lifts my dress, exposing me to the breezy spring air, takes his hand to my back and without saying a word bends me forward and pulls my thong to the side and then enters my hot little pocket.

He thrusts deep and slowly. I exhale at the amazing sensation. He whispers in my ear questions that I don't think he intends for me to answer, "Do you like that? I have been thinking about you all night, thinking about our day yesterday and I am hungry this morning."

I shiver and sigh, "Mm you feel amazing, keep doing that."

His hands hold my hips firm as he pushes into me. It's a bit cold this morning but I can no longer feel the cold. My body is on fire with passion and excitement. What am I thinking; someone at work may see me? No Jordan don't be silly, it's still early.

This is a quickie I know it and I know that I am about to explode, and he can feel it too. He reaches around me and rubs my clit with his fingers and whispers in my ear, "Explode for me." That sets me off and like his good girl I get mine while trying to hold in my moans. He replies, "That a girl."

I can hear him licking my desire from his finger then he places his hand back on my hip and goes at me that much harder. His is building fast and his dick feels so warm inside me. He slows and lets out a sigh and I can feel his dick throbbing, pumping everything that I so crave deep inside.

I know well enough to stay still and allow him to finish before doing anything he sighs a sound of relief and says, "Best breakfast ever." He slowly pulls out, zips up and like a gentleman helps me up and pulls my dress down so that I am no longer exposed.

I ask him, "Speaking of breakfast have you had one?"

He says, "No not yet, only a taste of you." He smirks.

I reply, "Dirty Cowboy; let's go get you something to eat and maybe a coffee? I have a great place in mind." We go through a drive through to my favorite coffee shop and pick up some bacon, egg and cheese sandwiches and drinks and he drives us to where he wants to go. The day has just begun, and it is still very early. We beat the morning traffic back to his hotel and head up to his room.

As we get in, I have to ask, it's bugging me, "Devon?"

He glances over, "Yes?"

I ask. "So back there in the parking lot, was that the thing that you had planned for us?"

He has that grin on his face, the grin that says, I am hiding something, he explains, "That was one of them." I grin back at him with a sideways glance, and he explains some more. "While we were apart, I did some shopping." Oh boy, if it's gifts, I didn't buy him anything. I feel a little nervous with not knowing what he means by it.

He walks over to the corner of the room, on the other side of the bed on the floor he lifts a bag and puts it on the bed. The bag is a plain white one, so I am still not sure where he did his shopping. He pulls out a couple of packages and lays them on the bed. I look at the packages and then look back at him. He chuckles, "Are you just going to stand there and stare, come over and see." I'm still not sure what's on the bed and approach, taking my time with each step because I came empty handed. Oh boy I see what it is; I must have made a face because he starts laughing. "You know just taking home a pair of your soaked panties wasn't going to cut it." There is a dildo and a pussy mold kit on the bed.

I tilt my head and ask, "How does that work?"

He smiles saying, "Oh, don't you worry my dear, I have got that covered. First let's get started."

He approaches, lifts me up and places me on the bed and joins me. As I lay back, he starts kissing me tenderly, his tongue is so gentle, and he does it in a way that makes me crave him more. His taste, his soft lips, and the way that he holds me, it is like I am the only person that matters in his world.

My hands go down to him and as always, he is ready. He takes my wondering hand and holds it in his own. He doesn't wish me to play with him. My cowboy wants to stay in control and that is okay with me.

His kisses move down my neck, and he goes in for a feel, my dress is still on however he manages to find a nipple and squeezes lightly. "Cold, are we?"

I admit, "I am horny actually." I play back.

He says, "Good, I like it when you want me. Shall we get you out of your clothes?"

I pull my dress up over my head and remove my bra and then my soaked thong.

I am about to just toss the thong on the floor with my other clothing and Devon catches my wrist. Surprised, I had forgotten for a split second. He shakes his head no, and says, "Those are now mine, hand them over."

I smirk; he did all of that just to make my girl's scent get onto that thong. I hand the thong over like I lost some bet, and with that he takes them in his hand then smells, "Jordan you have no idea how good you smell." I watch him and he even takes a lick. I have not had a man do that. This is different for me to watch a man go nuts over my scent and as weird as it is, I am flattered that he is that into me. For a moment he leaves the bed and tucks the thong away in his luggage and returns with the dildo and pussy mold kits with all of the packaging already removed and ready to go. He removes his clothing.

Je says, "Now I just need one more thing to remember you." I lie there as he puts the mold on me.

I say, "I feel like I am at the doctor's office or something." I make a face at him. This is sort of killing the mood with having the stuff placed over my clit.

He glances up, "Has the doctor made a mold of your pussy also?"

I reply, "No!" I stick my tongue out at him.

He demands, "Stop being a goof Jordan let me have what is mine and take it home with me so that I can have it forever." His words have a bit of seriousness to them and when he speaks, he says so politely, his assertion makes me listen to his desires and I allow that for him. I lay still as the mold sets. The least I can do is give him a parting gift that will help his memories of me last longer. He carefully removes the mold, and I watch curiously. He smiles as he holds it.

I ask, "Let me, see?"

He lies down next to me with it in his hand and shows me. I comment, "Oh, my so that's what it looks like up close."

He says, "You are silly; you know what you look like."

I explain, "I do but just haven't quite seen it from this angle. It looks a little different to me up close like this."

Devon admits, "You have the nicest looking pussy that I have ever seen. Mind you, I have only slept with four women before you. You have a beautiful little clit that swells up so fast. It makes me want to munch on you so badly." He gives me another kiss, a slow and tender peck on the cheek and then takes the mold and places it on the table to set completely and returns once more.

He has a permanent boner; just like me being so responsive to him with being wet. This time it's his turn to make a mold of himself, and with all his pent-up lust his dick is a huge, massive, thick, veined erection. I don't have to do much and just watch him make a mold of himself for me.

"What color is it going to be?" I ask.

He says, "Green"

I reply, "Green, it will be like I am masturbating to an alien dick." I make another playful face at him.

He shakes his head saying. "Oh Jordan, I know you will like it, besides what does the color mean to you anyway? Knowing how horny you are all the time I would imagine that my mold will be in you a hell of a lot." He winks.

I shrug, "Yes, you got me there. So, what's with the color green? Did you pick it, or did it just come in that color?"

He confirms, "I picked it. It's my favorite color." He does a little half shrug as he holds the kit in place.

I nod, "Ah yes, I remember you telling me that. Okay green, great color, I am sure it's going to get plenty of use my sexy cowboy."

He growls, "I know that it will, and you know I am going to have to ask for a video of you using it."

I chuckle, "You think of everything don't you?"

He says, "You know it." Devon leaves the bed for a moment to take care of the mold and returns, still hard and ready to go. We hardly need to talk. We know what the other wants and go with the motion of desire and fulfill each other's needs.

First, he climbs on top, he knows what I crave, and he pumps me hard but slowly, trying to make this one last longer than the quickie we had earlier in the parking lot. His rhythm with me is amazing and I lie still for him to move and allow my hands without even thinking about it to feel his body, his strong chest and shoulders and then draw his face close to mine to get his kisses that I crave. He is the best kisser I have ever locked lips with, and I enjoy tasting him. After some time, he takes my legs and bends my knees up to my shoulder so that my pelvis is raised for him. I know that he is getting close. He plunges back into my warm wetness, and I feel his body shake, he is trying to hold onto his for me to get mine.

I am so incredibly close, I bite my bottom lip from the tension building up inside and I catch him watching me, his eyes are full of lust while I enjoy him. My breathing is strong, and I know mine is here. I let out a cry of passion as I vibrate, my juices engulf him as I throb with his massive shaft there to feel it and he keeps me pinned beneath him. My eyes open and close at the sensation as I let go and I force myself to look up at him.

He says, "You have no idea how that makes me feel." I feel him shudder with all his own built-up passion and he starts to pump into me, harder and deeper and I know his own is here. His second explosion of the morning is let go. His pulses are similar to mine, and he lets a grunt escape his lips. I love this, this moment that we are sharing, he wants to hold onto this memory of us and so do I. I watch my secret lover with the total look of bliss on his face. His loads are a lot, and he is still pulsing as I draw him in and hold onto him as he is over top of me.

Chapter 65
With Him

I lay there with him. Devon now beside me, the warmth of his body is comforting and the feeling I get after this is I believe that the gift he has given me will work. I relax to allow the passion that he gives so tenderly the chance to work.

His hand is lightly touching my body, tracing, feeling, and touching my perky breasts then moving lightly down my smooth abdomen and rest on my stomach he asks, "What's on your mind?"

I turn to face him, "I think this will work, I just have a feeling that I can't explain and it's different from when I had tried with the IUI treatment. This time it's different."

He smiles, "It will work. You just have to allow it and relax." His warm hand on me is comforting and I feel at home in his arms. He continues, "I want this to work for you. I know that we have talked about this meeting for a long time and for me, it wasn't just about getting laid, you are my best friend and I want to give you what you desire, it will work I know."

I smile shyly at him, looking into those honest warm brown eyes of his. I say, "You and I would make some beautiful babies."

He laughs, "Oh you know it Jordan, you are gorgeous and hey when you add a sexy cowboy to the mix it's a win, win."

I give him a playful shove, he says, "What? It's true."

I reply, "Yah I know." This time I roll myself on top of his naked body and kiss him again.

After a few moments he asks, "What would you like to do my friend?"

I yawn, "Oh I don't know, what time is it now?"

He glances at his watch and says, "10:35 AM"

I joke, "We are making good use of our time, two encounters and it's still mid-morning." I glance at him for his reaction.

He chuckles, "Yes, this sounds wrong to say it, but my boys need some time to relax for a bit. I will have you, no doubt before the day is done, it's just I know that I emptied everything I had into you."

I smirk at him, "Can't keep up, can you?"

He tickles me, "Oh I can keep up, I need a bit of time to build up another good load for you. Come let's shower and maybe we can go exploring."

This shower is tamer than the one yesterday, however it is intimate. We take care in washing each other and exchanging a few kisses in the process and before we know it, we are out on the road on our adventure for today.

I guess in his time away from me last night he did some research online to see where all the landmarks are in the city for the drive, he hasn't asked me for any direction and is on route to places he had in mind. We find ourselves parked downtown in the market and are soon walking the street and browsing from shop to shop. It is a sunny spring day. The air still has a hint of the fading coolness that winter leaves behind, but the air has that smell, of budding trees and things coming to life.

He says, "You know Jordan, you really do live in a beautiful city."

I look at him and say, "I know; I just like to complain, I guess. If I could change one thing about it, that would be the fact that it gets cold. I would rather live in a warmer climate. That's just me. I guess I could hope that global warming sets in eventually." I make a face at him to show that I was only kidding.

He puts his arm around me as we walk down the street, "You are such a goof. You know how I used to live in Rochester, I do miss the seasons changing, and it's different from in Texas. Texas is nice don't get me wrong but there is no history like with the cities in the north and with no seasons it gets a little tiring at times."

I explain, "You already know that I have only really lived here my entire life, so I don't really know any different. I have visited other cities, so I know that in comparison this is a nice place."

Lunchtime is fast approaching, and we know this because as we walk there are rich smells in the air of many different kinds of food, it's consuming our senses. We stop in front of a New Orleans themed restaurant, and he asks, "How about we eat here?"

"Sure" I smile. I have eaten here before, and the food is amazing. Devon has good taste. We are greeted and seated, and a waiter comes within moments to take our order.

Devon orders for the two of us, "We will have a pitcher of your white wine, an order of Creole Mussels as a starter and two orders of the Jambalaya."

The waiter smiles and tells him, "Good choice." He collects the menus from the table and departs.

I look at Devon a little surprised that he ordered all that and he knows I am about to comment when he explains, "Remember way back when, we had a conversation on how we met our current partners?"

I answer, "I do."

He explains, "Well, I remember telling you how I met mine at a party where the main dish was mussels and you questioned me on the dish, if eating mussels really makes people horny and I recall you saying that you had never tried them and wanted to one day." I chuckle, and before I can say anything the waiter returns with our pitcher of white. I extend my hand to pour a glass, but Devon beats me to it and fills our glasses up.

He remarks, "Are you thirsty babe, or just speechless?" He hands me my glass.

I admit, "I am a little of both."

He says, "Well, I have a feeling that you will enjoy what I have ordered for us and if you don't you can punish me in the hotel room later." He smiles and takes a sip of his wine.

I grumble, "Bad boy"

He replies, "Bad boy, that you love, like a moth to the flame, is that how the saying goes?"

I say, "Yes, it's something like that." I feel my cheeks flush and my eyes fall to the table for a second knowing that Devon knows me too well.

The waiter returns with our mussels' appetizer, and I am already a little nervous because I have no idea how to eat them. He sets the dish down at our table and provides us two bowls with water and a lemon wedge as well as two empty bowls.

The waiter says before departing, "Enjoy your meal."

I look at the intimidating dish with these large black opened shells where I can see the meat inside and there is some sort of red based sauce that is slathered in and oh yes two bread sticks. My first thought is to go for the bread, and I reach out and Devon stops me, knowing what I am going for.

He swats my hand away and says, "Ah, ah, ah, it would be a shame if you filled up on bread. Give them a chance."

I confess, "You know I have no idea how to eat these."

He acknowledges, "I figured as much. Watch me." He picks up a shell and breaks it open, one side has the meat and the other is just the shell. He takes the empty shell and uses it as a spoon to scoop out the meat and then eats it. He smiles as he finishes his first one and says, "You're up my dear, these are good." He puts his shells into one of the bowls that have been provided.

I follow his lead and slowly put it to my mouth. I can smell the light scent of garlic, onion powder and the scents that come with a spicy dish. There is not a fishy smell that I had imagined with this sort of dish. Putting on a brave face I put it in my mouth and take a taste and to my surprise he is right, the texture, sort of reminds me of eating a really good mushroom, the meat is tender but is a little chewy too, I swallow and being the type of person who wears her emotions on her sleeve, I smile.

He laughs, "You are too cute. You like them, don't you?"

I nod, "I do, thank you for ordering them. If it were me, I would have been too much of a chicken to order these."

He goes for another and in between chews he answers, "Yes, I figured as much."

I brag to him, "So, I have had another first with you with tasting mussels for the first time."

His eyes are happy, and he answers, "I am honored."

We eat, laugh and flirt. I look around the restaurant, there are others dining but the restaurant isn't packed, and I don't recognize anyone which is just perfect because I don't need to make up any lies. We finish the appetizer, and the waiter returns with our main dish. The best way to describe jambalaya is it is a rice-based dish with vegetables and shrimp. This is another first for me, but I feel a little more confident in trying this one because there is nothing weird to do like opening shells with the mussels.

I take a bite and it's another flavorful dish, spicy and good, Devon is two for two. He asks, "Do you like your food?"

I smile, "I do, a man with good taste that is sexy." I admit to him.

He replies, "I think that's the mussels talking."

I giggle, "Yes maybe." By the time we finished I know I have already eaten too much. I was stuffed, and now I have some more favorites to keep in mind when ordering at restaurants. The waiter asks if we would like dessert and coffee, Devon looks at me and I shake my head no.

He answers the waiter, "No thank you, just the bill please." The waiter departs.

Devon turns back to me and leans forward to get closer and says, "No dessert, hunh?"

I finish my last sip of wine and respond in a hungry voice, "You are my dessert."

The waiter returns with the bill, Devon takes his wallet out and puts a couple of bills within the pocket that the bill is placed in, folds it closed and places it on the table. He gets up and extends his arm for me to take, "Let's not keep you from your dessert." I smile take his arm and we head back to the hotel.

Chapter 66
Craving for Him

It is the early afternoon, and I am already craving for him to be inside me. The elevator ride up to his room is all hands, touching, feeling, rubbing, I don't even know if we were alone on the ride up, that's how much I didn't care.

He swipes his card, and we stumble in, each removing our clothes as fast as we can, and he lays me down and has me deep and hard. Heavy breathing, passion, and the scent of wine on our breath, his pants somehow managed to land beside us on the bed and in the moment, he stops for a second.

"What?" I ask.

"I forgot I wanted something else to remember you by." He says.

I laugh, "Isn't the mold of my pussy and my wet panties enough?" I am growing hungrier for him because I have gotten close to getting my own and I try to lure him back in with pressing my body up against him.

He says in a breath, "I want something to remember this by." With him still inside me he reaches over to the pocket of his pants and pulls out his phone and that's when my heart stops and I slide out from under him.

I beg, "Please no pictures; it's not a good idea for you or me."

He is careful in his reply, "Jordan, I promise I won't take a picture of our faces. I just want to snap a couple of photos of me halfway in you." I'm worried, he continues, "I wouldn't put us in a compromising situation. I promise you that and I would keep these pictures safe."

"Okay" I answer.

He puts the phone back down on the bed and focuses his attention back on me, leaning over me, kissing me, and guiding me down beneath him. As I inch my way back, I feel his warm erection on my stomach then move its way down and it's soon resting just above my opening. I want him inside and try to guide him there. He stops kissing me for a second to say, "Jordan not yet, my picture."

He leans over to grab his phone. The first pictures are of his swollen member resting at the entrance to my wet lips. He slowly places himself inside me and I steal a thrust bringing him in some more.

"Bad girl" He grins.

"Bad girl, you are the one taking photos of us." I reply.

He smiles and warns, "Stay still and behave."

He takes another couple of photos and this time it's of himself halfway inside my wet, slimy pocket. He takes a moment to view all the photos and I let out a sigh, "God Jordan you are so demanding. Let your cowboy at least have a look at his photos." He smiles down at me, and I smile back, sexually frustrated but I know he will deliver so I wait for him to review his pictures. I watch his face as he swipes with his phone and smiles and then places the phone back on the bed.

"Satisfied?" I ask.

He confirms, "Very much" He enters me with a tantalizing deep thrust that makes my entire body shiver with pleasure.

"You like how I feel?" he asks in a labored voice.

I whisper, "Yes, I love the way that you fuck me."

This time there is no switching up positions or anything like that. It's just two greedy people having their way with one another and each time we do this, it gets better. Devon always has felt amazing, it's just that every time we do it, we learn more about what pleases the other and this time is no different. I close my eyes and try to stay in this moment as long as I can. His breathing, his scent his passion filled thrusts; I know that he is enjoying me as much as I am him. He knows my rhythm and is working on my climax.

I don't want to come; I want to hold on for just a bit longer, but Devon is getting really good at knowing me and I let go and vibrate. I open my eyes to see him watching me and enjoying the fact that I am enjoying him so much. He smiles and without skipping a beat he starts on his own.

I am sensitive and slicker than ever. His rhythm is faster than mine and I lay there and enjoy the sensation, his is building, faster and harder, and then right before he lets go, he slows and lets a grunt of satisfaction leave his lips as he fills me up with passion.

We lie there for a few moments. I know that this day is coming to an end, and we will eventually part ways for who knows how long. Time will only tell. I try not to think about it and just lie there in his arms as I allow my body to accept his gift in hopes that it works.

This life of mine, what a tease, I am in love with two very different men. I still have Devon here for the bit of time I have left. We kiss and he knows with having had the experience of having his own family knows that I need to remain for a bit to let his gift get settled in.

He says to me, "I know our time is coming to an end. I want you to know that you have made me the happiest man in the world. I know that this is going to work for you, and I am happy and honored that you allowed me to give you, my gift."

"Thank you" is all I can let out. I know that I mean more to him than just sex, we have become the closest of friends and for him to make this commitment to me, words cannot describe. I don't feel used in anyway and I know he doesn't either. It means so much to me that this gift is coming from him, my friend, and my smart, sexy, southern gentleman.

Devon suggests, "We should shower." He takes my hand and leads me to the washroom. It's a quick wash off as time is starting to speed up and I must return to my car soon.

I dress and he is just doing up his pants when I say, "Wait"

He asks, "What Jordan?"

I say, "One more parting gift, lie on the bed." He doesn't want to object but he shows concern because he is aware that's it is getting late in the afternoon. I explain, "It is okay, I have time, Josh and I took two cars to work today, I don't need to pick him up."

He smiles like he has won the lottery and says a simple, "Okay"

He lies back on the bed, and I open the zipper to his pants. Wow what a guy, after all the sex today he is swelling to the occasion, and I start off with gently stroking him. His soft smooth skin is growing warm as the blood swells in his member. I take him in my mouth and suck like I would a flavorful lollypop.

He loves this and loves that I love giving him this. My licks and sucks are light and gentle as I taste him on my tongue. I start to take him deeper into my mouth and with that I hear him sigh, "Wow Jordan."

I'm smiling on the inside; he is enjoying this as I continue, up and down and deep into my mouth. I continue for my own guilty pleasure. I touch his testicles with my warm hand. Feeling the texture of the skin and I begin to speed up with each suck and lick. He reaches his hand to my head, and I know that he is about to release, his hand is like a warning, and it hits the back of my throat with force as I swallow his warm love.

He whispers, "Wow Jordan"

I lick his tip clean and give him a kiss on his purple head which makes him shiver and then I zip his pant back up. I say, "You have been more than just a good friend in these last couple of days. I just wanted to give you one more thank you."

He sits up and says, "You're welcome and thank you for giving this man something that he hadn't felt in a long time."

I ask, "What is that?"

He replies, "To be loved and desired by someone as beautiful as you."

I say, "Ah Devon, I am going to miss you so much, you have no idea."

He says, "Oh, I know, I have an idea of it, I'm in the same boat, I'm going to return home and will be already planning my next escape to see you, trust me."

There isn't a rush to get back to my car like there was the day before. However, I still need to part ways as I know Josh will be calling the home phone during the evening to check in on me and if I am not home to take his call it will cause alarm.

We leave the hotel room for the last time. Devon will be spending one more night. His plane departs early the next morning. On the drive back to the car I can't help but hold one of his hands in my own. I can be so clingy at times, but I don't care. This is what my heart wants and touching him in our final moments together brings me happiness.

It's a bit later in the evening when Devon pulls into my work parking lot, it is almost empty.

He puts the car in park and says, "So this is it."

I look at him as the words leave his lips and unsuspecting to my own reaction my eyes start to swell with tears. I say nothing and a tear runs down my cheek.

He whispers, "Ah Jordan come here." I lean in and he wraps his arms around me in a warm embrace. "Don't think of it as goodbye." He gently wipes away a tear with his thumb.

I say, "I know it's just that time passes so fast with the ones that you love." He smiles at me, and he is trying to play the tuff guy, but I catch a tear escape him too and its reassurance that he feels the same.

I calm myself and give him a brave smile and with that he takes that as one final invitation for a kiss. It is a kiss that I can't get tired of. I desire Devon's kiss and all the passion that comes with it, he holds me in his arms and whispers the words, "I love you."

I whisper the words back to him and it's hard to let go. As seconds pass the silliness in me is rising up. Deep down I don't want this to be a sad moment, so I hold onto him a little longer. There is a length of time when a hug starts to become awkward, and my silly side wants it to go to that length and I feel him start to squirm a little and that is when I tighten my grip.

He finally says, "Ah Jordan?"

I glance at him and reply, "Yes?"

"You, need to let go." He says politely.

"Just a bit longer" I am not sure how long he will let me, and I just hold him in my tight embrace.

After another moment Devon asks again, "Jordan, are you done hugging me?"

"Not yet." I smile and I know he hears it in my voice.

He starts to tickle my sides, "Okay silly, you turned this into a long creepy hug."

I giggle, "Hey, I thought you liked my hugs?"

He makes a face at me, "You know what I am talking about."

I let go and ask, "So, what time does your plane depart?"

Devon says, "6:00 AM it will be an early morning for me." He smiles.

I ask, "Send me a message when you are safe on the ground?"

He says, "Will do, have a safe drive home."

I step out of the rental and before I close the door, I hear him say, "Wait!"

I smile, "What?"

He mentions, "Remember, your parting gift. You know to remember me by." He reaches over his seat and hands me a bag. I open it and see the green dildo he made. I start to laugh, and he grins seeing my amusement. "You know I want a video of you using that."

I chuckle, "Yes Devon, in time, it won't be the same as having you for real, but it will have to do." I roll my eyes at him as I walk around the rental to the driver's side, and he brings down the window one last time. I give him one last parting gift and we say our goodbyes.

The drive home is a quiet one for me. I will arrive in time to receive Josh's telephone call that he makes on his break.

These last two days have brought me passion, lust, desire. It has sparked a fire in me that I haven't felt in years, and I feel so alive. I feel good about all of this and to have this moment with a friend and then go back to reality without interruption. It couldn't have gone more smoothly.

Before I know it, I am back at home, pulling into the garage. I waste no time in changing out of my clothes to run a wash, I change into some pajamas, brush my teeth, and tidy up around the house, and oh yes, hide my Devon toy.

Chapter 67
Like it Always is

The next morning life is like it always is, Josh doesn't suspect a thing which means that I pulled this off and my Devon is already somewhere in the sky on his way home. The only thing different for today is I tested positive for ovulation, so I have to call the doctor's office to make an appointment for treatment tomorrow.

By the afternoon I check my social media and sure enough I have received a message from Devon to say that he landed and Sara is on her way to pick him up at the airport.

I reply back to him. "That's good to hear and thank you so much."

I guess Devon has nothing else to do but wait and a moment later I receive a response, "I had a great time thank you!"

I tell him the news, "I am going in for treatment tomorrow. I think yours will work; they are already there but you know just going through the motions to not blow our cover."

He replies, "Gotcha, well relax tomorrow and take it easy. I know that this time will work for you." He sends one last message, "Okay I see Sara pulling up, I am dropping off for today, and talk to you tomorrow maybe?"

I reply, "Yes, bye Dev" I send him a string of kisses and hugs.

He writes, "Bye" He copies me and does the same. I look at his last message he always has to beat me with the hugs and kisses. I smile and return back to my work.

Chapter 68
Josh and I

Josh and I take the day off work for this procedure. Josh is excited and, on the drive, he feels it's important to tell me to relax and if it doesn't work this time, there is always next time. I take his chatter as nothing but positive and am happy that he wants this to work as much as I do. I know this time will be different because I have taken matters into my own hands instead of using the frozen stuff that the doctors inject into me.

Before I know it, I am lying in a room with my privates exposed to the doctor as she injects the tube of sperm into my stomach. Josh is with me for support. He is a hand to hold to calm my nerves. To be honest I am not nervous this time. This is my third attempt with this procedure, so I know what to expect and I lie there for fifteen minutes after they have done the task.

Josh asks, "How are you doing?"

I smile, "I am good. It gets less stressful with every attempt."

"What do you mean?"

"I just mean that I know what to expect so I am not really nervous, that's all." I explain.

"I think the third time is the charm." He admits to me.

"I think so too." I smile back and behind that smile is the thought of everything that Devon has done for me.

The nurse comes in to give us the routine talk of what to expect and when our next appointment to check for pregnancy will be. It's set almost two weeks from today. I take a look at my calendar and that is day two or three of when my next period is due, which is the norm. They scheduled it like that for the two previous attempts.

We return home for the rest of the day and relax. Other than the procedure this has been a pretty easy-going day for us, and we find ourselves in our recliners catching up on our television shows.

During a show that Josh picked to watch I grab my phone to check my social media. Josh likes watching those police themed shows that I don't care so much for. Trust me I used to enjoy them but there has got to be at least fifteen different police shows on television and the thing is Josh likes to watch each one.

I have a message from Devon in my inbox.

"Hey Jordan, hoping that everything went good for you today, thinking about you." I noticed that he sent the message about fifteen minutes ago. What a sweetheart to check in on things. This is why I like this man so much. Even with being so far away, I feel like he is in some strange way here for me through all of this.

I respond back, "Hey Devon, yes things went well, procedure is done, and I took the afternoon to relax." I click send and then send out my daily broadcasts on my different media feeds.

Another message pops into my inbox, "How is your stomach, do you feel any different?"

I glance over at Josh, he is into his police show and I respond again, "Well I have a bit of cramps, but it should pass in a bit. I feel like I did after the first two procedures." I click send again.

Another message comes in, "I want you to take it easy today, okay?"

His concern it's touching. The procedure isn't extreme in any way, so I am a little surprised by his message. I respond, "I will, I promise but I got to ask what's up? I told you about the procedures before; they are nothing to be concerned over."

Devon replies, "Yes I know it's just I care for you, and I really do hope that my gift works. You mean more to me than just any old friend and I want to make you happy in the way that I can. Do you understand what I mean?"

I smile and respond, "Thanks Devon, you know you mean more to me also and I would be yours if I could. I will take care of myself I promise and hope that this works, and hope that it's yours."

He sends me a smiley face, "If it works, I am confident that it will be mine, besides, mine were there first!"

I chuckle, which causes Josh to turn his attention to me, "What's up Jordan?"

I say, "Oh nothing, I just saw something funny online, did you want to see?" I offer.

Josh replies, "No, it's okay, you have a terrible sense of humor. The stuff you think is funny is often not. I'll pass."

I do an internal phew, I hate having him look at my phone especially when I am in the middle of a live conversation with Devon.

I turn my attention back to Devon's last text and respond, "You are silly, time will tell my stud." I receive a response from him moments later.

Devon asks, "Is Josh home with you right now?"

I write, "Yes, why what's up?"

He explains "Oh, just curious, well I won't take up your time seeing that you are with him."

I text, "It's okay Devon; he is just watching his cop show. I can talk for a bit." I click send. I look at my message and I can't help but reread it and it looks a tad bit desperate. Ah well I don't care; my heart wants what it does, and I may as well try to keep it happy.

His reply comes in, "Oh no worries, I have to drop off anyways. I have a pile of work that I need to return to anyway. Enjoy the rest of your day and catch up tomorrow?"

I write, "Sure, bye Sexy."

He replies, "Bye gorgeous!"

I love our little pet names. I lean back in the recliner and reminisce on the time I had with Devon and make a point to not smile even though on the inside I beam at the fond memories.

The conversation with Devon seemed to end just in sequence with the ending to the cop show so I guess it was for the best that he dropped off.

Josh looks over to me and asks, "Do you want to watch another show or do something else?"

"Can I pick the next show?" I ask.

Josh nods, "Sure."

Chapter 69
Jumping Ahead

Jumping ahead about a week and I still have no news yet with the results. The appointment isn't for another few days. It's Saturday morning and not surprisingly I find myself alone this morning. Josh went into town for his part-time job. Usually, my social media is quieter on the weekend, and I don't usually expect to hear from Devon since Sara is home, so when I review my messages and to my surprise there is something in my inbox from him.

He wrote, "Hey girl, wishing you an amazing day"

I reply back, "Good morning cowboy, I wasn't expecting to hear from you this morning. How are things?" I click send and right away another reply comes in.

He writes, "Things are good. Sara decided to take the day to go shopping with friends. I knew that you would be on your own so I thought that I would say howdy."

I ask, "So, what's on your mind?"

He mentions, "Oh, just you, I was wondering if you happened to use that toy yet."

Oh, I know where this is going, I type back to him, "Yes, I may have used it once or twice."

He teases, "Only once or twice, I play with yours every day."

I scold him, "Dirty cowboy; I'm sticking my tongue out at you."

He asks, "Say, how about sending your dirty cowboy a video of you playing with your toy?

I chuckle to myself as I read the message; yes, I knew he would ask besides he mentioned something about it while we were together.

I write, "Yes, I can work on something would you like me to start on it now?"

He replies, "That would be amazing my hot Canadian girl!"

Whenever I talk to him, I get turned on. Not sure what it is but just knowing that he is there gets me every time. I explain, "Okay Sexy I will be back in a bit I am doing it now because I am alone."

He says, "Okay ping me when you are ready to send."

"Okay" I click the send button and go get my green Devon dildo and get soaked to the thought of my lover.

I enter one of my spare bedrooms, the one where I keep all of my workout clothes and my old dresser set. I hid my Devon dildo deep in the top right dark antique wood drawer.

I take it out and just having it in my hands, bring back the fond memories. I place my Devon toy on the bed and set up my phone against some pillows. I can't really hold the phone while pleasuring myself. The morning sun is trickling through the blinds, but I know Devon had said that some of my images were a little dark; I need more light so I turn on the main light and the bedside reading lamp. There that should be enough, it's bright in here.

I remove my pants and panties and get up close to the camera. He enjoys the close-ups and that works great for me because to keep it as discreet as possible none of my intimate videos contain my face or anything that could identify me.

I start off with lightly stroking my clit and pressing my palm against the area and lather up just getting off on the fact that he will be watching this soon. I keep the image of him in my head, and us together, how he felt, the way that he made me feel, the sound of his voice and the scent of him and it doesn't take long to bring myself to the edge.

The thing with emailing videos to each other is they have to be kept short because of the size of the file so I bring myself to the edge and then press record. I feel myself with my fingers one more time and then give my Devon toy a stroke before putting it in. This is only for him and normally I would be shy but for him I have gotten over it. I moan while I thrust my awesome toy inside, moving it in and out to get used to its size. I am so close. I press the toy deep and then start to move a little quicker, the same way he moved when he was here. It builds up, and I talk to him through the video. "Devon, I'm wishing this is you, deep inside me with your large hard dick. I want you." I set myself off at the thought and vibrate, letting out little moans with each pulse. As soon as I finish, I turn off the recording. I think recording yourself for someone else makes the activity so much more intense just knowing that the other is going to get off to seeing you.

I sit on the bed and replay the video, watching me play with my toy and myself, wow that's hot, he will love this one. I trim it down just a touch so that it fits in the email and then send it his way.

I send him a text, "Are you alone? I ask because I just sent."

Dev responds in seconds, "Got it and watching."

My heart flutters knowing that in a few moments he is going to send me his approval. I get up and straighten up the ruffled blankets from me squirming around on the bed. I take my toy, rinse it off and return it to its hiding spot in the drawer.

Like clockwork his message comes in. He writes, "You just made me pre-cum in my pants that is so hot."

I reply, "I'm smiling, happy that you liked it."

He tells me, "You girl are amazing. I just want to lick and suck those nice lips of yours. I am going to rub one off."

Oh, this sexy man of mine makes me happy in that I can still please him even though we are apart, and it will be for a while. I send him one final text, "I'm going to run some errands, talk to you later."

I need to head to the store to pick up some groceries.

Chapter 70
Nearing the End

It's Sunday morning and nearing the end of the waiting period and soon I will know. My period is a day late; normally it's on schedule like clockwork. I realize that it could be just a fluke. Once in a while it's late and my anticipation grows.

Josh, being the man that he is, is trying to hide his excitement. I know that he does this because until he knows for sure he doesn't want to get worked up for nothing and I can appreciate that as I try to keep my own emotions in check although it's hard when the news is close.

Sure, I could probably just go to the store and pick up a pregnancy test kit and test myself now, but I rather wait for the blood work, my reason is a friend had used the test kit and got a positive result, then days later got her blood test back from the doctor's office and found out that her test kit had given her a false positive. She was heartbroken in going from an extreme high to being absolutely crushed.

I can't help but think about it, am I? Did Devon's gift to me work and if I am could it be his and not the frozen donor sperm?

Josh interrupts, "Hey Jordan you are out in la la land, what's on your mind?"

We are in the home office; Josh is working on some photo editing at his desk, and I am working on the text for my next novel. I realized that I was just staring blankly at my screen while deep in thought. I stretch and let out a yawn before answering, "Oh you know things are on my mind. Just the same old stuff going through my head, anyway you already know what that stuff is."

He assures, "We will know soon Jordan. I know that it's hard, but you just have to keep your mind off of it, just for a little longer."

I agree, "Yah I know."

He asks, "How are you feeling?"

I reflect then say, "I feel sort of bloated like I am going to start, but I haven't." I shrug.

Josh asks, "Any cramps?"

"No" I reply.

He says, "Well, that is good. Say, did you want to go out and get some fresh air? We can go for a walk."

I give him a sideways glance. Josh isn't the one to normally want to go for walks so the suggestion is out of character. I ask, "Really, you want to go for a walk?"

He sounds enthusiastic when he answers, "Sure, I know that you need to get your mind off of things, just trying to help. So, would you like to go?"

I smile, "Yes, I could use the fresh air."

We live in a nice little town that is almost an hour's drive from the main city. The town has a small downtown with some mom-and-pop restaurants and stores and a grand church in the center of Main Street. The town even has its own train station. The surrounding streets have a variety of homes, some are century homes and moving away from Main Street there are newer homes. Some streets were built within the last year. Josh and I live in a home that was built in the nineties so it's a bit older, but we have taken good care of it with renovations and such that it doesn't feel dated. The community that we live in has a few parks, schools, and a sports complex and in the winter the town has an outdoor skating rink. Josh and I take a walk around a few of the blocks near our home, taking in the fresh air and looking at all of the pretty homes.

Josh knows how much this all means to me and he can't help but check and double check that I will be alright.

He says, "You know with whatever the result is tomorrow, if it doesn't work out you realize that we can just try again."

I glance up at him as we walk, "Yes, I know. I think I will be okay; we have been through it a couple of times. I am just anxious, that's all."

He admits, "I know me too."

Josh has changed tremendously over the months and when I started telling you my story, I described him as an asshole of a husband, because he was back then, but now I can say that he is caring, loving, I know that life isn't perfect, but he is becoming the person that I first fell in love with.

Chapter 71
My Alarm

Today is the day. I wake before my alarm has the chance to go off and I roll over to find that Josh is awake also. His eyes are closed, but I can tell with his breathing that he is just resting his eyes. I put my arm around him and leaned in to give him a kiss.

His eyes open, "Hey honey, did you sleep well?"

I reply, "As best as I could." I smile and then we are startled by the alarm going off. I roll over towards my nightstand to silence the alarm.

Josh says, "Well that was rude."

I say, "Tell me about it."

We go through our morning routine, getting dressed, having breakfast, driving to town and this morning brings us to the waiting room of the doctor's office.

A nurse comes into the waiting room, "Jordan, we are ready for you."

I give Josh a glance and get up and follow the nurse to the room while Josh waits patiently for me. She has me sit down in a chair with large arm rests.

She asks, "So how are things today?"

"Things are good." I answer. I am a funny creature. At times I have the capacity to chat people's ears off but in situations like this I can get pretty quiet and closed off. I try not to be, besides finding the results, I think in this moment I am more fearful of the needle than anything and coach myself silently, don't faint.

I have given blood in the past and they always test you before donating, but I have found through the process that I am a fainter and the feeling after fainting isn't fun.

It usually means having a headache for the rest of the day.

The nurse sits on a stool in front of me, puts a band over my upper arm, wipes the spot where the needle is to go and sets the empty vials in front of me. She gives me a stress ball to hold, and I know that the prick is coming. I close my eyes and turn my head as I feel her touch.

I hear her say, "Okay Jordan, here it comes." She is gentle and I hardly feel it going in, which is nice of her, but I continue to keep my eyes shut and head turned. I can feel the tube that is running down my arm has grown heavy and warm with blood, and I can hear her picking up and putting down each vial as she fills it.

She says, "One more vial Jordan and we will be done."

I say, "Okay."

She confirms, "There we go all done. I am just taking the needle out. Could I have you hold the swab please?" I open my eyes and do what she asks as she leaves with the filled vials and returns with a Band-Aid.

She asks, "How do you feel?"

I tell her, "I am okay. I just faint sometimes but I know that I am fine right now."

She smiles, "Okay great. Well, you will be receiving a call this afternoon with the result, good luck."

She walks me back to the waiting room. I met Josh and the nurse calls her next patient. Josh whispers, "So?"

I explain to him, "Oh, it's the same as the last two times. They will call me with the results this afternoon." He is trying to play it cool. He wants to know as much as I do. Josh hates surprises so I think the waiting is starting to get to him.

I drive him back to work and as I drive up to the roundabout to drop him off at the front door of his building he reminds me, "Call me the moment you find out."

I smile and give him an exaggerated rolling of the eyes, "Yes Josh, of course."

He jabs back playfully, "I know how sometimes you like to forget, that's all." He winks.

I speak. "Yes Josh, have a good day, love you." I lean in and give him a kiss on the cheek.

He replies, "Love you too, and don't forget." He smiles and closes the car door; I blow him a kiss and then continue the drive to my work.

Within twenty minutes after dropping off Josh at his work I arrived at my desk. Two ladies that I work with know where I was this morning and both of them stop by my desk to find out.

"So?" They ask, like Snoopy little gossip queens but I don't mind.

I smile and say, "No news yet. A nurse will be giving me a call this afternoon with the result."

I receive well wishes from them and thank them for their kind words.

Besides the doctor's appointment in the morning the day is pretty normal. I have to admit, no pun intended that I am feeling a little drained. It is likely due to my light sleep and the combination of the blood work. I sip water at my desk and nibble on snacks throughout the morning and find it helps.

By late morning I receive my check in from the one and only Devon. He asks, "So, if I have my day's right, today is the day you find out, right?"

I reply, "Hey Devon, Yep I had my blood work this morning and the nurse is calling me this afternoon with the result."

Devon asks, "You have no news yet?" He is obviously just as excited as Josh is to find out.

I assure, "Not yet but I promise to send you a text as soon as I know."

He writes, "My fingers are crossed; I really do hope this works for you."

I text, "Thanks Devon, I do too. Even if it doesn't just know that everything that you have done for me, I hold so close to my heart and am forever thankful that you had given me that chance."

He explains, "Jordan, you have made me feel a way that I never felt before with any other person. The love that you have given to me, I have never felt that sort of passion from anyone and I hold on to those memories. Just to have someone as beautiful as you and know that you desire me means the world."

A tear wells up as I read his kind words and it gives me chills knowing that for some reason the universe brought two complete strangers together. We needed each other, lifted the other up and gave each other love.

With the months that have passed in knowing Devon, he is an honest straight forward man and has risen in his own personal life with landing his dream job and to top it off, as a writer his book is starting to get noticed. Without sounding conceited, I think that I played a small factor in building his confidence to the success that he is starting to see.

Devon did the same in playing a factor by helping me realize my own confidence. I had been a mess with having found out that my first procedure of IUI treatment didn't work. Right from the start we became the best of friends, and he was someone there in my world, there to listen and not judge and he was completely removed from my world which made it a little easier to let loose and confide in him.

With Devon, I started to smile again, feel that I wasn't alone as Josh is often called into work and I am left alone. In no time he became more than a friend and found myself thinking about him and feeling a desire for him and found that he also had for me and so it brings us to now, where he has given me a chance, the chance that I have been longing for, for so long.

A co-worker peeks into my office and asks, "Everything okay Jordan?"

I jump a little startled, "Oh yes, just a friend sending me well wishes for the results today. I am just full of emotions." I give her a brave smile.

She says, "Okay, just keep us in the loop."

I nod and she goes back to her own office, and I respond to Devon, "Ah Devon you know the key to this girl's heart, I can't say it as eloquently as you but know that I am ditto on everything that you have said."

He replies, "Smiling big, well Jordan I have to step into a meeting. Please message me later with the news. I will be checking throughout the day."

I text, "Okay Devon, talk to you later."

Lunch hour soon arrives, and I step out and go for a walk. I need fresh air to clear my mind. The nurse hasn't called yet but should soon and just in case I have my phone with me and the ring tone on the loudest setting. I follow my normal path down the street and through the flower gardens near my work and then down to the pathway next to the water and then back to the building. It's time well spent to calm myself down for the little time that I have left to wait.

Okay Jordan the truth is you will soon know so just be cool and relax. The worst thing that can happen is the result will be that I am not, and I can always try again. You need to tell Josh and Devon the result either way. They asked that of you, and it is the least you can do and besides, you have their complete support however way this turns out. I continue to ponder, trying to understand my senses. The first time I had tried I was certain that I was and when I found out that I wasn't I couldn't have been more surprised and shocked. The second attempt, I intentionally tried not to think about it, or get my hopes up and it sort of worked, the thought was in the back of my mind for the two week wait but the thing with that is towards the end I just had that sinking feeling that I wasn't and I ended up being right. Now this time just like the first two attempts gives me a different feeling once again. I am hopeful that I am and still trying to keep my emotions in check as to not be disappointed but with the love that Devon had given me, I know that I was more relaxed this time around and somehow, I just feel like everything happened for this reason. I can't explain it. It feels like my mind set with the first attempt but different because I have that connection with Devon. Anyway, Jordan you are just pondering yourself in circles back to work and soon you will know.

I settled back at my desk and looked over my email. I received an email from Josh over my lunch hour that reads,

Hey Jordan,

Do you have any news yet?

-Josh

Oh boy it's starting. I just let out a sigh and clicked reply. I am about to send him back a message when my phone rings and I startle. I glance at the display. It's a private number which means that it's likely the nurse's line. My heart starts to pound but I manage to pick up on the second ring.

"Hello?"

"Hi, is this Jordan?" I hear a woman's voice ask.

"Yes" I answer in a gasp.

"This is Selena from the Fertility Clinic. I have your results from this morning's blood work."

I am overcome with nerves but manage to blurt out an "Okay"

Her pause feels like forever then she finally answers, "Congratulations you are pregnant!"

I am struck stupid for a moment, "What?" I murmur into the phone. I sense that the ladies in the office are now ease dropping on my phone call and trying my best to lower my voice.

The nurse explains, "Yes Jordan, your results came back positive, you are expecting." I can tell that she is speaking with a smile.

I stutter out, "Okay, so what now?"

"In about a week you will receive a call from one of our Admin's to schedule a scan." The nurse explains.

I feel my hands shaking as I hold the phone up to my ear, I am so clueless right now I never thought to line up any questions should I receive positive news and now I am all over the map and not sure what to ask. I know with myself and especially Josh we are going to have tons of questions.

I blurt out as if to just confirm, "So I will get a follow up call from the doctor's office with the next steps?"

"Yes." She answers with a certainty that is calming to me in this moment. She goes through the process of confirming all of my contact information and then I am left sitting there at my desk with the phone down.

I am just staring blankly at my desk and am not sure for how long I hear a noise and look up. The two women are standing in my office.

One asks, "So was that the call?"

"Yes" I take a moment to gulp and in disbelief I answer, "I'm pregnant."

"Congratulations! We were rooting for you." The ladies are all over the place and all smiles. I smile back and reality is sinking in. Wow, I touch my stomach. There is someone in there and a sudden sense of relief comes over me. This day has been a roller coaster of nerves. Actually, let me correct myself, this entire year has been a roller coaster of nerves and emotions.

I look back at my computer screen to find that I still have Josh's email opened but unanswered. I respond.

Hey Josh,

Just got the news, I am pregnant. The doctor's office is going to call back within the next week to schedule the next appointment.

-Jordan

I click send, watch the email window close and go back to my inbox view. That feels so weird to type the words and say them after all this time. Oh yes, I forgot about Devon.

I open up my social media on my phone and send a text to Devon, "I am pregnant." My heart flutters again at those words. My office telephone rings, it's Josh.

I answer, "Hey, so you got my email?" I ask, while trying to contain my excitement.

Josh, just as I was with the nurse is stumbling over his own words all that he can say is, "Really?"

I chuckle, "Yes, really!"

He starts to come around and playfully says, "Like, really, really?"

I laugh, "Yes, the blood work says that I am."

"I am so happy, for you, for us, how do you feel?" Josh asks.

I admit, "Happy, relieved. It feels good to know. I have been a ball of nerves all day and now I can just relax."

He asks, "Do you want to go out for dinner tonight? You know, to celebrate?"

"Are you asking me out on a date?" I flirt back to him.

He teases, "Jordan don't get all weird, I just want to take my beautiful wife out for dinner."

I reply to him, "That sort of sounds like a date, well I would love to."

Josh says, "Okay well I'll see you after work and we can decide where to go, bye Jordan."

I say, "Bye, I love you."

Josh says, "Love you too, bye."

I hang up the phone and get distracted with the screen of my phone alerting me of a message from Devon that reads, "Congratulations! I knew it would work!"

I reply back, "You're so confidant in yourself."

He texts, "I take pride in my work." He sends it with a winking face following the message.

I write, "Well, I am happy that you do. Thank you, a million times!" I send him a string of hugs and kisses.

Devon says, "You're welcome, just happy that you allowed me to help. Every woman deserves the chance to be a mother."

I sent him a smiley face as a response and he sends me one final text, "Well, my dear I am super busy today with all this new job training. I have to get back to it, have a great day and thinking about you. Sending some hugs and kisses right back at you!"

I read his message and know that I do need to get back to my own work. The rest of the day is nothing short of being fantastic. My own emotions towards all of this even take me by surprise that I can't begin to describe.

The workday ends and dinner with Josh is nothing short of awesome. It is like we are on one of our very first dates all over again. We are laughing, kidding, and flirting throughout the entire date. The stress of this entire process has been lifted for the two of us and we are back to ourselves again.

Afterward

I can say that at this moment I feel complete. This was nothing short of amazing, mind blowing and a laundry list of other reasons. I know that what I did essentially was wrong to society's standard. I admit to cheating and the lies that I had to keep from everyone, my friends and family. I didn't whisper a mention of Devon to anyone for the sake of burdening others in keeping my secret. You know, if I was reading my own story as an outsider looking in on the entire situation, if you had asked me a year or two ago what I thought about the premise of this story, I would say that if you are married you have no right to go behind their back and cheat on them. People marry each other for love and that you shouldn't go looking outside of your marriage for affection.

When I watched talk shows and heard news in the media of celebrities caught cheating and what not, I didn't understand the motive for the cheater looking for love elsewhere, but in this moment after it is all said and done, I have a different opinion.

For Devon and me, we were not looking for this. I can promise you that. We were two strangers, countries apart, that stumbled upon each other through social media because of like interests. We were both in our own relationships not contemplating, "How can I cheat on my spouse?" I can tell you that it doesn't work like that.

We connected as friends, and it mutually blossomed into more. We both tried to fight it but with all seriousness how can you fight with what the heart wants? Devon had tried to end it early on when we both knew that we were crossing the line. He was trying to be the stronger one in all of this, but it didn't last, and we ended up letting our feelings and hearts have what they desired. I still struggle with this and to answer it you can't. You can't tell your heart to stop loving someone because society says it's wrong. You can't ignore someone that you feel connected to in such an unexplainable way. We lived two separate lives and were joined together by chance or destiny; I still don't know which? All I know is that I love Devon with all my heart, and I love Josh with all of my heart.

Today, if I was looking in as an outsider and if asked the question, why do people cheat? I would say that I don't believe that they are looking to cheat, at least for me and Devon it didn't work that way. As weird as this comes across, I think that the universe delivers to us what we ask for.

I don't approve of my own actions, but I don't think that Devon and I were completely in the wrong. When this all started, the truth is I needed a friend and just like that Devon was there for me. I know that Devon needed a friend too. We needed each other and just like that it happened and let me add that I wasn't searching for a friend. In that moment I didn't know that I needed a friend. I have thousands of followers on social media, and I do get the odd crazy fan but when Devon and I started talking, it was simply, two authors sharing their experiences with one another.

For a long time, I had wished and hoped to start a family and with my first two failed attempts things were starting to look impossible. I think that somehow Devon and I were meant to meet in order to start this next chapter and as strange as this is I look back on it all and know that I wished for something to happen and just like that the handsome, smart, caring, sexy, perfect man comes into my life and is willing to assist. Do things like this happen? The life that I have lived and the stories that I have heard, I can say that I have not heard of a story quite like my own, maybe this happens a lot but kept secret, maybe not, I am not sure.

I know that Devon needed to feel loved and experience an intimacy that he was missing with his own partner who had stopped with it entirely. Devon needed to feel alive again and feel desired and that came from me. I was able to give him that.

I know that no matter how much I explain my actions not everyone will agree. I know for myself I don't feel guilty for what I did. In this process no one got hurt and everyone gained something from it. This is a secret that I don't feel guilty about keeping. This is the end of a journey and the start of another. As I write this I am with child, and I believe that it's Devon's. I know that Devon and my secret are safe and that we are both in a good spot with our loved ones.

To the people who read this story, like I said in the beginning, believe what you will, I will never confirm and leave it to you to decide and P.S. This isn't the end.

About the Author

C.R. Misty is an accomplished author who has enchanted readers with her captivating romance novels. Misty finds solace in both the written word and the silver screen, where she delights in witnessing tales come alive. When she's not crafting extraordinary stories, Misty channels her creativity into the vibrant strokes of a paintbrush, nurturing beautiful blooms in her garden, and embarking on thrilling adventures in unexplored destinations. Sharing her life's journey with her ruggedly handsome husband and a devoted German Shepherd fur baby, she calls Ottawa, Canada, home. Simple Affair is the first novel in The International Boundaries Series. You can track her progress on book retailer sites and social media.

If you enjoyed this novel, please show your support for this book by writing a review online.

www.ingramcontent.com/pod-product-compliance
Lightning Source LLC
Chambersburg PA
CBHW050540260626
47157CB00002B/376